The Best from

Fantasy &
Science Fiction

24th Series

The Best from

Fantasy &
Science Fiction

24th Series

edited by

EDWARD L. FERMAN

CHARLES SCRIBNER'S SONS/NEW YORK
A *Magazine of Fantasy & Science Fiction* Book

For Art and Eva ... *ens*

Library of Congress Cataloging in Publication Data

Main entry under title:

The Best from Fantasy & science fiction, 24th series.

Summary: An anthology of short stories and readers' contributions to contests published in "Fantasy & Science Fiction."

1. Science fiction, American. 2. Fantastic fiction, American. [1. Science fiction. 2. Fantasy. 3. Short stories.] I. Ferman, Edward L. II. Magazine of fantasy and science fiction. III. Title: The best from fantasy and science fiction, 24th series.

PS648.S3B48   1981   813'.0876'08 [Fic]   82-696
ISBN 0-684-17490-1   AACR2

1 3 5 7 9 11 13 15 17 19   F/C   20 18 16 14 12 10 8 6 4 2

Printed in the United States of America.

The editor hereby makes grateful acknowledgment of the following authors and authors' representatives for giving permission to reprint the material in this volume:

Bob Leman for "Window"
Writers House, Inc. for "The Fire When It Comes" by Parke Godwin
Algis Budrys for "Books: The Secret Language of Science Fiction"
Lisa Tuttle for "Wives"
Scott Meredith Literary Agency, Inc. for "The Alien Mind" by Philip K. Dick, copyright © 1981 by Philip K. Dick, and " 'A Day at the Fair' " by Neal Barrett, Jr.
A. W. Petrey for "Spidersong" by Susan C. Petrey
Curtis Brown Ltd. for "Out There Where the Big Ships Go" by Richard Cowper, copyright © 1979 by Colin Murry
Baird Searles for "Films and TV: Lost Rewards," copyright © 1982 by Baird Searles
Eric Norden for "The Curse of the Mhondoro Nkabele"
Michael Shea for "The Autopsy"
Virginia Kidd for "The Most Illuminatingly Doleful and Instructively Affecting Demise of Flo, Late of Upper Blooton" by Russell Griffin
Isaac Asimov for "Science: The Word I Invented"
Kirby McCauley for "The Pusher" by John Varley
Thomas M. Disch for "The Brave Little Toaster"

Contents

EDWARD L. FERMAN

Introduction

F OR many years *The Best from Fantasy & Science Fiction* series
offered the best fiction from a year or more of magazine publication. In the 22nd edition, I added the ingredient of sample
columns from *F&SF*'s long-running and popular departments. In
this, the 24th series, Isaac Asimov ("Science") answers questions
about his invention of the term "robotics," Algis Budrys ("Books")
explains how fans influence SF publishing, and Baird Searles
("Films and TV") contributes a brand-new piece on "lost" fantasy and SF movies. Also included are samples from *F&SF* com-
petitions, ranging from "Unwieldy SF Titles" ("Feed Me Young
Virgins or I Will Turn Off the World Cried the Computer Who
Sat At the Center"), through "Title Misprints" (*Oi, Robot*) and
"Imaginary Collaborations" (*If All Men Were Androids, Would
You Let One Marry Your Electric Sheep?* by Sturgeon and Dick).

Of course, the fiction remains at the heart of the series, and this volume includes eleven stories and a poem that reflect *F&SF*'s simply stated policy of publishing well-written, varied entertainment. The stories range from deep space SF (Lisa Tuttle, Richard Cowper) through traditional fantasy (Susan C. Petrey), a contemporary ghost tale (Parke Godwin), SF/horror (Michael Shea), humor (Philip K. Dick, Eric Norden), along with the usual number of stories that refuse to be jammed into any category at all.

This edition also marks a thirtieth anniversary of sorts, since the first *The Best from Fantasy & Science Fiction*, edited by Anthony Boucher and J. Francis McComas, was published by Little, Brown in 1952. After the first two volumes the series went to Doubleday; this book, released in 1982, is the first to be published under the combined imprint of the magazine and Charles Scribner's Sons.

According to Neil Barron's excellent critical guide to science fiction, *Anatomy of Wonder* (Bowker, 1981), the SF anthology is only about forty years old, originating with books by Phil Stong and Donald Wollheim in the early 1940s. Which means that this series has been around for quite a long time, as anthologies go; it is certainly the longest-running and most regular of the magazine series anthologies. Our goal has been to present something like a very good and very big issue of *F&SF*, and along the way we've accomplished something else, according to the Barron book, which says that: "these volumes comprise a comprehensive postwar library of superior SF and fantasy." And if that sounds at all intimidating, take our word that in this case "superior" also means "enjoyable." You'll have fun with this book.

Bob Leman is one of F&SF's *most valued contributors, because his stories are always polished and entertaining and because the quality holds up through a remarkable range of different types of work, from horror to humor to the science fiction stunner you are about to read. "Window" concerns a military project that is investigating telekinesis and that experiences an incredible accident: the disappearance of an entire building, along with one researcher, and the appearance, in its place, of something strange that is not exactly what it appears to be.*

BOB LEMAN

Window

WE don't know what the hell's going on out there," they told Gilson in Washington. "It may be pretty big. The nut in charge tried to keep it under wraps, but the army was furnishing routine security, and the commanding officer tipped us off. A screwball project. Apparently been funded for years without anyone paying much attention. Extrasensory perception, for God's sake. And maybe they've found something. The security colonel thinks so, anyway. Find out about it."

The Nut-in-Charge was a rumpled professor of psychology named Krantz. He and the colonel met Gilson at the airport, and they set off directly for the site in an army sedan. The colonel began talking immediately.

"You've got something mighty queer here, Gilson," he said. "I never saw anything like it, and neither did anybody else. Krantz here is as mystified as anybody. And it's his baby. We're just

I

security. Not that they've needed any, up to now. Not even any need for secrecy, except to keep the public from laughing its head off. The setup we've got here is—"

"Dr. Krantz," Gilson said, "you'd better give me a complete rundown on the situation here. So far, I haven't any information at all."

Krantz was occupied with the lighting of a cigar. He blew a cloud of foul smoke, and through it he said, "We're missing one prefab building, one POBEC computer, some medical machinery, and one, uh, researcher named Culvergast."

"Explain 'missing,' " Gilson said.

"Gone. Disappeared. A building and everything in it. Just not there any more. But we do have something in exchange."

"And what's that?"

"I think you'd better wait and see for yourself," Krantz said. "We'll be there in a few minutes." They were passing through the farther reaches of the metropolitan area, a series of decayed small towns. The highway wound down the valley beside the river, and the towns lay stretched along it, none of them more than a block or two wide, their side streets rising steeply toward the first ridge. In one of these moribund communities they left the highway and went bouncing up the hillside on a crooked road whose surface changed from cobblestones to slag after the houses had been left behind. Beyond the crest of the ridge the road began to drop as steeply as it had risen, and after a quarter of a mile they turned in at a lane whose entrance would have been missed by anyone not watching for it. They were in a forest now; it was second growth, but the logging had been done so long ago that it might almost have been a virgin stand, lofty, silent, and somewhat gloomy on this gray day.

"Pretty," Gilson said. "How does a project like this come to be way out here, anyhow?"

"The place was available," the colonel said. "Has been since World War Two. They set it up for some work on proximity fuzes. Shut it down in '48. Was vacant until the professor took it over."

"Culvergast is a little bit eccentric," Krantz said. "He wouldn't work at the university—too many people, he said. When I heard this place was available, I put in for it, and got it—along with the colonel, here. Culvergast has been happy with the setup, but I guess he bothers the colonel a little."

"He's a certifiable loony," the colonel said, "and his little helpers are worse."

"Well, what the devil was he doing?" Gilson asked.

Before Krantz could answer, the driver braked at a chain-link gate that stood across the lane. It was fastened with a loop of heavy logging chain and manned by armed soldiers. One of them, machine pistol in hand, peered into the car. "Everything O.K., sir?" he said.

"O.K. with waffles, Sergeant," the colonel said. It was evidently a password. The noncom unlocked the enormous padlock that secured the chain. "Pretty primitive," the colonel said as they bumped through the gateway, "but it'll do until we get proper stuff in. We've got men with dogs patrolling the fence." He looked at Gilson. "We're just about there. Get a load of this, now."

It was a house. It stood in the center of the clearing in an island of sunshine, white, gleaming, and incongruous. All around was the dark loom of the forest under a sunless sky, but somehow sunlight lay on the house, sparkling in its polished windows and making brilliant the colors of massed flowers in carefully tended beds, reflecting from the pristine whiteness of its siding out into the gray, littered clearing with its congeries of derelict buildings.

"You couldn't have picked a better time," the colonel said. "Shining there, cloudy here."

Gilson was not listening. He had climbed from the car and was staring in fascination. "Jesus," he said. "Like a goddamn Victorian postcard."

Lacy scrollwork foamed over the rambling wooden mansion, running riot at the eaves of the steep roof, climbing elaborately up towers and turrets, embellishing deep oriels and outlining a long, airy veranda. Tall windows showed by their spacing that the rooms were many and large. It seemed to be a new house, or perhaps just newly painted and supremely well-kept. A driveway of fine white gravel led under a high porte-cochère.

"How about that?" the colonel said. "Look like your grandpa's house?"

As a matter of fact, it did: like his grandfather's house enlarged and perfected and seen through a lens of romantic nostalgia, his grandfather's house groomed and pampered as the old farmhouse never had been. He said, "And you got this in exchange for a prefab, did you?"

"Just like that one," the colonel said, pointing to one of the seedy buildings. "Of course we could use the prefab."

"What does that mean?"

"Watch," the colonel said. He picked up a small rock and tossed it in the direction of the house. The rock rose, topped its arc, and began to fall. Suddenly it was not there.

"Here," Gilson said. "Let me try that."

He threw the rock like a baseball, a high, hard one. It disappeared about fifty feet from the house. As he stared at the point of its disappearance, Gilson saw that the smooth green of the lawn ended exactly below. Where the grass ended, there began the weeds and rocks that made up the floor of the clearing. The line of separation was absolutely straight, running at an angle across the lawn. Near the driveway it turned ninety degrees, and sliced off lawn, driveway and shrubbery with the same precise straightness.

"It's perfectly square," Krantz said. "About a hundred feet to a side. Probably a cube, actually. We know the top's about ninety feet in the air. I'd guess there are about ten feet of it underground."

" 'It'?" Gilson said. " 'It'? What's 'it'?"

"Name it and you can have it," Krantz said. "A three-dimensional television receiver a hundred feet to a side, maybe. A cubical crystal ball. Who knows?"

"The rocks we threw. They didn't hit the house. Where did the rocks go?"

"Ah. Where, indeed? Answer that and perhaps you answer all."

Gilson took a deep breath. "All right. I've seen it. Now tell me about it. From the beginning."

Krantz was silent for a moment; then, in a dry lecturer's voice he said, "Five days ago, June thirteenth, at eleven thirty a.m., give or take three minutes, Private Ellis Mulvihill, on duty at the gate, heard what he later described as 'an explosion that was quiet, like.' He entered the enclosure, locked the gate behind him, and ran up here to the clearing. He was staggered—'shook-up' was his expression—to see, instead of Culvergast's broken-down prefab, that house, there. I gather that he stood gulping and blinking for a time, trying to come to terms with what his eyes told him. Then he ran over there to the guardhouse and called the colonel. Who called me. We came out here and found that a quarter of an acre of land and a building with a man in it had disappeared and been replaced by this, as neat as a peg in a pegboard."

"You think the prefab went where the rocks did," Gilson said. It was a statement.

"Why, we're not even absolutely sure it's gone. What we're seeing can't actually be where we're seeing it. It rains on that house when it's sunny here, and right now you can see the sunlight on it, on a day like this. It's a window."

"A window on what?"

"Well—that looks like a new house, doesn't it? When were they building houses like that?"

"Eighteen seventy or eighty, something like—oh."

"Yes," Krantz said. "I think we're looking at the past."

"Oh, for God's sake," Gilson said.

"I know how you feel. And I may be wrong. But I have to say it looks very much that way. I want you to hear what Reeves says about it. He's been here from the beginning. A graduate student, assisting here. Reeves!"

A very tall, very thin young man unfolded himself from a crouched position over an odd-looking machine that stood near the line between grass and rubble and ambled over to the three men. Reeves was an enthusiast. "Oh, it's the past, all right," he said. "Sometime in the eighties. My girl got some books on costume from the library, and the clothes check out for that decade. And the decorations on the horses' harnesses are a clue, too. I got that from—"

"Wait a minute," Gilson said. "*Clothes?* You mean there are people in there?"

"Oh, sure," Reeves said. "A fine little family. Mamma, poppa, little girl, little boy, old granny or auntie. A dog. Good people."

"How can you tell that?"

"I've been watching them for five days, you know? They're having—*were* having—fine weather there—or then, or whatever you'd say. They're nice to each other, they *like* each other. Good people. You'll see."

"When?"

"Well, they'll be eating dinner now. They usually come out after dinner. In an hour, maybe."

"I'll wait," Gilson said. "And while we wait, you will please tell me some more."

Krantz assumed his lecturing voice again. "As to the nature of it, nothing. We have a window, which we believe to open into the past. We can see into it, so we know that light passes through; but it passes in only one direction, as evidenced by the fact that the people over there are wholly unaware of us. Nothing else goes through. You saw what happened to the rocks. We've shoved poles through the interface there—there's no resistance at all—but anything that goes through is gone, God knows where. Whatever you put through stays there. Your pole is cut off clean. Fascinating. But wherever it is, it's not where the house is. That interface isn't between us and the past; it's between us and—someplace else. I think our window here is just an incidental side-effect, a—a twisting of time that resulted from whatever tensions exist along that interface."

Gilson sighed. "Krantz," he said, "what am I going to tell the secretary? You've lucked into what may be the biggest thing that ever happened, and you've kept it bottled up for five days. We wouldn't know about it now if it weren't for the colonel's report. Five days wasted. Who knows how long this thing will last? The whole goddamn scientific establishment ought to be here—should have been from day one. This needs the whole works. At this point the place should be a beehive. And what do I find? You and a graduate student throwing rocks and poking with sticks. And a girlfriend looking up the dates of costumes. It's damn near criminal."

Krantz did not look abashed. "I thought you'd say that," he said. "But look at it this way. Like it or not, this thing wasn't produced by technology or science. It was pure psi. If we can reconstruct Culvergast's work, we may be able to find out what happened; we may be able to repeat the phenomenon. But I don't like what's going to happen after you've called in your experimenters, Gilson. They'll measure and test and conjecture and theorize, and never once will they accept for a moment the real basis of what's happened. The day they arrive, I'll be out. And damnit, Gilson, this is *mine*."

"Not any more," Gilson said. "It's too big."

"It's not as though we weren't doing some hard experiments of our own," Krantz said. "Reeves, tell him about your batting machine."

"Yes, *sir*," Reeves said. "You see, Mr. Gilson, what the professor said wasn't absolutely the whole truth, you know? Sometimes something *can* get through the window. We saw it on the first day. There was a temperature inversion over in the valley, and the stink from the chemical plant had been accumulating for about a week. It broke up that day, and the wind blew the gunk through the notch and right over here. A really rotten stench. We were watching our people over there, and all of a sudden they began to sniff and wrinkle their noses and make disgusted faces. We figured it had to be the chemical stink. We pushed a pole out right away, but the end just disappeared, as usual. The professor suggested that maybe there was a pulse, or something of the sort, in the interface, that it exists only intermittently. We cobbled up a gadget to test the idea. Come and have a look at it."

It was a horizontal flywheel with a paddle attached to its rim, like an extended cleat. As the wheel spun, the paddle swept around a table. There was a hopper hanging above, and at intervals something dropped from the hopper onto the table, where it was immediately banged by the paddle and sent flying. Gilson peered into the hopper and raised an interrogatory eyebrow. "Ice cubes," Reeves said. "Colored orange for visibility. That thing shoots an ice cube at the interface once a second. Somebody is always on duty with a stopwatch. We've established that every fifteen hours and twenty minutes the thing is open for five seconds. Five ice cubes go through and drop on the lawn in there. The rest of the time they just vanish at the interface."

"Ice cubes. Why ice cubes?"

"They melt and disappear. We can't be littering up the past with artifacts from our day. God knows what the effect might be. Then, too, they're cheap, and we're shooting a lot of them."

"Science," Gilson said heavily. "I can't wait to hear what they're going to say in Washington."

"Sneer all you like," Krantz said. "The house is there, the interface is there. We've by God turned up some kind of time travel. And Culvergast the screwball did it, not a physicist or an engineer."

"Now that you bring it up," Gilson said, "just what *was* your man Culvergast up to?"

"Good question. What he was doing was—well, not to put too fine a point upon it, he was trying to discover spells."

"Spells?"

"The kind you cast. Magic words. Don't look disgusted yet. It makes sense, in a way. We were funded to look into telekinesis—the manipulation of matter by the mind. It's obvious that telekinesis, if it could be applied with precision, would be a marvelous weapon. Culvergast's hypothesis was that there are in fact people who perform feats of telekinesis, and although they never seem to know or be able to explain how they do it, they nevertheless perform a specific mental action that enables them to tap some source of energy that apparently exists all around us, and to some degree to focus and direct that energy. Culvergast proposed to discover the common factor in their mental processes.

"He ran a lot of putative telekinecists through here, and he reported that he had found a pattern, a sort of mnemonic device functioning at the very bottom of, or below, the verbal level. In one of his people he found it as a set of musical notes, in several as gibberish of various sorts, and in one, he said, as mathematics at the primary arithmetic level. He was feeding all this into the computer, trying to eliminate simple noise and the personal idiosyncrasies of the subjects, trying to lay bare the actual, effective essence. He then proposed to organize this essence into *words;* words that would so shape the mental currents of a speaker of standard American English that they would channel and manipulate the telekinetic power at the will of the speaker. Magic words, you might say. Spells.

"He was evidently further along than I suspected. I think he must have arrived at some words, tried them out, and made an attempt at telekinesis—some small thing, like causing an ashtray to rise off his desk and float in the air, perhaps. And it worked, but what he got wasn't a dainty little ashtray-lifting force; he had opened the gate wide, and some kind of terrible power came through. It's pure conjecture, of course, but it must have been something like that to have had an effect like *this*."

Gilson had listened in silence. He said, "I won't say you're crazy, because I can see that house and I'm watching what's happening to those ice cubes. How it happened isn't my problem, anyhow. My problem is what I'll recommend to the secretary that we do with it now that we've got it. One thing's sure, Krantz: this isn't going to be your private playpen much longer."

There was a yelp of pure pain from Reeves. "They can't *do* that," he said. "This is ours, it's the professor's. Look at it, look at that house. Do you want a bunch of damn engineers messing around with *that?*"

Gilson could understand how Reeves felt. The house was drenched now with the light of a red sunset; it seemed to glow from within with a deep, rosy blush. But, Gilson reflected, the sunset wasn't really necessary; sentiment and the universal, unacknowledged yearning for a simpler, cleaner time would lend rosiness enough. He was quite aware that the surge of longing and nostalgia he felt was nostalgia for something he had never actually experienced, that the way of life the house epitomized for him was in fact his own creation, built from patches of novels and films; nonetheless he found himself hungry for that life, yearning for that time. It was a gentle and secure time, he thought, a time when the pace was unhurried and the air was clean; a time when there was grace and style, when young men in striped blazers and boater hats might pay decorous court to young ladies in long white dresses, whiling away the long drowsy afternoons of summer in peaceable conversations on shady porches. There would be jolly bicycle tours over shade-dappled roads that twisted among the hills to arrive at cool glens where swift little streams ran; there would be long sweet buggy rides behind somnolent patient horses under a great white moon, lover whispering urgently to lover while nightbirds sang. There would be excursions down the broad clean river, boats gentle on the current, floating toward the sound from across the water of a brass band playing at the landing.

Yes, thought Gilson, and there would probably be an old geezer with a trunkful of adjectives around somewhere, carrying on about how much better things had been a hundred years before. If he didn't watch himself he'd be helping Krantz and Reeves try to keep things hidden. Young Reeves—oddly, for someone his age—seemed to be hopelessly mired in this bogus nostalgia. His description of the family in the house had been simple doting. Oh, it was definitely time that the cold-eyed boys were called in. High time.

"They ought to be coming out any minute, now," Reeves was saying. "Wait till you see Martha."

"Martha," Gilson said.

"The little girl. She's a doll."

Gilson looked at him. Reeves reddened and said, "Well, I sort of gave them names. The children. Martha and Pete. And the dog's Alfie. They kind of look like those names, you know?" Gilson did not answer, and Reeves reddened further. "Well, you can see for yourself. Here they come."

A fine little family, as Reeves had said. After watching them for half an hour, Gilson was ready to concede that they were indeed most engaging, as perfect in their way as their house. They were just what it took to complete the picture, to make an authentic Victorian genre painting. Mama and Papa were good-looking and still in love, the children were healthy and merry and content with their world. Or so it seemed to him as he watched them in the darkening evening, imagining the comfortable, affectionate conversation of the parents as they sat on the porch swing, almost hearing the squeals of the children and the barking of the dog as they raced about the lawn. It was almost dark now; a mellow light of oil lamps glowed in the windows, and fireflies winked over the lawn. There was an arc of fire as the father tossed his cigar butt over the railing and rose to his feet. Then there followed a pretty little pantomime, as he called the children, who duly protested, were duly permitted a few more minutes, and then were firmly commanded. They moved reluctantly to the porch and were shooed inside, and the dog, having delayed to give a shrub a final wetting, came scrambling up to join them. The children and the dog entered the house, then the mother and father. The door closed, and there was only the soft light from the windows.

Reeves exhaled a long breath. "Isn't that something," he said. "That's the way to live, you know? If a person could just say to hell with all this crap we live in today and go back there and live like that. . . . And Martha, you saw Martha. An angel, right? Man, what I'd give to—"

Gilson interrupted him: "When does the next batch of ice cubes go through?"

"—be able to— Uh, yeah. Let's see. The last penetration was at 3:15, just before you got here. Next one will be at 6:35 in the morning, if the pattern holds. And it has, so far."

"I want to see that. But right now I've got to do some telephoning. Colonel!"

Gilson did not sleep that night, nor, apparently, did Krantz and Reeves. When he arrived at the clearing at five a.m. they were still there, unshaven and red-eyed, drinking coffee from thermos bottles. It was cloudy again, and the clearing was in total darkness except for a pale light from beyond the interface, where a sunny day was on the verge of breaking.

"Anything new?" Gilson said.

"I think that's my question," Krantz said. "What's going to happen?"

"Just about what you expected, I'm afraid. I think that by evening this place is going to be a real hive. And by tomorrow night you'll be lucky if you can find a place to stand. I imagine Bannon's been on the phone since I called him at midnight, rounding up the scientists. And they'll round up the technicians. Who'll bring their machines. And the army's going to beef up the security. How about some of that coffee?"

"Help yourself. You bring bad news, Gilson."

"Sorry," Gilson said, "but there it is."

"Goddamn!" Reeves said loudly. "Oh, goddamn!" He seemed to be about to burst into tears. "That'll be the end for me, you know? They won't even let me in. A damn graduate student? In *psychology?* I won't get near the place. Oh, damn it to hell!" He glared at Gilson in rage and despair.

The sun had risen, bringing gray light to the clearing and brilliance to the house across the interface. There was no sound but the regular bang of the ice cube machine. The three men stared quietly at the house. Gilson drank his coffee.

"There's Martha," Reeves said. "Up there." A small face had appeared between the curtains of a second-floor window, and bright blue eyes were surveying the morning. "She does that every day," Reeves said. "Sits there and watches the birds and squirrels until I guess they call her for breakfast." They stood and watched the little girl, who was looking at something that lay beyond the scope of their window on her world, something that would have been to their rear had the worlds been the same. Gilson almost found himself turning around to see what it was that she stared at. Reeves apparently had the same impulse. "What's she looking at, do you think?" he said. "It's not necessarily forest, like now. I think this was logged out earlier. Maybe a meadow? Cattle or horses on it? Man, what I'd give to be there and see what it is."

Krantz looked at his watch and said, "We'd better go over there. Just a few minutes, now."

They moved to where the machine was monotonously batting

ice cubes into the interface. A soldier with a stopwatch sat beside it, behind a table bearing a formidable chronometer and a sheaf of charts. He said, "Two minutes, Dr. Krantz."

Krantz said to Gilson, "Just keep your eye on the ice cubes. You can't miss it when it happens." Gilson watched the machine, mildly amused by the rhythm of its homely sounds: *plink*—a cube drops; *whuff*—the paddle sweeps around; *bang*—paddle strikes ice cube. And then a flat trajectory to the interface, where the small orange missile abruptly vanishes. A second later, another. Then another.

"Five seconds," the soldier called. "Four. Three. Two. One. *Now.*"

His timing was off by a second; the ice cube disappeared like its predecessors. But the next one continued its flight and dropped onto the lawn, where it lay glistening. It was really a fact, then, thought Gilson. Time travel for ice cubes.

Suddenly behind him there was an incomprehensible shout from Krantz and another from Reeves, and then a loud, clear, and anguished, "Reeves, *no!*" from Krantz. Gilson heard a thud of running feet and caught a flash of swift movement at the edge of his vision. He whirled in time to see Reeves' gangling figure hurtle past, plunge through the interface, and land sprawling on the lawn. Krantz said, violently, *"Fool!"* An ice cube shot through and landed near Reeves. The machine banged again; an ice cube flew out and vanished. The five seconds of accessibility were over.

Reeves raised his head and stared for a moment at the grass on which he lay. He shifted his gaze to the house. He rose slowly to his feet, wearing a bemused expression. A grin came slowly over his face, then, and the men watching from the other side could almost read his thoughts: Well, I'll be damned. I made it. I'm really here.

Krantz was babbling uncontrollably. "We're still here, Gilson, we're still here, we still exist, everything seems the same. Maybe he didn't change things much, maybe the future is fixed and he didn't change anything at all. I was afraid of this, of something like this. Ever since you came out here, he's been—"

Gilson did not hear him. He was staring with shock and disbelief at the child in the window, trying to comprehend what he saw and did not believe he was seeing. Her behavior was wrong, it was very, very wrong. A man had materialized on her lawn, suddenly, out of thin air, on a sunny morning, and she had evinced no surprise or amazement or fear. Instead she had smiled—instantly, spontaneously, a smile that broadened and broadened until it seemed to split the lower half of her face, a smile that showed too many teeth, a smile fixed and incongruous and terrible below her bright blue eyes. Gilson felt his stomach knot; he realized that he was dreadfully afraid.

The face abruptly disappeared from the window; a few seconds later the front door flew open and the little girl rushed through the doorway, making for Reeves with furious speed, moving in a curious, scuttling run. When she was a few feet away, she leaped at him, with the agility and eye-dazzling quickness of a flea. Reeves' eyes had just begun to take on a puzzled look when the powerful little teeth tore out his throat.

She dropped away from him and sprang back. A geyser of bright blood erupted from the ragged hole in his neck. He looked at it in stupefaction for a long moment, then brought up his hands to cover the wound; the blood boiled through his fingers and ran down his forearms. He sank gently to his knees, staring at the little girl with wide astonishment. He rocked, shivered, and pitched forward on his face.

She watched with eyes as cold as a reptile's, the terrible smile still on her face. She was naked, and it seemed to Gilson that there was something wrong with her torso, as well as with her mouth. She turned and appeared to shout toward the house.

In a moment they all came rushing out, mother, father, little boy, and granny, all naked, all undergoing that hideous transformation of the mouth. Without pause or diminution of speed they scuttled to the body, crouched around it, and frenziedly tore off its clothes. Then, squatting on the lawn in the morning sunshine, the fine little family began horribly to feed.

Krantz's babbling had changed its tenor: "Holy Mary, Mother of God, pray for us. . . ." The soldier with the stopwatch was noisily sick. Someone emptied a clip of a machine pistol into the interface, and the colonel cursed luridly. When Gilson could no longer bear to watch the grisly feast, he looked away and found himself staring at the dog, which sat happily on the porch, thumping its tail.

"By God, it just can't be!" Krantz burst out. "It would be in the histories, in the newspapers, if there'd been people like that here. My God, something like that couldn't be forgotten!"

"Oh, don't talk like a fool!" Gilson said angrily. "That's not the past. I don't know what it is, but it's not the past. Can't be. It's— I don't know—someplace else. Some other—dimension? Universe? One of those theories. Alternate worlds, worlds of If, probability worlds, whatever you call 'em. They're in the present time, all right, that filth over there. Culvergast's damn spell holed through to one of those parallels. Got to be something like that. And, my God, what the *hell* was its history to produce *those?* They're not human, Krantz, no way human, whatever they look like. 'Jolly bicycle tours.' How wrong can you be?"

It ended at last. The family lay on the grass with distended bellies, covered with blood and grease, their eyelids heavy in repletion. The two little ones fell asleep. The large male appeared to be deep in thought. After a time he rose, gathered up Reeves' clothes, and examined them carefully. Then he woke the small female and apparently questioned her at some length. She gestured, pointed, and pantomimed Reeves' headlong arrival. He stared thoughtfully at the place where Reeves had materialized, and for a moment it seemed to Gilson that the pitiless eyes were glaring directly into his. He turned, walked slowly and reflectively to the house, and went inside.

It was silent in the clearing except for the thump of the machine. Krantz began to weep, and the colonel to swear in a monotone. The soldiers seemed dazed. And we're all afraid, Gilson thought. Scared to death.

On the lawn they were enacting a grotesque parody of making things tidy after a picnic. The small ones had brought a basket and, under the meticulous supervision of the adult females, went about gathering up the debris of their feeding. One of them tossed a bone to the dog, and the timekeeper vomited again. When the lawn was once again immaculate, they carried off the basket to the rear, and the adults returned to the house. A moment later the male emerged, now dressed in a white linen suit. He carried a book.

"A Bible," said Krantz in amazement. "It's a Bible."

"Not a Bible," Gilson said. "There's no way those—things could have Bibles. Something else. Got to be."

It looked like a Bible; its binding was limp black leather, and when the male began to leaf through it, evidently in search of a particular passage, they could see that the paper was the thin, tough paper Bibles are printed on. He found his page and began, as it appeared to Gilson, to read aloud in a declamatory manner, mouthing the words.

"What the hell do you suppose he's up to?" Gilson said. He was still speaking when the window ceased to exist.

House and lawn and white-suited declaimer vanished. Gilson caught a swift glimpse of trees across the clearing, hidden until now by the window, and of a broad pit between him and the trees. Then he was knocked off his feet by a blast of wind, and the air was full of dust and flying trash and the wind's howl. The wind stopped, as suddenly as it had come, and there was a patter of falling small objects that had momentarily been windborne. The site of the house was entirely obscured by an eddying cloud of dust.

The dust settled slowly. Where the window had been there was a great hole in the ground, a perfectly square hole a hundred feet across and perhaps ten feet deep, its bottom as flat as a table. Gilson's glimpse of it before the wind had rushed in to fill the vacuum had shown the sides to be as smooth and straight as if sliced through cheese with a sharp knife; but now small landslides were occurring all around the perimeter, as topsoil and gravel caved and slid to the bottom, and the edges were becoming ragged and irregular.

Gilson and Krantz slowly rose to their feet. "And that seems to be that," Gilson said. "It was here and now it's gone. But where's the prefab? Where's Culvergast?"

"God knows," Krantz said. He was not being irreverent. "But I think he's gone for good. And at least he's not where those things are."

"What are they, do you think?"

"As you said, certainly not human. Less human than a spider or an oyster. But, Gilson, the way they look and dress, that house—"

"If there's an infinite number of possible worlds, then every possible sort of world will exist."

Krantz looked doubtful. "Yes, well, perhaps. We don't know anything, do we?" He was silent for a moment. "Those things were pretty frightening, Gilson. It didn't take even a fraction of a second for her to react to Reeves. She knew instantly that he was alien, and she moved instantly to destroy him. And that's a baby one. I think maybe we can feel safer with the window gone."

"Amen to that. What do you think happened to it?"

"It's obvious, isn't it? They know how to *use* the energies Culvergast was blundering around with. The book—it has to be a book of spells. They must have a science of it—tried-and-true stuff, part of their received wisdom. That thing used the book like a routine everyday tool. After it got over the excitement of its big feed, it didn't need more than twenty minutes to figure out how Reeves got there, and what to do about it. It just got its book of spells, picked the one it needed (I'd like to see the index of that book) and said the words. Poof! Window gone and Culvergast stranded, God knows where."

"It's possible, I guess. Hell, maybe even likely. You're right, we don't really know a thing about all this."

Krantz suddenly looked frightened. "Gilson, what if—look. If it was that easy for him to cancel out the window, if he has that kind of control of telekinetic power, what's to prevent him from getting a window on *us*? Maybe they're watching us now, the way we were watching them. They know we're here, now. What kind of ideas might they get? Maybe they need meat. Maybe they—my God."

"No," Gilson said. "Impossible. It was pure, blind chance that located the window in that world. Culvergast had no more idea what he was doing than a chimp at a computer console does. If the Possible-Worlds Theory is the explanation of this thing, then the world he hit is one of an infinite number. Even if the things over there do know how to make these windows, the odds are infinite against their finding us. That is to say, it's impossible."

"Yes, yes, of course," Krantz said, gratefully. "Of course. They could try forever and never find us. Even if they wanted to." He thought for a moment. "And I think they do want to. It was pure reflex, their destroying Reeves, as involuntarily as a knee jerk, by the look of it. Now that they know we're here, they'll have to try to get at us; if I've sized them up right, it wouldn't be possible for them to do anything else."

Gilson remembered the eyes. "I wouldn't be a bit surprised," he said. "But now we both better—"

"*Dr. Krantz!*" someone screamed. "*Dr. Krantz!*" There was absolute terror in the voice.

The two men spun around. The soldier with the stopwatch was pointing with a trembling hand. As they looked, something white materialized in the air above the rim of the pit and sailed out and downward to land beside a similar object already lying on the ground. Another came; then another, and another. Five in all, scattered over an area perhaps a yard square.

"It's bones!" Krantz said. "Oh, my God, Gilson, it's bones!" His voice shuddered on the edge of hysteria. Gilson said, "Stop it, now. Stop it! Come on!" They ran to the spot. The soldier was already there, squatting, his face made strange by nausea and terror. "That one," he said, pointing. "That one there. That's the one they threw to the dog. You can see the teeth marks. Oh, Jesus. It's the one they threw to the dog."

They've already made a window, then, Gilson thought. They must know a lot about these matters, to have done it so quickly. And they're watching us now. But why the bones? To warn us off? Or just a test? But if a test, then still why the bones? Why not a pebble—or an ice cube? To gauge our reactions, perhaps. To see what we'll do.

And what *will* we do? How do we protect ourselves against *this?* If it is in the nature of these creatures to cooperate among themselves, the fine little family will no doubt lose no time in spreading the word over their whole world, so that one of these days we'll find that a million million of them have leaped simultaneously through such windows all over the earth, suddenly materializing like a cloud of huge, carnivorous locusts, swarming in to feed with that insensate voracity of theirs until they have left the planet a desert of bones. Is there any protection against that?

Krantz had been thinking along the same track. He said, shakily, "We're in a spot, Gilson, but we've got one little thing on our side. We know when the damn thing opens up, we've got it timed exactly. Washington will have to go all out, warn the whole world, do it through the U.N. or something. We know right down to the second when the window can be penetrated. We set up a warning system, every community on earth blows a whistle or rings a bell when it's time. Bell rings, everybody grabs a weapon and stands ready. If the things haven't come in five seconds, bell rings again, and everybody goes about his business until time for the next opening. It could work, Gilson, but we've got to work fast. In fifteen hours and, uh, a couple of minutes it'll be open again."

Fifteen hours and a couple of minutes, Gilson thought, then five seconds of awful vulnerability, and then fifteen hours and twenty minutes of safety before terror arrives again. And so on for—how long? Presumably until the things come, which might be never (who knew how their minds worked?), or until Culvergast's accident could be duplicated, which, again, might be never. He questioned whether human beings could exist under those conditions without going mad; it was doubtful if the psyche could cohere when its sole foreseeable future was an interminable roller coaster down into long valleys of terror and suspense and thence violently up to brief peaks of relief. Will a mind continue to function when its only alternatives are ghastly death or unbearable tension endlessly protracted? Is there any way, Gilson asked himself, that the race can live with the knowledge that it has no assured future beyond the next fifteen hours and twenty minutes?

And then he saw, hopelessly and with despair, that it was not fifteen hours and twenty minutes, that it was not even one hour, that it was no time at all. The window was not, it seemed, intermittent. Materializing out of the air was a confusion of bones and rent clothing, a flurry of contemptuously flung garbage that clattered to the ground and lay there in an untidy heap, noisome and foreboding.

*This impressive **F&SF** debut is a gripping contemporary ghost story that also presents a fascinating and convincing picture of a young actress. Mr. Godwin is a reformed actor whose latest novel,* Firelord, *was published in 1980. He is the co-author (with Marvin Kaye) of* The Masters of Solitude *and its recently completed sequel,* Wintermind.

PARKE GODWIN

The Fire When It Comes

G OT to wake up soon.

I've been sick a long time, I mean really sick. Hard to remember why or how long, but it feels like that time I had hundred-and-three fever for a week. Sleep wasn't rest but endless, meaningless movement, and I'd wake up to change my sweaty nightdress for a clean one which would be soaked by sunup.

But this boring, weary dream has gone on for ages. I'm walking up and down the apartment trying to find the door. The furniture isn't mine. People come and go, replaced by others with even tackier sofas in colors loud enough to keep them awake, and I flutter around and past them on my own silly route as if I'd lost an earring and had to find it before I could get on with life. None of it's very real, murky as *cinema-verité* shot in a broom closet. I have to strain to recognize the apartment, and the sound track just mumbles. No feeling at all.

Just that it's gone on so long.

All right, enough of this. Lying around sick and fragile is romantic as hell, but I have to get it together, drop the needle on the world again and let it play. I'm—

Hell, I am out of it, can't even remember my name, but there's a twinge of pain in trying. Never mind, start with simple things. Move your hand, spider your fingers out from under the covers. Rub your face, open your eyes.

That hasn't worked the last thousand times. I can't wake up, and in a minute the stupid dream will start again with a new cast and no script, and I'll be loping up and down after that earring or the lost door. Hell, yes. Here it comes. Again.

No. It's different this time. I'd almost swear I was awake, standing near the balcony door with the whole long view of my apartment stretching out before me: living room, pullman kitchen, the bedroom, bathroom like an afterthought in the rear. It's clear daylight, and the apartment is bare. Sounds are painfully sharp. The door screams open and shuts like thunder.

A boy and a girl.

She's twenty-two at the outside, he's not much older. He looks sweet, happy and maybe a little scared. Nice face, the kind of sensitive expression you look at twice. The girl's mouth is firmer. Small and blonde and compact. I know that expression, tentative only for a moment before she begins to measure my apartment for possibilities, making it hers.

"Really a lot of room," she says. "I could do things with this place if we had the money."

My God, they're so *loud*. The boy drifts toward me while she bangs cupboard doors, checks out the bathroom, flushes the toilet.

"The john works. No plumbing problems."

"Al, come here. Look, a balcony."

"Wow, Lowen, is that for real?"

Of course it's real, love. Open the door, take a look and then get the hell out of my dreams.

"Let's look, Al." He invites the girl with one hand and opens the balcony door. He's in love with her and doesn't quite know how to handle it all yet. They wander out onto my tiny balcony and look down at 77th Street and out over the river where a garbage scow is gliding upstream. It's a lovely day. Jesus, how long since I've seen the sun? Kids are romping in the playground across Riverside Drive. Lowen and Al stand close together. When he pulls her to him, her hand slips up over his shoulder. The gold ring looks new.

"Can we afford it, Lowen?"

"We can if you want it."

"If? I never wanted anything so much in my life."

They hold each other and talk money as if it were a novelty, mentioning a rent way over what I pay. The frigging landlord would love to hang that price tag on this place. Lowen points to the drainpipe collar bedded in a patch of cement, monument stone to my epic battle with that bastard to clear the drain and anchor it so every rain didn't turn my balcony into a small lake. Lowen's pointing to letters scratched in the cement.

"GAYLA."

That's right, that's me. I remember now.

They look through the apartment again, excited now that they think they want it. Yes, if they're careful with their budget, if they get that cash wedding present from Aunt Somebody, they can work it. I feel very odd; something is funny here. They're too real. The dream is about them now.

Hey, wait a minute, you two.

The door bangs shut after them.

Hey, wait!

I run out onto the balcony and call to them in the street, and for the first time in this fever dream, I'm conscious of arms and legs that I still can't feel, and a fear growing out of a clearing memory.

Hey, hello. It's me, Gayla Damon.

Lowen turns and tilts his head as if he heard me, or perhaps for one more look at where he's going to live with Al-short-for-Alice. I can't tell from his smile, but I lean to it like a fire in winter, out over the low stone parapet—and then, oh Christ, I remember. For one terrible, sufficient flash, the memory flicks a light switch.

If I could cry or be sick, I'd do that. If I screamed loud enough to crack the asphalt on West End Avenue, nobody would hear. But I let it out anyway, and my scream fills the world as Lowen and Al stroll away toward Riverside Drive.

As if they could actually see me hunched over the balcony edge, head shaking back and forth in despair. They could will their real bodies to stop, real eyes lift again to a real, vacant balcony.

Because they're real. I'm not. Not sick or dreaming, just not.

You died, Gayla baby. You're dead.

The last couple of days have been bad. Panic, running back and forth, scared to death or life, I don't know which, trying to find a way out without knowing where to go or why. I know I died, God, am I sure of that, but not how or how to get out.

There's no frigging door! Lowen and Al sail in and out unloading their junk, but when I try to find the door, it's Not, like me. I'm stuck here. I guess that's what frightens all of us because you can't imagine Not. I never bought the MGM version of heaven. For me, being dead was simply not being, zero, zilch, something you can't imagine. The closest you can come is when a dentist knocks you out with pentothol or how you felt two years before you were born.

No. I don't end, you say. Not me, not the center of the universe. And yet it's happened and I'm stuck with it, no way out, trying to hack the whole thing at once, skittering back and forth from the bedroom to the living room, through the kitchen with its new cream paint, crawling like cigarette smoke in the drapes, beating my nothing-fists against the wall sometimes, collapsing out of habit and exhaustion into a chair or bed I can't feel under me, wearing myself out with the only sensation left, exhaustion and terror.

I'm not dead. I can't be dead, because if I am, why am I still here. Let me out!

To go where, honey?

There's a kind of time again. Al's pinned up a Japanese art calendar in the kitchen, very posh. This month it's a samurai warrior drawing his sword; either that or playing with himself. I can't see it that well, but the date is much too clear. 1981. No wonder the rent's gone up. Seven years since I—

No, that word is a downer. Exited is better. Just how is still a big fat blank wrapped in confusion. All I remember is my name and a few silly details about the apartment. No past, no memory to splice the little snippets of film that flash by too swiftly to catch. Not that it matters, but where's my body? Was I buried or burned, scattered or canned in memoriam in some mausoleum? Was there a husband, a lover? What kind of life did I have?

When I think hard, there's the phantom pain of someone gone, someone who hurt me. That memory is vaguely connected with another of crying into the phone, very drunk. I can't quite remember, just how it made me feel. Got to organize and think, I've worn myself out running scared, and still no answers. The only clear thought is an odd little thing; there must have been a lot of life in me to be kept so close to it.

Don't ask me about death. The rules are all new. I might be the first of the breed. It's still me, but unable to breathe or sleep or get hungry. Just energy that can still run down from overuse, and when that happens, Lowen and Al grow faint. That's all there is to me now, energy, and not much of that. I have to conserve, just float here by Al's painfully correct window drapes and think.

Does anyone know I'm here. I mean, Anyone?

A few more days. Al and Lowen are all moved in. Al's decor works very hard at being House Beautiful, an almost militant graciousness. Style with clenched teeth. And all her china matches —hell, yes, it would. But let's face it: whatever's happening to me is because of them. When they're close, I get a hint of solid objects around me, as if I could reach out and touch tables and chairs or Lowen, but touching life costs me energy. The degree of nearness determines how much of my pitiful little charge is spent. Like being alive in a way. Living costs. I learned that somewhere.

Just got the hell scared out of me. Al has a mirror in the bedroom, a big antique affair. Sometimes when she brushes her hair, I stand behind her, aching out of habit to get that brush into my own mop. Tonight as I watched, I saw myself behind her.

I actually jumped with fright, but Al just went on pumping away with the brush while I peered over her head at Gayla Damon. Thirty-three—I remember that now—and beginning to look it. Thank God that won't bother me any more. Yes, I was tall. Brownish-black hair not too well cut. Thin face, strong jaw, eyes large and expressive. They were my best feature, they broadcast every feeling I ever had. Lines starting around my mouth. Not a hard mouth but beginning to turn down around the edges, a little tired. Hardness would have helped, I guess. Some of Natalie Bond's brass balls.

Nattie Bond: a name, another memory.

No, it's gone, but there was a kind of pain with it. I stared at the mirror. Cruddy old black sweater and jeans: was I wearing them? You'd think I could check out in something better. Hey, brown eyes, how did they do you for the curtain call? Touch of pancake, I hope. You always looked dead without it. Oh, shit. . . .

A little crying helps. Even dry it's something.

I watch Lowen more and more, turning to him as a flower follows the sun, beginning to learn why I respond to him. Lowen's a listener and a watcher. He can be animated when he's feeling good or way down if he's not. Tired, depressed or angry, his brown eyes go almost black. Not terribly aggressive, but he does sense and respond to the life going on around him.

He likes the apartment and being quiet in it. He smokes, too, not much but enough to bother Al. They've worked out a compromise: anywhere but the bedroom. So, sometimes, I get a surprise visit in the living room when Lowen wakes up and wants a smoke. He sits for a few minutes in the dark, cigarette a bright arc from his mouth to the ashtray. I can't tell, but sometimes it seems he's listening to pure silence. He turns his head this way and that—toward me sometimes—and I feel weird; like he was sifting the molecules of silence, sensing a weight in them. Sometimes in the evening when he and Al are fixing dinner, Lowen will raise his head in that listening way.

It's a long-shot hope, but I wonder if he can feel *me.*

Why has he brought me back to time and space and caring? All these years there's been only blurred shadows and voices faint as a radio in the next room. Real light and sound and thought came only when he walked in. When Lowen's near, I perk up and glow; when he leaves, I fade to drift, disinterested, by the balcony door.

Lowen Sheppard: twenty-four at most, gentle, unconsciously graceful, awkward only when he tries to be more mature than he is. Don't work at it, lover, it'll come. Soft, straight brown hair that he forgets to cut until Al reminds him, which is often. She's great on detail, lives by it. Faces this apartment like a cage of lions to be tamed. Perhaps it's the best she ever had.

Lowen seems used to this much or maybe better. Mister nice guy, not my type at all, and yet I'm bound to him by a kind of fascination, bound without being able to touch his hair or speak to him. And it's no use wondering why, I'm learning that, too. Like that old Bergman flick where Death comes to collect Max von Sydow. Max says, "Tell me what eternity is like." And Death says, "Who knows? I just work here."

Don't call us. We'll call you.

Well, damnit, *someone* is going to know I'm here. If I can think, I can do, and I'm not going to sit here forever just around the corner from life. Lowen and Al are my world now, the only script left to work with. I'm a part of their lives like a wart on the thigh, somewhere between God and a voyeur.

Wait, a memory just . . . no. Gone too quick again.

If I could touch Lowen somehow. Let him know.

Lowen and Al are settled in, place for everything and everything in its place, and Al daring it to get out of line. Lowen works full time, and Al must do some part-time gig. She goes out in the early afternoon. The lights dim then. Just as well; I don't like what she's done with my apartment. Everything shrieks its price at you, but somehow Al's not comfortable with it. Maybe she never will be. That mouth is awful tight. She wanted to keep plastic covers over the sofa and chairs, the kind that go *crunkle* when you sit on them and make you feel like you're living in a commercial. But Lowen put his foot down on that.

"But, Al, they're to use, not just to look at."

"I know, but they're so nice and new."

"Look, I wear a rubber when we make love. I don't need them on the furniture."

She actually blushed. "Really, Lowen."

Son of a—she makes him—? Do guys still wear those things? Whatever happened to the sexual revolution?

It's indicative of their upbringing the way each eats, too. Al sits erect at the table and does the full choreography with her knife and fork, as if disapproving mama was watching her all the time. Cut the meat, lay the knife down, cross the fork to her right hand, spear, chew, swallow, and the whole thing over again. Left hand demurely in her lap.

Lowen leans slightly into his plate, what-the-hell elbows on the table. More often than not, he uses the fork in his left hand, placing things on it with his knife. The way he handles them both, he's definitely lived in England or Europe. Not born there, though. The fall of his speech has a hint of softness and mid-South nasal. Virginia or Maryland. Baltimore, maybe.

Perhaps it's just plain jealousy that puts me off Alice. She's alive. She can reach out and touch, hold, kiss what I can only look at. She's the strength in this marriage, the one who'll make it work. Lowen's softer, easier, with that careless assurance that comes from never having to worry about the rent or good clothes. He's been given to; Al's had to grab and fight. Now he's got a job and trying to cut it on his own for the first time. That's scary, but Al helps. She does a pretty fair job of supporting Lowen without letting him notice it too much.

She has her problems, but Lowen comes first. She gets home just before him, zips out to get fresh flowers for the table. A quick shower and a spritz of perfume, another swift agony at the mirror. And then Lowen is home and sitting down to dinner, telling her about the day. And Al listens, not so much to the words but the easy, charming sound, the quality she loves in him, as if she could learn it for herself. She's from New York, probably the Bronx. I remember the accent somehow. Petite and pretty, but she doesn't believe it no matter how much attention Lowen gives her. Spends a lot of time at the mirror when he's gone, not admiring but wondering. What does she really look like. What type is she, what kind of an image does she, should she, project; and can she do it? Lipstick: this shade or that? So she fiddles and narrows her eyes, scrutinizing the goods, hopes for the advertised magic of Maybelline and ends up pretty much the same: more attractive than she thinks, not liking what she sees.

Except she doesn't see. She's carried it around all her life, too busy, too nervous and insecure to know what she's got. Stripped down for a bath, Al looks like she never had a pimple or a pound of fat in her life, but I swear she'll find something wrong, something not to like.

Don't slop that goo on your face, girl. You're great already. God, I only wish I had your skin. The crap I had to put on and take off every night, playing parts like—

Parts like. . . .

My God, I remember!

I was an actress. That's what I remember in quick flashes of hard light. The pictures whiz by like fast cars, but they're slowing down: stage sets, snatches of dialogue, dim faces in the front rows. Bill Wrenn giving me a piece of business to work out. Fragments of me like a painting on shattered glass. I grope for the pieces, fitting them together one by one.

Bill Wrenn: there's a warm feeling when I think of him, a trusting. Where did I meet him? Yes, it's coming back.

Bill directed that first season at Lexington Rep. Gentle and patient with a weariness that no longer expected any goodies from life, he always reminded me of a harried sheepdog with too many sheep to hustle. Forty years old, two marriages and struck out both times, not about to fall hard again.

But he did for me. I made it easy for him. We were out of the same mold, Bill and I. He sensed my insecurity as a woman and found ways to make it work for me onstage, found parts in me I'd never dream of playing. With most men, my whole thing began in bed and usually ended there. Bill and I didn't hurry; there was a love first. We enjoyed and respected each other's work, and theater was a church for us. We'd rehash each performance, sometimes staying up all night to put an extra smidge of polish on business or timing, to get a better laugh, to make something good just a hair better. We started with a love of something beyond us that grew toward each other, so that bed, when it came, was natural and easy as it was gorgeous.

I made him love me, my one genuine conquest. We even talked about getting married—carefully skirting around a lot of if's. I seem to remember him asking me one night in Lexington. I *think* he asked then; there's a thick haze of vodka and grass over that night. Did I say yes? Not likely; by that time the old habits were setting in.

It was too good with Bill. That's not funny. Perfection, happiness, these are frightening things. Very few of us can live with them. After a while, I began to resent Bill. I mean, who the hell was he to take up so much of my life? I began to pick at him, finding things not to like, irritating habits like the nervous way he cleared his throat or dug in his ear when he was thinking out some stage problem; the way he picked his feet in bed and usually left the bathroom a mess. Just bitchiness. I even over reacted when he gave me notes after a performance. All bullshit and panic; just looking for a way out. How dare you love me, Bill Wrenn? Who asked you? Where did I get that way, where did it begin?

When Nick Charreau came into the company, he was tailor-made for me.

He was alone onstage the first time I saw him, a new cast replacement going through his blocking with the stage manager. Everything his predecessor did, Nick adjusted to show himself in a better light. He wasn't a better actor, but so completely, insolently sure of himself that he could pull off anything and make it look good, even a bad choice. Totally self-centered: if there were critics in the house, Nick lit up like a sign, otherwise it was just another working night in the sticks.

Nick was a lot better looking than Bill and eighteen years younger. Even-featured with a sharp, cool, detached expression. Eyes that looked right through you. He could tell me things wrong with myself that would earn Bill Wrenn a reaming out, but I took it from Nick. He didn't get close or involved all the way down. Perhaps that's why I chose him, out of cowardice. He wouldn't ever ask me to be a person.

When he finished the blocking session, I came down to lean on the stage apron. "You play that far back, you'll upstage everyone else in the scene."

"It's my scene. I'm beautifully lit up there." Nick's smile was friendly with just the right soupçon of cockiness. A little above us all, just enough to tickle my own self-doubt and make me want to take him on. I can handle you, mister. You're not so tough.

But he was. There was always part of Nick I couldn't reach or satisfy. I started out challenged, piqued, to cut him down to size in bed and ended up happy if he'd just smile at me.

Looking over Al's shoulder in the mirror, I know it's not what we're born but what we're made into. The game is called Hurt me, I haven't suffered enough. I needed a son of a bitch like Nick. You don't think I'd go around deserving someone like Bill, do you?

Call that weird, Alice? You're the same song, different verse. You have that wary, born-owing-money look yourself. You handle it better than I did—you knew a good man when you saw one—but you still feel like a loser.

The fights with Bill grew large, bitter and frequent. He knew what was happening and it hurt him. And one night we split.

"When will you grow up, Gayla?"

"Bill, don't make it harder than it has to be. Just wish me luck."

Dogged, tired, plopping fresh ice-cubes into his drink. "I care about you. About you, Gayla. That makes it hard. Nick's twenty-two and about an inch deep. He'll split in six months and you'll be out in the cold. When will you learn, Gay? It's not a game, it's not a great big candy store. It's people."

"I'm sorry, Bill."

"Honey," he sighed, "you sure are."

I still hovered, somehow needing his blessing. "Please? Wish me luck?"

Bill raised his glass, not looking up. "Sure, Gay. With Nick you'll need it."

"What's that mean?"

"Nothing, forget it."

"No, you don't just say things like that."

"Sorry, I'm all out of graciousness."

"What did you mean? I'll need it."

Bill paused to take a swallow of his drink. "Come on, Gay. You're not blind."

"Other women? So what."

"Other anybody."

"Oh boy, you're—"

"Nick swings both ways."

"That's a lie!"

"He'd screw a light socket if it helped him to a part."

That was the nastiest thing Bill ever said about anyone. I felt angry and at the same time gratified that he made it easier to walk out mad. "Good-bye, Bill."

And then he looked up at me, showing what was hidden before. Bill Wrenn was crying. Crying for me, the only person in this fucking world who ever did. All the pain, anger, loss, welling up in those sad sheepdog eyes. I could have put my arms around him and stayed . . . no, wait, the picture's changing. I'm here in the apartment. *Get him out of here, Nick—*

No, it goes too fast or I will it to go. I can't, won't remember that yet because it hurts too much, and like a child I reach, cry out for the one thing I could always trust.

Bill-l-l—

Not a scream, just the memory of sound.

Lowen looks up from his book, puzzled. "Al? You call me?"

No answer. It's late, she's asleep.

Once more Lowen seems to listen, feeling the air and the silence, separating its texture with his senses. Searching. Then he goes back to his book, but doesn't really try to read.

He heard me. He heard *me*. I can reach him.

Sooner or later, he'll know I'm here. Bust my hump or break my heart, I'll do it. Somehow. I've got to live, baby. Even dead, it's all I know how to do.

I've hit a new low, watched Lowen and Al make love. At first I avoided it, but gradually the prospect drew me as hunger draws you to a kitchen; hunger no longer a poignant memory but sharp need that grows with my strength.

I've never watched love-making before. Porn, yes, but that's for laughs, a nowhere fantasy. One of the character men in Lexington had a library of films we used to dig sometimes after a show, hooting at their ineptness. They could make you laugh or even horny now and then, but none of them ever dealt with reality. Porn removes you from the act, puts it at a safe distance.

Real sex is awkward, banal and somehow very touching to watch. It's all the things we are and want: involvement, commitment, warmth, passion, clumsiness, generosity or selfishness. Giving and receiving or holding back, all stained with the colors of openness or fear, lovely—and very vulnerable. All that, and yet the words are inadequate; you can't get any of that from watching. Like the man said, you had to be there.

Rogers and Astaire these two are not. It's all pretty straight missionary and more of an express than a local. Lowen does certain things and Al tries a few herself, sort of at arm's length and without much freedom. I don't think Lowen's had much experience, and Al, though she needs sex, probably learned somewhere that she oughtn't like it all that much. She's the new generation; she's heard it's her right and prerogative, but the no-no was bred in early. So she compromises by not enjoying it, by making it uphill for both of them. She inhibits Lowen without meaning to. He has to wait so long for her to relax and then work so hard to get her going. And of course at the best moment, like an insurance commercial in the middle of a cavalry charge, he has to stop and put on that stupid rubber. I wonder if Al's Catholic, she never heard of a diaphragm? Or maybe it's money. That's not so far out. Maybe she's up-tight about getting pregnant because she remembers how it was to grow up poor. Maybe it's a lot of things adding up to tense ambivalence, wondering why the bells don't ring and the earth shake like she read in *Cosmopolitan*. I seem to remember that trip.

She doesn't give herself much time to relish it afterward, either. Kiss-kiss-bang-bang, then zip with the kleenex and pit-pat into the shower as if someone might catch them. Maybe that's the way it was before they married, a habit that set before either of them realized it.

But I've touched Lowen. God, yes, for one galvanized split-second I felt his body against me. I paid for it, but it had to be.

It was after they made love and Al did her sprint from bed through the shower and into her nightie-cocoon. Lowen went into the bathroom then. I heard the shower running and drifted in after him.

His body looked marvelous; smooth light olive against Al's blue flower-patterned bath curtains, the soap lather standing out sharp white against the last of his summer tan. Not too muscular; supple like Nick. It'll be a while before he has to worry about weight.

Lowen soaped and rinsed, and I enjoyed the shape of his chest and shoulders when he raised his arms over his head.

You're beautiful, Mr. Sheppard.

I had to do it then. I moved in and kissed him, *felt* his chest, stomach, his hardness against the memory of my pelvis. Only a second, a moment when I had to hold him.

The sensation that shivered through me was like a sudden electric shock. I pulled back, frightened and hurt, hovering in the shower curtain. Lowen jerked, grabbing for the towel rack, taut, scared as myself. Then, slowly, the fear faded and I saw that listening, probing attitude in the lift of his head before the instinctive fear returned. Lowen snapped the water off, stumbled out of the tub and just sat down on the john, dripping and shaking. He sat there for minutes, watching the water drying on his skin, runneling down the sides of the tub. Once he put a hand to his lips. They moved, forming a word I couldn't hear.

You felt me, damn you. You know I'm here. If I could just talk to you.

But the exhaustion and pain ebbed me. We slumped at opposite ends of the small bathroom, Lowen staring through me, not hearing the sob, the agony of the pictures that flashed into life. Touching him, I remember. After the shock of life comes the memory, filling me out by one more jagged fragment, measuring me in pain.

Al, Al, frowning at your mirror, wondering what magic you lack—I should have your problem. The guys probably lined up around the block when you were in school. Not for Gayla Damon; hell, that wasn't even my real name, not for a long, hard time. First there was big, fat Gail Danowski from the Bronx like you, and at seventeen what your men prayed for and likely never got, I couldn't give away.

Why do I have to remember that? Please, I tried so hard to get away from it. My father who worked for the city as a sandhog, my dumpy mother with her permanent look of washed-out disgust, both of them fresh off the boat in 1938. My sister Sasha who got married at seventeen to get away from them. Big change: all Zosh did after that was have kids for that beer-drinking slob husband of hers. Jesus, Charlie disgusted me. Sunday afternoons he'd come over and watch football with my father, swill beer and stuff potato chips. Every once in a while he'd let out a huge belch, then sigh and pat his pot gut like he was so goddamn pleased with himself. For years, while Zosh's teeth went and her skin faded to chalk delivering five kids.

And me growing up in the middle of it, waiting for the big event of the day in the south Bronx, the Good Humor truck out on the street.

"Mommy, Mommy, the goojoomer's here! C'n I have a dime for the goojoomer?"

"Y'fadda din leave me no money."

Urgent jingling from the Good Humor, ready to leave and take excitement with it. "Mommy!"

"Geddouda here. I ain't got no dime, now shaddup."

I used to think about that a lot: a lousy dime. So little and so much to a kid. Go to hell, Momma. Not for the dime, but for a whole beauty you never had and never missed. You weren't going to keep me from it.

It wasn't much better in high school. I was embarrassed to undress for gym because of the holes in my underwear. And the stains sometimes because I had to use Momma's Kotex and she didn't care if she ran out. I could have used Tampax; virgin or not, I was a big, healthy ox like her and Zosh. I could have conceived an army. When Momma found the Tampax I bought, she slapped me halfway across the room.

"What's this, hah? *Hah?* I ain't got enough trouble, you started already? You sneakin around, you little bitch?"

No such luck, Momma. They didn't want me. The closest I got to boys was talking about them. Sitting in a coffee shop over the debris of my cheap, starchy lunch, the table a garbage dump of bread crusts, spilled sugar and straw wrappers, shredding food bits and paper ends like our envious gossip dissected the girls we knew and the boys we wanted to know.

I never had any sense about men or myself. That happens when you're five foot seven in high school and still growing. A sequoia in a daisy bed, lumpy and lumbering, addicted to food, my refuge when I lost the courage for school dances. I fled home to the ice box and stayed there, eating myself out of my clothes, smearing my acne with Vis-o-Hex, or huddled for hours in a movie, seeing it twice over to pretend I was Hepburn or Bacall, slim, brittle and clever. Or Judith Anderson, tearing hell out of *Medea*. I read the play and practiced the lines at my mirror with stiff approximations of her gestures.

But it was *A Streetcar Named Desire* that changed my life. I hardly spoke for days after seeing it. The play stabbed me deep and sparked something that was going to be. I bought more plays and devoured them. Fewer trips to the movies now and more downtown to Broadway and the Village. Live theater, not unreeling on a spool, but happening the moment I saw it.

I was still a lump, still a hundred and fifty pounds of un-lusted-after virgin bohunk, and nobody was going to star Gail Danowski in anything but lunch. I walked alone with my dreams while the hungers grew.

You can go a little mad with loneliness, past caring. Virginity? I couldn't give it away, Momma; so I threw it away. No big Zanuck production, just a boy and a party I can't picture too clearly. We were drinking and wrestling, and I thought: all right, why not? Just once I'm gonna grab a little happiness even if it's just getting laid, what am I saving it for? But I had to get drunk before he fumbled at me. If there was pain or pleasure, I barely felt them, only knew that at last I tasted life where it sprang from the fountain. A meager cup, the cut version, the boy pulling at his clothes afterward, distant, disgusted.

"Shit, whyn't you tell me, Gail?"

Tell you what, lover? That I was a virgin, that by accident you were first? Is that a guilt trip? Whatever I lost, don't mourn it. Cry for the other things we lose in parked cars and motel beds because we're too drunk or there's too much guilt or fear for beauty. It was the beauty I missed. Be first any time, score up a hundred stiff, clumsy girls, say the silly words, break a hundred promises, brag about it afterwards. But leave something of yourself, something of beauty. Only that, and you part with a blessing.

He didn't.

The next morning, hung over and miserable, I looked at that frazzled thing in the mirror, had clean through and down to rock bottom, and knew from here on out I'd have to be me or just another Zosh. That day I started to build Gayla Damon.

I graduated an inch taller and thirty pounds lighter, did hard one-week stock as an apprentice. Seventeen hours a day of walk-ons, painting scenery, fencing and dance classes. Diction: practicing for hours with a cork between my teeth—

"Baby, the word is dance. DAAnce, hear the A? Not de-e-ance. Open your mouth and *use* it when you speak."

—Letting my hair grow and moving down to Manhattan, always running away from that lump in the mirror. I never outran her. She was always there, worrying out of my eyes at a thousand auditions, patting my stomach and thighs, searching a hundred dressing room mirrors, plastering pancake on imagined blemishes, grabbing any man's hand because it was there. The years just went, hurrying by like strangers on a street, trailing bits of memory like broken china from a dusty box: buses, planes, snatches of rehearsal, stock, repertory, old reviews.

Miss Damon's talent is raw but unmistakable. When she's right, she *is* theater, vivid, filled with primordial energy that can burn or chill. If she can learn to control . . . she was superbly cast as. . . .

—A self-driven horse record-time springing from nowhere to noplace. Life? I lived it from eight to eleven o'clock every night and two matinees a week. For three hours each night, I loved, hated, sang, sorrowed enough for three lifetimes. Good houses, bad houses, they all got the best of me because my work had a love behind it. The rest was only fill, and who cared? Season after season of repertory, a dozen cities, a dozen summer towns barely glimpsed from opening night to closing, a blur of men and a lot of beds, flush or broke, it didn't matter.

Zosh caught a show once when I was playing in Westchester. Poor Zosh: pasty and fat as Momma by then, busting out of her dresses and her teeth shot. She came hesitantly into my dressing room, wondering if someone might throw her out. The first stage play she ever saw. She didn't know really what to make of it.

"Oh, it was great and all. You look good, Gail. God, you really got some figure now, what size you wear? I never knew about plays. You know me'n school, I always got my girlfriend to write my reports."

She barely sipped the scotch I poured her. "Charlie never buys nothin' but beer." I wanted to take her out for a good dinner, but, no, she had a sitter at home and it was expensive, and Charlie would yell if she came home too late when he was out bowling.

"Let the dumb ox yell. You're entitled once in a while."

"Hey, you really gettin' a mouth on you, Gail."

"Speaking of that, doesn't Charlie ever look at yours? Doesn't he know you need a dentist?"

"Well, you know how it is. The kids take it out of you."

I gave Zosh a hundred dollars to get her teeth fixed. She wrote that she spent it on the house and kids. *There was the gas bill and Christmas. You cant complain theres nobody on the other end of the phone. Ha-ha. My friends all want to know when your on TV.*

Are you still around, Zosh? Not that it matters. They buried you years ago. No one was going to do that to me.

And then suddenly I was thirty, that big, scary number. Working harder, running harder without knowing where, doing the where-did-it-all-go bit now and then (while the lights caught her best, most expressive angle). Where are you now, Bill? You must be pushing fifty. Did you find someone like me or just the opposite. I wouldn't blame you.

And how about you, Nick?

He'll split in six months. You'll be out in the cold.

When Bill said that, I remember thinking: hell, he's right. I'm thirty-two and after that comes thirty-three. Fourteen years, seven dollars in the bank, and where the hell am I?

But I was hung up on Nick's body and trying to please him. Perhaps there were other, unspoken things that have nothing to do with loving or sex. You get used very early to not liking yourself. You know you're a fraud, someday they'll all know. The Lump hiding inside your dieted figure and with-it clothes knows you haven't changed, no matter what. The Lump doesn't want to like you. How can she tolerate anyone who does? No, she'll sniff out someone who'll keep her in her lovely place.

Crimes and insanities. Hurting Bill was a very countable sin, but I knew what I needed. So it was Nick, not Bill, who moved in here with me.

And where are you this dark night, Nick? Did you make the big time? I hope so. You're almost thirty now. That's getting on for what you had to sell. Your kind of act has a short run.

My mind wanders like that when Lowen's not around.

Energy builds again, the lights dim up. I drift out onto the balcony, feeling that weight of depression it always brings. My sense of color is dimmed because the kids are asleep. 77th Street is a still shot in black and white. Not a soul, not even a late cab whispering up Riverside Drive.

Hey, look: there's a meteor, a falling star. Make a wish: be happy, Bill Wrenn.

And listen! A clock tower. Even with Lowen asleep, I can hear it. Two-three-four o'clock. Definitely, I'm getting stronger. More and more I can feel and sometimes see my legs when I walk, less like floating in a current. I move back through the apartment to hover over Lowen as he sleeps. Wanting. Wondering.

After all this time, why should it be Lowen who wakes me? Nothing's clear but that I can touch life again with him. It that's wrong, I didn't write the script. Name any form of life you want. A cold germ is just a bug trying to make a living in the only way it knows, in a place it doesn't understand, and it only takes a little out of the place trying. That's me, that's all of us. I'll take what I need to live. If there's air to breathe, don't tell me I can't. That's academic.

Al sleeps tiny and still beside Lowen, hardly a bump under the covers. It must be wonderful to sleep like that. I could never stay out more than two hours at a time. No, wait: here she comes up out of it with a sigh and turnover that barely whispers the covers. She slides out of bed and pit-pats to the bathroom. Bladder the size of an acorn, up three times a night like I was.

When the john flushes, Lowen stirs and mumbles, flops over and sinks again. The bathroom door creaks, Al slips back in beside him. She doesn't settle down yet, but rests on one elbow, a momentary vigil over Lowen, a secret protecting. I'll bet he doesn't know she watches him like that. Then she slides under the covers very close, one arm over him, fingers spread lightly on his skin.

To lie beside Lowen like that, to touch him simply by willing it. If that were my hand resting on his skin. What wouldn't I give for that?

The idea is sudden and frightening. Why not?

If I could get inside Al, stretch out my arm inside hers, wear it like a glove; just for a moment move one real finger over Lowen's skin. It couldn't hurt her, and I need it so.

I wait for Al to fall asleep, scared of the whole notion. It could hurt. It hurt to touch Lowen before. Maybe it's against some natural law. They're flesh, I'm a memory. Lots of maybe's, but I have to try. Slow and scared, I drift down over Al and will what shape there is to me into the attitude of her body. There's no shock when I touch her, but a definite sensation like dipping into swift-running water. So weird, I pull away and have to build up my nerve to try again, settling like a sinking ship as the current of Al's healthy young life surges and tingles around me, and her chest rises and falls like a warm blanket over cozy sleep. My breasts nestle into hers, my arm stretching slowly to fill out the slim contour of her shoulder, elbow, wrist. It's hard and slow, like half-frozen syrup oozing through a hose. My fingers struggle one by one into hers.

So tired. Got to rest.

But I feel life, I *feel* it, humming and bubbling all around me. Jesus, I must have sounded like a steel mill inside, the way I drove myself. The power, such a wonder. Why did I waste so much time feeling miserable?

The electric clock glows at 5:03. More minutes pass while each finger tests itself in Al's, and then I try to move one on Lowen's skin.

The shock curdles me. I cringe away from it, shiveling back up Al's arm, all of me a shaky little ball in her middle. Just as in the shower, I felt skin against skin, even the tiny moisture of pores, but it drains me as if I've run five miles.

Rest and try again. Slow, so slow, so hard, but my fingers creep forward into Al's again. Same thing: the instant I let myself feel with Al's flesh, there's a bright shock and energy drains. If that's not enough, those delicate fingers weigh ten pounds each. I push, poop out, rest, try again, the hardest battle of my life, let alone death, and all in dogged silence broken only by their breathing and the muted *whir* of the clock.

6:32. The dark bedroom grays up to morning. I can see Lowen's face clearly now: very young, crumpled with sleep. He can't hear my soundless, exhausted panting like the heartbeat of a hummingbird.

6:48. Twelve minutes before the clock beeps the beginning of their day, one finger, one slender thread binding me to Lowen . . . moves. Again. I go dizzy with the sensation but hang on, pouring the last strength into one huge effort. The small hand flexes all five fingers like a crab, sliding over the sparse hair on Lowen's chest. A flash-frame of Bill, of Nick, and a thrill of victory.

Hi, baby. I made it.

Then Al stirs, moves, *don't, please, wait!* and flips over on her other side, unconcerned as a pancake. I let go, used up, drifting out to nowhere again, barely conscious of space or objects, too burned out even to feel frustrated after all that work.

But I did it. I know the way now. I'll be back.

Night after night I kept at it, fitting to Al's body, learning how to move her fingers without burning myself out. Stronger and surer, until I could move the whole hand and then the arm, and even if Lowen pressed the hand to his mouth or nestled his cheek against it, I could hold on.

And then I blew it, the story of my life. Klutz-woman strikes again. I tried to get in when they were making love.

I said before they're not too dexterous in the bedroom. Al gets uptight from the start, and I can see her lying there, eyes tight shut over Lowen's shoulder, hoping he'll come soon and get it over with. Not always; sometimes she wants it as much as him, but the old hangups are always there. She holds back, so he holds back. It's usually one-sided and finished soon.

But that evening everything seemed perfect. They had a light supper, several drinks rather than the usual one, and Lowen didn't spare the vodka. They just naturally segued to the bedroom, not rushed or nervous, undressing each other slowly, enjoyably, melting into each other's arms. Al brought in a candle from the supper table. Nice touch: Nick and I used to do that. They lie there caressing each other, murmuring drowsily. Lowen looks gorgeous in the soft glow, Al like a little Dresden doll. And me—poor, pathetic afterthought—watching it all and yearning.

Jesus, Al, act like you're alive. That's a man. Take hold of him.

Damn, it was too much. The hell with consequences. I draped myself over Al with the ease of practice, stretched my arms and legs along hers. Foolhardy, yes, but at last *my* arms went around Lowen, smoothing, then clawing down his back.

Love me, baby. Love all of me.

My mouth opened hungrily under his, licking his lips and then nipping at them. I writhed Al's slim body under his, pushed her hands to explore him from shoulders to thighs. I never had much trouble in bed. If the guy had anything going and didn't run through it like a fire drill, I could come half a dozen times, little ones and big ones, before he got there.

With Lowen it was like all the best orgasms I ever had. The moment before you start to go, you want to hold back, prolong it, but you can't. I was dependent on Al's chemistry now. Her body was strangely stiff as I hauled her over on top of Lowen. Something new for her. She went taut, resisting it.

"Lowen, wait."

He can't wait, though I'm the only one who sees the irony and the lie. Lowen is coming, I certainly want to, but Al is out of it. I want to *scream* at her, though I should have guessed it long before this. She always times her cries with his, as if they came together.

But it's a lie. She's faking it. She's learned that much.

My God, you're alive, the greatest gift anyone ever got. Does a past tense like me have to show you how?

With a strength like life itself, I churned her up and down on

Lowen, hard, burning myself out to tear Al's careful controls from her emotions. She moaned, fighting me, afraid.

"Lowen, stop. Please stop."

You don't fake tonight, kid.

"Stop!"

No way. Go . . . *go!*

Lowen gripped her spasmodically, and I felt his hips tremble under mine/hers. He couldn't hold back any longer. With the last ounce of my will, I bent Al's body down over his, mouth to mouth.

"Now, Lowen. Now!"

Not Al's voice but mine, the first time I've heard it in seven years. Deeper, throatier than Al's. In the middle of coming, an alien bewilderment flooded Lowen's expression. Al stiffened like she was shot. With a cry of bleak terror, she tore herself loose and leaped clear off the bed, clawing for the lamp switch, big-eyed and terrified in the hard light.

"Oh, God. Oh, Jesus, what's happening?"

Confused, a little out of it himself now, Lowen sat up to stare back at her. "Al, what's the matter?"

She shuddered. "It's not me."

"What?"

"It's not *me*." She snatched up her bathrobe like the last haven in the world. Lowen reached for his instinctively, comforting.

"It's all right, honey, it's—"

"No. It's like something hot inside me."

He went on soothing her, but he knew. I could see that in his eyes as he pulled Al down beside him. He knew: the last thing I saw, because the lights were going down for me, their last spill playing over memory-fragments before fading. A confused montage: Nick putting on his jacket, me fumbling for the phone, then pulling at the balcony door, and the darkness and the silence then were like dying again.

I've had some hangovers in my time, mornings of agony after a messy, screaming drunk. Coming back to queasy consciousness while the night's party repeats in your mind like a stupid film loop, and you wonder, in a foggy way, if you really spilled that drink on somebody, and—oh, no—you couldn't have said *that* to him, and if you're going to be sick right then or later.

Then the smog clears and you remember. Yeah. You spilled it and did it and you sure as hell said it, and the five best bloody mary's in the world won't help.

I blew it good this time, a real production number. Now they both know I'm here.

December 23. I know the date because Al's carefully crossed the days off her calendar where she never bothered before. I've been turned off for days. Almost Christmas, but you'd never know it around here. No holly, no tree, just a few cards opened and dropped on the little teakwood desk where they keep their bills. When Lowen brushes one aside, I can see a thin line of dust. Al hasn't been cleaning.

The kitchen is cluttered. The morning's dishes are still in the sink. Three cardboard boxes stand on the floor, each half full of wrapped dishes and utensils.

So that's it. They're moving. A moment of panic: where do I go from here, then? All right, it was my fault, but . . . don't go, Lowen. I'm not wild about this script myself, but don't ask me to turn out the lights and die again. Because I won't.

There's a miasma of oppression and apprehension all through the apartment. Al's mouth is tighter, her eyes frightened. Lowen comes out into the living room, reluctant and dutiful. Furtively, he tests the air as if to feel me in it. He sits down in his usual chair; 3:13 by the miniature grandfather clock on the book case. The lights and sound come up slowly with Lowen's nearness. He's home early this afternoon.

Al brings out the Waterford sherry set and puts it on the coffee table. She sits down, waiting with Lowen. The whole scene reminds me of actors taking places before the curtain rises; Al poised tensely on the sofa, revolving her sherry glass in white fingers: Lowen distant, into his own thoughts. The sound is still lousy.

". . . feel silly," Lowen ventures. ". . . all this way . . . time off from . . . just to . . ."

"No! . . . live here like this, not with . . ." Al is really shook; takes a cigarette from Lowen's pack on the coffee table and smokes it in quick, inexpert puffs. "You say you can feel her?"

Lowen nods, unhappy. He doesn't like any of this. "I loved this place from the first day."

"Lowen, answer me. Please."

"Yes."

"Where?"

"Somewhere close. Always to me."

Al stubs out the cigarette. "And we sure know it's *she,* don't we?"

"Al—"

"Oh, hell! I loved this place too, but this is crazy. I'm *scared,* Lowen. How long have you known?"

"Almost from the start."

"And you never told me."

"Why?" Lowen looks up at her. "I'm not a medium; nothing like this ever happened before. It was weird at first, but then I began to feel that she was just *here*—"

"What!"

"—and part of things . . . like the walls. I didn't even know it was a woman at first."

"Until that time in the shower," Al finishes for him. "Bitch."

Thanks a lot, kid. At least I know what to do with him.

"Look, Al, I can't tell you how I know, but I don't think she means any harm."

Al gulps down her sherry and fills the glass. "The—hell—she—doesn't. I'm not into church anymore. Even if I were, I wouldn't go running for the holy water every time a floor creaked, but don't tell me she doesn't mean anything, Lowen. You know what I'm talking about." Her hands dry-wash each other jerkily. "I mean that night, the way we made love. I—always wanted to make love to you like that. That . . . free."

The best you ever had, love.

Al gets up and paces, nervous. "All right, I've got these god-damned problems. You get taught certain things are wrong. If it's not for babies, it's wrong. It's wrong to use contraceptives, but we can't afford a baby, and—I don't know, Lowen. The world is crazy. But that night, it wasn't me. Not even my voice."

"No, it wasn't."

Lowen must be way down, depressed, because my energy is wavering with his, and sound fades in and out. There's a muffled knock at the door. Lowen opens it to a bald little man like a wizened guru in a heavy, fur-collared overcoat.

Wait, I know this guy. It's that little weasel, Hirajian, from

Riverside Realty. He rented me this place. Hirajian settles himself in a chair, briefcase on his knee, declining the sherry Al offers. He doesn't look too happy about being here, but the self-satisfied little bastard doesn't miss Al's legs, which make mine look bush league in retrospect.

I can't catch everything, but Hirajian's puzzled by something. Al's saying. No problem about the lease, he allows, apartments rent in two days now, but she's apparently thrown him a curve.

Al now: ". . . not exactly our wish, but . . ."

"Unusual request . . . never anything. . . ."

Now Al is flat and clear: "Did you find out?"

Hirajian opens his briefcase and brings out a sheet of paper while I strain at his through-the-wall mumble.

"Don't know why . . . however . . . before you. . . ." He runs through a string of names until I make the connection. The tenants who came after me, all those damned extras who wandered through my dreams before Lowen.

Lowen stops him suddenly. He's not as depressed as Al; there's an eagerness in the question. "Did anyone die here?"

"Die?"

"It's very important," Al says.

Hirajian looks like an undertaker's assistant now, all professional solemnity and reluctance. "As a matter of fact, yes. I was getting to that. In 1974, a Miss Danowski."

Lowen's head snaps up. "First name?"

"Gail."

"Anyone named Gayla? Someone cut the name Gayla in the cement on the balcony."

"That was the Danowski woman. Gayla Damon was her stage name. She was an actress. I remember because she put that name on the lease and had to do it again with her legal signature."

"Gayla."

"You knew her, Mr. Sheppard?"

"Gayla Damon. I should, it's awfully familiar, but—"

"Single?" Al asks. "What sort of person was she?"

Hirajian cracks his prim little smile like a housewife leaning over a back fence to gossip. "Yes and no, you know show people. Her boyfriend moved in with her. I know it's the fashion nowadays, but *we*," evidently Riverside and God, "don't approve of it."

There's enough energy to laugh, and I wish you could hear me, you little second-string satyr. You made a pass when you showed me this place. I remember: I was wearing that new tan suit from Bergdorf's, and I couldn't split fast enough. But it was the best place yet for the money, so I took it.

Damn it, how did I die? What happened. Don't fade out, weasel. Project, let me hear you.

Al sets down her sherry glass. "We just can't stay here. It's impossible."

Don't go, Lowen. You're all I have, all there is. I won't touch Al, I promise never again. But don't go.

Of course there were promises, Nick. There's always a promise. No one has to spell it out.

I said that once. I'm starting to remember.

While Hirajian patters on, Lowen's lost in some thought. There's something in his eyes I've never seen before. A concern, a caring.

"You mean he didn't come back even when he heard Gayla was dead?"

I love the way he says my name. Like a song, new strength.

"No end of legal trouble," Hirajian clucks. "We couldn't locate him or any family at first. A Mister . . . yes, a Mister Wrenn came and made all the arrangements. An old boyfriend, I suppose."

You did that for me, Bill? You came back and helped me out. Boy, what I had and threw away. Sand through my fingers.

"Gayla. Gayla Damon." I grow stronger as Lowen repeats my name, stronger yet as he rises and takes a step toward the balcony door. I could touch him, but I don't dare now. "Yes. Just the name I forgot. It's hard to believe, Al, but it's the only thing I can believe."

Such a queer, tender look. Al reads it too. "What, Lowen?"

He strides quickly away to the bedroom, and the lights dim a little. Then he's back with a folded paper, so lost in some thought that Al just stares at him and Hirajian is completely lost.

"The things we learn about life," Lowen says. "An English professor of mine said once that life is too coincidental for art; that's why art is structured. Mr. Hirajian, you said no one else ever complained of disturbances in this apartment. I'm not a medium, can't even predict the weather. But I'm beginning to understand a little of this."

Will you tell me, for Christ's sake?

He hands the paper to Al. It looks like an old theater program. "You see, Mister Hirajian, she's still here."

He has to say it again, delicately as possible. Hirajian pooh-poohs the whole notion. "Oh, really, now, you can't be sure of something like that."

"We know," Al says in a hard voice. "We haven't told you everything. She, it, something's here, and it's destructive."

"No, I don't think so." Lowen nods to the program. I can't see it too well. "Eagle Lake Playhouse, 1974. I saw her work."

You couldn't have. You were only—

"She played Gwendolyn in *Becket*. That's her autograph by her name."

Where the hell is Eagle Lake? Wait a minute. Wait—a—minute. I'm remembering.

"My father was taking me back to school. I spent my whole life in boarding schools all the way through college. Dad thought for our last night together, he'd take me to an uplifting play and save himself making conversation. My parents were very efficient that way.

"Gayla only had one scene, but she was so open, so completely translucent that I couldn't take my eyes off her."

I did play Eagle Lake, and there's a faint memory of some double-breasted country-club type coming back for an autograph for his kid.

"I still remember, she had a line that went: 'My lord cares for nothing in this world, does he?' She turned to Becket then, and you could see a *line* in that turn, a power that reached the other actor and came out to the audience. The other actors were good, but Gayla lit up the stage with something—unbearably human."

Damn right, love. I was gangbusters in that role. And you saw me? I could almost believe in God now, though He hasn't called lately.

"I was sixteen, and I thought I was the only one in the world who could be so lonely. She showed me we're all alike in that. All our feelings touch. Next day I hitchhiked all the way back to the theater from school. . . ." Lowen trails off, looking at Al and the apartment. "And this was her place. She wasn't very old. How did she die?"

"Depressing," Hirajian admits. "Very ugly and depressing, but then suicide always is."

What!

"But as regards your moving out just because—"

The hell I did, no *way,* mister. No. No. NO! I won't listen to any more. Don't believe him, Lowen.

Lowen's on his feet, head tilted in that listening attitude. Al puts down her glass, pale and tense. "What is it?"

"She's here now. She's angry."

"How do you know?"

"Don't ask me how, damnit. I know. She's here."

No, Lowen. On the worst, weakest day of my life, I couldn't do that. Listen. Hear me. Please.

Then Al's up, frightened and desperate. "Go away, whoever you are. For the love of God, go away."

I barely hear her, flinging myself away from them out onto the balcony, silent mouth screaming at the frustration and stupid injustice of it. A lie, a lie, and Lowen is leaving, sending me back to nothing and darkness. But the strength is growing, born of rage and terror. Lowen. Lowen, Lowen. Hear me. I didn't. *Hear me.*

"Lowen, don't!"

I hear Al's voice, then the sudden, sharp sound of the balcony door wrenching open. And as I turn to Lowen, the whole, uncut film starts to roll. And, oh Jesus, I remember.

Eagle Lake. That's where it ended, Lowen. Not here, no matter what they tell you. That's where all the years, parts, buses, beds, the whole game came to an end. When I found that, no matter what, none of it worked any more. Maybe I was growing up a little at last, looking for the *me* in all of it.

Funny: I wasn't even going to audition for stock that summer. Bill called me to do a couple of roles at Eagle Lake, and Nick urged me to go. It was a good season, closing with *A Streetcar Named Desire.* The owner, Ermise Stour, jobbed in Natalie Bond for Blanche DuBois, and I was to be her understudy. Nattie's name wasn't smash movie box office any more, but still big enough for stock and star-package houses. She's be Erm's insurance to make up whatever they lost on the rest of the season.

Erm, you tough old bag. You were going to sell that broken-down theater after every season. I'll bet you're still there, chain-smoking over a bottle of Chivas and babying that ratty poodle.

Ermise lived in a rambling ex-hotel with a huge fireplace in the lounge. We had all our opening-night parties there with a big blaze going because Eagle Lake never warmed up or dried out even in August.

At the opening party for *Becket,* all of us were too keyed up to get drunk, running on adrenaline from the show, slopping drinks and stuffing sandwiches, fending off the local reviewers, horny boy scouts with a course in journalism.

Dinner? No thanks. I've got a horrible week coming up, and it's all I can do to shower and fall into bed. Bill, let's get *out* of here. Thank's, you're a jewel, I needed a refill. Gimme your sweater. Jesus, doesn't it ever get warm in this place? You could age beef in our dressing room.

Nick was down for a few days the week before. Bill rather pointedly made himself scarce. He was still in love with me. That must have hurt, working with me day after day, keeping it inside, and I didn't help matters by dragging Nick everywhere like a prize bull: hey, look what I got! Smart girl, Gayla. With a year's study, you could be an idiot.

But Nick was gone, and we'd managed to get *Becket* open despite failing energy, colds, frayed nerves and lousy weather. It was good just to stand with Bill against the porch railing, watching moths bat themselves silly against the overhead light. Bill was always guarded when we were alone now. I kept it light and friendly, asked about his preparations for *Streetcar*. He sighed with an Old Testament flavor of doom.

"Don't ask. Erm had to cut the set budget, first read-through is tomorrow morning, and Nattie's plane won't get in until one. I'm going to be up all night and I'll still only be about five pages ahead of you people on blocking."

"Why's she late?"

"Who the hell knows? Business with her agent or something. You'll have to read in for her."

Good. One more precious rehearsal on my Blanche, one more time to read those beautiful words and perhaps find one more color in them before Natalie Bond froze it all in star glitter. That was all I had to look forward to now. The fatigue, the wet summer, lousy houses, all of it accumulated to a desolation I couldn't shrug off. I had a small part in *Streetcar,* but understudying Natalie Bond meant watching her do my role, never to touch the magic myself. Maybe her plane could crash—just a little—but even then, what? Somehow even the thought of Nick depressed me. Back in New York he'd get in to see the right agents where I couldn't, landing commercials, lining up this, grabbing that, always smarter at business than me.

That night before the party, I sat on my bed, staring glumly at the yellow-green wallpaper and my battered Samsonite luggage, and thought: *I'm tired of you. Something's gone. There's gotta be more than this.* And I curled up in my old gray bathrobe, wallowing in self-pity. Nick, you want to get married? Bring me the towel and wash my back? Baby me a little when I feel rotten, like now? There's a big empty place in me wants to be pregnant with more than a part. Tired, negative, I knew Nick would never marry me; I was kidding myself.

So it was good to have Bill there on the porch for a minute. I leaned against him and he put an arm around me. We should have gone to bed and let it be beautiful one more time. It would have been the last.

"Tired, Gay?"

"I want to go home."

Except I never in my whole life found where it was.

Natalie Bond came and conquered. She knew her lines pretty well going in and crammed the rest with me in her room or the restaurant down our street. No one recognized her at first with her hair done just the right shade of fading dishwater blonde for Blanche, most of her thin face hidden behind a huge pair of prescription sunglasses.

She was near-sighted to blindness; some of her intensity on film must have come from trying to feel out the blocking by Braille. But a pro she was. She soaked up Bill's direction, drove herself and us, and I saw the ruthless energy that made Nattie a star.

I saw other things, too. Nattie hadn't been on a live stage for a lot of years. She missed values left and right in Blanche and didn't have time to pick them up on a two-week stock schedule. Film is a director's medium. He can put your attention where he wants with the camera. Stage work takes a whole different set of muscles, and hers were flabby, unused to sustaining an action or mood for two and a half hours.

But for the first time that season, we were nearly sold out at the box office. Erm was impressed. Bill wasn't.

"They're coming to see a star. She could fart her way through Blanche and they'll still say she's wonderful."

Maybe, but life wasn't all skittles for Nattie. She had two children in expensive schools and got endless phone calls from her manager in California about taxes.

"I gotta work, honey," she told me over black coffee and dry toast. "The wolf's got my ass in his chops already."

She meant it. Another phone call, and that same afternoon between lunch and rehearsal call, Nattie Bond was gone, and I was sitting in Ermise's living room again while Erm swore back and forth across the worn carpet, waving her drink like a weapon, and Bill tried to look bereaved. He always wanted me for Blanche. He had me now.

"Screwed me from the word go." Ermise sprayed ashes over the rug and her poodle. "She knew this when she signed and never said a goddamn word."

The facts filtered through my rosy haze. Natalie's agent had a picture deal on the coast so close to signing that it was worth it to let Ermise sue. They'd just buy up her contract—if she could be in Los Angeles tomorrow.

Ermise hurled her cigarette into the trash-filled fireplace, gulped the last of her drink and turned a mental page. Nattie was one problem, the show another. "You ready to go, Gayla?"

"In my sleep, love."

I was already readjusting the role to the Blanche in my ear and not as sorry for the box office as Erm. Screw 'em all, they were going to see ten times the Blanche Nattie Bond could give them on the best day she ever worked.

"Bill wants me to give you a raise," Ermise said. "Wish I could, Gay, but things are tight."

I pulled the worn script out of my jeans, grinning like a fool back at Bill, who couldn't hide his glee any more. "Just pay on time, Erm. Keep out of my hair and don't clutter up my stage. Bill, let's go to work."

From my first rehearsal, the play convulsed and became a different animal. The whole cast had to shift gears for me, but no longer suffused by Nattie's hard light they began to find themselves and glimmer with life. I ate and slept with the script while Blanche came sure and clear. Hell, I'd been rehearsing her for fourteen years. It wasn't hard to identify: the hunger for love half appeased in bed-hopping and sexual junk food, and what that does to a woman. The blurred, darkening picture of a girl waiting in her best dress to go to the dance of life with someone who never came.

Then, just as it seemed to be coming together, it went flat, deader than I am now. But out of that death came a beautiful, risky answer.

Blanche DuBois is a bitch of a role and demands a powerhouse actress. That's the problem. Like the aura that surrounds Hamlet, the role accumulates a lot of star-shtick, and something very subtle can get lost. I determined to strip away the layers of gloss and find what was there to begin with.

"The part's a trap, Bill. All those fluttery, curlicued lines reach out and beg you to *act* them. And you wind up with dazzle again, a concert performance."

"Cadenzas," he agreed with me. "The old Williams poetry."

"Right! Cadenzas, scales. No, by God. I've played the Deep South. There's a smothered quality to those women that gets lost that way. The script describes her as a moth. Moths don't dazzle. They don't glitter."

"Remember that night on the porch," Bill said thoughtfully. "They don't glitter, but they do need the light."

And that was it. Blanche aspired to the things she painted with foolish words. A dream of glitter seen by a near-sighted person by a failing candle. The lines are ornate, but just possibly, Blanche is not quite as intelligent as she's been played.

A long artistic chance, but they're the only ones worth taking. If you don't have the guts to be wrong, take up accounting.

So my Blanche emerged a very pathetic woman, a little grotesque as such women are, not only desperate for love but logical in her hopes for Mitch. For all Belle Reeve and the inbred magnolias, she's not that far above him. Bill gave me my head, knowing that by finding my own Blanche, even being wrong for a while, I'd find the play's as well. On my terms and with my own reality.

I had three lovely labor-pained days of seeing her come alive.

On the third day, I was sitting in a corner of the stage with coffee and a sandwich, digging at the script while the others lunched. When Sally Kent walked in, I snapped at her.

"Where's the rest? It's two o'clock. Let's go."

"They want you over at the office, Gay."

"What the hell for? I don't have time. Where's Bill?"

"At the office," Sally admitted reluctantly. "Natalie Bond is here. She's back in the show."

The kiss of death. Even as I shook my head, no, Erm wouldn't do this to me, I knew she would.

Ermise hunched in a chair by the fireplace, bitter with what she had to do, trying not to antagonize Bill any further. He poised on the sofa, seething like a malevolent cat.

"Nattie will do the show after all," Ermise said. "I have to put her back in, Gay."

I couldn't speak at first; sick, quivering on my feet with that horrible end-of-the-rope hollowness in my stomach. No place to go from here. No place. . . .

"When we pulled her name off the advertising, we lost more than a third of our reservations." Erm snorted. "I don't like it. I don't like her right now, but she's the only thing'll keep my theater open."

Bill's comment cut with the hard edge of disgust. "You know what this does to the cast, don't you? They've readjusted once. Now they have to do it again and open in two days. They were an ensemble with Gayla. Now they're the tail of a star vehicle."

Bill knew it was already lost, but he was doing this for me.

Ermise shook her head. "Gay, honey, I can't afford it, but I'm gonna raise you retroactive to the first week of your contract." Her hands fluttered in an uncharacteristically helpless gesture. "I owe you that. And you'll go back in as Eunice. But next season—"

I found my voice. It was strange, old. "Don't do this to me. This role, it's mine, I earned it. She'll ruin it."

"Don't look at me," Bill snapped to Ermise. "She's right."

Ermise went defensive. "I don't care who's right. You're all for Gay. Fine, but I can't run a theater that way. Lucky to break even as it is. Nattie's back, she plays, and that's the end of it. Gay's contract reads 'as cast.' She's Eunice. What else can I say?"

I showed her what else. I ripped the *Streetcar* script in four parts and threw them in the fireplace. "You can say good-by, Ermise. Then you can take your raise and shove it." I was already lurching toward the door, voice breaking. "Then you can put someone in my roles, because I'm leaving."

I meant it. Without Blanche, there was no reason to stay another minute. Finished. Done.

Except for Natalie Bond. I found her in her hotel room, already dressed for rehearsal and running over the script.

"Come on in, Gayla. Drink?"

"No."

She read my tension as I crouched with my back against the door. "All right, hon. Get it off your chest."

"I will."

I told the bitch what I felt and what I thought and didn't leave anything out. It was quite a speech for no rehearsal, beginning with my teens when I first knew I had to play Blanche, and the years and hard work that made me worthy of it. There wasn't a rep company in the east I hadn't worked, or a major role from Rosalind to Saint Joan I hadn't played. To walk out on the show like she did was pure shit. To crawl back was worse.

"Right," said Nattie. She faced me all through it, let me get it all out. I was crying when I finished. I sank down on a chair, grabbing for one of her Kleenex.

"Now do you want a drink?"

"Yes, what the hell."

She wasn't all rat, Nattie. She could have put me down with the star routine, but she fixed me a stiff gin and soda without a word. I remember her fixing that drink: thick glasses and no make up, gristly thin. She had endless trouble with her uterus, infection after painful infection and a work schedule that never allowed her to heal properly. A hysterectomy ended the whole thing. Nattie's face was thinner than mine, all the softness gone, mouth and cheeks drawn tight. No matter how sincere, the smile couldn't unclench.

And this, I thought, is what I want to be? Help me, Nick. Take me home. There's gotta be a home somewhere, a little rest.

"Know what we're like?" Nattie mused. "A little fish swimming away from a big, hungry fish who's just about to be eaten by a bigger fish. That's us, honey. And that's me in the middle."

She screwed Ermise, but someone shafted her too. The picture deal was a big fat fake. The producer wanted someone a little bigger and hustled Nattie very plausibly to scare the lady into reaching for a pen.

"I'm broke, Gayla. I owe forty thousand in back taxes, my house is on a second mortgage, and my kids' tuition is overdue. Those kids are all I have. I don't know where the hell to go from here, but Ermise needs me and I sure as hell need the job."

While I huddled over my drink, unable to speak, Nattie scribbled something on a memo pad.

"You're too good to waste, you're not commercial, and you'll probably die broke. But I saw your rehearsal this morning."

I looked up at her in weepy surprise. The smile wasn't quite so hard just then.

"If I can do it half that well, Gay. Half."

She shoved the paper into my hand. "That's my agent in New York. He's with William Morris. If he can't get you work, no one can. I'll call him myself." She glanced at her dressing table clock. "Time, gotta run."

Nattie divined the finality in my shoulders as I sagged toward the door. "You going to play Eunice?"

"No. I'm leaving."

Pinning her hair, she shot me a swift, unsmiling appraisal through the mirror. "Good for you. You got a man in New York?"

"Yeah."

"Get married," she mumbled through a mouthful of pins. "It's not worth it." As the door closed, she raised her voice. "But call my agent."

My bags were packed, but I hadn't bothered to change clothes. That's why my permanent costume, I suppose. Who knew then I'd get very tired of black. Bill insisted on driving me to the airport. When he came for me, I must have looked pathetic, curled up on the bed in one more temporary, damp summer room just waiting to eject me. No love lost; I got damned sick of yellow-green wallpaper.

Bill sat on the edge of the bed. "Ready, love?"

I didn't move or answer. Done, finished. Bill put aside the old hurt and lay down beside me, bringing me into his arms. I guess something in him had to open in spite of his defenses. He opened my heart gently as a baby's hand clutched around something that might harm it, letting me cry the last of it out against his shoulder. The light faded in the room while we lay together.

We kissed good-by like lovers at the departure gate. Bill was too much a part of me for anything less. Maybe he knew better than I how little was waiting for me.

"Be good, Gay."

"You too." I fiddled with his collar. "Don't forget to take your vitamins, you need them. Call me when you get back."

He hugged me one last time. "Why don't you marry me some-time?"

For a lot of reasons, Bill. Because I was a fool and something of a coward. The stunting begins in the seed when we learn not to like ourselves. The sad thing about life is that we usually get what we really want. Let it be.

Funny, though: that was my first and last proposal, and I kissed him good-by, walked out of his life, and four hours later I was dead.

There was time on the plane to get some of it together. Natalie was a star, at the top where I wanted to be, and look at her: most of the woman cut out of her, flogged to work not by ambition but need. Driven and used. She reminded me of a legless circus freak propelling herself on huge, overdeveloped arms, the rest of her a pitiful afterthought cared for by an expensive gynecologist. I thought: at least when I get home there'll be Nick. Don't call him from the airport; let it be a surprise. We'll get some coffee and cold-cuts, make love and talk half the night. I needed to talk, to see us plain.

Get married, Nattie said. It isn't worth it.

Maybe not the way I chased it for fourteen years. I'd call her agent, keep working, but more New York jobs with time left over to be with Nick, to sit on my balcony and just breathe or read. To make a few friends outside of theater. To see a doctor and find out how tough I really am, and if everything in the baby box is working right, so that maybe—

Like she said, so maybe get married and have kids while I can. A little commitment, Nick, a little tomorrow. If the word sounds strange, I just learned it. Give me this, Nick. I need it.

The light was on in our living room as I hauled my suitcase

out of the cab and started up. Hell, I won't even buzz, just turn the key in the lock and reach for him.

I did that.

There was—yes, I remember—one blessed moment of breathing the good, safe air of my own living room as I set down the luggage. I heard a faint stirring from the bedroom. Good, I've surprised him. If Nick was just waking from a nap, we'd have that much more time to touch each other.

"It's me, baby."

I crossed to the bedroom door, groping inside for the light switch. "I'm home."

I didn't need the switch. There was enough light to see them frozen on the torn-up bed. The other one was older, a little flabby. He muttered something to Nick. I stood there, absurd myself, and choked: "Excuse me."

Then, as if someone punched me in the stomach, I stumbled to the bathroom, pushed the door shut and fell back against it.

"Get him out of here, Nick!"

The last word strangled off as I doubled over the john and vomited all the horrible day out of me, with two hours left to live, retching and sobbing, not wanting to hear whatever was said beyond the door. After a short time, the front door closed. I washed my face, dried it with the stiff, clumsy movements of exhaustion, and got out to the living room somehow, past the bed where Nick was smoking a cigarette, the sheet pulled up over his lean thighs.

I remember pouring a drink. That was foolish on an empty stomach, the worst thing anyone could have done. I sat on the sofa, waiting.

"Nick." The silence from the bedroom was the only thing I could feel in my shock. "Nick, please come out. I want to talk to you."

I heard him rustle into his clothes. In a moment Nick came out, bleak and sullen.

"Why are you back so early?"

"No, they—" My reactions were still disjointed, coming out of shock, but the anger was building. "They put Nattie Bond back in the show. I walked out."

That seemed to concern him more than anything else. "You just walked out? They'll get Equity on you."

"Never mind about Equity, what are *we* gonna do?"

"What do you mean?" he asked calmly.

"Oh, man, are you for real?" I pointed at the door. "What was that?"

"That may be a Broadway job." He turned away into the kitchen. "Now get off my back."

"The hell I—"

"Hey look, Gayla. I haven't made any promises to you. You wanted me to move in. Okay, I moved in. We've had it good."

I began to shake. "Promises? Of course there were promises. There's always a promise, nobody has to spell it out. I could have gone to bed with Bill Wrenn plenty of times this summer, but I didn't."

He only shrugged. "So whose fault is that? Not mine."

"You bastard!" I threw my glass at him. He ducked, the thing went a mile wide, then Nick was sopping up whisky and bits of glass while I shook myself apart on the couch, teeth chattering so hard I had to clamp my mouth tight shut. It was all hitting me at once, and I couldn't handle half of it. Nick finished cleaning up without a word, but I could see even then the tight line of his mouth and the angry droop of his eyelids. He had guts of a kind, Nick. He could face anything because it didn't matter. All the important things were outside, to be reached for. Inside I think he was dead.

"The meanest thing Bill ever said to me," I stuttered. "When I left him for you, h-he said you played both sides of the fence. And I c-called him a goddamn liar. I couldn't believe he'd be small enough to— Nick, I'm falling apart. They took my show, and I came home to you because I don't know what to do."

Nick came over, sat down and held me in his arms. "I'm not, Gayla."

"Not what?"

"What Bill said."

"Then w-what was this?"

He didn't answer, just kissed me. I clung to Nick like a lost child.

Why do we always try to rewrite what's happened? Even now I see myself pointing to the door and kissing him off with a real Bette Davis sizzler for a curtain. Bullshit. I needed Nick. The accounting department was already toting up the cost of what I wanted and saying: *I'll change him. It's worth it.*

I only cried wearily in his arms while Nick soothed and stroked me. "I'm not that," he said again. "Just that so many guys are hung up on role-playing and all that shit. Oh, it's been said about me."

I twisted in his lap to look at him "Nick, why did you come to me?"

The question gave him more trouble than it should. "I like you. You're the greatest girl I ever met."

Something didn't add up. Nothing ever bugged Nick before; he could always handle it, but he was finding this hard.

"That's not enough," I persisted. "Not tonight."

Nick disengaged himself with a bored sigh. "Look, I have to go out."

"Go out? Now?" I couldn't believe he'd leave me like this. "Why?"

He walked away toward the bedroom. I felt the anger grow cold with something I'd never faced before, answers to questions that gnawed at the back of my mind from our first night. "Why, Nick? Is it him? Did that fat queer tell you to come over after you ditched the hag?"

Nick turned on me, lowering. "I don't like that word."

"Queer."

"I said—"

"Queer."

"All right." He kicked viciously at the bedroom door with all the force he wanted to spend stopping my mouth. "It's a fact in this business. That's why I get in places you don't. It's a business, cut and dried, not an *aht fawm* like you're always preaching."

"Come off it, Nick." I stood up, ready for him and wanting the fight. "That casting couch bit went out with Harlow. Is that how you get jobs? That, and the cheap, scene-stealing tricks you use when you know and I know I played you against the wall in Lexington, you hypocritical son of a bitch."

Nick threw up a warning hand. "Hey, wait just one damn minute, Bernhardt. I never said I was or ever could be as good as you. But I'll tell you one thing." Nick opened the closet and snaked his jacket off a hanger. "I'll be around and working when nobody remembers you, because I know the business. You've been around fourteen years and still don't know the score. You won't make rounds, you don't want to be bothered waiting for an agent to see you. You're a goddamn *ahtist.* You won't wait in New York for something to develop, hell no. You'll take any show going out to Noplaceville, and who the hell ever sees you but some jerkoff writing for a newspaper no one reads. Integrity? Bullshit, lady. You are *afraid* of New York, afraid to take a chance on it."

Nick subsided a little. "That guy who was here, he produces. He's got a big voice where it counts." Again he looked away with that odd, inconsistent embarrassment. "He didn't want to sleep with me, really. He's basically straight."

That was too absurd for anger. "Basically?"

"He only wanted a little affection."

"And you, Nick. Which way do you go basically. I mean was it his idea or yours?"

That was the first totally vulnerable moment I ever saw in Nick. He turned away, leaning against the sink. I could barely hear him. "I don't know. It's never made much difference. So what's the harm? I don't lose anything, and I may gain."

He started for the door, but I stopped him. "Nick, I need you. What's happened to me today, I'm almost sick. Please don't do this to me."

"Do what? Look." He held me a moment without warmth or conviction. "I'll only be gone a little while. We'll talk tomorrow, okay?"

"Don't go, Nick."

He straightened his collar carefully with a sidelong glance at the mirror. "We can't talk when you're like this. There's no point."

I dogged him desperately, needing something to hang onto. "Please don't go. I'm sorry for what I said. Nick, we can work it out, but don't leave me alone."

"I have to." His hand was already on the door, cutting me off like a thread hanging from his sleeve.

"Why!" It ripped up out of the bottom, out of the hate without which we never love or possess anything. "Because that fat faggot with his job means more than I do, right? How low do you crawl to make a buck in this business? Or is it all business? Jesus, you make me sick."

Nick couldn't be insulted. Even at the end, he didn't have that to spare me. Just a look from those cool blue eyes I tried so hard to please, telling me he was a winner in a game he knew, and I just didn't make it.

"It's your apartment. I'll move."

"Nick, don't go."

The door closed.

What did I do then? I should remember, they were the last minutes of my life. The door closed. I heard Nick thumping down the carpeted stairs, and thank God for cold comfort I didn't run after him. I poured a straight shot and finished it in one pull.

A hollow, eye-of-the-storm calm settled on me and then a depression so heavy it was a physical pain. I wandered through the apartment drinking too much and too fast, talking to Nick, to Bill, to Nattie, until I collapsed, clumsy, hiccuping drunk on the floor with half an hour to live.

Another drink. Get blind, drunk enough to reach . . . something, to blot out the Lump. Yeah, she's still with you, the goddamn little loser. Don't you ever learn, loser? No, she won't ever learn. Yesterday did this day's madness prepare. What play was that and who cares?

I tried to think but nothing came together. My life was a scattered Tinkertoy, all joints and pieces without meaning or order. A sum of apples and oranges: parts played, meals eaten, clothes worn, he said and I said, old tickets, old programs, newspaper reviews yellowed and fragile as Blanche's love letters. Apples and oranges. Where did I leave anything of myself, who did I love, what did I have? No one. Nothing.

Only Bill Wrenn.

"Christ, Bill, help me!"

I clawed for the phone with the room spinning and managed to call the theater. One of the girl apprentices answered. I struggled to make myself understood with a thickening tongue. "Yeah, Bill Wrenn, 'simportant. Gayla Damon. Yeah, hi, honey. He's not? Goddamnit, he's gotta be. I *need* him. When'll he be back? Yeah . . . yeah. Tell'm call Gayla, please. Please. Yeah, trouble, Real trouble. I need him."

That's how it happened. I dropped the phone in the general vicinity of the hook and staggered to the pitching sink to make one more huge, suicidal drink, crying and laughing, part drunk, part hysteria. But Bill was going to bail me out like he always had, and, boy, ol' Gay had learned her lesson. I was a fool to leave him. He loved me. Bill loved me and I was afraid of that. Afraid to be loved. How dumb can you get?

"How dumb?" I raged mushily at the Lump in the mirror. "You with the great, soulful eyes. You never knew shit, baby."

I was sweating. The wool sweater oppressed my clammy skin. Some sober molecule said take it off, but no. It's cooler out on my balcony. I will go out on my beautiful, nighted balcony and present my case to the yet unknowing world.

I half fell through the door. The balcony had a low railing, lower than I judged as I stumbled and heaved my drunken weight behind the hand flung out to steady myself and—

Fell. No more time.

That's it, finished. Now I've remembered. It was that sudden, painless, meaningless. No fade out, no end title music resolving the conflict themes, only torn film fluttering past the projector light, leaving a white screen.

There's a few answers anyway. I could get a lump in my throat, if I had one, thinking how Bill came and checked me out. God, let's hope they kept me covered. I must have looked awful. Poor Bill; maybe I gave you such a rotten time because I knew you could take it and still hang in. That's one of the faces of love, Mister Wrenn.

But I'd never have guessed about Lowen. Just imagine: he saw me that long ago and remembered all those years because I showed him he wasn't alone. I still can't add it up. Apples and oranges.

Unless, just maybe. . . .

"Lowen!"

The sound track again, the needle dropped on time. The balcony door thunders open and slams shut. Al calls again, but Lowen ignores her, leaning against the door, holding it closed.

"Gayla?"

His eyes move searchingly over the balcony in the darkening winter afternoon. From my name etched in the cement, around the railing, Lowen's whole concentrated being probes the gray light and air, full of purpose and need.

"Gayla, I know you're here."

As he says my name, sound and vision and my own strength treble. I turn to him, wondering if through the sheer power of his need he can see me yet.

Lowen, can you hear me?

"I think I know what this means."

I stretch out my hand, open up, let it touch his face, and as I tingle and hurt with it, Lowen turns his cheek into the caress.

"Yes, I feel you close."

Talk to me, love.

"Isn't it strange, Gayla?"

Not strange at all, not us.

"When I saw you that night, I wanted to reach out and touch you, but I was just too shy. Couldn't even ask for my own autograph."

Why not? I could have used a little touching.

"But I hitched all the way from school next day just to catch a glimpse of you. Hid in the back of the theater and watched you rehearse."

That was Blanche. You saw that?

"It was the same thing all over again. You had something that reached out and showed me how we're all alike. I never saw a lonelier person than you on that stage. Or more beautiful. I cried."

You saw Blanche. She did have a beauty.

"Oh, Gayla, the letters I wrote you and never sent. Forgive me. I forgot the name but not the lesson. If you hear me: you were the first woman I ever loved, and you taught me right. It's a giving."

I can hear Al's urgent knock on the other side of the door. "Lowen, what is it? Are you all right?"

He turns his head and smiles. God, he's beautiful. "Fine, Al. She loves this place, Gayla. Don't drive her away."

I won't, but don't go. Now when I'm beginning to understand so much.

He shakes his head. "This is our first house. We're new, all kinds of problems. Parents, religion, everything."

Can you *hear* me?

"We were never loved by anyone before, either of us. That's new, too. You pray for it—"

Like a fire:

"—like a fire to warm yourself."

You do hear me.

"But it's scary. What do you do with the fire when it comes?" Lowen's hands reach out, pleading. "Don't take this away from her. Don't hurt my Al. You're stronger than us. You can manage."

I stretch my hand to touch his. With all my will, I press the answer through the contact.

Promise, Lowen.

"Don't make me shut you out, I don't know if I could. Go away and keep our secret? Take a big piece of love with you?"

Yes. Just that I was reaching for something, like you, and I had it all the time. So do you, Lowen. You're a—

I feel again as I did when the star fell across the sky, joyful and new and big as all creation without needing a reason, as Lowen's real fingers close around the memory of mine.

You're a *mensche,* love. Like me.

Lowen murmurs: "I feel your hand. I don't care what anyone says. Your kind of woman doesn't kill herself. I'll never believe it."

Bet on it. And thank you.

So it was a hell of a lot more than apples and oranges. It was a giving, a love. Hear that, Bill? Nattie? What I called life was just the love, the giving, like kisses on the wind, thrown to the audience, to my work, to the casual men, to whom it may concern. I was a giver, and if the little takers like Nick couldn't dig that, tough. That's the way it went down. All the miserable, self-cheating years, something heard music and went on singing. If Nattie could do it half as well. If she was half as alive as me, she meant. I loved all my life, because they're the same thing. Man, I was beautiful.

That's the part of you that woke me, Lowen. You're green, but you won't go through life like a tourist. You're going to get hurt and do some hurting yourself, but maybe someday. . . .

That's it, Lowen. That's the plot. You said it: we all touch, and the touching continues us. All those nights, throwing all of myself at life, and who's to say I did it alone?

So when you're full up with life, maybe you'll wake like me to spill it over into some poor, scared guy or girl. You're full of life like me, Lowen. It's a beautiful, rare gift.

It's dark enough now to see stars and the fingernail sliver of moon. A lovely moment for Lowen and me, like a night with Bill a moment before we made love for the first time. Lowen and I holding hands in the evening. Understanding. His eyes move slowly from my hand up, up toward my face.

"Gayla, I can see you."

Can you, honest?

"Very clear. You're wearing a sweater and jeans. And you're smiling."

Am I ever!

"And very beautiful."

Bet your ass, love. I feel great, like I finally got it together.

One last painful, lovely current of life as Lowen squeezes my hand. "Good-by, Gayla."

So long, love.

Lowen yanks open the door. "Al, Mister Hirajian? Come on out. It's a lovely evening."

Alice peeks out to see Lowen leaning over the railing, enjoying the river and the early stars. His chest swells; he's laughing and he looks marvelous, inviting Al into his arms the way he did on their first day here. She comes unsurely to nestle in beside him, one arm around his waist. "Who were you talking to?"

"She's gone, Al. You've got nothing to be afraid of. Except being afraid."

"Lowen, I'm not going to—"

"This is our house, and nobody's going to take it away from us." He turns Al to him and kisses her. "Nobody wants to, that's a promise. So don't run away from it or yourself."

She shivers a little, still uncertain. "Do you really think we can stay? I can't—"

"Hey, love." Lowen leans into her, cocky and charming, but meaning it. "Don't tell a *mensche* what you can't. Hey, Hirajian."

When the little prune pokes his head out the door, Lowen sweeps his arm out over the river and the whole lit-up West Side. "Sorry for all the trouble, but we've changed our minds. I mean, look at it! Who could give up a balcony with a view like this?"

He's the last thing I see before the lights change: Lowen holding Al and grinning out at the world. I thought the lights were dimming, but it's something else, another cue coming up. The lights cross-fade up, up, more pink and amber, until—my God, it's gorgeous!

I'm not dead, not gone. I feel more alive than ever. I'm Gail and Gayla and Lowen and Bill and Al and all of them magnified, heightened, fully realized, flowing together like bright, silver streams into—

Will you look at that *set*. Fantastic. Who's on the lights?

So that's what You look like. Ri-i-ght. I'm with it now, and I love You too. Give me a follow-spot, Baby.

I'm on.

This competition, suggested by Philip Michael Cohen, asked competitors to retell a pointless anecdote about a man on a bus in the style of any SF writer. The idea was originally presented in the excellent book Exercises in Style *by Raymond Queneau.*

From Competition 22: Anecdotes in the Style of a SF Writer

In the style of Jack Vance

The shimmering blues and violets from the midday suns cast multiple shadows beneath the orange and pink roof slats of the Tarquay to Munhill denham.* Arzal Gherkin used a green and purple kerchief to pat at the rivulets of perspiration that ran down his neck as he and his fellow passengers jounced along the poorly cobbled streets toward their destination. He was dolefully passing the time by surreptitiously observing another occupant of the denham, a man of the obscure Grey Abbey sect which was known almost solely for its disdain of local fashion. The stark, drab grey of his costume, especially that of his felt hat encircled by plaited

* A contrivance for public transportation on Homyl:281; its gaudy color scheme reflects its owner's social status, and the intricacies of design about the headboard reveal much about his mental stability.

cords instead of the more popular brightly colored ribbons and feathers, drew attention by virtue of its subdued uniqueness.

The man suddenly turned to a fellow passenger and began to berate him quite vigorously, accusing him of purposefully scuffing the toes of his boots at every stop when moving aside to allow other passengers to board or to alight. Just as suddenly he ceased his harangue and seated himself in a recently vacated side-seat from which he glowered for the remainder of the journey at the passing tree-beet forests.

Later in the day while partaking of some Green Moss wine and reed cakes along the esplanade near the station in Munhill, Arzal Gherkin noticed the man again, this time engaged in earnest conversation with another member of his drab sect. The man was apparently being advised to seek the assistance of a nearby tailor in order to re-situate the top button on his lapelled overjacket, to what advantage one could only speculate.

—Paul Major
Baton Rouge, La.

In the style of Philip K. Dick

Returning to his conapt on a bus, he felt the *koinos kosmos* slip away. What would happen, he thought, if he asked the bus driver? But, no. Everyone else thought they were riding the S bus; only he knew it was now No. 84. Yes. He opened his eyes and looked around for evidence to support this theory. The bus continued on through the Parc Monceau district.

Or did it?

After all, he had boarded the bus in Marin County, and there was no Parc Monceau district in California. Perhaps if he asked a passenger. He glanced ahead at the Longnecker, but the plaited cord around the Longnecker's felt hat identified him as a PEAK-man; so he decided to remain silent. I think, he thought, the other passengers on this bus are mere props. So it would be useless to ask them. The bus passed a vacant lot.

Suddenly, the PEAK-man threw himself on to a seat which had become vacant. The whole row of seats, in fact, had become vacant. So had the PEAK-man. Molecules dispersed. The bus went out of existence. In its place was a sheet of paper with all of these words printed on it. He turned it over. On the other side were the words, "Please retype other side and enter in Competition 22."

—Robert Stewart
Somerville, Mass.

In the style of Robert Heinlein

The triple suns of Herculon B danced a jig high overhead. Tom felt a sharp elbow jab him through the double-bind pleats of his mono-thread suit. He turned to face the gangly, long necked man leaning on the aft rail of the Herculon B to Sirius star cruiser. As he hit his ancient meershaum pipe with a pocket laser, Tom noticed something odd about him.

Why, Tom thought, *he's using nickel-steel for space helmet reinforcing instead of ferro-cement!*

"You've been stepping on my toes, partner," said the gangly man, dense clouds of pumice smoke leaking through the pipe's complex zero-g filtering system.

"I-I'm sorry," said Tom, blushing. *Just two hours away from Aunt Zeb and Uncle Eke's nuclear breeding farm and already I show I'm a hick!*

The tall man waved away the smoke. "Think nothing of it," he said, lowering himself to the floor. The memory plastic of the deck anticipated and flowed upwards, forming a chair beneath him. "I could see you're lost in thought. Me, too. I'm going to Sirius Major IV to see a man about modifying certain cosmetic designs on my outer protective suit."

—Buzz Dixon
Van Nuys, Calif.

In the style of Barry Malzberg

The bus map is a small mockery, printed without street names, as if to tell me that I no longer deserve to know where I am going. I will have to do something about this. I am not like these others, not like the woman next to me with the sparse beard and shopping bag, not like the man nearby in the torn fatigue jacket and tan chinos. I do not belong on a bus. But even as I form the thought, the map betrays me with its illiterate defiance; I have almost missed my transfer. I lunge for the exit, brushing past the man in fatigues, and he turns to accost me, accusing me of deliberately stepping on his feet. I know that I have done no such thing, but I mumble a few words of apology; in the face of his madness, argument would only be futile. An elderly black woman reassures me that he does the same thing to every other rider who passes him. Even this reassurance is a reproach; I need not have wasted even an automatic apology on him.

Two hours later, I pass my fatigue-clad nemesis talking with another man in a similar costume. He plucks at the fatigue jacket, pulling it into some semblance of shape, demonstrating his faith that a pin here and there, a tear sewn together, can somehow alter its basic nature.

—Marc Desmond
Brooklyn, N.Y.

ALGIS BUDRYS

Books:
The Secret Language
of Science Fiction

MANY of you out there in Readerland possess a close acquaintance with the world of Fandom. But if *F&SF*'s readership is anything like what I picture when I peer out at you from my basement window, many of you do not. Some of you have never even heard of it. Whether you know it or not, that has affected your SF reading. And so a brief introductory discussion precedes this month's book review, and perhaps even the more sophisticated among us will profit from it.

No one can be certain of why there are Fans.* A number of plausible theories exist. Mine are the correct ones, but other ob-

---

* The time has come to begin using the term as a proper noun, since a specific interest in SF is meant when distinguishing between Fans and fans in the generic sense of persons who simply have a liking for something.

servers of the SF scene offer differing hypotheses which they stubbornly refuse to abandon. The important thing for our present purposes is that SF supports a very large community of individuals who draw their principal psychic energy from the community—i.e., Fandom—rather than from the literature around which it coalesced in the late 1920s. For many people—thousands; tens of thousands, ranging in age from the single-digit numbers on up through Nonagenaria—Fandom is a way of life. Even those who insist that Fandom is just a God-damned hobby must enter that community, and adopt its morés and idioms, in order to communicate that opinion.

The thing that must be grasped, incredible as it may seem to the uninitiated, is that Fandom represents the most prominent instance in all world literature of a reader-generated, positively acting, organized (though not single-minded), effective force whose effect is to condition its literateurs from birth. In some cases, some SF stories cannot be fully understood except by Fans, and while that is an extreme case it is a frequent case, and growing more frequent.

At first glance some may think that even if true this is no more than a microcosm of what literacy in general accomplishes, in ensuring that writers are replaced as they run out their careers, and that any given generation of writers for the most part reflects the cultural biases of its own time. But the difference is sharply more qualitative than it is quantitative. It is more nearly as if, for instance, the island of Trinidad traditionally fostered nearly all the writers who would supply the next generation of all writing for English-speaking people everywhere.

Fandom is in many ways as attractive a place as Trinidad can be, and its inhabitants are sharply engaged with the universe at large. It is one of their principal tenets that one cannot be a good member of the culture without taking an inordinately deep interest in aspects of art and science, and a far broader than usual interest in the world in general. But it is, nevertheless, an enclave risen from the days when "science fiction" and "fantasy" were circumscribed popular literatures promulgated by ephemeral media. From about 1940 until quite recently, it was *the* source of new SF writers, artists, and editors, who typically first served an apprenticeship in the very large and proliferated Fannish amateur publishing establishment . . . itself a phenomenon without significant parallel.

Fans are incessantly in communication with each other, through these media, by private correspondence, or face-to-face in groups ranging in size from the carful of visitors on up through the local and regional convention to the national and world conventions whose attendances routinely attain several thousand. They communicate about everything under the Sun. Some no longer read SF, having burned out on it but not on Fandom. They are a singularly unorganizable culture—even the conventions are created by ad hoc groups which, essentially, form for that purpose and dissolve afterward. There is no central organizing body, no hierarchical process of any great note or endurance, but obviously at any given time there will be an unspoken but feelable consensus whose general import is detected in the bones.

Thus, as you might expect, there are a secret language and a body of tradition, both nurtured by the Fannish publishing establishment and then disseminated in person-to-person contact as older Fans encounter and indoctrinate newer ones.

The core of the secret language lies not in the nonce-words and thieves' language whose existence is apparent to any observer and is frequently flaunted. It is in the Fannish use of perfectly ordinary terms. "Mundane," to take the most obvious example, is pejorative when used by literati in general. In Fannish, it simply means "not related to SF," usually a far more neutral connotation, if a revealing one. Few professional SF writers, well aware that the bulk of their audience does not speak it, use blatantly Fannish words in their work. But few professional SF writers are as scrupulously aware of the large body of connotative Fannish concealed within the mundane portions of their vocabularies, and a fair measure of that does get through into the text.

Still, it's the Fannish traditions that most influence SF, most notably by preserving certain favorite icons. To the extent that this is not knowable to non-Fan readers, its reflection in the reading can be both puzzling and not accessible to unaided rational analysis. You cannot see to find your glasses because your glasses are lost.

Passages within books, and books within a canon, and canons within the field, may then seem oddly motivated and out of focus.

Books which have received critical acclaim, award-winning books, and new books already bearing lavish advance endorsements from respected SF personalities, can seem plainly undeserving of such encomia when one applies reasonable, ordinary and reliable critical standards learned from general literature. Conversely, an SF book which has been largely ignored, or castigated, may seem on reading it to have been treated with manifest unfairness.

I bring all this up because we're about to look at a piece of work I think will prove an apt example of this phenomenon. I feel it's important to bring up because by far the most frequent conversation that occurs whenever I meet a non-Fannish reader of this column centers around this species of puzzlement. I've been looking for an opportunity to move the discussion out to where it is accessible to us all at once.

The manner in which these conversations are usually initiated is with a sincere question about whether the award committees, the contributors of the book-jacket endorsements, and some of my fellow reviewers are venal or just stupid. I believe this is an attempt to flatter me by implication—an attempt that always makes me squirm, for all that I don't mind feeling like an unusually perceptive and rectitudinous fellow. And, yes, since the opportunities in SF to express a literary opinion of some kind are open to many, and frequent, a certain percentage of corrupt performance must exist. When I think I have detected some of that, I twit it with great satisfaction while keeping my fingers crossed that I'm not being stupid or prejudiced in that particular instance. But I hope that the foregoing passages have contained the materials of a less invidious explanation, and furthermore of the explanation that applies most accurately in the greatest number of such instances.*

* Incidentally, and alas all systems, I have always conducted my criticisms from a complex and partially intuitive base. Most of the time, I proceed as if addressing literate ladies and gentlemen whose interest in SF is the most reasoned of all the SF magazine readerships', and whose appreciation of traditional literary values is high and informed. I do not assume any "inside" viewpoint on their part.

Some of the time, however, when dealing with a book whose chief validity lies in its connections with traditional magazine "science fiction" and the kind of "fantasy" found in magazines sister to science fiction magazines, I will concentrate on Fannish aspects.

And some of the time the Devil just gets into me.

All right, what are the signatures of Fandom?

Let us look at Julian May's *The Many-Colored Land* (Houghton Mifflin, 1981), an enjoyable book, and see what there is in it to enjoy; but let us also look at the literary choices the author made, and how many other sorts of book might have occurred.

The Guderian Effect, discovered some centuries in the future, is a means of opening a one-way portal to the Pliocene Era, a geological epoch in Earth's past when the climate was equable, mammals—including early hominids, but not true humans—had appeared and proliferated, and, according to some paleontologists but not all, the Earth was as near Eden as it has ever gotten. Doctor Guderian's rather small and immovable portal on this past, operated from his cottage in France, can trap things—an eohippus, for instance—and bring them forward across the millions of years into his cottage. But unfortunately they age through every one of the intervening years, so that what arrives are the molecules left over after the fossilized bones of the eohippus have disintegrated.

This is the point at which an author like James P. Hogan, for example, who is characteristically Nulleff—non-Fannish—would have exploited the obvious fact that the field from Guderian's effect could not really be so discrete; it would take not only the animal, but a hemispherical or hemilobal portion of the sod under its hooves and the soil under the sod. From a Pliocene point of view, it would be a disintegrator ray of mysterious origins and unknown limitations. Hogan's resulting "hard science" novel would revolve around that idea. But Julian May is a Fan, of very long standing, once deeply involved in the Fannish community and such signature activities as the writing of Fannish verses to Sullivan melodies, her subsequent scientific career and credentials notwithstanding. So at the same time that she devotes much attention to making her Pliocene verisimilitudinous, she sketches the physics of Guderian's machine. They are detailed only to the extent required to establish that it cannot be used to return, should one choose to use it to enter the Pliocene. This can be done without growing millions of years younger, as is repeatedly demonstrated by the people who, over the years, now for various reasons begin passing through the portal.

The portal—the stargate, the massive doors of the forbidding castle, the path between the worlds, the matter-transmitter—is an icon of central stature in SF. Perhaps there is no direct correlation between the frequency of its appearance in our literature and the fact that many who enter Fandom do so while in the throes of pubescence. But perhaps there is.

In May's novel, the cast of these many voluntary exiles is considerably varied. Some are failed careerists, some are simply mad, some are motivated by love or lost love, one is a young woman accidentally deprived of her telepathic powers, one is a recently widowed ageing scientist who cannot endure continued life in an environment full of reminders, one is a nun in spiritual crisis, and one is even Guderian's widow, moved at last to share the unknown fate of the many people she has been sending through the portal. Here is the *Bridge of San Luis Rey* again, but with the SF-added dimension that the explorable question is not Why did these people die? It is How will they live? Many a novelist in and out of SF could proceed from there to explore the interactions of these characters, given on the one hand a sentence of absolute removal from their habituated lives and on the other a clean slate.

But this is not allowed to play out as an unhindered process. The Pliocene unexpectedly turns out to be populated by members of an alien race from another galaxy, whose women have breasts that hang to their waists and who enslave all the humans as they come through the portal.

It is too much cocktail-party Freudianism to simply call this a disguised child's-eye view of the world. It is anyone's view of the world, expressed within very limited parameters whose crudity is the crudity of those limitations, not of the concept toward which that particular vocabulary is directed. Julian May is at this point a mature individual for whom a great deal of life and work has intervened since her famous 1951 novella, "Dune Roller." But there is no question in my mind that the presence of this almost omnipotent, capricious and conditionally human race beyond the portal, with its cruelties far overshadowing whatever wisdom and beauty it might also offer, constitutes a particularly attractive feature in many Fannish eyes. From a purely literary point of view, of course, it is an intrusion on the potential elegance and clean line of extrapolation offered by the uncluttered situation first presented by the Guderian effect.

Whatever prospects May had of writing a great book were not crucially compromised until the appearance of the aliens. But such an appraisal presumes that May at some point wanted to attempt a great—i.e., directly penetrating, obfuscation-killing—book. All the evidence instead indicates that she wanted from the beginning to write a sprawling, proliferated "epic"—that is, a story with many sub-plots not directly bearing on the inner lives of the central characters, containing a fair number of events which exist essentially for their own sake as set-pieces modeled on similar events in earlier well-received SF novels; an entertaining book.* Nor blushed to do so. Nor, I hasten to stress, ought to have blushed. We are discussing choices here, not transgressions.

The remainder of the novel—a sufficiently self-contained Part One of a two-part epic of "The Pliocene Exile"—is best read as a physical contention for mastery of the domain beyond the portal. Individuals can, do, and have escaped from their masters, gathered as rebel bands in the outlying forests and mountains, and made alliances among themselves. They have also made variously trustworthy alliances with a spectrum of subsidiary alien races other than the main one. (These are actually other aspects of the one alien race, which is not as straightforward in its corporealizations as our own is.) In due course, they gather the physical resources to strike the first blow of what will be a long campaign.

Here is where the independent sub-plots occur most thickly. In a literarily gratuitous but Fannishly potent stratagem, May is weaving the structure of a "rational" explanation for the legends of fairies, kobolds, leprechauns, were-people, fey Celtics, and even possibly of UFOs, that will somehow penetrate the massive intervention of Ice Ages and persist into our own time. Here again, in attempting to account for every fantasy manifestation ever known, May is forced to digress from a fairly concentrated premise —the one alien race—into a diffuse one.

She also appears to be getting ready to account for Neanderthal

---

* And thus, incidentally, far more likely to be an immediately popular book, but more important a book the author found it enjoyable to write and to contemplate the daily writing of. The need to maintain one's own elan in the face of doing a thousand words a day, day after day, when one is unaccustomed to the lifelong routines of the professional writer, also conditions many a Fannish novel.

Man and the Cro-Magnons; it's as if she felt unable to journey into just one past, but instead felt obliged to tour her own Fannish awareness of every icon that has ever existed in the rather large body of SF devoted to prehistorical milieux. She repeatedly asserts that the Pliocene cannot in any meaningful way be connected to our own time, which is rationally true, but in her heart she feels otherwise. Which is, perhaps by coincidence, exactly how Fandom would want her to feel.

With so much physical activity going on—battles, skirmishes, escapes, rapes, confrontations—this book could readily have become simply another compendium of hugger-mugger punctuated by brief lectures, a mode not unknown to faithful readers of the old Ace double-novel or, for that matter, of most of the present-day SF product of fringe imprints such as Zebra and Pinnacle. But another Fannish requirement comes into play here. Fans as a matter of fact have a considerable contempt for the mere action novel, dismissing it as juvenile and mindless. A novel of action, in Fannish eyes, can be worthy of serious attention only if it displays obvious mindedness. One frequent representation of mindedness is precisely the sort of rationalization May employs in scrupulously proposing a "scientific" basis for supernatural legend. Another is "character development."

It is a requirement of the Fannish SF novel that the characters "grow"—that is, display the results of a capacity to learn life's lessons. This is a particularly stringent requirement, reflected in Fannish critical articulations as well as in Fannish lists of work regarded with special approval. A list of Hugo winners, for example, or to some extent winners of the putatively non-Fannish Nebula Award, and particularly of work which appears on the award nomination lists at the behest of nominators with relatively sparse professional credentials, will reveal that over the years the one sort of story that almost never makes it is the story in which no one "learns better." I am also here to assert my opinion that, by and large, the story in which the process of learning better is particularly visible and particularly easy to express as a homily is the story that stands the best chance.

Homiletics of course is the residue of experience. There is something to be said for the incessant stream of memorizable axioms that constitute the bulk of human educational material, since each represents the core of some initially complex and tumultuous process of human trial-and-error that had to be worked out over decades, centuries, and eventually millennia. Such aphorisms as "A rolling stone gathers no moss" or "A stitch in time saves nine" are the result of what must have been very extended processes of observation, and for that matter are still being cross-checked against observed data every day. There must have been a time when they were less refined; when their prototypes were expressed as "Wandering around is bad" and "You'd better tuck-point that wall."

Any number of homilies are still at that prototypical stage, and a case might be made for an assertion that it's particularly the still imprecise and less helpfully expressed homily-situations that define the area in which Fannish SF—Effseff—works. Effseff is notably fond of scenarios testing such propositions as "You shouldn't bottle-up anger," "You'd better be sure what you're sure of," "Pride creates mistakes," and any number of other such variously profound open-ended statements which are in the same relationship to a fully formed aphorism as the *Reader's Digest* is to a good encyclopedia.

This is natural enough. The Fannish community in its articulations has always displayed an energetic predilection for testing the latest in intellectualization, a process usually described as "being at the forefront of human thought." What this means is that Fans tend to become engaged with the least precisely formed proto-aphorisms because they have caught them early in their development. Nulleff SF is not free of this trait, either, but it is particularly exaggerated in Effseff.*

Since such imprecise maxims are what the protagonist in an Effseff situation must work *toward* discovering, and since dramatic values first require that there be an extended intervening process of trial-and-error—to validate by its effortfulness the viability of the climactic proposition—this forces a peculiar constraint. When first encountered, Effseff protagonists can often seem particularly

---

* Ah, secret languages growing before our very eyes! Were we to continue this trend here, a few months would suffice to make this column totally incomprehensible to newcomers. Wouldn't we feel proud and good and cozy?

limited and unperceptive, since even where they get to is often a rather elementary and circumscribed enlightenment.

It would take a writer of first-rate genius to create a transcendent Effseff novel, since that writer would have to produce a genuinely formed, first-rate aphorism, with self-evident applicability to the human condition, that thousands of articulate and intelligent Fans had not already thought of, but were sufficiently developed intellectually to understand at once. That is a very tall order, since all of SF contains no more first-rate geniuses at any given time than any other literature does—that is, some number statistically quite near zero.

Which is a long and weighty way 'round to characterizing the characterization in *The Many-Colored Land,* a novel which, by the way, is gaining enthusiastic reviews in the Fannish media, with fervent declarations that its stature and potential are comparable to those of *The Lord of the Rings,* the *Foundation* Trilogy, and the Lensman series—to name three creations that have few literary mutualities with each other or the May novel, but which are at about the same point on the Fannish scale of adulability. Some such otherwise inexplicable comparison will almost certainly appear in the selling copy blurbed upon the covers of the eventual paperback reprint. And so those of you who did not previously possess a key to the logic of SF blurbing now have one.

Now, mind you—as we lumber toward my conclusion here— while I have struck hard and deeply at some of Fandom's most cherished tenets; or, far more precisely, while I have re-expressed some of those tenets in language that seemed more useful, without even once passing judgment upon the institutions represented by that language—Julian May's novel remains an enjoyable book. It is a careful and sapient construct, by someone who for all that she is not a professional writer certainly could be a rather good one if she chose to abandon her other careers.* It is a page-turner on an intelligent level, and some of the characters are notably easy

---

* In SF generally, the distinction between the amateur and the professional is far more often than not a distinction in career-choice, not in talent or skill. In all of literature, there are actually very few full-time writers who do nothing else in the sense that writers of advertising copy do nothing else. It may reflect my own parochialism when I say that it seems to be truer in SF than elsewhere.

to take into one's acquaintance, for all that even the oldest of them does not seem to have lived very much or thought about life with the depth one might expect. It is written in a lucid style—for all that its construction also caters to the Fannish liking for the cryptic prologue, supposed to whet the Effseff reading appetite but sometimes giving Nulleff readers the sensation of forging through a dark room thick with cobwebs. It is not only an enjoyable but a trustworthy book; May proliferates her theses, but she never cheats; there is a Fannish taboo against proffering intellectual constructs without concluding them, which is more than the Nulleff milieu can say.

So we have come a long way here, and employed a tone not usual even to this journal; I crave your pardon if you would much rather have had the mixture as before. It shall return promptly and any future excursions will be infrequent. But it seemed to me we had a unique opportunity here to discuss some things that might have value for you. And I say, again, that the opportunity is unique not because I haven't had all this thinking on tap and ready for expression at almost any time, but because *The Many-Colored Land* seems to me to be a book which signally rewards both the Nulleff and the Effseff reader, for all that it does not reward them each in the same way.

This story angered many readers because it extrapolates certain domestic situations in a most pointed fashion. But for all that, it is a strong and moving science fiction tale that takes place on a settlement far from home.

LISA TUTTLE

Wives

A SMELL of sulfur in the air on a morning when the men had gone, and the wives, in their beds, smiled in their sleep, breathed more easily, and burrowed deeper into dreams.

Jack's wife woke, her eyes open and her little nose flaring, smelling something beneath the sulfur smell. One of those smells she was used to not noticing, when the men were around. But it was all right, now. Wives could do as they pleased, so long as they cleaned up and were back in their proper places when the men returned.

Jack's wife—who was called Susie—got out of bed too quickly and grimaced as the skintight punished her muscles. She caught sight of herself in the mirror over the dressing table: her sharp teeth were bared, and she looked like a wild animal, bound and struggling. She grinned at that, because she could easily free herself.

She cut the skintight apart with scissors, cutting and ripping carelessly. It didn't matter that it was ruined—skintights were plentiful. She had a whole boxful, herself, in the hall closet behind the Christmas decorations. And she didn't have the patience to try soaking it off slowly in a hot bath, as the older wives recommended. So her muscles would be sore and her skintight a tattered rag— she would be free that much sooner.

She looked down at her dead-white body, feeling distaste. She felt despair at the sight of her small arms, hanging limp, thin and useless in the hollow below her ribs. She tried to flex them but could not make them move. She began to massage them with her primary fingers, and after several minutes the pain began, and she knew they weren't dead yet.

She bathed and massaged her newly uncovered body with oil. She felt terrifyingly free, naked and rather dangerous, with the skintight removed. She sniffed the air again and that familiar scent, musky and alluring, aroused her.

She ran through the house—noticing, in passing, that Jack's spider was eating the living room sofa. It was the time for building nests and cocoons, she thought happily, time for laying eggs and planting seeds; the spider was driven by the same force that drove her.

Outside, the dusty ground was hard and cold beneath her bare feet. She felt the dust all over her body, raised by the wind and clinging to her momentary warmth. She was coated in the soft yellow dust by the time she reached the house next-door—the house where the magical scent came from, the house which held a wife in heat, longing for someone to mate with.

Susie tossed her head, shaking the dust out in a little cloud around her head. She stared up at the milky sky and around at all the houses, alien artifacts constructed by men. She saw movement in the window of the house across the street and waved—the figure watching her waved back.

Poor old Maggie, thought Susie. Old, bulging and ugly, unloved, and nobody's wife. She was only housekeeper to two men who were, rather unfortunately Susie thought, in love with each other.

But she didn't want to waste time by thinking of wives and men, or by feeling pity, now. Boldly, like a man, Susie pounded at the door.

It opened. "Ooooh, Susie!"

Susie grinned and looked the startled wife up and down. You'd never know from looking at her that the men were gone and she could relax—this wife, called Doris, was as dolled-up as some eager-to-please newlywed and looked, Susie thought, more like a real woman than any woman had ever looked.

Over her skintight (which was bound more tightly than Susie's had been) Doris wore a low-cut dress, her three breasts carefully bound and positioned to achieve the proper, double-breasted effect. Gaily patterned and textured stockings covered her silicone-injected legs, and she tottered on heels three centimeters high. Her face was carefully painted, and she wore gold bands on neck, wrists and fingers.

Then Susie ignored what she looked like, and her nose told her much more. The smell was so powerful now that she could feel her pouch swelling in lonely response.

Doris must have noticed, for her eyes rolled, seeking some safe view.

"What's the matter?" Susie asked, her voice louder and bolder than it ever was when the men were around. "Didn't your man go off to war with the others? He stay home sick in bed?"

Doris giggled. "Ooooh, I wish he would, sometime! No, he was out of here before it was light."

Off to see his mistress before leaving, Susie thought. She knew that Doris was nervous about being displaced by one of the other wives her man was always fooling around with—there were always more wives than there were men, and her man had a roving eye.

"Calm down, Doris. Your man can't see you now, you know." She stroked one of Doris' hands. "Why don't you take off that silly dress, and your skintight. I know how constricted you must be feeling. Why not relax with me?"

She saw Doris' face darken with emotion beneath the heavy make-up, and she grasped her hand more tightly when Doris tried to pull away.

"Please don't," Doris said.

"Come on," Susie murmured, caressing Doris' face and feeling the thick paint slide beneath her fingers.

"No, don't . . . please . . . I've tried to control myself, truly I have. But the exercises don't work, and the perfume doesn't cover the smell well enough—he won't even sleep with me when I'm like this. He thinks it's disgusting, and it is. I'm so afraid he'll leave me."

"But he's gone now, Doris. You can let yourself go. You don't have to worry about him when he's not around. It's safe, it's all right, you can do as you please now—we can do anything we like and no one will know." She could feel Doris trembling.

"Doris," she whispered and rubbed her face demandingly against hers.

At that, the other wife gave in, and collapsed in her arms.

Susie helped Doris out of her clothes, tearing at them with hands and teeth, throwing shoes and jewelry high into the air and festooning the yard with rags of dress, stockings and under-garment.

But when Doris, too, was naked, Susie suddenly felt shy and a little frightened. It would be wrong to mate here in the settlement built by men, wrong and dangerous. They must go somewhere else, somewhere they could be something other than wives for a little while, and follow their own natures without reproach.

They went to a place of stone on the far northern edge of the human settlement. It was a very old place, although whether it had been built by the wives in the distant time before they were wives or whether it was natural, neither Susie nor Doris could say. They both felt that it was a holy place, and it seemed right to mate there, in the shadow of one of the huge, black, standing stones.

It was a feast, an orgy of life after a season of death. They found pleasure in exploring the bodies which seemed so similar to men's, but which they knew to be miraculously different, each from the other, in scent, texture, and taste. They forgot that they had ever been creatures known as wives. They lost their names and forgot the language of men as they lay entwined.

There were no skintights imprisoning their bodies now, barring them from sensation, freedom and pleasure, and they were part-ners, not strangers, as they explored and exulted in their flesh. This was no mockery of the sexual act—brutishly painful and brief as it was with the men—but the true act in all its meaning.

They were still joined at sundown, and it was not until long after the three moons began their nightly waltz through the clouds that the two lovers fell asleep at last.

"In three months," Susie said dreamily, "we can. . . ."

"In three months we won't do anything."

"Why not? If the men are away. . . ."

"I'm hungry," Doris said. She wrapped her primary arms around herself. "And I'm cold, and I ache all over. Let's go back."

"Stay here with me, Doris. Let's plan."

"There's nothing to plan."

"But in three months we must get together and fertilize it."

"Are you crazy? Who would carry it then? One of us would have to go without a skintight, and do you think either of our husbands would let us slop around for months without a skintight? And then when it's born how could we hide it? Men don't have babies, and they don't want anyone else to. Men kill babies, just as they kill all their enemies."

Susie knew that what Doris was saying was true, but she was reluctant to give up her new dream. "Still, we might be able to keep it hidden," she said. "It's not so hard to hide things from a man. . . ."

"Don't be so stupid," Doris said scornfully. Susie noticed that she still had smears of make-up on her face. Some smears had transferred themselves to Susie in the night. They looked like bruises or bloody wounds. "Come back with me now," Doris said, her voice gentle again. "Forget this, about the baby. The old ways are gone—we're wives now, and we don't have a place in our lives for babies."

"But someday the war may end," Susie said. "And the men will all go back to Earth and leave us here."

"If that happens," Doris said, "then we would make new lives for ourselves. Perhaps we would have babies again."

"If it's not too late then," Susie said. "If it ever happens." She stared past Doris at the horizon.

"Come back with me."

Susie shook her head. "I have to think. You go. I'll be all right."

She realized when Doris had gone that she, too, was tired, hungry and sore, but she was not sorry she had remained in the place of stone. She needed to stay awhile longer in one of the old places, away from the distractions of the settlement. She felt that she was on the verge of remembering something very important.

A large, dust-colored lizard crawled out of a hole in the side of a fallen rock, and Susie rolled over and clapped her hands on it. But it wriggled out of her clutches like air or water or the wind-blown dust and disappeared somewhere. Susie felt a sharp pang of disappointment along with her hunger—she had a sudden memory of how that lizard would have tasted, how the skin of its throat would have felt, tearing between her teeth. She licked her dry lips and sat up. In the old days, she thought, I caught many such lizards. But the old days were gone, and with them the old knowledge and the old abilities.

I'm not what I used to be, she thought. I'm something else, now—a "wife," created by man in the image of something I have never seen, something called "woman."

She thought about going back to her house in the settlement and of wrapping herself in a new skintight and then selecting the proper dress and shoes to make a good impression on the returning Jack; she thought about painting her face and putting rings on her fingers. She thought about burning and boiling good food to turn it into the unappetizing messes Jack favored and about killing the wide-eyed "coffee fish" to get the oil to make the mildly addictive drink the men called "coffee." She thought about watching Jack, and listening to him, always alert for what he might want, what he might ask, what he might do. Trying to anticipate him, to earn his praise and avoid his blows and harsh words. She thought about letting him "screw" her and about the ugly jewelry and noisome perfumes he brought her.

Susie began to cry, and the dust drank her tears as they fell. She didn't understand how this had all begun, how or why she had become a wife, but she could bear it no longer.

She wanted to be what she had been born to be—but she could not remember what that was. She only knew that she would be Susie no longer. She would be no man's wife.

"I remembered my name this morning," Susie said with quiet triumph. She looked around the room. Doris was staring down at her hands, twisting in her lap. Maggie looked half-asleep, and the other two wives—Susie didn't remember their names; she had simply gathered them up when she found them on the street—looked both bored and nervous.

"Don't you see?" Susie persisted. "If I could remember that, I'm sure I can remember other things in time. All of us can."

Maggie opened her eyes all the way. "And what would that do," she asked, "except make us discontented and restless, as you are?"

"What *good* . . . why, if we all began to remember, we could live our lives again—our *own* lives. We wouldn't have to be wives, we could be . . . ourselves."

"Could we," said Maggie sourly. "And do you think the men would watch us go? Do you think they'd let us walk out of their houses and out of their lives without stopping us? Don't you—you who talk about remembering—don't you remember how it was when the men came? Don't you remember the slaughter? Don't you remember just who became wives, and why? We, the survivors, became wives because the men wouldn't kill their wives, not if we kept them happy and believing we weren't the enemy. If we try to leave or change, they'll kill us like they've killed almost everything else in the world."

The others were silent, but Susie suspected they were letting Maggie speak for them.

"But we'll die," she said. "We'll die like this, as wives. We've lost our identities, but we can have them back. We can have our world back, and our lives, if we only take them. We're dying as a race and as a world, now. Being a wife is a living death, just a postponement of the end, that's all."

"Yes," said Maggie, irony hanging heavily from the word. "So?"

"So why do we have to let them do this to us? We can hide— we can run far away from the settlement and hide. Or, if we have to, we can fight back."

"That's not our way," said Maggie.

"Then what *is* our way?" Susie demanded. "Is it our way to let ourselves be destroyed? They've already killed our culture and our past—we have no "way" anymore—we can't claim we do. All we are now is imitations, creatures molded by the men. And when the men leave—*if* the men leave—it will be the end for us. We'll have nothing left, and it will be too late to try to remember who we were."

"It's already too late," Maggie said. Susie was suddenly impressed by the way she spoke and held herself, and wondered if

Maggie, this elderly and unloved wife she once had pitied, had once been a leader of her people.

"Can you remember why we did not hide or fight before?" Maggie asked. "Can you remember why we decided that the best thing for us was to change our ways, to do what you are now asking us to undo?"

Susie shook her head.

"Then go and try to remember. Remember that we made a choice when the men came, and now we must live with that choice. Remember that there was a good reason for what we did, a reason of survival. It is too late to change again. The old way is not waiting for our return, it is dead. Our world has been changed, and we could not stop it. The past is dead, but that is as it should be. We have new lives now. Forget your restlessness and go home. Be a good wife to Jack—he loves you in his way. Go home and be thankful for that."

"I can't," she said. She looked around the room, noticing how the eyes of the others fell before hers. So few of them had wanted to listen to her, so few had dared venture out of their homes. Susie looked at Maggie as she spoke, meaning her words for all the wives. "They're killing us slowly," she said. "But we'll be just as dead in the end. I would rather die fighting, and take some of them with me."

"You may be ready to die now, but the rest of us are not," Maggie said. "But if you fought them, you would get not only your own death, but the deaths of all of us. If they see you snarling and violent, they will wake up and turn new eyes on the rest of us and see us not as their loving wives but as beasts, strangers, dangerous wild animals to be destroyed. They forget that we are different from them now; they are willing to forget and let us live as long as we keep them comfortable and act as wives should act."

"I can't fight them alone, I know that," Susie said. "But if you'll all join with me, we have a chance. We could take them by surprise, we could use their weapons against them. Why not? They don't expect a fight from us—we could win. Some of us would die, of course, but many of us would survive. More than that—we'd have our own lives, our own world, back again."

"You think your arguments are new," said Maggie. There was a trace of impatience in her usually calm voice. "But I can remember the old days, even if you can't. I remember what happened when the men first came, and I know what would happen if we angered them. Even if we managed somehow to kill all the men here, more men would come in their ships from the sky. And they would come to kill us for daring to fight them. Perhaps they'd simply drop fire on us, this time being sure to burn out all of us and all life on our world. Do you seriously ask us to bring about this certain destruction?"

Susie stared at her, feeling dim memories stir in response to her words. Fire from the sky, the burning, the killing. . . . But she couldn't be certain she remembered, and she would rather risk destruction than go back to playing wife again.

"We could hide," she said, pleading. "We could run away and hide in the wilderness. The men might think we had died—they'd forget about us soon, I'm certain. Even if they looked for us at first, we could hide. It's our world, and we know it as they don't. Soon we could live again as we used to, and forget the men."

"Stop this dreaming," Maggie said. "We can never live the way we used to—the old ways are gone, the old world is gone, and even your memories are gone, that's obvious. The only way we know how to live now is with the men, as their wives. Everything else is gone. We'd die of hunger and exposure if the men didn't track us down and kill us first."

"I may have forgotten the old ways, but you haven't. You could teach us."

"I remember enough to know what is gone, to know that we can't go back. Believe me. Think about it, Susie. Try—"

"Don't call me that!"

Her shout echoed in the silence. No one spoke. Susie felt the last of her hope drain out of her as she looked at them. They did not feel what she felt, and she would not be able to convince them. In silence, still, she left them, and went back to her own house.

She waited for them there, for them to come and kill her.

She knew that they would come; she knew she had to die. It was as Maggie had said: one renegade endangered them all. If one wife turned on one man, all the wives would be made to suffer. The look of love on their faces would change to a look of hatred, and the slaughter would begin again.

Susie felt no desire to try to escape, to hide from the other wives as she had suggested they all hide from the men. She had no wish to live alone; for good or ill, she was a part of her people, and she did not wish to endanger them nor to break away from them.

When they came, they came together, all the wives of the settlement, coming to act in concert so none should bear the guilt alone. They did not hate Susie, nor did she hate them, but the deadly work had to be done.

Susie walked outside, into their midst. To make it easier for them—to act with them, in a sense—Susie offered not the slightest resistance. She presented the weakest parts of her body to their hands and teeth, that her death should come more quickly. And as she died, feeling her body pressed, pounded and torn by the other wives, Susie did not mind the pain. She felt herself a part of them all, and she died content.

After her death, one of the extra wives took on Susie's name and moved into her house. She got rid of the spider's gigantic egg-case first thing—Jack might like his football-sized pet, but he wouldn't be pleased by the hundreds of pebble-sized babies that would come spilling out of the egg-case in a few months. Then she began to clean in earnest: a man deserved a clean house to come home to.

When, a few days later, the men returned from their fighting, Susie's man Jack found a spotless house, filled with the smells of his favorite foods cooking, and a smiling, sexily dressed wife.

"Would you like some dinner, dear?" she asked.

"Put it on hold," he said, grinning wolfishly. "Right now I'll take a cup of hot coffee—in bed—with you on the side."

She fluttered her false eyelashes and moved a little closer, so he could put his arm around her if he liked.

"Three tits and the best coffee in the universe," he said with satisfaction, squeezing one of the bound lumps of flesh on her chest. "With this to come home to, it kind of makes the whole war-thing worthwhile."

This short and surprising tale grew from an encounter at a Santa Ana, Ca., grocery store. The author was buying cat food and met a teen-ager who was editor of the Yuba City High School student paper and was enterprising enough to ask Mr. Dick to write a story for the paper. Phil agreed, and here is the happy result.

PHILIP K. DICK

The Alien Mind

INERT within the depths of his Theta Chamber he heard the faint tone and then the synthovoice. "Five minutes."

"Okay," he said, and struggled out of his deep sleep. He had five minutes to adjust the course of his ship; something had gone wrong with the autocontrol system. An error on his part? Not likely; he never made errors. Jason Bedford make errors? Hardly.

As he made his way unsteadily to the control module, he saw that Norman, who had been sent with him to amuse him, was also awake. The cat floated slowly in circles, batting at a pen that somehow had gotten loose. Strange, Bedford thought.

"I thought you were unconscious with me." He examined the read-out of the ship's course. Impossible! A fifth-parsec off in the direction of Sirius. It would add a week to his journey. With grim precision he reset the controls, then sent out an alert signal to Meknos III, his destination.

"Troubles?" the Meknosian operator answered. The voice was

dry and cold, the calculating monotone of something that always made Bedford think of snakes.

He explained his situation.

"We need the vaccine," the Meknosian said. "Try to stay on course."

Norman the cat floated majestically by the control module, reached out a paw and jabbed at random; two activated buttons sounded faint *bleeps* and the ship altered course.

"So you did it," Bedford said. "You humiliated me in the eyes of an alien. You have reduced me to idiocy vis-a-vis the alien mind." He grabbed the cat. And squeezed.

"What was that strange sound?" the Meknosian operator asked. "A kind of lament."

Bedford said quietly, "There's nothing left to lament. Forget you heard it." He shut off the radio, carried the cat's body to the trash sphincter and ejected it.

A moment later he had returned to his Theta Chamber and, once more, dozed. This time there would be no tampering with his controls. He dozed in peace.

When his ship docked at Meknos III, the senior member of the alien medical team greeted him with an odd request. "We would like to see your pet."

"I have no pet," Bedford said. Certainly it was true.

"According to the manifest filed with us in advance—"

"It is really none of your business," Bedford said. "You have your vaccine; I'll be taking off."

The Meknosian said, "The safety of any life form is our business. We will inspect your ship."

"For a cat that doesn't exist," Bedford said.

Their search proved futile. Impatiently, Bedford watched the alien creatures scrutinize every storage locker and passage-way on his ship. Unfortunately, the Meknosian found ten sacks of dry cat-kibble. A lengthy discussion ensued among them, in their own language.

"Do I have permission," Bedford said harshly, "to return to Earth now? I'm on a tight schedule." What the aliens were thinking and saying was of no importance to him; he wished only to return to his silent Theta Chamber and profound sleep.

"You'll have to go through decontamination procedure A," the senior Meknosian medical officer said. "So that no spore or virus from—"

"I realize that," Bedford said. "Let's get it done."

Later, when decontamination had been completed and he was back in his ship starting up the drive, his radio came on. It was one or another of the Meknosians; to Bedford they all looked alike. "What was the cat's name?" the Meknosian asked.

"Norman," Bedford said, and jabbed the ignite switch. His ship shot upward and he smiled.

He did not smile, however, when he found the power supply to his Theta Chamber missing. Nor did he smile when the back-up unit could also not be located. Did I forget to bring it? he asked himself. No, he decided; I wouldn't do that. They took it.

Two years before he reached Terra. Two years of full consciousness on his part, deprived of theta sleep; two years of sitting or floating or—as he had seen in military-preparedness training holofilms—curled up in a corner totally psychotic.

He punched out a radio request to return to Meknos III. No response. Well, so much for that.

Seated at his control module, he snapped on the little inboard computer and said, "My Theta Chamber won't function; it's been sabotaged. What do you suggest I do for two years?"

THERE ARE EMERGENCY ENTERTAINING TAPES

"Right," he said. He would have remembered. "Thank you." Pressing the proper button, he caused the door of the tape compartment to slide open.

No tapes. Only a cat toy—a miniature punching bag—that had been included for Norman; he had never gotten around to giving it to him. Otherwise . . . bare shelves.

The alien mind, Bedford thought. Mysterious and cruel.

Setting the ship's audio recorder going, he said calmly and with as much conviction as possible, "What I will do is build my next two years around the daily routine. First, there are meals. I will spend as much time as possible planning, fixing, eating and enjoying delicious repasts. During the time ahead of me I will try out every combination of victuals possible." Unsteadily, he rose and made his way to the massive food-storage locker.

As he stood gazing into the tightly packed locker—tightly packed with row upon row of identical snacks—he thought, On the other hand there's not much you can do with a two-year supply of cat-kibble. In the way of variety. Are they all the same flavor?

They were all the same flavor.

Susan C. Petrey wrote several stories for F&SF *during 1979 and 1980; she was just at the point of gaining recognition as one of the fine new talents in the field when she died suddenly in December 1980. She was only in her mid-thirties. "Spidersong" was her second published story.*

SUSAN C. PETREY

Spidersong

BRENNEKER, the lyre spider, lived inside a lute, a medieval instrument resembling a pear-shaped guitar. The lute was an inexpensive copy of one made by an old master and had rosewood walls and a spruce sounding board. Her home was sparsely furnished, a vast expanse of unfinished wood, a few sound pegs reaching from floor to ceiling like Greek columns, and in one corner, near the small F-shape sound holes, the fantasy of iron-silk thread that was Brenneker's web. Brenneker's home was an unusual one for a lyre spider. Most of them spin their webs in hollow tawba stalks, which echo the music of these tiny fairy harps seldom heard by ears of men. Lyre spiders play duets with each other, sometimes harmonizing, sometimes bouncing counterpoint melodies back and forth across the glades between the tall bamboo-like tawba. They play their webs to attract prey, to win a mate, or for the sheer joy of music. They live alone except for the few weeks in mother's silken egg case and one day of spiderlings climbing up the tawba to cast their threads into the wind and fly away. When they mate, the embrace lasts but a few moments. Then the female eats the male, who gives himself gladly to this deepest union of two souls.

Originally, Brenneker had lived in the forest, surrounded by the music of her own kind. Although she lived alone, she was never lonely, for she could always hear the mandolin-like plucking of Twinklebright, her nearest neighbor, the deep, droning chords of old Birdslayer, and occasionally the harpsichord tones of Klavier, carried on the breeze.

One hot afternoon as Brenneker experimented with augmented fifths, she noticed that some of her neighbors had stopped mid-song. She suddenly realized she was the only one still playing and she stopped abruptly, leaving a leading tone hanging on the air like an unfinished sentence.

"These ones should do," she heard a man's voice say. An angry blow struck the base of her tawba stalk. She felt herself falling as the tawba that was her home broke at the base, tumbling her to the floor of the glade below. Bruised and frightened, she scampered quickly back inside her home and clung to her silent, broken web. She felt herself lifted up and then dropped with a jar as her tawba was tossed into a wagon.

Over many hours of jolting and rattling, she fell asleep, and when she awoke, all was quiet and dark. She climbed out of her stalk and began to explore her new surroundings, a workbench with many hollow wooden objects lying about. Although she had never seen a musical instrument such as men make, she recognized with the eye of a musician that their shape was intended to give sound. She chose a lute and squeezed her plump body through one of the sound holes, saying, "Certainly this will give greater tone than my old home." She began to string her web.

At night there was no music in the instrument maker's shop, and she was lonely without the songs of her friends to cheer her. Since she was also hungry, she played her hunger song, and a fat, stupid moth came, aching to be devoured. When she'd finished with him, she tossed his powdery wings out the sound hole.

In the morning, the old instrument maker, Sanger, came to open up his shop. He paused in the shop doorway rattling his keys and then turned on the overhead light. Brenneker watched him from the sound holes of her new home as he ran a wrinkled hand through his sparse, gray hair, stuffed his keys back into a deep pocket, and picked a viola from the wall. Carefully, he adjusted the tuning of the strings, and then, picking up the bow, he played a short, lilting tune and then replaced the instrument on its peg on the wall. He made his way along the wall, pausing at each instrument to check the tuning. When he came to Brenneker's lute, he did the same, tightening the strings briefly and then playing a few bars of melody. Brenneker felt her whole surroundings vibrate with the tone and her web pulsed in sympathetic vibration. Timidly, she picked out a few notes of the song.

"Odd," said Mr. Sanger, "I'd never noticed that it had such lovely overtones. Too bad I had to use such cheap materials in its construction." He placed the lute back on the wall and was about to pick up a zither, when the shop bell rang to announce that someone had come in from the street.

A young girl and her father came through the door and paused to look at violins.

"But I don't want to play violin," said the girl, who was about ten years old. "Everyone plays violin. I want something different."

"Well, what about a guitar," said her father. "Your friend Marabeth plays one quite well. It seems like a proper instrument for a young lady."

"But that's just it," said the girl, whose name Brenneker later found out was Laurel. "I don't want to copycat someone else. I want an instrument that isn't played by just anyone. I want something special."

Sanger interrupted this conversation to say, "Have you considered the lute?" He removed Brenneker's home from the wall and strummed a chord. The vibration in the web tickled Brenneker's feet as she strummed the same chord an octave higher.

"What a lovely tone it has!" said Laurel, touching the strings and plucking them one by one.

"Be careful," said her father. "That's an antique."

"Not so," said Sanger, "it's a copy. Made it myself. And I intended it to be played, not just looked at like a dusty old museum piece."

"May I try?" asked the girl. Sanger gave the instrument to her and she sat down on a stool, placing the lute across her lap. She strummed a discord which caused Brenneker to flinch and grip her strings tightly so they wouldn't sound.

"Let me show you how," said the instrument maker. "Put your first finger in that fret and your middle finger there, like so." He indicated where the fingers should fret the strings to make a chord. Laurel plucked the strings one by one. The tone was tinny but true. The second time she plucked, Brenneker plucked inside, on her own instrument. Rich, golden tones emanated from the lute.

"Oh, Father, this is the instrument for me," said Laurel.

"But who will teach you to play such an antiquated instrument?"

"I would be glad to," said Sanger. "I have studied medieval and Renaissance music and I would like to share it with an interested pupil."

"Please, Father?"

"Well, perhaps . . . there is the question of cost. I can't afford a very expensive instrument," said her father.

"This lute, although made with loving care and much skill," said Sanger, "is unfortunately made of inexpensive wood, and for that reason it is very reasonably priced."

Mr. Sanger and Laurel's father were able to make agreeable terms for the lute and the cost of lessons. That morning Laurel took the lute, Brenneker and all, home with her.

The first few weeks of lessons were torture for Brenneker, who sat huddled, clenching her strings to her body to damp them. But as Laurel improved, Brenneker rewarded her by playing in unison. This was great incentive to Laurel, who did not realize that she was only partial author of the lovely music. Mr. Sanger was himself at a loss to explain how such beautiful tones came from such a cheaply built instrument. He did not credit his workmanship, although this was in some measure responsible, but told Laurel that the lute was haunted by a fairy harpist, and he advised her to leave a window open at night and put out a bowl of milk and honey before she went to bed. Perhaps he had been the beneficiary of such a fairy in the past, for Brenneker found that the milk and the open window provided her with a bountiful supply of flies and insects, which she tempted by song through the sound holes of the lute to make her supper.

Sanger valued highly the virtue of two playing in harmony. "For the ability to blend with another in duet is a mark of maturity in a true musician," he would say. "Harmony between two players recaptures for us briefly that time when the universe was young, untainted by evil, and the morning stars sang together."

Brenneker never played by herself unless she was sure that she was alone. She played when Laurel played or at night when everyone was sleeping. When spring came that year, she played the mating song and waited, but no lover came. The next night she tried again, this time varying the tune and adding trills, but still no one came. Brenneker tried for several nights before she finally admitted to herself that there was no fault in her song, but that none of her folk dwelt in this faraway land and so there was no one to answer. But this reasoning made her feel unhappy, and she preferred to think that it might be some imperfection in her song, which could be righted by practice.

As Laurel grew older, Brenneker noticed that the quality of their music changed. Whereas she had formerly been a lover of sprightly dance tunes, Laurel became more interested in old ballads and would sing as she accompanied herself on the lute. One of her favorites was "Barbara Allen," another, "The Wife of Ushers Well."

She was often asked to perform at weddings and parties. She met other lovers of medieval music and even other lute players. Laurel would sometimes allow others to play her instrument, which drew a mixed response. If Brenneker knew the tune of the strange artist, she would pick along. If not, she held her strings silent, leaving others to wonder how Laurel got such rounded tones where they only strummed dull, tinny notes.

One summer evening Laurel took a blanket, the lute and Brenneker to a woodsy place and sat down alone to play. She sang many of the old ballads and then she would stop for a while and listen. Then she would play another song. Brenneker wondered at this until she heard answering notes from a recorder in a grove nearby. The two instruments played a duet, with occasional counterpoint melody, and then the recorder player drew near, and Brenneker saw that it was a young man.

"Aha," she thought, "Laurel plays to attract a mate."

The young man sat down beside Laurel on the grass.

"I knew you'd come," he said to her.

She moved over toward him and he put an arm around her waist and kissed her.

This went on for quite some time. After a while the two said goodbye, and Laurel picked up her blanket and trudged homeward, while her love went in the other direction.

"Strange," thought Brenneker. "She did not eat him." This bothered the lyre spider until she stopped to reflect; "Birds do not eat their mates. Perhaps the humans are like birds, but I had always thought them more intelligent than that."

A few nights later, Laurel took her blanket and went to the grove again. The young man, whose name was Thomas, was there waiting for her. They played a few songs and then they made love. As she walked home, Laurel sang "Barbara Allen."

"And still she does not eat him," thought Brenneker. "Their way of being together is different from ours. Yet I'm sure it must mean as much to them as ours does to us. Yet it seems so incomplete. Impermanent."

The presence of the human lovers made Brenneker more aware of her own loneliness. "If I could mate," she thought, "I would make the most beautiful egg-sack all of silk, and my eggs would sway to the music of the lute until they hatched. Then they would fly to neighboring trees and build their own lyres and play to me and I wouldn't be alone anymore." But when she played her love songs, softly on the night air, no lover came. She was used to it by now, but she never gave up hope.

One evening the two lovers had a quarrel.

"You must marry me this fall," Thomas insisted.

"But we have no money," Laurel objected. "You are only an apprentice at your trade, and it will be a long time before you bring home a journeyman's wage. I would not be able to go to the university to study music."

"We would get by somehow," said Thomas. "You could take in music students and teach the lute. We could pick up a little extra money playing for gatherings."

"But I do so much want to go to the university," said Laurel. "We could go to the city and both take jobs. That way we could be together and I could study for my degree."

"I can't get as good a job in the city as here," said Thomas, "and besides, you could not earn enough to support yourself and pay tuition. So you might as well settle here with me."

"There has to be a way for me to continue my study of music," said Laurel, "and I intend to find it."

When Thomas left, he did not kiss Laurel goodbye.

Laurel, thoughtful and concerned, put her lute aside and went to bed early. She did not forget to leave a window open, however, or set out milk to feed the fairy. Brenneker pondered their dilemma and could see no solution. While she was brooding over this, she heard the unmistakable sound of a lyre spider tuning up its instrument, and this caused her to listen intently. It was a curious song, having a haunting quality, a shadowing of minor key but not quite. This was no spider song, Brenneker was sure, but it was definitely played by one of her own kind. She strummed an answering chord and the other player stopped in midphrase as if startled. Brenneker played part of an old song she'd played many times at home. The other answered her with the refrain of the song, and so they played back and forth for a while until the other stopped. Brenneker was somewhat disappointed that the song had ended, but a few moments later she discovered why. A gentle tapping on the sounding board roused her attention and she went to the F holes to peer out. The other spider, a male, had followed her music and had come to investigate. He clambered up the side of the instrument to her vantage point.

"How lovely," he said, "to hear the songs of home in a strange land. Tell me, Lady, how did you come here?"

"By accident," said Brenneker. "The humans picked my tawba stalk for a flute and brought me here. But I have never seen another of our kind here until now."

"I came in similar fashion," said the male. "My name is Wisterness, and, until now, I had thought I was the only one of our kind that had ranged so widely."

"What was that strange tune you played? Is it in a minor key? I have heard none like it before," said Brenneker.

"It's neither major or minor," said Wisterness. "It is based on a modal scale like some of the Renaissance music I've heard you play. I've noticed that you sometimes play in the Dorian mode, which is somewhat similar. Actually, I was playing a southern mountain tune 'June Apple.' The tuning is called 'mountain minor,' or 'A to G' tuning among them, but it is actually the older double-tonic scale, based on the highland bagpipe tuning, or, according to some sources, the Irish Harp."

"My goodness," said Brenneker, "you certainly know a lot about music. I haven't heard half of those words. I do remember playing 'Scarborough Fair' in the Dorian mode, but that's about the extent of my music theory."

"I may know more theory, but you are the better musician, Lady. I am always barely learning one tune and then going on to something new. Consequently my playing lacks polish. I have listened to your songs for several nights before summoning the courage to answer."

"I certainly have no complaint against your playing," said Brenneker. "I thought it was quite beautiful. I am curious about one thing, though, and that is your age. I never knew male spiders lived much more than a few years, yet you seem quite mature and well-read. Have you never mated?"

Wisterness shuffled his pedipalps and appeared slightly embarrassed.

"No, I never have," he said. "There was one once in my youth that I cared for, but she chose to devour another. Then one day I followed a woodsman to listen to his song, and I was carried off in a load of wood and eventually came to this place. Since then I have devoted myself to the study of humans and their music, but it has been lonely at times."

Since it was not the mating time, Wisterness left after awhile and went back to his lyre, which was strung in a hollow tree not far from the window, and he and Brenneker played duets most of the night. But sometimes she paused to listen to the piercing modal sweetness of Wisterness, as he experimented with different tunings from the lonely southern mountains.

The next morning, Laurel did not sit down to her music at the usual time, but instead put on her coat and went out with a purposeful look in her eyes. The next day, at the practice hour, a younger girl came to Laurel's door carrying a lute under her arm, and Laurel taught her a lesson. It was "Greensleeves," a favorite of Brenneker's, and she played along at first, but the student had troubles, and they kept stopping midverse and starting over until Brenneker decided it was more pain than pleasure and gave it up. Before the student left, she counted out a small sum of money which Laurel put in a large jar on her dresser. This money, Brenneker learned, was to go toward Laurel's university tuition.

As the weeks passed, more students came, until Laurel had five beginners to teach. One student came twice a week from a distant township. Sanger, the old instrument maker, still came by once in a while to teach Laurel a song, but she had long ago surpassed him in musical skill, and he never charged for his "lessons" anymore. His fingers had grown arthritic and he could not play as well as he had in the past. He no longer took students, which made Laurel one of the few teachers of the lute in her part of the country. The money piled up slowly in the jar, but it was nowhere near enough, and sometimes Brenneker would overhear Laurel arguing with her father at night about her plans to go to the university.

"Even if you get a degree in music," he would say, "that doesn't guarantee that you'll be able to support yourself. Why not study something practical that you can find a good job in."

Laurel agreed to take courses in handicrafts and midwifery to pacify her father, whom she still depended upon for support, but her heart belonged to music, and she refused to give up her plans for further study.

When she saw Thomas now, they both avoided talking about future plans, as this always provoked a fight, and he did not come to see her as often. Brenneker fretted about this, as she saw Laurel suffering in silence. When Laurel played, Brenneker sometimes wove her mating song into the web of sound hoping that Thomas would hear and return to renew his love. But he did not hear, or if he did, he didn't come.

One warm spring night, Brenneker alone played her mating song hopefully to the open window, and after a short time Wisterness came, tapping shyly on her sound box to announce his presence.

"You must come out," he said, "for the sound holes are too small for me to get in."

Brenneker had failed to recognize her predicament. As a young spider, she had entered through the holes with ease, but now she was bigger, and therefore trapped within the lute. She forced her legs out the F holes, and she could feel the tantalizing closeness of his belly fur, but try as they might, they could not negotiate across the wooden barrier.

Finally he said, "Brenneker, I fear our love must go unconsummated, for you can't get out and I can't get in. But then perhaps it's better that way, for even if we could somehow manage to mate, we could not partake of the deeper sharing, with you in there and me out here."

And so he left sadly. She did not hear his song for several days, and then one day the wind carried the distant strains of "Billy in the Lowground" to her window. The sad Irish mode echoing in the lonely Appalachian melody, told her that he had moved his harp farther away to avoid the pain of their unsatisfied need. He was too far to answer any of her musical questions or play the counterpoint games.

One day Laurel invited Thomas over to her home. She was very anxious to share a piece of news with him.

"The university is offering a music scholarship," she said. "There will be a contest and I intend to participate. If I win, my tuition would be paid, and if we both found jobs, we could be together while I go to school in the city."

Thomas thought about this before answering and then said, "It's not the money that really bothers me, it's your attitude. I get the feeling that I am not as important to you as your music. I want you to be happy, but I don't wish to play second fiddle to a lute."

"But my work is as important to me as yours is to you," said Laurel. "The truth is that neither of us wish to make the sacrifice of our career goals to be with the other."

"I had hoped our love meant more to you than your music," said Thomas, "but I see I was wrong."

"It means equally as much to me," said Laurel, "I just don't think I should be the one to have to make the sacrifice of my career. There is no reason you couldn't get a job in the city. It would not be forever, only a few years. Then we could come back here and you could take up where you left off."

"I don't see it that way," he said. "In a few years I would be behind everyone in my training and I'd be competing with younger men whom they don't have to pay as much. If I stay, I have opportunity for advancement in a few years."

"Well, I suppose we will part, then, when the summer's over," said Laurel. "I shall miss you terribly, but that's the way things work out sometimes. There is one last request I want to make of you, and that is, will you accompany me playing when I go to the contest?"

"I'm afraid I can't do that," said Thomas. "It would be adding insult to injury if I participated in the very thing that takes you away from me."

After Thomas left, Laurel cried. She went to bed early and even forgot about the milk for the fairy. This did not disturb Brenneker very much, for she had lost her appetite listening to their argument. She was pondering Laurel's problem in her mind (it seemed strange that humans could have barriers to love more complex than her wooden cage) when she heard a strange grinding noise as of a small drill emanating from one corner of the lute. She scampered to the source of the sound and stood watching the smooth surface of the unfinished wood as the sound came nearer. Suddenly a little bump appeared in the surface, and then the bump dissolved in a small pile of sawdust, and an ugly bulbish head poked out of the newly formed hole. Brenneker pounced at the woodworm but missed as it pulled back into its tunnel. Frustrated, she stood tapping at the hole with her forelegs, as the worm withdrew and burrowed in a different direction.

"You must leave," said Brenneker to the worm. "You are destroying my home and Laurel's lute."

"There is plenty of wood here for both of us," came the muffled reply of the woodworm. "You may have the rosewood, and I'll eat only the spruce."

"But I don't eat wood," said Brenneker, "and you shouldn't eat this lute. There is plenty of other wood that you can eat. Leave my home alone. You are destroying a musical instrument. Have you no appreciation for music?"

"Hmm, yes, music," said the worm, whose name was Turkawee. "I've never cared for that funny-sounding stuff. Leave it to the birds, I always say."

"You ignorant barbarian!" exclaimed Brenneker.

"I think spiders are more barbaric than our kind," said Turkawee, "for spiders eat their cousins the insects, and even their own mates. You should take care whom you go calling a barbarian."

"Philistine, then!" snorted Brenneker. "You obviously have no concept of a higher culture than your own."

"Culture, you say?" said Turkawee. "That's a term my snooty

Aunt Beetle used to use. She was always admiring the wings of butterflies. She knew an artist who made pictures of the wings. She ended up stuck with a pin to a cork board because all her interest in culture led her to follow a butterfly too closely into a collector's net. Culture is also for the birds, I say."

Brenneker, having no answer for this, retreated to her web and played the angriest song she could think of, which was a military march. The worm ignored her and continued gnawing at the wood of the lute.

Two days later, Brenneker was surveying the damage done by Turkawee. She was dismayed to find one part of the sounding board completely riddled with holes. She set about to mend it, binding the remaining wood with the steely white thread that she extruded from her spinnerets. The patch was actually quite strong, perhaps more so than the surrounding wood, but the discrepancy in the surface weakened the instrument structurally. The tension of the lute strings could cause the instrument to break, if the patch didn't hold.

Brenneker returned to her web by the sound posts and fell asleep. She wasn't used to making so much new thread, and the effort had drained her strength. In the night when she awoke, she called many insects to her supper with song, for she was ravenously hungry due to her exertion. The next day when Laurel tuned up the lute to play for a wedding, Brenneker noted with satisfaction that the patch held. But the ravages of the woodworm continued.

Old Sanger, the instrument maker, when he heard that Laurel intended to enter the scholarship contest, came by the house to offer his advice. He had played in competition in the past, and he knew what sort of artistry was apt to attract the notice of the judges and what displays of skill might sway their opinion.

"It is always a good idea to include in your repertoire a few songs that are not well known and played by everyone. And in the songs that are better known, try to display some different interpretation or more rare harmony. A few classical pieces in your presentation are in order, and playing a duet, or having some- one accompany you, is essential; so be sure to play your arrange- ment of 'The Ash Grove' with that young-man friend of yours. Your counterpoint harmony mixes very well with his recorder, and such a presentation will be sure to impress the judges. They will be looking for that particular blending of tones that displays your sense of harmony not only with your partner but with yourself and the universe."

"Poor Laurel," thought Brenneker. "What will she do without Thomas' accompaniment?"

Laurel said nothing to Sanger about her falling out with Thomas, and after he left she practiced "The Ash Grove" unaccompanied and tried to develop some new variations on the old theme. Brenneker was tempted to play the recorder part, but since to do so would reveal her presence, she contented herself with her usual practice of playing in unison or one octave higher than the melody.

That night Brenneker made a tour of the inside of her home and found that the woodworm had damaged the bond where the neck of the lute joins the body. She set about to repair the damage as best she could, plugging the holes with spidersilk and binding the weakened seam with long, tough strands. It was hard work and took much of her strength. She could barely stay awake long enough to eat the cricket that came chirping to hear her music.

Finally the greatly anticipated day came and Laurel took the coach to the big city where the contest was to be held. She refused to surrender her lute to the baggage rack and carried it in her lap, where it provoked much comment among the other passengers.

"What is that strange instrument?" they would ask. Or, "Please play us a tune."

Laurel consented and filled the coach with dulcet tones as her clear voice transported all the listeners to "Scarborough Fair."

When they arrived in the city, Laurel spent some of her hard-earned lesson money on a room at the inn. That night when Laurel was asleep, Brenneker found more holes to fill. Turkawee had almost destroyed one of the interior braces of the frame. And not only that, but also he had eaten away most of the surface below the bridge. If this were to give way, the strings would go slack and the instrument would be unplayable. Brenneker worked far into the night, binding the lute with her webbing. So far her spider silk, being stronger in tensile strength than steel wire of its same proportions, had held the lute together. But Brenneker was worried that the damage was too extensive. The inside of the lute was completely webbed and re-webbed in silk and she knew it would not hold forever. She ate sparsely that night of the few insects that inhabit an inn and then forced her body to make more thread to continue the repairs. By daybreak she was nearly exhausted. She tried to get some sleep, but Laurel woke early, concerned about the contest, and practiced her pieces, causing Brenneker to get no sleep at all.

Brenneker dozed on the carriage trip across town to the university but awoke in time to restring and tune her musical web before the contest began.

Both Brenneker and Laurel fidgeted nervously as they awaited their turn to play. There were many contestants, including a few lutists. One young man held the very antique instrument of which Laurel's was a copy. He allowed Laurel to stroke the strings once to demonstrate the superiority of its sound. But he was quite impressed when Laurel strummed a few bars on her own instrument with Brenneker's lute in tandem. "I don't understand it," he said. "Your cheaply made modern instrument sounds almost as good as mine."

"Better," thought Brenneker, smugly, but then she remembered the damaged bridge and hoped it would stand the strain. She roused herself wearily and went to find a few more holes which she hastily filled with silk.

When Laurel's time came to play, she mounted a stool on the edge of the stage. Brenneker peered out through the sound holes and saw a sea of faces watching. As Laurel tuned up, Brenneker heard an unnerving creak as the wood near the bridge shifted slightly. To her horror she saw daylight between the bridge and the body of the lute. She jumped to the ceiling of her home, bound the gap quickly, and prayed that the mend would hold. Her spinnerets ached with the strain of making so much silk, and she was very tired, but forced herself to pick the strings nimbly as Laurel began with a lively dance tune. Apparently the lovely tone impressed the judges, for Laurel was selected from a large field of competition to enter the finals.

The young man with the antique instrument was also one of the finalists, and he stopped to wish Laurel good luck. Laurel asked him if he would accompany her on "The Ash Grove," but he excused himself, saying that time would be too short for him to learn the intricate counterpart melody. He also assured her that without a duet piece, she didn't have a chance in the competition.

This point was emphasized by the lovely duet played by the young man and a woman who accompanied him on the psaltry. They received a standing ovation from the audience and high marks from the judges.

"Mercy," thought Brenneker. "Now Laurel won't be able to win the scholarship," and spider tears dampened the silk of her web.

"Hey! It's raining on my picnic," said a small voice near her.

She looked over and saw Turkawee calmly munching a chunk of spruce.

Without thinking, Brenneker pounced and bit with just enough venom to cause the woodworm to fall into a swoon.

"That should keep you from doing more damage!" she snapped. But the damage had already been done. One of the sounding pegs looked as if it were ready to crumble into dust. Brenneker could feel, through her feet, the ominous vibrations as the tension of the strings pulled against the ravaged wood.

Finally Laurel's turn came again. She played a few classical pieces, a rondo, and sang "The Wife of Ushers Well," accompanying herself beautifully with an intricate rhythm she had worked out. For her last song, she began "The Ash Grove." Her first variation was neatly composed, but Brenneker thought it lacked the clever harmony of the previous duet. The second variations sounded very lonely without accompaniment, and this provoked Brenneker to try something she'd never done before. On the third verse she began to play her web in the counterpoint harmony as she had heard Thomas play so many times on the recorder. Laurel paused abruptly, but then, true performer that she was, began to play the melody in clear, bold tones which complemented Brenneker's descant. Laurel played every variation, and Brenneker knew them all and answered back. The people in the audience were amazed that someone could play two-part harmony on one instrument. This was the most lovely duet arrangement of "The Ash Grove" that the judges had ever heard.

"That's the first time I ever heard anyone play a duet alone," said the young man with the lute as she came down from the stage. "Your harmony was better than any duet I've ever heard. How did you ever do that?"

Flustered, Laurel answered, "I don't know. I guess sometimes one must be alone to truly be in harmony with one's self."

A few more contestants got up to play, but they seemed half-hearted. The contest went of course to Laurel, who was almost as bewildered at her music as was everyone else. When she ascended the stage to accept the scholarship, the audience cheered and whistled for an encore.

Laurel sat down and prepared to play again, but just then there came a terrible wrenching sound and a loud snap. Brenneker saw the roof fly off her home, pulling a tangle of cobwebs after it. She cowered by the sound pegs, weak and frightened, and saw the face of Laurel staring down at her. Raising one timorous leg, she strummed a chord on her music web and thought she saw recognition in Laurel's eyes.

One of the judges came onstage to help pick up the debris. When he saw the large spider, he said, "How ugly! Let me kill it for you."

"No," said Laurel. "It's the fairy harpist that Sanger told me about. See how she plays her web like a harp. She's been my secret friend all these years."

Because Brenneker appeared to be in a very weakened state and near death, Laurel kept her in a bottle for a few days and fed her all the crickets she could catch. Then, when it appeared that the spider would live, she took her back to the small town and turned her loose in the woods.

It was not the woods of home, but Brenneker found a hollow tree in which to string her harp and was quite content to play her songs alone for a while, although she missed Laurel's music. When spring came that next year, she played her love song to the open air, and it was Wisterness who came, tapping shyly on her web strings to attract her attention.

"I have always loved your songs," she said. "I had hoped you would come."

"Now you shall play my songs," he said, and he sacrificed himself to their mutual need.

Weeks later, she watched her young spiderlings float away on their kiteless strings, and she knew she would not play alone anymore. Then, feeling the deep harmony of the universe in her soul, she returned her web to the Dorian mode and played the gentle, lilting sadness that was now Wisterness.

This competition, suggested by David Vereschagin, asked for long, unwieldy, and entertaining titles of fifty words or less.

From Competition 23:
Unwieldy SF Titles

I Have Heard the Star-Sounds in the Sea-Shell and Felt the Living Hatred in the Storm

Oh, Daisy Mae, Please Nurture Me; For I Have Plumbed the Empty Places and Found Them Out of True

—Elizabeth Singleton
Houston, Tex.

Blue Fingertips, Sea-Green Breasts, Hair of Ebony Darker Than the Midnights of Winter, and a Schnozz on Her Like You Wouldn't Believe

Stranded Shoeless at Night in the Jungles of Beta Hydri V With Thingies Writhing Underfoot That Can Only Be Described as Icky, Squishy, and Yucchy: A Threnody

—Bruce Berges
Lennox, Calif.

An Account of the Singular Events Which Befell Captain Hilbert Armstrong and the Passengers and Crew of the Space Cruiser Leviathan Featuring the Unseemly Asides of Pulchritudia, Courtesan of the Cosmos, and Adorned with Musings of a Philosophical Nature by Xymurgklxsz, Antarean Cabin Boy and Metaphysician

Neat Things I Did in What Was the Bronx Over My Summer Vacation from MIT, with Just a Few Fissionable Isotopes and Stuff I Bought from a Hardware Store With My Allowance
—Robert Werner
Albany, N.Y.

Feed Me Young Virgins or I Will Turn Off the World Cried the Computer Who Sat At the Center

Oh, Tell the Lady to Dance Again While the Moons of Krooth Swing Greenly Over Her Heads
—Miki Magyar
Boulder, Colo.

On the Day That History Almost Repeated Itself on the Day That Hiftory Almost Repeaded Itslef on thi Dag Thah Flitsphory Amherst Defeated Instealth

I Was an Ancient Astronaut on a Visit to Earth Who Stayed Around Long Enough to Dig Some Miniature Landing Strips and Teach Astronomy to a Primitive Tribe That Hadn't Even Discovered Shoelaces, the Wheel, or Dental Floss Yet
—David Lubar
Edison, N.J.

Oh Dad, Poor Dad, Mom's Hung You in the Closet and when the Lobster Invaders from NGC 3077 Conquered Earth Last Week They Mistook You For A Three-Button Cashmere Sport Jacket and Now They've Burned A Hole in Your Lapel and I'm Feelin So Sad

—Harlan Ellison
Sherman Oaks, Calif.

How Princess Lindora, On Dark Teleportvoyage III, Told Her
Mass from that of a Troll in the Ground

—Larry Dan Frost
Bismarck, Ark.

If Bushes Were Men, Would Redwoods Be Gods?

—Niles Gwinn
Brownsburg, Ind.

Richard Cowper is the pen name for John Middleton Murry, Jr.,
an Englishman who lives in South Wales. His SF novels include
The Road to Corlay, Kuldesak, *and* The Twilight of Briareus. *He*
has written several superior stories for F&SF, *including "The*
Custodians," "Piper At the Gates of Dawn," and the tale you are
about to read, which concerns a starship that makes contact with
an intelligent civilization and brings back a somewhat
mysterious gift.

RICHARD COWPER

Out There Where the Big Ships Go

IT was at breakfast on the second day that Roger first noticed the grey-haired man with the beard. He was sitting at the far corner table, partly shadowed by the filmy swag of the gathered gauze curtain. It was the ideal vantage point from which to observe what ever might be going on outside the long vista-window or to survey the guests as they came into the hotel dining room. But the bearded man was doing neither. He was just sitting, staring straight ahead of him, as though he could see right through the partition wall which divided the dining room from the hotel bar, and on out across the town and the azure bay to where the giant clippers unfurled their glittering metal sails and reached up to grasp the Northeast Trades.

"Don't stare, Roger. It's rude."

The boy flushed and made a play of unfolding his napkin and arranging it on his lap. "I wasn't staring," he muttered. "Just looking."

A young waiter with a sickle-shaped scar above his left eyebrow moved across from the buffet and stood deferentially at the shoulder of Roger's mother. He winked down at Roger, who smiled back at him shyly.

"You go on cruise today maybe, Senor? See *Los dedos de Dios,* hey?"

Roger shook his head.

Mrs. Herzheim looked up from the menu. "Is the fish real *fresh?*"

"*Si,* they bring him in this morning."

"We'll have that then. And grapefruits for starters. And coffee."

"*Si,* Senora." The young waiter flapped his napkin at Roger, winked again and hurried away.

Mrs. Herzheim tilted her head to one side and made a minuscule adjustment to one of her pearl eardrops. "What're your plans, honey?" she enquired lazily.

"I don't know, Mom. I thought maybe I'd—"

"Yoo-hoo, Susie! Over here!"

"Hi, Babs, Hi, Roger. Have you ordered, hon?"

"Yeah. We're having the fish. Where's Harry?"

"Collecting his paper."

The dining room was beginning to fill up, the waiters scurrying back and forth with laden trays, the air redolent with the aroma of fresh coffee and hot bread rolls. A slim girl with a lemon-yellow cardigan draped across her shoulders came in from the bar entrance. She was wearing tinted glasses, and her glossy, shoulder-length hair was the color of a freshly husked chestnut. She passed behind Roger's chair, threading her way among the tables until she had reached the corner where the bearded man was sitting. She pulled out a chair and sat down beside him so that her profile was towards the other guests and she was directly facing the window.

Roger watched the pair covertly. He saw the man lean forward and murmur something to the girl. She nodded. He then raised a finger, beckoned, and as though he had been hovering in readiness just for this, a waiter hurried over to their table. While they were giving their breakfast order, Roger's waiter reappeared with the grapefruits, a pot of coffee and a basket of rolls. As he was distributing them about the table, Susie Fogel signed to him.

He bent towards her attentively.

She twitched her snub nose in the direction of the corner table. "Is that who I think it is?" she murmured.

The waiter glanced swiftly round. "At the corner table? *Si, Senora*, that is him."

"Ah," Susie let out her breath in a quiet sigh.

"When did he arrive?"

"Late last night, Senora."

The waiter took her order and retreated in the direction of the kitchens. Mrs. Herzheim poured out a cup of coffee and handed it to Roger. As he was reaching for it, Harry Fogel appeared. He wished Roger and his mother a genial good morning and took the seat opposite his wife.

Susie lost no time in passing on her news.

Harry turned his head and scanned the couple in the corner. "Well, well," he said. "That must mean Guilio's around too. How's *that* for a turn-up?"

Roger said, "Who is he, Mr. Fogel?"

Harry Fogel's round face transformed itself into a parody of wide-eyed incredulity. "*Oi vai,*" he sighed. "Don't they teach you kids *any* history these days?"

Roger flushed and buried his nose in his grapefruit.

"Aw, come on, son," protested Harry. "Help an old man to preserve his illusions. Sure even a twelve-year-old's heard of *The Icarus?*"

Roger nodded, acutely conscious that his ears were burning.

"Well, there you are then. That's Mr. Icarus in person. The one and only. Come to add luster to our little tourney. Very big deal, eh, Babs?"

Roger's mother nodded, reached out for the sugar bowl and sprinkled more calories than she could reasonably afford over her grapefruit.

Roger risked another glance at the corner table. To his acute consternation the bearded man now appeared to be gazing directly across at him. For a moment their eyes met, and then, in the very act of glancing away, Roger thought he saw the old man lower his left eyelid ever so slightly.

At ten o'clock, Roger accompanied his mother to the youth salon. It was a trip he had been making in innumerable resorts for almost as long as he could remember. Hitherto, it had not occurred to him to resent it any more than it would have occurred to the poodles and chuhuahuas to resent their diamante studded leashes. Had anyone thought to ask him, he would probably have admitted that he genuinely enjoyed the warm, familiar femininity of the salons with their quiet carpets, their scents of aromatic waxes and lacquers, their whispered confessions which came creeping into his ears like exotic tendrils from beneath the anonymous helmets of the driers while, mouselike and unobserved, he turned the pages of the picture magazines. But today, when they reached the portico of the salon he suddenly announced: "I think I'll go on down to the harbor and take a look at the clippers, Mom."

Mrs. Herzheim frowned doubtfully. "All on your *own,* honey? Are you *sure?* I mean it's—well. . . ."

Roger smiled. "I'll be fine. You don't have to worry about me."

"But we can go together this afternoon," she countered. "I'm looking forward to seeing those clippers too, honey."

Roger's smile remained inflexible, and suddenly it dawned upon his mother that the only way she would get him inside that salon would be to drag him in by main force. The realization shocked her profoundly. She gnawed at her bottom lip as she eyed askance her twelve-year-old son, who had chosen this moment to challenge, gently, her absolute authority over him. She consulted her Cartier wristwatch and sighed audibly. "Well, all right then," she conceded. "But you're to be right back here on this very spot at noon sharp. You hear that? Promise me, now."

Roger nodded. "Sure, Mom."

Mrs. Herzheim unclipped her handbag, took out a currency bill and passed it over. Roger folded it carefully, unzipped the money pouch on his belt and stuffed the note inside. "Thanks," he said.

They stood for a moment, eying each other thoughtfully; then Mrs. Herzheim leant forward and kissed him lightly on the forehead. "You're going to tell me all about it over lunch," she said. "I'm counting on it."

Roger grinned and nodded as he watched her turn and vanish through the swing doors of the salon; then he too turned lightly on his heel and began skipping down the cobbled street towards the harbor. After a few seconds he broke into a trot which gradually accelerated into a sort of wild, leaping dance which lasted until he hurtled out, breathless, through the shadow of an ancient arched gateway and found himself on the quayside.

He clutched at a stone stanchion while he got his breath back. Then he blinked his eyes and looked about him. The sunshine striking off the ripples was flinging a shifting web of light across the hulls of the fishing boats. The very air seemed to swirl like the seabirds as they circled and swooped and dived for floating fragments of fishgut. Dark-eyed women in gaudy shawls, brass combs winking in their black hair, shouted to one another across the water from the ornate iron balconies of the waterside tenements. Donkey carts rattled up and down the slabbed causeway. Huge swarthy men, sheathed in leather aprons, their bare arms a-shimmer with fish scales, trotted past crowned with swaying pagodas of baskets and flashed white teeth at him in gleaming grins. A posse of mongrels queued up to cock their legs against a shell-fish stall only to scatter, yelping, as the outraged owner swore and hurled an empty box at them. Roger laughed, relinquished his stanchion, and began dodging among the fishermen and the sightseers, heading past the dim and echoing warehouses towards the light tower on the inner harbor mole.

When he reached his goal he sat down and drew a deep breath of pure delight. On a rock ledge some ten meters beneath him, two boys of about his own age were fishing. He watched them for a moment, then raised his eyes and looked up at the dark volcanic hills. He noted the scattering of solar "sunflower" generators; the distant globe of the observatory; the tumbling, trade-driven clouds; the lime-washed houses clambering on each other's shoulders up the steep hillside; the great hotels squatting smugly high above. By screwing up his eyes he just managed to make out in one of them the shuttered windows of the rooms which, for the next fortnight, were to be his and his mother's.

Suddenly, for no particular reason, he found himself remembering the old man and the girl with auburn hair. He tried to recall what he had read about *The Icarus,* but apart from the fact that she had been the last of the starships, he could not recall very much. As Mr. Fogel had said, that was history, and history had never been his favorite subject. But there was something about that grey-haired, bearded man which would not let his mind alone.

And suddenly he knew what it was! "He just wasn't *seeing* us," he said aloud. "He didn't *care!*"

Hearing his voice, the two boys below glanced up *"Cigarillo, Senor?"* one called hopefully.

Roger smiled and shook his head apologetically.

The boys looked at one another, laughed, shouted something he could not understand, and returned to their fishing.

Far out to sea, sunlight twinkled from the dipping topsails of an eight-masted clipper. Roger thrust out his little finger at the full stretch of his arm and tried to estimate her speed, counting silently to mark off the seconds it took her to flicker out of his sight and back again. Twenty-four. And an eight-master meant at least 200 meters overall. Two hundred in twenty-four seconds would be one hundred in twelve would be . . . five hundred in a minute. Multiply 500 by 60 and you got . . . 30 kilometers an hour. Just about average for the Northeast Trade route. But, even so, six days from now she would be rounding Barbados and sniffing for the Gulf. Very quietly he began to hum the theme of *Trade Winds,* the universal hit of a year or two back, following the great ship with his dreaming eyes as she dipped and soared over the distant swells and vowing that one day he too would be in command of such a vessel, plunging silver-winged along the immemorial trade routes of the world.

He sat gazing out to sea long after the great ship had slipped down out of sight below the horizon. Then with a sigh he climbed to his feet and began making his way back along the harbor, dimly conscious that some part of him was still out there on the ocean but not yet sufficiently self-aware to know which part it was.

A clock in a church tower halfway up the hillside sent its noonday chimes fluttering out over the roofs of the town like a flock of silver birds. Roger suddenly remembered his promise to his mother and broke into a run.

Mrs. Herzheim discovered that the youth salon had given her a headache. So after lunch she retired to her bedroom leaving Roger to spend the afternoon by the hotel pool. He had it to himself, most of the other guests having opted for one or other of the organized excursions to the local beauty spots, or, like Roger's mother, chosen to rest up prior to the ardors of the night's session.

Roger swam the eight lengths he had set himself, then climbed out and padded across to the loafer where he had left his towel and his micomicon. Who was it to be? He sat down, gave a cursory scrub to his wet hair, then flipped open the back of the cabinet and ran his eye down the familiar index. Nelson, Camelot, Kennedy, Pasteur, Alan Quartermain, Huck Finn, Tarzan, Frodo, Titus Groan—his finger hovered and a voice seemed to whisper deep inside his head *"each flint a cold blue stanza of delight, each feather, terrible. . . ."* He shivered and was on the point of uncoiling the agate earplugs when he heard a splash behind him. He glanced round in time to see the head of the girl who had shared the old man's breakfast table emerging from the water. A slim brown hand came up, palmed the wet hair from her eyes; then she turned over on her back and began threshing the water to a glittering froth, forging down the length of the pool towards him.

Five meters out, she stopped kicking and came gliding in to the edge upon her own impetus. She reached up, caught hold of the tiled trough, and turned over. Her head and the tops of her shoulders appeared above the rim of the pool. She regarded Roger thoughtfully for a moment then smiled. "Hello there."

"Hi," said Roger.

"Not exactly crowded, is it?"

"They're all out on excursions," he said, noting that she had violet eyes. "Or taking a siesta."

"All except us."

"Yes," he said. "Except us."

"What's your name?"

"Roger Herzheim."

"Mine's Anne. Anne Henderson."

"I saw you at breakfast this morning," he said. "You were with. . . ."

She wrinkled her nose like a rabbit. "My husband. We saw you too."

Roger glanced swiftly round. "Is—is he coming for a swim too?"

"Pete? No, he's up at the observatory."

Roger nodded. "Are you here on holiday?"

She flicked him a quick, appraising glance. "Well, sort of. And you?"

"Mom's playing in the tourney. She's partnering Mr. Fogel."

"And what do *you* do, Roger?"

"Oh, I come along for the trips. In the vacations, that is."

"Don't you get bored?"

"Bored?" he repeated. "No."

The girl paddled herself along to the steps and climbed out. She was wearing a minute token costume of gold beeswing, and the sunlight seemed to drip from her. She skipped across and squatted down beside him. "May I see?" she asked, pointing to the micomicon.

"Sure," said Roger amicably. "I guess they'll seem a pretty old-fashioned bunch to you."

She peered at the spool index and suddenly said, "Hey! You've got one of mine there!"

"Yours?"

"Sure. I played Lady Fuchsia in *Titus* for Universal."

Roger stared at her with the sort of absorbed attention a connoisseur might have given to a rare piece of Dresden. "You," he repeated tonelessly. "You're Lady Fuchsia?"

"I *was*," she laughed. "For nine solid months. Seven years ago. It was my first big part. Gail Ferguson. You'll find me among the credits."

"I wiped those off," he said. "I always do."

She glanced up at him sideways. "How old are you, Roger?"

"Twelve and a half."

"You like *Titus*, do you?"

"It's my favorite. Easily."

"And Fuchsia?"

He looked away from her out to where the distant aluminized dishes of the solar generators, having turned past the zenith, were now tracking the sun downhill towards the west. "I wish . . ." he murmured and then stopped.

"What do you wish?"

"Nothing," he said.

"Go on. You can tell me."

He turned his head and looked at her again. "I don't know how to say it," he muttered awkwardly. "Not without seeming rude, I mean."

Her smile dimmed a little. "Oh, go on," she said. "I can take it."

"Well, I just wish you hadn't told me, that's all. About you being Fuchsia, I mean."

"Ah," she said and nodded. There was a long pause, then: "You know, Roger, I think that's about the nicest compliment anyone's ever paid me."

Roger blinked. "Compliment?" he repeated. "Really?"

"Really. You're saying I made Fuchsia come alive for you. Isn't that it?"

He nodded. "I guess so."

"Here. Close your eyes a minute," she said. "Listen." Her voice changed, not a lot, but enough, became a litle dry and husky. "*Sunflower,*" she murmured sadly, "*Sunflower who's broken, I found you, so drink some water up, and then you won't die—not so quickly anyway. If you do I'll bury you anyway. I'll dig a long grave and bury you. Pentecost will give me a spade. If you don't die you can stay. . . .*"

She watched his face closely. "There," she said, in her own voice. "You see? Fuchsia exists in me and apart from me: in you and apart from you. Outside of time. She won't grow older like the rest of us."

Roger opened his eyes. "You speak about her as if she was real," he said wonderingly.

"*Real!*" There was a sudden, surprising bitterness in the girl's voice. "I don't know what the word means. Do you?"

"Why, yes," he said, puzzled by the change in her tone. "You're real. So am I. And this"—he waved a hand towards the pool and the hotel—"that's real."

"What makes you so sure?"

He suspected that she was laughing at him. "Well, because I can touch it," he said.

"And that makes it real?"

"Sure."

She lifted her arm and held it out to him. "Touch me, Roger."

He grinned and laid his right hand lightly on the sun-warmed flesh of her forearm. "You're real, all right."

"That's very reassuring," she said. "No, I mean it. Some days I don't feel real at all." She laughed. "I should have you around more often, shouldn't I?"

She stood up, walked to the edge of the pool, flexed her coral-tipped toes and plunged in, neatly and without fuss.

Roger watched her slender body flickering, liquid and golden against the tiled floor. Then he snapped shut the micomicon, sprinted across the paved surround, and dived to join her.

The tourney was due to start at eight o'clock. Mrs. Herzheim was all a-flutter because she had just learnt that she and Harry Fogel were drawn against the co-favorites in her section for the first round. "Do you think it's a good omen, Roger?" she asked. "Be honest now."

"Sure, Mom. A block conversion at the very least."

"Wouldn't that be marvelous? Certain sure Harry would muff it though. Like that time in Reykjavik, remember? I could've *died!*" She leant close to the dressing table mirror and caressed her eyelashes with her mascara brush. "You going to watch So-Vi, honey?"

"I expect so."

Mrs. Herzheim eyed her reflection critically and then sighed. "That's the best you'll do, girl. Can't turn mutton into lamb. How do I look, baby?"

"You look great."

"That's my pet." She restored the mascara brush to its holder and zipped up her toilet case. "Well, all you can do for me now is wish me luck, honey."

"Good luck, Mom."

She walked over to the bed where her son was lying, bent over and kissed him, but lightly as to avoid smearing her lips. "I'll mouse in so's not to wake you," she said.

He smiled and nodded and she went out, wafting him a final fingertip kiss from the doorway.

Roger lay there for a few minutes, his fingers laced behind his head, and gazed up at the ceiling. Then he got up from his mother's bed and walked through into his own room. From the drawer of the bedside cabinet he took out his recorder, ran it back for a while and listened to the letter to his father which he had started taping the previous evening. He added a description of his visit to the harbor and was about to move on to his meeting with Anne Henderson when he suddenly changed his mind. He switched off the recorder, when back into his mother's room and retrieved his micromicon. Having slotted home the *Titus* cartridge, he uncoiled the earphones and screwed the plugs into his ears. Then he lay on the bed, reached down, pushed the button which activated the mechanism, and, finally, dragged the goggles down over his eyes.

At once the familiar magic began to work. The wraiths of milk-white mist parted on either side; gnarled specters of ancient trees emerged and lolloped past to the slow pacing of his horse; he heard the bridle jingle and the whispering waterdrops pattering down upon the drifts of dead and decaying leaves. At any moment now he would emerge upon the escarpment and, gazing down, behold by the sickly light of a racing moon, the enormous crouching beast of stone that was the castle of Gormenghast. Then, swooping like some huge and silent night bird down over the airy emptiness and up again towards the tiny pinprick of light high up in the ivied bastion wall, he would gaze in through the latticed, candlelit window of Fuchsia's room. He heard the telltale rattle of the pebble dislodged, and the mist veils thinned abruptly to a filmly gauze. He had reached the forest's edge. His horse moved forward one more hesitant pace and stood still, awaiting his command. He leant forward and was about to peer down into The Valley That Never Was when the vision dimmed abruptly and, a second later, had flickered into total darkness.

Roger swore, dragged off the goggles and hoisted the machine up from the floor beside the bed. The ruby telltale was glowing like a wind-fanned spark. He pushed the OFF button, and the light vanished. He stared glumly at the all-but-invisible thread, then activated the rewind mechanism and plucked the slender cartridge from its slot. Perhaps he would be able to find a repair depôt in the town somewhere. It did not seem likely. He unfastened the earplugs, restored them to their foam-molded cache beside the goggles and closed up the inspection panel. Then he let himself out into the corridor and rode the elevator down to the reception hall.

His spirits revived a little when the desk clerk informed him that there was indeed a Universal Elektronix shop in the town. He added regretfully that, so far as he knew, it ran no all-night service. Roger thanked him and was about to head for the So-Vi lounge when an impulse persuaded him to change his mind and he walked out on to the terrace instead.

The sun had set a quarter of an hour past, but the western horizon was still faintly fringed with a pale violet glow that deepened precipitately to indigo. Directly overhead, the equatorial stars were trembling like raindrops on the twigs of an invisible tree. Roger walked slowly to the edge of the pool and gazed down at the quivering reflections of unfamiliar constellations. The air was soft and warm, balmy with the scent of spice blossom. From somewhere on the dark hillside below him he could hear the sound of a guitar playing and a girl's voice singing. He listened, entranced, and suddenly, unaccountably, he was struggling in the grip of an overwhelming sadness, an emotion all the more poignant because he could ascribe it to no specific cause. He felt the unaccustomed pricking of tears behind his eyelids and he stumbled away towards the dark sanctuary of the parapet which divided the pool area from the steeply terraced flower gardens.

There was a flight of steps, carpeted with some small creeping plant, which he remembered led down to a stone bench where earlier he had seen a small green lizard sunning itself. He scuttled down into the comforting shadows, skirted a jasmine bush and, with eyes not yet fully adjusted to the deeper darkness, felt his cautious way forward. The bench was occupied.

The shock of this discovery froze the sob in his throat. His heart gave a great painful leap and he stared, open-mouthed, at the suddenly glowing end of a cigar. There was a faint chuckle from the shadows, and a deep voice said, "Well, hello there. Roger, isn't it?"

Roger swallowed. "I'm sorry, sir," he gulped. "I didn't know. . . ."

"Sure you didn't. Why should you? So help yourself to a seat, son. And mind the bottle."

Roger hesitated for a moment, then edged carefully forward and sat down on the very far end of the bench.

"Saw you at breakfast, didn't I?" said the voice, and added, parenthetically: "The name's Henderson, by the way."

"Yes, sir," said Roger. "I know. You're The Master."

"Ah," said the deep voice thoughtfully. There was a long pause, then: "So, tell me, what brings you out roaming in the gloaming?"

Roger said nothing.

"Me, I come to look at the stars," said the old man. "That sound crazy to you?"

"No, sir."

The cigar flower bloomed bright scarlet and slowly faded. "Well, it does to a lot of people," said the deep voice, once more dis-embodied.

"Not to me," said Roger, surprised to hear how firm his own voice sounded.

There was a clink of glass against glass, followed by a brisk gurgle. "Care for a mouthful of wine?"

"No, thank you, sir."

There was a moment of silence and then the sound of a glass being set down again. "I gather you met Anne this afternoon."

"Yes, sir."

"You like her?"

"Yes, sir," Roger affirmed fervently.

"Beautiful, isn't she?"

Roger said nothing, partly because he could think of nothing to say, partly because he had just realized that his recollection of touching Anne's sun-warmed arm had been a primal cause of his sudden loneliness.

"Well, she is," said The Master. "And let me assure you, Roger, I know what I'm talking about."

"Yes, she's lovely," murmured Roger, and wondered where she was now.

"Beauty isn't just *shape,* boy. It's spirit too. A sweet harmony. Did you know that?"

"I—I'm not sure I know what you mean, sir."

"Well, take The Game. What grade are you, Roger?"

"Thirty-second Junior, sir."

"Ever make a clear center star?"

"I did nearly. About a year ago."

"How'd it feel?"

"I don't really know, sir. It just sort of happened. I wasn't even thinking about it."

"Of course not. It's a sort of natural flow. You lose yourself in it. That's the secret of The Game, boy. Losing yourself." The cigar tip described a rosy, fragrant arabesque in the air and ended up pointing towards the heavens. "Out there beyond Eridanus.

That's where I found that out. Might just as well have stayed at home, hey?" Again the glass clinked. "How old are you, son?"

Roger told him.

"Know how old I am?"

"No, sir."

"Take a guess."

Roger groped. "Sixty."

The Master gave a brusque snort of laughter and said, "Well, I'm surely flattered to hear you say so, Roger. Tell me, do the names Armstrong and Aldrin mean anything to you?"

"No, sir."

The Master sighed. "And why should they, indeed? But when I was your age, they were just about the two most famous names on this whole planet. '68 that was—the year all the kids in our neighborhood grew ten feet tall overnight!" He gave another little mirthless snort. "We were the ones who bought the dream, Roger, the whole goddamn, star-dream package, lock, stock and barrel. And in the end one or two of us even got there. The chosen few. Hand-picked. Know what they called us? Knights of the Grail!" He spat out into the darkness, and a moment later the tiny furnace of the cigar glowed bright and angry as he dragged hard at the invisible teat.

"Like Sir Lancelot and Sir Gawain?" suggested Roger timidly.

"Maybe," said The Master. "All I know is they told us we'd been privileged to live out man's eternal dream on his behalf. And we believed them! Thirty-nine years old I was, boy, and I still swallowed that sort of crud! Can you credit it?"

Some small creature rustled dryly in the jasmine bush and was silent again. Down below in the scarf of shadow that lay draped across the shoulder of the hill between the hotel and the twinkling lights of the town, the sound of the girl's voice came again, singing sweetly and sadly to the accompaniment of the plucked strings.

Roger said, "What was it *really* like out there, sir?"

There was a pause so long that Roger was beginning to wonder whether the old man had heard his question, then: "There comes a moment, boy, when for the life of you you can't pick out the sun from all the rest of them. That's when the thread snaps and you slip right through the fingers of God. There's nothing left for you to relate to. But if you've been well-trained, or you're as thick as two planks, or maybe just plain lucky, you come through that and out on the other side. But something's happened to you. You don't know what's *real* any more. You get to wondering about the nature of Time and how old you *really* are. You question everything. But *everything*. And in the end, if you're like me, the dime finally drops and you realize you've been conned. And that's the second moment of truth."

"Conned?"

"That's right, son. Conned. Cheated. Hood-winked. Look." He took the cigar from between his lips and blew upon the smoldering cone of ash until it glowed bright red. "Now what color would you say that was?"

"Why, red, of course."

"No. I'm telling you you're wrong. That's blue. Bright blue."

"Not *really*," said Roger.

"Yes, really," said The Master. "You only say it's red because you've been told that's what red is. For you blue is something else again. But get enough people to say that's blue, and it *is* blue. Right?"

"But it's still red, really," said Roger, and gave a nervous little hiccup of laughter.

"It's what it is," said The Master somberly. "Not what anyone *says* it is. That's what I discovered out there. Sometimes I think it's all I did discover."

Roger shifted uneasily on the stone bench. "But you said . . ." he began and then hesitated. "I mean when you said before about spirit . . . about its being beautiful. . . ."

"That too," admitted The Master. "But it's the same thing."

Was it? Roger had no means of knowing.

"Spirit's just another way of saying 'quality'—something everyone recognizes and no one's ever defined. You can recognize quality, can't you, Roger?"

"I—I'm not sure, sir."

"Sure you're sure. You recognized it in Anne, didn't you?"

"Oh, yes."

"I suspect it's what you were out looking for down by the harbor this morning. It's what brought you out here tonight when you could have been sitting there snug and pie-eyed in front of the So-Vi with all the rest of the morons."

"My micomicon broke," said Roger truthfully.

The Master chuckled. "You win, son," he said.

"Did you know that Anne was Lady Fuchsia in *Titus Groan?*"

"She was?"

"Yes. She told me this afternoon. I was going to see if it seemed any different now I know."

"Ah," said The Master. "And was it?"

"I don't know. The spool broke before I got to her."

"That's life, son," said The Master, and again gave vent to one of his explosive snorts of laughter. "Just one long series of broken spools. You're here for the tourney, are you?"

"Mom is."

"And your father?"

"He's in Europe—Brussels. He's a World Commodity Surveyor. He and mom are separated."

"Ah." The sound was a verbal nod of understanding.

"I get to go on vacation with him twice a year. We have some great times together. He gave me the micomicon. He's fixing a clipper trip for us next spring."

"You're looking forward to that, are you?"

Roger sighed ecstatically, seeing yet again in his mind's eye the silver-winged sea-bird dipping and soaring over the tumbling, trade-piled Atlantic hills, wreathed in spraybows.

"You like the sea?"

"More than anything," avowed Roger. "One day I'm going to be master of my own clipper."

The cigar glowed and a pennant of aromatic smoke wavered hesitantly in the vague direction of far-off Eridanus. "That's your ambition, is it?"

"Yes, sir," said Roger simply.

"And how about The Game?"

Before Roger could come up with an answer, a voice called down from the terrace above them: "Hey! Isn't it time you were getting robed-up, Pete?"

"I guess it must be, if you say so," responded The Master.

"Guilio's in the hall already. Who's that down there with you?"

"A fan of yours, I gather."

"Roger?"

"Hello," said Roger.

With a faint groan The Master rose from the bench, dropped his cigar butt on the stone-slabbed parterre and screwed it out beneath the sole of his shoe. Then he picked up his glass and the almost empty wine bottle. With eyes now fully accustomed to the gloom, Robert saw that the old man was bowing gravely towards him. "I must beg you to excuse me, Roger," he said, "but as you will have realized, duty calls. I have greatly enjoyed our conversation. We shall meet again. Perhaps tomorrow, heh?"

"Thank you, sir. Good luck."

"Luck?" The Master appeared to consider the implications of the courtesy for a moment. He smiled. "It's a long, long time since anybody wished me that, Roger. But thank you, nonetheless."

Mercifully the darkness hid the bright flush of mortification on the boy's cheeks.

The Master and his challenger, Guilio Romano Amato, sat facing each other on a raised dais at one end of the tourney hall, separated from the other players by a wide swath of crimson carpet and the token barrier of a thick, gilded cord. On the wall above their heads a huge electronic scoreboard replicated the moves in this, the third session of the Thirty-Third World Kalire Championship.

Besides the two contestants seven other people shared the dais: the Supreme Arbitrator, The Master's two Seconds, Amato's Seconds, and the two Official Scorekeepers, one of whom was Anne. They all sat cross-legged on cushions at a discreet distance from the two principals. If they were conscious that their every movement, every facial expression, was being relayed by satellite to a million Kalire temples around the world, they evidenced no sign of it. They dwelt apart, isolated, enthralled by the timeless mystery and wonder of The Game of Games, the Gift from Beyond the Stars.

Into those silent, fathomless, interstellar reaches, the mere contemplation of which had once so terrified Pascal, Man in the person of The Master had dared to dip his arm. Two full centuries later, long after he had been given up for dead, he had returned to Earth, bearing with him the inconceivable Grail he had gone to seek.

He had emerged to find a world exhausted and ravaged almost

beyond his recognition—a world in which the fabulous mission of *The Icarus* had dwindled to little more than an uneasy folk memory of what was surely the purest and most grandiloquent of all the acts of folly ever perpetrated in the whole crazy history of the human race.

When the great starship, scorched and scarred from its fantastic odyssey, had finally dropped flaming out of the skies to settle as gently as a seed of thistledown upon its original launching site on the shore of Lake Okeechobee, few who witnessed its arrival could bring themselves wholly to believe the evidence that was so manifestly there before them. The huge, tarnished, silver pillar standing there among the rusting debris and the crumbling gantries whispered to them of those days, long since past, when their forefathers still had the capacity to hope.

A hastily convened reception committee had driven out to welcome the wanderers home. Grouped in a self-conscious semicircle on the fissured and weed-ribbed concrete of the ancient launch pad, the delegation stood waiting for the port to open and the Argonauts to descend.

At last the moment came. The hatch inched open, slowly cranking itself back to reveal a solitary figure standing framed in the portal and gazing down upon them.

"Who is it?" They whispered to one another. "Dalgleish? Martin? No, I'll swear that's Henderson himself. God, he hardly looks a day older than the pictures, does he? Are you *sure* it's him? Yeah, that's Henderson all right. Christ, it doesn't seem possible, does it?"

And then someone had started to clap. In a moment everyone had joined in, beating the palms of their hands together in the dry, indifferent air.

Thirty feet above them, Peter Henderson, Commander of *The Icarus,* heard the strange, uncoordinated pattering of their applause and slowly raised his left hand in hesitant acknowledgment. It was then that some sharp-eyed observer noted that beneath his right arm he was carrying what appeared to be an oblong wooden box.

At first practically nobody took Henderson seriously, and who could blame them? Yet the memory banks of *The Icarus* appeared to confirm much of what he said. The gist of it was that out there, beyond Eridanus, on a planet they had called "Dectire III," they had finally discovered that which they had gone forth to seek. The form it took was that of a fabulous city which they called "Eidothea," a city which, if Henderson was to be believed, was nothing less than all things to all men. It was inhabited by a race of gentle, doe-eyed creatures who differed from themselves only in being androgynous and in possessing an extra finger upon each hand. They were also, by human standards, practically immortal. The Eidotheans were the professed devotees of an hermaphrodite deity they called Kalirinos, who, they maintained, held sway over one half of the existing universe. The other half was the ordained territory of her counterpart (some said her identical twin) Arimanos. Kalirinos and Arimanos were locked in an eternal game of Kalire (The Game) whose counters were nothing less than the galaxies, the stars and the planets of the entire cosmos. By reaching Eidothea, humanity, in the persons of the crew of *The Icarus,* had supplied the evidence that their species was ready to join The Game and, by so doing, to take another step up the evolutionary ladder.

There had followed a period of roughly six months devoted to their initiation and instruction in the rudiments at Kalire, at the end of which Henderson alone had gained admission to the very lowest Eidothean rank of proficiency in The Game—a grade approximately equivalent by our own standards to the First Year Primary Division. After his victory he had been summoned before the High Council, presented with his robe of initiation, with the board marked out in the one hundred and forty-four squares, each of which has its own name and ideogram, and with the box containing the one hundred and forty-three sacred counters, colored red on one side and blue on the other, which alone constitute the pure notes from which the divine harmonies of The Game of Games are derived. "And now you shall return to your own world," they had told him, "and become the teacher of your people. Soon, if we have judged correctly, your world will be ready to take its place in the timeless federation, and Kalirinos will smile upon you."

Henderson had protested passionately that he was wholly unworthy of such an honor, but the truth was that he could not bear the thought of having to tear himself away from the exquisite delights of Kalire, which, like those of the fabled lotus, once they have been enjoyed, must claim the soul forever. However, the Eidotheans had seemingly been prepared for this. The commander was placed in a mild hypnotic trance, carried aboard *The Icarus,* and the ship's robot brain was instructed to ferry him back to his own planet. The rest of the crew were graciously permitted to remain behind in Paradise.

Within the terms of the eternal symbolic struggle between Kalirinos and Arimanos (and certainly against all the odds), the conversion of the Earth was accomplished with a swiftness roughly commensurate to the reversal of a single counter upon the Divine Board. Within twenty-four hours of his setting foot once more upon his native soil, Commander Henderson had been interviewed upon International So-Vi. There, before the astonished eyes of about a billion skeptical viewers, he had unfolded his board, set down in his four opening counters in the prescribed pattern, and had given an incredulous world its very first lesson in Kalire.

The Japanese, with their long tradition of Zen and Go, were the first to become enmeshed in the infinite subtleties of The Game, and within a matter of weeks the great toy factories of Kobe and Nagoya were churning out Kalire sets by the million. The Russians and Chinese were quick to follow. And then—almost overnight it seemed—the whole world had gone Kalire-crazy. It leapt across all barriers of language and politics, demanding nothing, offering everything. Before it armies were powerless, creeds useless. Time-hallowed mercenary values, ancient prejudices, long-entrenched attitudes of mind—all these were suddenly revealed as the insubstantial shadows of a childhood nightmare. Kalire was all. But was it a religion, or a philosophy, or just a perpetual diversion? The answer surely is that it was all these things and more besides. The deeper one studied it, the more subtle and complex it became. Layer upon layer upon layer of revelation awaited the devotee, and yet there was always the knowledge that however profoundly he delved he would never uncover the ultimate penetralia of the mystery.

Soon international tourneys were being organized, and the champions started to emerge. They too competed among themselves for the honor of challenging Peter Henderson. The first contender so to arise was the Go Master, Subi Katumo. He played six games with Henderson and lost them all. From that point on Henderson was known simply as "The Master." He traveled the world over playing exhibition games and giving lectures to rapt audiences. He also founded the Kalirinos Academy at Pasadena, where he instructed his disciples in those fundamental spiritual disciplines so vital to the mastery of the art of Kalire and into which he himself had been initiated by the Eidotheans. He wrote a book which he called *The Game of Games* and prefaced it with a quotation taken from "The Paradoxes of the Negative Way" by St. John of the Cross—

In order to become that which thou art not,
Thou must go by a way which thou knowest not. . . .

The Game of Games became a world best-seller even before it had reached the bookshops, and within six months of publication had been translated into every language spoken on Earth.

And so Henderson grew old. Now, in the thirty-fourth year of his return, at the physical age of seventy-eight, he was defending his title yet again. His challenger, Guilio Amato, the twenty-eight-year-old Neapolitan, was the premier graduate from the Kalirinos Academy. In his pupil's play The Master had detected for the first time a hint of that ineffable inner luminosity which others ascribe to genius but which he himself recognized as supreme quality. Having recognized it, he dared to permit himself the luxury of hoping that his long vigil might at last be drawing to its close.

So far, they had played two games of the ordained six: one in Moscow and one in Rome. The Master had won both. But in each, in order to ensure victory, he had had to reach deeper than ever before into his innermost resources for a key to unlock his pupil's strategy. Now the third game had reached its critical third quarter. If The Master won (and who could doubt that he would?), the title would remain his. Even if, by some miracle, Amato managed to win the three remaining games, the resulting draw would still count as a victory for the title holder. To state the matter in a way wholly foreign to the spirit of the contest—let alone of Kalire itself—to keep his chances alive, Amato had to win this third game.

Such was the situation when The Master, having entered the hall, bowed to the Supreme Arbitrator, sat down, touched hands formally across the board with his challenger and then accepted the envelope containing Amato's sealed move. He opened it, scanned the paper, nodded to his pupil, and permitted himself the ghost of a smile. It was exactly the move he had expected. He leant forward and placed a blue counter upon the designated square. On the display board above their heads a blue light winked on and off. A faint sigh went up from the main body of the hall. The struggle was rejoined.

Immediately after breakfast the following morning, Roger took his micomicon down to the depôt in the town and left it for the broken spool to be repaired. Having been assured that it would be ready for him to collect within the hour, he elected to retrace his path of the previous day, wandering out along the stone-flagged quay to where the mole jutted out across the harbor mouth.

The morning sun was shining just as brilliantly upon the flanks of the volcanic hills and scooping up its shimmering reflections from the restlessly looping wavelets in the inner basin; the brightly shawled women were still crying out to each other in their strange parrot-patois from their ornate balconies; the gulls were still shrieking and swirling as they dived for the scraps; ostensibly it was all just as it had been the day before. And yet the boy was conscious that, in some not quite definable way, things were subtly different. Something had changed. Frowning, he scanned the horizon for signs of clippers plying the trade routs but could see nothing. Then, moved by a sudden impulse, he clambered over the parapet and scrambled down the rocks to the ledge where he had last seen the two boys fishing.

There were dried fish scales glinting like chips of mica on the rocks, and he picked one or two of them off with his fingernail. Having examined them, he flipped them into the green, rocking waters below him. Then he squatted down, cupped his chin in his hands and stared down at the flickering shadows of the little fish as they came darting to the surface attracted by the glittering morsels.

He thought of Anne finning her golden way across the bottom of the sunlit pool, and from there his memory winged on to the curious conversation he had had with the old man. As he started to recall it, he began to realize that it was his recollection of their meeting in the darkness which had contrived to insinuate itself between him and the brilliant scene about him. "It's what it *is,* not what anyone *says* it is." What was that supposed to mean? And how could red *be* blue? Even if everyone *called* it blue, it would still *be* red. Or would it? A sharp splinter of sunlight struck dazzling off a wave straight into his eyes. He covered them with his hands, and suddenly, bright as an opal on his retina, he seemed to see again the glowing spark of The Master's cigar and above it the shape of the bearded lips blowing it brighter. Yet, even as he followed the point of light, its color began to change, becoming first mauve, then purple, and finally a brilliant aquamarine. And yet, indisputably, it was still the original spark.

He opened his eyes wide, blinked, and gazed about him. As he did so, he heard a voice calling down to him from above. He looked up and saw the silhouette of a head against the arching blue backdrop of the morning sky. He screwed up his eyes, smiled, and shook his head.

The man's voice came again, and Roger guessed it must be one of the waiters from the hotel. He spread his hands helplessly. "*No habla Espanol,* senor," he tried. "*Scusi. Estoy Americano.*"

The man laughed. "I was only asking what it was like down there," he said in perfect English.

Roger shrugged. "Well, it's OK. I guess," he said. "If you like sitting on rocks, that is."

"Nothing I like better. Mind if I join you?"

"Sure. Come on down."

The man stepped over the low parapet and descended, sure-footed, to the ledge. Once there, he glanced about him, selected a smoothish rock and sat down, letting his long legs dangle over the waters. He drew a deep breath and let it out in a luxurious sigh. "That's great," he murmured. "Just great."

Roger scrutinized him out of the tail of his eye. He was dark-haired, his face was tanned, and he had pale smile creases at the corners of his eyes and mouth. Roger placed him as being in his middle twenties. "Are you here for the tourney?" he asked.

"That's right."

"I thought you must be."

"How so? I speak a pretty fair Espanol, don't I?"

"Yes. I guess so. But you're not Spanish, are you?"

"No."

"Where are you from?"

"California mostly."

Roger poked his little finger up his nose and scratched around thoughtfully for a moment. Then he glanced sideways at the newcomer, removed his finger and said, "Would you mind if I asked you a question?"

"Well, that all depends, doesn't it? I mean there are questions and questions."

"Oh, it's not personal," said Roger hastily.

"Then I'd say there's just that much less chance of my being able to answer it. But go ahead anyway."

Roger pointed across the inner harbor to where a woman in a flame-colored shawl was leaning over a fisherman on the water below her. "Do you see that woman in the red dress?" he asked.

The man followed his pointing finger. "I see her," he said.

"If I said she was wearing a *blue* dress, would I be right or wrong?"

The man glanced at him, and his brown eyes widened in fractional astonishment. "Would you mind repeating that?"

Roger did so.

"Yes, I thought that's what you said." The dark head turned and he stared again at the woman. "A *blue* dress?" he repeated. "What kind of a crazy question is that, for Godsake?"

"I don't know," Roger confessed. "But last night The Master told me that if enough people said red was blue, then it *was* blue."

The young man turned and stared at him. "Come again. *Who* said it?"

"The Master. I was talking to him out in the hotel garden after supper last night. But what I'm wondering is, if there's only *two* people and one says a thing's red and the other says it's blue— well, what *is* it?"

The young man lifted his right hand and drew it slowly across his mouth. "He said red *was* blue?"

"Well, not exactly. He said it's what it is. He said it's not *really* red or blue or anything—except itself."

The young man's eyes had taken on a curiously opaque expression, and though Roger knew he was looking *at* him, he also knew he wasn't really seeing him. "I guess it's a pretty dumb sort of question," he said at last. "But, I don't know, somehow it's been bothering me."

"How's that?"

"It's just been bugging me, that's all."

"Yes, I can see that." The young man nodded. "So. What kind of an answer are you hoping for?"

"I don't know."

"What's your name, son?"

"Roger. Roger Herzheim."

"Well, Roger, I don't know that I can help. But how's this for a start? Let's say these are *things* and there are the *names* of those things. Right? Well, it's from the names we derive our *ideas* of the things. D'you follow?"

Roger nodded.

"OK. Now if we play around with the *ideas* for long enough, then, sure as hell, we'll get to believing that the ideas *are* the things. But they're not. Not really. The things are the things themselves. They always have been and, I guess, they always will be. It's a pretty profound truth really. At least that's what *I* think he was saying. But, hell, Roger, I could be *way* out."

Roger nodded rather doubtfully, and as he did so, his attention was caught by a sudden silver flickering far out on the eastern horizon. "Hey! Look!" he cried. "That's the first today! Just look at her *go!*"

The young man grinned broadly as he turned and gazed out to sea. "Yep, she's a real beauty," he said. "*Leviathan* class, I'd guess."

"*Leviathan?*" echoed Roger scornfully. "With five t'gallants? Why sure she's an *Aeolian*. And on the Barbados run too. Do you know that bird can *average* thirty knots?"

"Thirty knots, eh?" repeated the young man reverently. "You don't say so? Incredible!"

Half an hour later they strolled back into town to collect Roger's micomicon. As they were walking up the main street, Roger heard someone cry out: "Guilio! Where the helluv you *been,* man? I've been scouring the whole goddamn *town* for you! Tuomati's done a depth analysis of the whole Mardonian sector and he reckons he's found us some real counter chances."

"That's great, Harry," said the young man, with what seemed

to Roger rather tepid enthusiasm. "Well, *ciao,* Roger. I'm really glad to have met you. I surely won't ever again mistake a *Leviathan* for an *Aeolian.*"

Roger smiled and waved his hand shyly, but Guilio Romano Amato was already striding away up the hill deep in conversation with his Second.

Roger spent the afternoon beside the pool hoping that Anne would reappear. She never did. Nor did she show up in the hotel dining room for the evening meal. Roger accompanied his mother up to their bedroom and, in response to her query as to how he intended to spend his evening, told her that he thought maybe he'd look in at the Spectators' Gallery for a while.

"I'm truly flattered to hear it, honey. But isn't *Clippers* on So-Vi tonight?"

"Sure it is. But not till ten. So I thought I'd finish off my letter to dad first, then take in a bit of the tourney. You've drawn 58, haven't you?"

"That's right, pet. Board 58, Section 7. I'll give you a wave."

It was not until his mother had wafted him her ritual kiss and left the apartment that it occurred to the boy to wonder why he had not told her of either of his meetings with the two champions.

At nine o'clock he rode the elevator down to the first floor and followed the indicators to the Spectators' Gallery. The sign STANDING ROOM ONLY was up, but Roger contrived to squeeze his way in and found a place to squat down on one of the steep gangways. The general tourney had already been in session for over an hour, but The Master and his challenger had only just taken their seats on the dais, and the red light which marked The Master's sealed move was still winking on the display board. There was an almost palpable atmosphere of tension in the hall as Amato surveyed the field before him.

Roger glanced across at one of the monitor screens and saw a huge closeup of the young man's face. It could almost have been a death mask, so total was its stillness. Then the picture flicked over to the board itself and showed Amato's hand dipping into his bowl of counters. The whole vast hall had become as silent as though everyone had been buried beneath a thick, invisible blanket of snow.

Beneath Guilio's slim fingers the counter slowly turned and turned again. Red, blue; red, blue; red, blue; and then he had reached out and laid it quietly on the board. The tip of the index finger of his right hand lingered upon it for a long, thoughtful moment and then withdrew.

As the blue light sprang out on the display, there came a sound which was part whisper, part sigh, as the spectators let out their pent breath. And then, from somewhere down below out of Roger's view, in the section of the tourney which held the players of the Premier Grade, there came the shocking sound of someone clapping. In a moment it had caught hold like a brush fire, and it was at least a minute before the controller's impassioned pleas for silence could make themselves heard above the unprecedented hubbub.

"What is it?" Roger demanded, shaking the arm of the person beside him. "What's he done?"

"I don't know, son. Frankly it seems crazy to me. But I guess it must be something pretty special to earn that sort of hand from the Premiers."

Roger turned to the monitor screen for enlighenment and was treated to a close-up of The Master's face. He was smiling the sort of smile that might have wreathed the face of a conquistador as he emerged from some high Andean jungle to find himself gazing down upon El Dorado. He leant across the board and murmured something to the impassive Amato. The concealed microphones picked up his voice instantly, and around the world was replayed one single vibrant word, the supreme accolade: *"Beautiful!"*

As he was fully entitled to do under the rules, The Master requested a statutory thirty-minute recess, which the Arbitrator immediately granted. The clocks were stopped; the two contestants touched hands; and The Master rose from his cushion, beckoned to Anne, and vanished with her through the curtained exit at the back of the dais.

The microphones picked up the whisper of conversation between Amato and his Seconds. As the cameras zoomed in on them, Roger saw that the two men were gazing at Guilio with what can only be described as awe. The young man simply shook his head and shrugged as if to signify that what they were saying scarcely concerned him. He was right.

That single move of Amato's has justly earned the title of "The Immortal," though, by today's standards, one must admit that it does have a distinctly old-fashioned air. The fact is that after an interval of close on thirty years, it is all but impossible to convey just how exceptional it was at the time it was first played. To appreciate it fully, one would have to re-create the whole electric atmosphere of that tourney and the seemingly impregnable position that The Master had established for himself in the match. It has been claimed with some substance that Amato's ninety-second move in the third game of the Thirty-Third World Series marked mankind's coming of age. But probably Amato himself came closer to the truth when he remarked to a reporter at the conclusion of the match: "Hell, man, it was just a matter of realizing that you can walk backwards through a door marked PUSH."

Twelve years later, in the preface to his monumental work *One Thousand Great Games,* Guilio elaborated upon this as follows: "I realized at that moment why The Master had chosen that particular paradox from St. John of the Cross as prefix to his *Game of Games.* Up to that instant in time, my whole approach to Kalire had been based upon the overwhelming desire to win. In order to become that which I was not (in my case, at that time, the winner of that vital third game), I had to go by a way which I did not know. There was only one such way available to me. I had to desire not defeat (that seemed inevitable anyway) but the achievement of a state of mind in which winning or losing ceased to have meaning for me. In other words, I had to gain access to the viewpoint from which Kalirinos and Arimanos are perceived to be one and the same being. In the timeless moment during which I turned that counter over between my fingers, I understood the significance of The Master's casual observation which I had heard for the first time that very morning: 'There is neither red nor blue, there is only the thing itself.' The thing itself was nothing less than the pure quintessence of The Game—an eternal harmonic beauty which obeys its own code of laws and whose sublime and infinite subtlety we are fortunate to glimpse perhaps once or twice in a lifetime. Let us call it simply 'the Truth of the Game.' At that moment I recognized it, and I laid my counter where I did for no other reason than my overwhelming desire to preserve the pattern forever in my own mind's eye."

So the shapes dissolve and reassemble in the swirl of Time. Everything changes; everything remains the same. We know now what we are, and some of us believe we have an inkling of what we may become.

Thirty-four years have passed since Guilio Romano Amato dethroned The Master and became The Master in his turn. He held the title for seven years, lost it to Li Chang, and then regained it two years later in the epic encounter of '57. In '62 the Universal Grade of Grand Master was established, and The Game moved into its present phase.

It only remains to outline briefly the subsequent histories of those persons who have been sketched in this little memoir.

First, The Master himself. He died peacefully at his home in Pasadena three years after relinquishing his title. At the time of his death his age by calendar computation was 273 years; by physical measurement, 81 years. Despite his insistence that he wished for no ostentatious ceremonial of any kind, his funeral was marked by a full week of mourning throughout the capitals of the world, and the memorial service at the academy was attended by the ambassadors from more than two hundred nations.

Guilio Amato retired from active play in '61 and since then has devoted his energies to supervising the work of the academy, of which he had been principal since The Master's death. His best known work—apart from the *Thousand Great Games* already mentioned—is undoubtedly his variorum edition of The Master's own *Championship Games,* which in itself probably constitutes the best standard world history of Kalire.

After The Master's death Anne Henderson returned to the theater, where she enjoyed a successful career up until her second marriage in '59. She now lives in Italy with her family. Her delightful *Memories of The Master* was published in '64.

Roger Herzheim never did become a clipper captain. At the age of fifteen he sat for a scholarship to the academy and soon proved that he had an outstanding talent for The Game. At 21 he won his first major tournament, emerging a clear four points ahead of all the other contestants. By 25 he was an acknowledged Master and acted as Second to Guilio Amato in his final Championship match. He gained his own Grand Master's Robe in '67 and was unsuccessful challenger for the World Title two years later. He won the Title conclusively in '71 and has held it ever since. But his days too are surely numbered. *Sic itur ad astra.*

(This fragment of autobiography was found among the papers of the ex-World Master, Roger Herzheim. He died on March 23, 2182, aged 68 years.)

BAIRD SEARLES

Films and TV:
Lost Rewards

O VER the dozen years I've been writing this column, one of the
greatest pleasures has been in those times when I have been
able to make note of, in detail or in passing, films outside of the
mainstream of science fiction or fantasy cinema (if that's not a
contradiction in terms) that had something going for them. These
were mostly found on the TV screen, and could be old or recent,
familiar to me or newly discovered. Some were major movies of
their time, others seem to have been distributed to only one drive-in
in Chillicothe. But each had something, if only momentarily, that
made me sit up, take notice, and feel that thrill of discovery, the
concomitant of which is the desire to share.

So let's share a few in this convenient spot. Let me say that
many of these have been mentioned in this column over the years,
some I've never had the chance to bring up because of the press
of current works. A couple are major enough to be considered

"lost," but nevertheless seem never to crop up in the increasing amount of discussion and literature being devoted to the science fiction, fantasy, and horror film.

Blood on Satan's Claw (1971) starts us off with a perfect example of a little-known film of great excellence. It's a mosaic of the events in an English village of the 17th century when a demonic artifact is turned from the earth during plowing. There is no real hero or heroine, and the influence of the object is deliberately vague (as opposed to infuriatingly ambiguous, as is so often the case). The production is one of those impeccable British period reproductions, the script is literate and chilling (intellectually as well as in the gut); if the master of the ghost story, M. R. James, had written a film, it could well have been this one.

The Borgia Stick (1967) is a taut little piece of ambiguity which takes some getting into, since it begins with a rather ordinary suburban couple whose entire life, one realizes slowly, is an intricately planned cover—the marriage, the job, everything. But for what? They know as little as we, and as the intrigue gets thicker, everything and everybody is suspect. The web as a whole is never really revealed; it's a neat, succinct comment on the potential phoniness of everything in our lives.

Carnival of Souls (1962), a small masterpiece whose budget must have consisted of the crew's loose change, follows a young woman traveler who has survived a curious accident along the way. Something else is following her, too, and it appears at particularly unnerving moments. Brilliant use is made of an empty church, a deserted, small-time amusement pier, and driving at that creepy time just after the sun has set. It still scares me whenever I see it.

Curse of the Crying Woman (1961) is a Mexican horror film, and Mexican horror films are always worth seeing because they're so blatantly bananas. (It could be the dubbing, but somehow I doubt it.) This one, however, has one moment which sent me straight up, and if you think I'm going to say any more about it, *you're* bananas.

Death Takes a Holiday (1934) was a prestige production back when it was made, and is said to have influenced Cocteau's classic *Orpheus*. In it, Death personified indeed takes a holiday in the mortal world, and falls in love with a human woman. There's an odd tension between its baroque premise and its modern (as of when it was made) setting; it's beautifully filmed and highly atmospheric.

Dr. Phibes Rises Again (1972) may be the most outrageously campy film ever made, and practically defies description. A sequel *The Abominable Dr. Phibes,* the good doctor does rise again, out of the ruins of his house, playing an organ with the lighting effects of a '40s juke box. Other ingredients include an attendant spirit in the form of a stunning lady whose taste in clothes runs to Russian sables and other high fashion outfits; some bizarre murders, one of which incorporates a life-sized statue of the RCA dog full of scorpions, and another in which a ship's passenger is thrown overboard in a very large bottle; a cast of British character actors all stealing scenes from one another; and a finale whose major theme, up and out, is "Over the Rainbow." There aren't many funny horror films, and even fewer witty ones. This is both.

Donkey Skin (*Peau d'Ane*) (1971) was done by Jacques (*Umbrellas of Cherbourg*) Demy as an homage to Cocteau's *Beauty and the Beast,* one of the great fantasy films of all time. The Demy film is lighter and cuter, as it tells the story of a princess whose father seeks to marry her (the dying Queen had bade him marry only someone more beautiful than herself, which left only guess who?). She flees, disguised in the skin of a magic donkey, to find her own prince eventually. There are lots of Cocteau in-jokes and themes, and one effect—a gown the color of weather—that is awe-inspiring.

The Emperor's Nightingale (1947) is a short film of the Anderson fairy tale, performed by Czech puppets, which are a far cry indeed from the rather obvious American Puppetoons. Exquisite images abound, such as Death walking in his garden, which is an endless and peaceful expanse of headstones.

Eye of the Devil (1967) is an intelligent handling of an original theme for cinema, an extension of the pagan king-must-die ritual into the present. The scion of a French winemaking family must return to his chateau *cum* vineyards and will not tell his wife why. She follows, to run into all sorts of grim goings-on. The story is told with a maximum of mystery, but a minimum of cheap effects.

Frankenstein: the True Story (1974) came along at a time when we felt that the last thing we needed was another Frankenstein spinoff, especially one made for TV. The 4-hour epic proved us wrong; scripted by the eminent author, Christopher Isherwood, it less tells the "true story" than move oddly in and out of the Mary Shelley original. Typical of the strange, but always successful directions it takes is that Victor, Elizabeth, the creature, and Prima, its "bride," are all flamboyantly handsome; in fact, the creature's first word, as he sees Victor, is "beautiful." The finale is a surrealist chase and encounter amid the ice of the Arctic. This *Frankenstein* is an amazing achievement.

The Innocents (1961), based on Henry James' *The Turn of the Screw,* can hardly be considered a lost film, but its reputation as a masterpiece of fright should be a good deal higher than it is. At least one viewer thinks it could well be the most chilling film he's ever seen. As everyone should know, it has to do with a neurotic Victorian governess in a lonely house who may or may not be seeing the ghosts of two dead servants. One reason for its lack of note may be that it doesn't really work on TV; its long-lined sustenance of atmosphere and tension should be uninterrupted.

Los Angeles: A.D. 2017 (1971) was an episode of the series *The Name of the Game,* using as principal one of the regular characters, the magazine mogul Glen Howard, who travels ahead in time to find what's left of the American population gone underground after a nuclear war. In this situation, a totalitarian state is in the process of forming. Not all that original, but the script is by Philip Wylie, no less, and it abounds in deft ideas and original touches.

The Man Who Haunted Himself (1970) is yet another of those little films with an idea so off the wall that you wonder how anyone was talked into making it. It's a paranoid's delight, concerning as it does a perfectly ordinary businessman whose life begins to be taken over by a doppelgänger, an exact duplicate. Low-keyed and effective, the word for it might be unnerving rather than frightening.

A Midsummer Night's Dream (1959) combines Czech puppets and Shakespeare; the results, as you might guess, are enchanting. Seldom has the film ever showed anything more lovely than the slim, high-cheekboned, ahuman elves, and Titania's "train" is both garment and attendants, a cloak made up of thousands of tiny beings.

Moon Zero Two (1969) is unabashedly a western on the moon: saloon, claim jumping, and all. But its tongue is firmly in its cheek, and the formula is redone with cleverness and moves right along; here is none of the heavy pretentiousness of *Outland*.

On the Beach (1959), also, is hardly a lost film, but the fact that it was big budgeted, star-studded, and given the slick (i.e., technically proficient) production movies got back then, seems to be held against it. Nonetheless, this story laid in Australia, the last continent to support life after nuclear holocaust and whose inhabitants are themselves eventually doomed, is rich, poignant, and splendidly unmelodramatic. I defy anyone to sit through this movie, which is lengthy and leisurely enough to really involve the viewer, and remain unaffected.

One Million Years B.C. (1966) brings to most people's minds Ray Harryhausen's dinosaurs and the poster of Raquel Welch clad in skins (mostly hers). The contributions of those two (certainly one of Harryhausen's better efforts and Ms. Welch looking even more monumentally beautiful than usual), however, added to others to make a film that was really fun, allowing for a certain basic silliness. The score was another plus, consisting mostly of rocks struck percussively together (an inspiration) and one of those good, BIG movie themes.

Phase IV (1973) seems at first glance another one of those man vs. Nature amok numbers; it took me three seeings to realize what an odd little film this is. Nature amok in this case is mutated ants; not bigger (that's *Them*), but better in the old intellect/initiative department. There is some amazing microphotography, and a highly original note is struck when communication with the ants is attempted; it's of the few screen portrayals of a really alien intelligence. They do indeed want to carry off the pretty girl, but why, and what results, will surprise you.

The Picture of Dorian Gray (1945) was something of a family joke in Hollywood in the 1940s, probably because this Oscar Wilde tale of a man who retains his youth and beauty while his portrait shows age and corruption was filmed with entirely too much style for that plebeian period. It captures a real sense of beauteous evil; the only ugly thing in the entire film is the portrait.

Salomé (ca. 1970) is another walk on the Wilde side; in fact,

I doubt if I've ever seen anything wilder on big or little screen than this production of Oscar's play produced for French television. The play itself is fantasy only by its association with legend and its supernatural overtones; here, the production itself is epitomal fantasy, filmed in the grotesquely bizarre Gaudi park and buildings in Barcelona, with costuming to equal them in flamboyance. The famous dance is performed on what appears to be a frozen lake in the desert; the "7 veils" are several acres of rippling cloth as backdrop. This is truly a lost movie; it showed on PBS briefly over a decade ago. I'd give my soul as quickly as Dorian did to see it again.

Somewhere In Time (1980), more recent than the others on this list and therefore probably more familiar, did not do well on its theatrical release and after the usual prime time TV showing, might well sink into oblivion. This would be a pity, because this none-too-original film, about a young man who falls in love with a girl in an old photograph and travels back in time to find her, may leave a few loose ends in the time travel department, but wears its heart so beautifully, romantically on its sleeve that any Romantic who has ever cried at a movie will find it irresistible.

The Uninvited (1943) is that rarity on screen, a true, unadorned ghost story. The ghosts inhabit an ancient house on the cliffs of Cornwall, and it's all done with an emphasis on subtly scarey moments, such as a rose wilting when brought into a certain room, rather than shock effect.

Now, of course, the question remains as to where you can see these goodies. Your best bet is, of course, television, to which the distribution of films is even more erratic than to theatres. Some of these may well show up there, though probably in the wee small hours, or in the case of s/f, on (yawn) Saturday mornings. *The Name of the Game* is well-distributed in syndication; if it shows in your area, keep an eye on the listings; the Wylie episode should turn up.

In the larger cities, revival houses might well screen some of these. And so much is being brought out on video cassette and disc, even obscure stuff, that one or more could show up there, though none have as of this writing.

"Good hunting!" as they say in *The Jungle Book*.

From Competition 24:
Author/Title Misprints

Asimov's *Oi, Robot*
Del Rey's *Gnerves*
Capek's *W.R.U.R.*
Budrys's *Whom?*
Brunner's *The Squarest of the City*
Biggle's *The Still, Small Voice of Strumpets*
> —Daniel P. Dern
> Brighton, Mass.

Lafferty's *The Flambé Is Green*
Laumer's *Retief Ate Large*

Leiber's *Ill Meat in Lankhmar*
Pohl's *Gladiator-at-Slaw*
Russ's *And Chaos Dined*
> —Tad Turner
> New Orleans, La.

Blish's *The Tissue at Hand*
Carter's *The Man Who Loved Mares*
Porges's *The Bruum*
Varley's *In the Bowel*
> —Mario Milosevic
> Waterloo, Ont., Canada

Tiptree's *Urp the Walls of the World*
Knight's *Ha for Anything*
MacDonald's *Swine of the Dreamers*
Sturgeon's *The Man Who Lost the Seat*
                    —Susan Milmore
                    New York, N.Y.

Rotsler's *Patron of the Tarts*
Tenn's *On Venus, Have We Got A Rabbit*
Bester's *The Four Hour Fudge*
McCaffrey's *Dragonslinger*
                    —Michael J. Padgett, Jr.
                    Atlanta, Ga.

Haldeman's *All My Sinks Remembered*

Lafferty's *Continued on Next Frock*
Delany's *The Feinstein Intersection*
Delany's *No Ova*
                    —Jeff Grimshaw
                    New York, N.Y.

Leiber's *I'll Meet in Lankhmar*
Bradbury's *Mary's Is Heaven*
Vance's *The Moon Mouth*
                    —David Finkelstein
                    Old San Juan, P.R.

Delany & Hacker's *Squark #1*
Blish's *Jack of Beagles*
Kotzwinkle's *Doctor Drat*
                    —Augustine Funnell
                    Perth, Ont., Canada

Here is a welcome addition to the small and not entirely serious body of science fiction stories about . . . science fiction! I do, in fact, have a golden retriever (named Howard, not Jenny, and who—last time I looked—was alive and well and chewing on unsolicited manuscripts). But nothing else in this incredible and incredibly funny gathering of editorial correspondence bears any resemblance to reality, past or future. I hope.

ERIC NORDEN

The Curse of the Mhondoro Nkabele

329 East 8th Street
New York, N.Y. 10009
May 10, 1980

Mr. Edward L. Ferman
Magazine of Fantasy & Science Fiction
Cornwall, Connecticut 06753

Esteemed Editor Ferman:

As one who peruses your illustrious periodical with great admiration and enjoyment, please permit me to submit for your attention one of my own humble literary efforts.

Hoping to hear from you forthwith, I remain

Your obedient servant,
O. T. Nkabele, Esq.

Cornwall, Connecticut 06753
May 23, 1980

Mr. O. T. Nkabele
329 East 8th Street
New York, New York 10009

Dear Mr. Nkabele:

Thank you for letting us see ASTRID OF THE ASTEROIDS. I'm afraid it does not meet our current editorial requirements.

Sincerely,
Edward L. Ferman

329 East 8th Street
New York, New York 10009
May 25, 1980

Mr. Edward L. Ferman
Magazine of Fantasy & Science Fiction
Cornwall, Connecticut 06753

PERSONAL & CONFIDENTIAL

Esteemed Editor Ferman:

I'm afraid, as is sometimes unavoidable in all great publishing enterprises, that there has been a clerical error on the part of your staff. I have just received a letter, bearing what can only be a facsimile of your signature, returning my manuscript ASTRID OF THE ASTEROIDS, which I know you will be most anxious to publish. At first I was sorely troubled by this misunderstanding, but I soon realized that one of your overzealous underlings, as yet unfamiliar with my name, took it upon himself to reject my work unread. Thus I am resubmitting ASTRID, as well as two more of my latest stories, with instructions that they are for your eyes only. Do not be too harsh on the unwitting culprit, dear Editor Ferman, as such debacles are not unknown in literary history. The initial reception of James Joyce's *Ulysses* is but one case in point. . . .

I should appreciate your check to be made out to cash, as I have not as yet opened a banking account in this city.

Hoping to hear from you forthwith, I remain

Your obedient servant,
O. T. Nkabele, Esq.

Cornwall, Connecticut 06753
June 12, 1980

Mr. O. T. Nkabele
329 East 8th Street
New York, N.Y. 10009

Dear Mr. Nkabele:

Thank you for letting us see SLIME SLAVES OF G'HARN and URSULA OF URANUS. I'm sorry to say that, as was the case with your original story, neither piece meets our present needs.

If you are contemplating further submissions, I should point out to you that as a matter of editorial policy we require all manuscripts to be *typed,* perferably on white, unlined paper, and on only one side of the page. Manuscripts should also be accompanied by a stamped, self-addressed return envelope.

Sincerely,
Edward L. Ferman

329 East 8th Street
New York, N.Y. 10009
June 19, 1980

Mr. Edward L. Ferman
Magazine of Fantasy & Science Fiction
Cornwall, Connecticut 06753

Esteemed Editor Ferman:

How clumsy I have been! Please excuse my unforgivable ignorance of publishing requirements in your great country, and my thoughtlessness in inflicting on you my, let us be frank, less than decipherable calligraphy. With considerable good fortune I have found an accomplished typist, Ms. Rachel Markowitz, a fellow student at New York University's Washington Square Campus where I am matriculating, who has most graciously consented to prepare my manuscripts in the prescribed manner, and at most reasonable rates. Ms. Markowitz, a most gracious and charming young lady, has also, if it is not immodest to say so, developed a great admiration for my *oeuvre,* and has volunteered to assist me in the intricacies of American publishing, with particular emphasis on what she refers to as subsidiary rights. If you have any questions on such matters, I suggest you address them directly to her. (She may be reached, for the time being, at the above address.)

In any case, I am happy to resubmit, in the desired format, ASTRID OF THE ASTEROIDS, SLIME SLAVES OF G'HARN and URSALA OF URANUS. If you should wish to make one check payable for all three works, that would be quite satisfactory.

Hope to hear from you forthwith, and with abject apologies for my execrable scrawl, I remain

Your obedient servant,
O. T. Nkabele, Esq.

P.S. I am enclosing Ms. Markowitz's typing bill, as well as a receipt for the unlined white paper you specified.

Cornwall, Connecticut 06753
June 25, 1980

Mr. O. T. Nkabele
329 East 8th Street
New York, N.Y. 10009

Dear Mr. Nkabele:

I'm afraid I'm somewhat at a loss for words. I had hoped my previous letter made it clear that I *had* read all three of your stories, despite their being handwritten, and could not use any of them. The fault, I'm afraid, lies least of all in format.

Sheer pressure of time normally precludes editorial evaluation of unsolicited manuscripts, but in this case I would strongly suggest you study the more recent work in the field, particularly Harlan Ellison's two DANGEROUS VISIONS anthologies and the annual collection of Nebula Award stories. Your own work, frankly, is unpublishable as it now stands, although I will admit you have rather neatly captured the tone and texture of 1940s "space opera." There have been vast changes in the field since the heyday of the pulps, however, and there is no longer a market for such material, even in juveniles. If you were aiming at parody, that fails too— why flog a long-dead b.e.m.? And I'm afraid your treatment is so relentlessly serious it might evoke the worst kind of literary laughter—the unintended.

I hope you won't be too discouraged by these comments. You display a flair for vivid action prose, and your plots, though hackneyed, are tightly structured. There does, however, seem to be a language problem on occasion. *"Zut alors!"*, *"sacre bleu"* and *"nom d'un chien"* are, so far as I know, no longer in common parlance, even in France. I am not sure of the etymological derivation of *"Zounds!"* but it, too, is an uncommon expletive in contemporary English-language s-f. Am I correct in assuming that French is your native language? If so, any problems in translation could be ameliorated by the wider reading in modern s-f I suggested earlier.

I would also caution you to beware the pitfalls of conceptual, as well as linguistic, anachronism. I.e., it is unlikely that the Mary Tyler Moore Show would be a weekly staple on the vidscreens of the humanoid colony on 31st Century Venus which you describe in SLIME SLAVES OF G'HARN, particularly after widespread intermarriage with the amphibious Mottled Marsh Marsupials and the attendant changes in sexuality and sensibility. In a different vein, but equally jarring, the Gargons of Ganymede you depict in URSULA OF URANUS are, so far as I can gather, no more than oversized purple lobsters, and it's unlikely they would have the capability, much less the desire, to ravish Ursula and her friends. (Avoid euphemism as well as anachronism, as in "Ursula's mammoth mammary protuberances heaved in horror as she watched the slimy giant crustacean approach. . . .")

I could go on, but I hope these criticisms have been both constructive and helpful. I'll be happy to see your future work, but remember: *study the market.* That is really the best advice I can give any aspiring writer.

Sincerely,
Edward L. Ferman

329 East 8th Street
New York, New York 10009
June 29, 1980

Mr. Edward L. Ferman
Magazine of Fantasy & Science Fiction
Cornwall, Connecticut 06753

My dear Mr. Ferman:

I am in receipt of your missive of 25th June, and, in all honesty, *I* am the one at a loss for words. I find it both shocking and profoundly disturbing that you have so totally misunderstood my work. My sole remaining hope at this stage of our relationship is that a frank and forthright discussion of our differences may dissuade you from the creatively suicidal course you are pursuing. I am thinking not only of your own reputation, Mr. Ferman, but of your periodical's; I should certainly regret being forced by your blindness (a temporary condition, I trust) to take my work to your competitors. Therefore, in a spirit of openness and good will that hopefully will lead to dialogue and understanding, let me confront the major issues you raise in your communication.

Yes, you are correct in surmising that English is not my native language, but neither is French. I was born twenty-nine years ago in the town of Kaolak, in the eastern recesses of Senegal, by the Falémé River. My "first" language was Diola, the tongue of my people, although under the colonial administration French was the official language of the country, and useful in that it allowed the main tribes—Diolas, Fulas and Mandingos—to communicate with one another. (You may have remarked that our illustrious President, His Excellency Léopold Senghor, the great poet and philosopher who first conceived "negritude" as a literary and cultural belief system, wrote in French so that he could be understood by all his people.) My father, Sikhalo, was paramount chief of our people and my uncle, Nbulamauti, was the *mganga,* or spiritual counselor of our tribe, and a learned master of *uchawi,* our indigenous religion. The Diolas are traditionally animist, but my father sent me at the age of nine to the mission school in Mbawne Province run by the Holy Ghost Fathers, a predominantly French and Belgian order. There I mastered not only French but, through the good offices of Father Devlin, the one Irish priest, English as well.

I originally had some doubts about the missionaries, but my father approved the doctrine of transubstantiation, viewing it as an affirmation of our own ancient practices. He himself, as a very young child, had once tasted a priest, of the Franciscan order I believe, and he felt that consuming the blood and flesh of Christ would be a salutary experience for me. You and I, Mr. Ferman, would of course interpret this as poetic allegory, as Mr. Melville did so evocatively in his great fish story, but my father is close to the earth. In any case, I was soon quite content at the school, due mainly to the blessed Father Devlin, a good and gentle man who took me, so to speak, under his wing. It was also due to Father Devlin that I had my first exposure to science fiction, at the age of eleven.

This brings me to your contention (the word "criticism" would unduly dignify what can most generously be adjudged a misapprehension) that I am not *au courant* with the science fiction field. It is to laugh! Due to Father Devlin, who had become a devotee while a parish priest in Newark, New Jersey, U.S.A., I was nurtured on science fiction as on my mother's milk. When Father Devlin arrived in Senegal in 1953 he had with him *three* steamer trunks packed with his lifetime collection of s-f, over five hundred magazines, ranging from the marvelous *Thrilling Wonder Stories, Famous Fantastic Mysteries, Super Science Stories* and *Planet* to the more intellectual journals such as *Startling* and *Amazing Stories,* and dating from 1936 to 1952. Under his diligent tutelage I pored over these treasure troves of the imagination, star-borne through their pages to the nethermost reaches of the cosmos. By the age of fourteen I had memorized many stories by heart, and was a particular fan of Robert Moore Williams, E. E. "Doc" Smith,

Nelson Bond, Ray Cummings, Eric Frank Russell, P. Schuyler Miller, Raymond Z. Gallun, the revered Stanley G. Weinbaum, L. Ron Hubbard and the magnificent Richard Shaver, so brilliantly discovered by my favorite editor, Ray A. Palmer of *Amazing Stories.* ("Dear Rap," where are you now? *Où sont les neiges d'antan?*) Study the market, Mr. Ferman? I dare say I know the market as well as any living fan. It is true that I have only been in the United States under my exchange scholarship for two months now, and have not yet read a great many of the more recent magazines and books, but what better apprenticeship could I have! Ever since I was a day-dreaming boy, Mr. Ferman, sometimes misunderstood by the other children because of my stocky build (which Ms. Markowitz, who is typing this, singularly admires, being similarly well-endowed herself), I have immersed myself in s-f, lived s-f, dreamed s-f, eaten s-f as my daily millet. How often were the times as an adolescent that I would slip away from school, clutching a treasured copy of *Amazing Stories,* and sit under a tamarind or baobab tree, mute in joy and wonder at the magical universes into which I was transported, oblivious to all around me. Even as the other lads stole into the bush with giggling young maidens to play hide-the-snake, I was riding the asteroid belts, or battling the dreaded deros in their eldritch caverns beneath the earth, or winning the hand of a Martian princess. And you suggest *I* am ignorant of this field? The mind boggles, Mr. Ferman. The mind positively boggles.

But let us return to our muttons. I will not deign to comment on your specific references to my work (others, less charitably inclined, might employ the word "nit-picking") or on the somewhat condescending tone of your letter. That, Mr. Fermen, is something better left to you and your conscience. I am, however, for the third and *final* time, submitting to you ASTRID OF THE ASTEROIDS, SLIME SLAVES OF G'HARN and URSULA OF URANUS. I hope and trust you will read them with a fresh insight and a new spirit, untainted by whatever animus perverted your initial perusal. (Could it be that you, like Father Devlin, are plagued by "the bottle sickness," and the distortions of mood and perception it engenders? This would explain much.) In any case, Mr. Ferman, I wish you well, and can only hope that the blinders will be struck from your eyes, and my work revealed to you as what it truly is—

the most significant contribution to the corpus of science fiction since Stanley G. Weinbaum. If not, I am afraid I will be forced to consider alternative markets.

Yours,

O. T. Nkabele, Esq.

P.S. Ms. Markowitz, who is conversant with such matters, points out that the only prominent black writer in s-f today is Samuel "Chip" Delany, and wonders if your obtuseness could be motivated by racialism. I will reserve judgment on this matter.

P.P.S. If my earlier surmise was correct, I commend to your attention a morning-after concoction I used to prepare for Father Devlin, and which appreciably improved both his health and temper: a calabash containing the juice of three paw-paws and two limes, leavened with the slightest *soupçon* of fresh palm oil and a dash of Tabasco. Ideally, this should be followed by a light repast of manioc, mealies and wild figs, the latter consumed in moderation.

Cornwall, Connecticut 06753
July 7, 1980

Mr. O. T. Nkabele
329 East 8th Street
New York, New York 10009

Dear Mr. Nkabele:

Mr. Ferman has asked me to return the enclosed manuscripts to you. Thank you for thinking of F&SF.

Sincerely,
James T. Leasor
Assistant to the Editor

329 East 8th Street
New York, New York 10009
July 10, 1980

Mr. Edward L. Ferman
Magazine of Fantasy & Science Fiction
Cornwall, Connecticut 06753

My dear Mr. Ferman:

I am dismayed at the evident breakdown in communication between us. I urgently suggest a face-to-face meeting to iron out the misunderstandings that have arisen, either in Connecticut or here in New York City. Please ring me any time of the day or night at area code 212, 675-4709. (Feel free to reverse the charges.) My calendar is free for the next two weeks, and I am completely at your disposal.

Dear Mr. Ferman, we must end this petty bickering and get down to a serious evaluation of my work. I am sure that if we sat together over a sundowner and discussed the situation, your attitude would soon change. We owe this not only to each other, but to the field of science fiction we both love so dearly.

With warmest affection,
O. T. Nkabele, Esq.

Cornwall, Connecticut 06753
July 19, 1980

Mr. O. T. Nkabele
329 East 8th Street
New York, New York 10009

Dear Mr. Nkabele:

I must admit that my irritation over your earlier letter has taken some time to subside. I was particularly put off by your veiled accusation of racism, which was really a cheap shot. There are relatively few black s-f writers for the same reason there are still relatively few blacks prominent in other areas of American life and literature: a 300-year-old legacy of oppression and exclusion does not die easily. There is, however, no conspiracy to exclude blacks from s-f; just the opposite, in fact. Furthermore, it would be the rankest kind of paternalistic condescension, if not reverse racism, for me to treat your work any differently, or to qualify my criticism, simply because of your skin color. So let's bury that red herring once and for all. You are obviously as defensive about your work as any fledgling writer, but I must warn you that your overly touchy attitude will only serve to antagonize other editors in the field.

Which brings me to the reason I am, after all, resuming our correspondence. I must admit that, after my initial annoyance had worn off, I was rather intrigued, and even touched, by your description of growing up on a diet of pulp s-f in the heart of Africa. One problem in our field, due both to parochialism and translation difficulties, is that we know regrettably little about s-f outside the English-speaking world. There have, of course, been some good volumes of Russian and Eastern European s-f published here (Sanislaw Lem, obviously), and we occasionally see some French work, while Judith Merrill has just begun translating Japanese s-f into English. There are also several foreign-language editions of F&SF, and we receive some feedback from writers and readers in the countries where they appear. But otherwise we are relatively ignorant of what is (or is not) being written in vast areas of the world. Africa, of course, is a case in point. I have heard there is some s-f being published in Nigeria, but this has only reached my attention because it's in English, which is still the *lingua franca* there. So the whole subject of African s-f fascinates me, as does your own story of your childhood addiction to the vintage pulps. This is obviously the root of your current literary problems, of course; you are still writing in a style that was out of date twenty years ago. But before you bridle, let me suggest that your background also holds the germs of an intriguing article idea.

I would like you to write up your childhood experiences for us, a personal memoir telling how you first came into contact with Western s-f and fell in love with it, and how it affected your life. What was it like to be a teen-ager from tribal Africa immersed in the alien world of American s-f? How did your family and fellow students react? How did it color your view of the United States when you first came here? Did you ever feel excluded by the technologically advanced, all-white societies depicted in most of the stories of that time? How did science fiction change your view of yourself, your village, your tribe? How did you translate the work into an African cultural matrix? I think the answers to all these questions would be fascinating to our readers, and provide them with a totally fresh perspective on s-f. We rarely run articles, with the exception of Dr. Asimov's monthly science column, but perhaps we could carry it as an extended book review section, or maybe, who knows, as part of a general symposium on Third World s-f. I obviously can't use your fiction, as I've tried so unavailingly to make clear, but this could break you into print at the same time you're updating your knowledge of contemporary s-f. (Believe me, my advice in that area is *not* condescending; it is vital.)

Now to the less pleasant side of this assignment. You would have to tone down your florid style, and avoid rhetorical overkill. Bear in mind Hemingway's wise adage: kill your darlings. And I'd have to exact a promise in advance that you won't quibble over my editorial blue pencil. Don't take this the wrong way, please; you have a talent, but it's not only anachronistic in content but stylistically undisciplined. The first may be more easily corrected than the second, but I'm willing to have a go.

Finally, let me add that I appreciate the conciliatory tone of your last letter. I hope it won't sound pompous if I say that I rarely enter into prolonged correspondence with unknown authors. I simply don't have the time; nor, to be frank, in most cases the inclination. But I was moved by your childhood experiences and I think our readers could be too. Think about it.

Best,
Edward L. Ferman

329 East 8th Street
New York, New York 10009
July 23, 1980

Mr. Edward L. Ferman
Magazine of Fantasy & Science Fiction
Cornwall, Connecticut 06753

Esteemed Editor Ferman:

I welcome your letter, as it reveals a distinct thaw in our relationship. I always knew that, on reflection, you would realize the futility, if not self-destructiveness, of your earlier attitude.

As to your suggestion, I am afraid it poses certain problems. I have always intended to write my autobiography, but I do not think the time is yet ripe. First my work must be accepted by a large audience in America and abroad, which is why publication of my short stories is a vital prerequisite. I would also publish initially in hard-cover, so that the book clubs and Hollywood could bid on the rights. Ms. Markowitz assures me this is most important. I would, of course, be happy for F&SF to serialize it in whole or part, subject, of course, to mutually satisfactory financial terms.

We are, however, getting a bit ahead of ourselves on this. Thus, I am enclosing a revised version of SLIME SLAVES OF G'HARN, tailored to meet your objection about the sexual preferences of the Gargons of Ganymede. They are no longer giant crustaceans but giant gerbils which, being mammalian, should have no difficulty consummating their lustful desires for Ursula. I hope this will prove a token of my willingness to meet you halfway.

I must reiterate my desire for a personal meeting, and as soon as possible. These matters should be ideally considered on what Ms. Markowitz so aptly terms a one-to-one basis. I would be more than happy to visit you in Connecticut at your convenience.

With warmest affection,
O. T. Nkabele, Esq.

Cornwall, Connecticut 06753
July 29, 1980

Mr. O. T. Nkabele
329 East 8th Street
New York, New York 10009

Dear Mr. Nkabele:

Mr. Ferman has asked me to return SLIME SLAVES OF G'HARN to you. He does not believe further correspondence on the matter would prove productive.

Sincerely,
James T. Leasor
Assistant to the Editor

Cornwall, Connecticut 06753
August 8, 1980

Mr. O. T. Nkabele
329 East 8th Street
New York, New York 10009

Dear Oginga:

Once again, I want to thank you for your most gracious gifts. The silver-chased *assegai* is hanging above the fireplace as I write this, and the beautiful carved wood fertility statue has a place of honor in my study. I really shouldn't have accepted such magnificent, and obviously valuable, presents from you; it must have been that last "sundowner" you prepared that undermined my resistance. (The next morning it seemed as if the sun *had* set, and permanently!) But be assured that I am grateful.

I am, in retrospect, very glad you came up. After my initial surprise wore off at encountering you in my local barber shop, of all places, I was relieved that you had reconsidered your earlier attitudes and were willing to make a serious effort to improve and update your work. I'm afraid I had rather given up on you after that last letter, which I hope explains my initial coolness when we met, but I am pleased my words had some impact, however belated. Anyway, that's all water under the bridge, and I anxiously await the first draft of your autobiographical article, SAFARI TO WONDER: THE PULPS AND I. (I think we should discuss that title further, but it will do for now.) I also hope the books I loaned you will be of some help in modernizing your knowledge of s-f.

By the way, my memories of the latter part of the evening are rather dim, but by any chance did you leave a small pouch of animal skin behind at my place? I found it under my pillow the next morning, and I assumed it was another of your generous gifts, perhaps a good-luck fetish. It is filled with bits of bone, feathers, dirt, hair, beads, cowrie shells, scraps of cloth, lumps of iron and a tiny clay figurine pinned down with wooden pegs and pierced with thorns in the head and heart. If it was a present, thanks once again, but if you lost it just let me know and I'll mail it off to you.

Good luck on the article!

> Best regards,
> Ed

P.S. You mentioned that your major at N.Y.U. is physiotherapy. Would you recommend massage as a cure for persistent headaches that are unresponsive to medication? I've had the granddaddy of them all for the past few days now, and nothing seems to work. (Or maybe I *do* need that recipe you concocted for your Irish mentor!) Seriously, if you have any suggestions let me know, as it's beginning to affect my concentration.

> 329 East 8th Street
> New York, New York 10009
> August 12, 1980

Mr. Edward L. Ferman
Cornwall, Connecticut 06753

My dear friend Ed:

Thank you so much for your gracious letter. I too shall treasure the delightful evening at your home, rendered doubly poignant by the turbulent course of our prior relationship. But, like the famous journalist Stanley and the intrepid explorer Livingstone, our reunion was memorable precisely because of those obstacles of mutual misunderstanding that preceded and impeded it. Now, however, our collaboration has begun! Let it be both creatively fruitful and financially remunerative. (The latter is the least of my considerations, of course, but, as a saying of my people has it, "The man without mealie does not sing songs.")

The pouch you refer to is, as you surmise, a good-luck charm or *ju-ju,* a small token of my affection for you. It may be worn around the neck or simply kept within the hut as a ward against malign spirits. And, yes, therapeutic massage is *very* good for headache.

I also want to thank you for the novels and collections of short stories. I have not as yet read them all, but I must confess I am shocked and depressed at the profound deterioration in our field since my apprenticeship in Africa. It is obvious that I was blessed with exposure to the Golden Age of science fiction, and that the downward spiral towards decadence and decay has accelerated horrendously since the mid-fifties. Writers like Theodore Sturgeon, whom I remember from an earlier, healthier stage in his career, particularly disturb me, as they must know the birthright they are betraying. (If I may be permitted a note of levity, the eggs Sturgeon lays are far from caviar!) Certainly, his current stories would never have been accepted by *Thrilling Wonder Stories* in the glorious days gone by. And this Barry Malzberg you suggested I read —my word, dear Edward, surely he is afflicted of the Gods! The man is a veritable pustulence on the face of the universe, a yellow dog barking in the night. We have another saying in my tribe, "The jackal dreams lions' dreams." How true! How tragically true. And how a creature such as Malzberg would cringe and whimper if ever confronted with the shade of Stanley G. Weinbaum, the Great Master himself. And these women, Ursula LeGuin and Joanna Russ, they should be beaten with stout sticks! I would not give one hamstrung goat for the pair of them. (It is apposite here to reflect on the words of the good Dr. Johnson, who pointed out that "A woman's preaching is like a dog walking on his hind legs; it is not done well, but you are surprised to find it done at all.") Of all the stories I have read recently, only Kilgore Trout's *Venus on the Half Shell* is worthy to bear the mantle of the giants of yesteryear. Truly, my good friend, the field we love is facing terrible times, and it is indeed providential that I have arrived on the scene to arrest the rot. Perhaps, in fact, there was a Larger Purpose of Father Devlin's introducing me to science fiction. We shall see.

I have not yet got around to Mr. Ellison's books, but I am glad you told me he experiments with new work in his DANGEROUS VISIONS series. I have sent him several of my stories, and expect a prompt and enthusiastic reply. And thank you once again for providing me with his home address and unlisted phone number. Perhaps the three of us, united, can yet cleanse the science fiction temple of this babbling *canaille!*

Once more, thank you for a delightful weekend. Looking out my window at the squalor of what the natives call the East Village, I can only wish I were back with you in Connecticut. Your Cornwall is so green and beautiful, I can understand why the game hens flourish. I hope on my next trip you will introduce me to Daphne de Maurier, an old favorite of mine, and we can find time to visit some of your picturesque tin mines and smugglers' coves.

Hoping to see you again soon, I remain

> Your devoted pal,
> Oginga
> (You may call me Oggy)

Cornwall, Connecticut 06753
August 16, 1980

Mr. Harlan Ellison
Villa Van Vogt
9263 Easton Drive
Beverly Hills, California 90210

Dear Harlan:

I'm afraid I owe you something of an apology. It's a long story, but I'm being pursued by a young African exchange student who fancies himself another Heinlein—or, God save us all, another Stanley G. Weinbaum. It's an interesting story, actually, he was brought up in a remote area of Senegal on a diet of 1940s pulp s-f, and he writes and thinks like a reincarnated ha'penny-a-word hack. (I thought I'd partially converted him, but after his last letter I have some doubts.) Anyway, after an exchange of letters that you wouldn't believe he showed up in Cornwall and collared me, all 300 pounds of him. (Wrapped in a *dashiki* that would blind you at forty paces.) I couldn't help feeling sorry for the kid, he's like a big fat puppy, so I took him back to the house for a talk and a few drinks. He seemed contrite, said he recognized the problems with his writing, and we worked up an article on how he grew up in the jungle on a diet of space opera. Could be quite good, really, though God knows I'll have a hell of a re-write job on my hands. But the point of all this is that I got royally plastered, for the first time in years—funny too, I don't remember drinking that much—and apparently gave him your address and phone number in a fit of alcoholic fugue. Your *home* number.

Now I know what you're going to say, Harlan, but have pity. Every Ellison has his Brutus, and you can always change your number and/or move. If you think I'm joking, wait 'till the phone calls start. I know my man. Actually, I hope he doesn't give you too hard a time, but he's a persistent cuss and I suggest you let him down gently. Otherwise, he's liable to turn up in *your* barber shop!

I haven't had a chance to read your new piece yet, the work is piling up and I haven't been too well lately. I've got the damndest headache, I can't seem to shake it, and I'm a little worried about my hearing. There's a kind of constant, staccato beating in my inner ear, it sounds almost like drums. I guess I'll have to go to an ee&t man if it keeps up. Ah, well, time's winged chariot hovers on all our heels.

Once again, I'm sincerely sorry for inadvertently violating your privacy. I hope we'll still be on speaking terms after this, and you'll let me buy you dinner at the Worldcon in atonement. Sans booze!

Best,
Ed

P.S. Could you ask one of your Japanese gardeners what, if anything, can be done about rose blight? All our roses just died overnight, I found the bushes shriveled and black in the morning. And the weather was perfect, too. I really can't understand it, and after all the work I put in it's a bit depressing. Christ, I moved to Connecticut in the first place to tend my garden and avoid the badgering of hot-eyed young geniuses fresh from the Famous Writers' School. Seems I'm not doing too well on either front.

ELLISON ENTERPRISES UNIVERSAL
"Heute gehörten Hollywood,
morgen die ganze welt"
9640 Sunset Boulevard
Los Angeles, California 90069
CABLE ADDRESS: ENEMU   ORDERS TO GO

August 21, 1980

Edward My Son:

You are forgiven, though reluctantly. Yes, your protege has been pursuing me, like a hound out of hell. I got a batch of his drek in the mail last week, and then the phone calls began. I was polite to the schmuck the first few calls because I hadn't got around to his stuff, and because he said you two were collaborating on some magnum opus or other. It was only because of that I finally sat down and waded through the crap. Jesus, it was god-awful, so ludicrously so that I thought the whole thing was a put-on at first. But nobody, I mean *nobody,* could write that consistently, humorlessly bad without sincerity. Shit, I haven't read such won-drously lobotomized prose in years, it was a real nostalgia trip. He kept calling up pestering me for a reaction and I tried to fob him off, but when he rang at two in the morning last Friday, and me making the beast with two backs on the casting couch, I really told him what I thought of the garbage. He hung up in a tiff and so far, Yahweh be praised, he hasn't called back, either here at the office or at home. It did get a bit hairy for a while though, calls every hour of the night and day. I got to wandering around muttering, "Who will free me from this turbulent scribe?" Well, so far so good.

The thing is, Ed, you weren't helping the poor turd by encour-aging him. To lumber toward a pun, this guy is not the *crème* of the *Senégalèse.* I mean, look, I'm as sympathetic as you are to all the no-talent hacks out there, but you don't do the schlemiels any good by feeding their delusions of grandeur; sometimes, to coin a phrase, you've gotta be cruel to be kind. I will admit that after I got your letter with all that stuff about growing up on the pulps out in Tarzan-land I felt a wee bit guilty about the way I'd dressed him down, but the putz's gotta find out someday that his stuff's unreadable, not to mention unpublishable. And without getting shirty with you, *cher maitre,* who needs it anyway? I mean, you should see the shit I'm getting from the *heavies* for LAST DANGER-OUS VISIONS. I sure don't need to comb the boondocks for something even worse. Christ, I've gotta tell writers I like and respect I can't use their pieces, and then you inflict this *merde* on me! No more, Edward. Peace, calm, I beg you. Become a solitary drinker, and spare your friends. The kooks can manage on their own, God knows there are enough of them out there. In fact, one of them left a little leather bag full of what looks like chicken guts and graveyard dirt on my doorstep the other night. Jesus, L.A. is really one huge out-patient clinic. Don't recruit *more* crazies for me!

About your roses, tough titty. My gardeners are at a loss, they say only a sudden frost could kill 'em off all at once, and that's hardly likely in August. Not in your part of the world anyway. But you think you've got problems? My fuckin' hair is falling out! Started yesterday, and it's going as fast as your roses. Jesus, I'm gonna need a friggin' rug soon. Cry your hearts out, ladies. Oh, well, this is the summer of our discontent.

You've got a date for the Worldcon, and it's gonna cost you.

Peace,
Harlan of the Bald Pate

Cornwall, Connecticut 06753
August 24, 1980

Mr. Harlan Ellison
Villa Van Vogt
9263 Easton Drive
Beverly Hills, California 90210

Dear Harlan:

   This will sound silly, but could you please describe, in detail, the contents of that pouch you mentioned? I have my reasons, and I would appreciate a quick response. I've tried to call you, but there is no answer.

   Our golden retriever, Jenny, is dead. Something seems to have eaten her. Our neighbor, Tom Gould, swears he saw a leopard slinking away into the night. Ridiculous, of course. Could you phone or wire me that information on the pouch? If you call, speak loudly. I can't hear too well over these goddamned drums.

Best regards,
Ed

9263 Easton Drive
Beverly Hills, Calif. 90210
August 27, 1980

Mr. Edward L. Ferman
Magazine of Fantasy & Science Fiction
Cornwall, Connecticut 06753

Edward me darlin':

   Sorry you couldn't reach me on the phone, but I've turned the damned thing off for a few days. Oddly enough, I've got a lousy headache myself, and nothing seems to help. Probably overwork. I've been batting my brains out on *The Sound of Screaming,* that TV musical comedy of mine about the Moors Murder Trial in England. Some asshole producer cast Julie Andrews as Myra Hindley, and she's breaking my chops with script revisions. It's my first score, too, and the bitch is ruining the title song. ("And the moors echo now/With the sound of screaminggg. . . .") I'm not too happy with their choice of Donny Osmond for Ian Brady, either.

Anyway, that's my problem. As to the pouch, I threw it away a couple of days ago. Why? Did you get one too? Maybe we're being hexed by that African pal of yours! God, to die so young, like Alexander, with the world in my grasp. . . . Listen, *mon vieux,* I don't have to go outside the field for my enemies; I can name a half-dozen Hugo winners who are probably fashioning wax images of me right now! But if I get another, I'll send it off to you. Hokay?

Be good, and don't send me any more Stanley Weinbaums, even in blackface.

Love and Kisses,
Harlan

P.S. Hey, seriously, were you playing straight about your dog? If so, I'm really sorry, that's a real bummer. Maybe it was a pack of wild dogs; I hear a lot of abandoned summer pets have gone feral. My sympathies.

329 East 8th Street
New York, New York 10009
August 28, 1980

Mr. Edward L. Ferman
Magazine of Fantasy & Science Fiction
Cornwall, Connecticut 06753

My dear friend Edward:

It was good talking to you last night. I'm sorry you'd been ringing for the past two days, but I was out of town on business, and Ms. Markowitz was visiting her parents in a place called Great Neck. (How one relishes these exotic, and evocative, American place names!) In fact, when you phoned I had just returned from the airport.

I am most desolate to hear of your troubles. First the headaches, then your roses, and now your poor dog. It is said that these things tend to run in threes, but that is scant consolation for you. I was surprised, I must admit, at your inclination to suspect a supernatural agency behind these sad events. Surely, dear Edward, we are living in the fourth quarter of the twentieth century, not in some primitive backwater of medieval times. I will grant you that among my own people such calamities would be ascribed to the intervention of malign spirits, or possibly to one's own guilt rebounding on one in punishment of a sin or grievous error of judgment, and thereby unleashing self-destructive psychic, manifestations. In my land it is believed that when one of royal blood is wronged and unable to redress that wrong himself a *mhondoro,* or "mouthpiece of the spirit," will appear to avenge him. It has been known for the spirit of a great warrior or medicine man to materialize on earth and enter into the body of a wild animal in order to torment and ultimately devour those ignorant or malicious humans who prey like insolent jackals on his hapless descendants. Only the intercession of the original victim, it is said, can break the curse and banish the avenging shades to eternal darkness. But whom have you wronged so deeply, whom have you misunderstood so profoundly, whom have you hurt so callously, as to bring down on your head the wrath of the victim's ancestral spirits? All such conjecture is, in any case, rank superstition, and I am surprised to find a man of your knowledge and sophistication succumbing to it. There must be a perfectly logical explanation for your travails. Must there not?

Without appearing overly sensitive I must also confess that I was troubled by your insinuation that my humble gifts were somehow related to your recent misfortunes. My dear Edward, must our friendship, so recently sealed, now be sundered by hysterical suspicion and paranoid allegation? Permit me to say, as gently as possible, that you are overwrought, and need a good rest. You mention that the noise in your head, which you fancifully describe as drums, is keeping you from sleep. Perhaps that is the root of your problem, and you should consult an alienist of good repute. But always feel free to call on your friend Oginga for advice or consolation.

I am afraid we can dismiss Harlan Ellison as an ally in our crusade to redeem science fiction. I have been in touch with him recently, and he was most crudely abusive and insensitive; in fact, at one point he went so far as to threaten legal action if I continued to contact him! I regret to say he is no gentleman, and can be written off as a force for progress in the field. I am afraid, my friend, that the struggle to wrest s-f from the hands of the obfuscators and pornographers is ours alone. It will be a lonely battle, but victory will be all the more sweet for that reason. And remember the tocsin sounded by Edmund Burke, which Father Devlin prophetically taught me so many years ago: "The triumph of evil is insured when good men do nothing."

I have a feeling that you are finally in a receptive mood for SLIME SLAVES OF G'HARN, ASTRID OF THE ASTEROIDS and URSULA OF URANUS, which I am enclosing. Though I hesitate to say so, my friend, it is not impossible that your failure to as yet fully appreciate these works is at the root of your present troubles. Your subconscious may be warring with you, urging you to reconsider and reevaluate my stories, and thus creating severe psychic stress which manifests itself in headaches and auditory hallucinations. Nothing, dear Edward, is impossible. I counsel you to remember that.

> With warmest affection,
> Your pal,
> Oggy

> Cornwall, Connecticut 06753
> September 1, 1980

Dr. Isaac Asimov
Asimov Hall
Asimov State University
Asimovia, New York 14603

Dear Isaac:

God, is it really true about Harlan? I couldn't believe the first press reports, but Fritz Lieber called me from L.A. a little while ago and confirmed it all. The poor devil. I knew it had to come some day, but I always thought it would be at the hands of a fellow writer. Not like this.

I know I was a little incoherent on the phone last night, but I

swear that this ties in with what's happening to me. Ellison re-
buffed the African too, and look what happened to him. Christ,
I may be next! The drums are getting louder every day, and I've
developed sharp, stabbing pains in my chest and joints. This
morning I found my parakeet dead in his cage, his little neck
snapped like a twig. And the cage was *locked,* Isaac, I had the
only key. I know you're a confirmed rationalist but I swear to
you, I am being hexed! Or voodooed, or hoodooed or whatever
the right African name for it is. I don't know whether the bastard
intends to kill me too or just terrify me to the point where I'll
agree to publish his abominable stories. God, psychic blackmail!
But I can't go on like this, I haven't slept for three days, and the
pain is getting unbearable. You've got to help me, Isaac, use your
encyclopedic knowledge, find an antidote to the curse. Remember
M. R. James' *The Casting of the Runes?* Maybe there's some way
I can hit back, make his damned magic boomerang on him! But I
know nothing about these matters, I used to be as thoroughgoing
a sceptic as you are. I tried to ask Fritz about it, he's an expert
on the occult and the whole thing is so bloody reminiscent of
Conjure Wife, but the minute I described the *ju-ju* bag and its
contents he got all stuttery, made some excuse about having to
leave for a trip to Mexico, and hung up. Some friend.

Listen, Isaac, I'm not crazy, no matter how it sounds. You and
I have both read about these things actually working in Haiti;
well, now they're working in Connecticut. For the love of God,
help me!!!! I'm enclosing the ju-ju bag, examine it, tell me what
I can do. Should we burn it? Or would that just make things
worse? My life and my sanity are in your hands, Isaac. Don't let
me down.

Desperately,
Ed

ASIMOV STATE UNIVERSITY

"The Intelligent Have A Right Over The Ignorant, The Right of Instructing Them."

—Ralph Waldo Emerson

September 6, 1980

Mr. Edward L. Ferman
Cornwall, Connecticut 06753

Dear Ed:

Yes, it was a great tragedy about Harlan. (Not in the Aristotelian sense that great tragedy requires the fall of a great man, of course, but on the human level; after all, even Harlan had a mother who will mourn him, and remember when Harlie was one.) When the first, fragmentary reports came over the news I suspected Harlan had perished by his own hand; he had toiled too long in the literary abattoir of locust-land, and I knew it was exacting a heavy toll. The last time I saw him I quoted Fred Allen's line that "You can take all the sincerity in Hollywood, place it in the navel of a fruit fly and still have room enough for three caraway seeds and a producer's heart." He said nothing, just smiled wanly and twitched several times. Poor Harlan. There will not be another like him.

I've just come back from the funeral in Los Angeles, which is why I'm a little late in responding to your letter. A senior police officer was there and I spoke to him in private, since I'm thinking of doing a mystery based on the case, in the vein of my *Murder at the A.B.A.* The cops still haven't located the zoo or circus from which the giant python escaped, but they are scouring the state. Apparently Harlan was attacked and devoured beside the swimming pool of the Beverly Hills Hotel, on his way to a ceremony in the Polo Lounge where he was to have received his fourth Atilla award from the Screen Writers' Guild West. What bitter irony! The police shot the snake shortly afterwards, when it attempted to consume an elderly lady walking her dog on Mulholland Drive. Apparently it was still hungry.

I was really glad I attended the funeral. There should have been someone there besides his accountant, whom I suspect showed up only to make sure. (Harlan was already partially digested when they autopsied the python, so the coffin was closed and he went away a bit disappointed.) It was a bittersweet occasion for all of us in s-f.

Now to address myself to the subject of your letter and phone call. Frankly, Ed, you put me in a difficult position. You know I have both respect and affection for you, but it would be dereliction of our friendship to encourage you in this delusion. I'm afraid you've been driving yourself too hard in recent years, far too hard, and this *idée fixe* is obviously the result. You know that I do not have a closed mind; in fact, I fully subscribe to Haldane's Law that the universe is not only queerer than we imagine, it is queerer than we *can* imagine. But that does not mean I have to swallow a lot of nonsensical mumbo-jumbo about hexes and curses and drums and leopards in the night. I'm sorry, Ed, but I'm afraid the problem is all in your troubled mind. Sure, people in Haiti can die of a voodoo hex, *if they believe totally and fanatically in the power of voodoo.* Psychosomatic medicine is still in its infancy, but we do know that individuals can *will* themselves to serious illness and even death. My fear is that this is precisely what is happening to you. I urgently suggest that you contact Dr. Joseph Rauschbusch in New York City, a highly qualified psychoanalyst who worked wonders for Malzberg. His number is 676-4350, and I've already spoken to him, so he's expecting your call.

Before a cure can be effective, Ed, you must grasp the fact that a logical, rational explanation is, in this case as in all others, the *only* explanation. Remember Sherlock Holmes' dictum, as true in science as in criminology: "When you have eliminated the impossible, whatever remains, *however improbable,* must be the truth." To you, old friend, the improbable truth is that you are having a nervous breakdown; rather than face that, you have taken refuge in consoling impossibilities. And do not quote back to me Aristotle's claim that "plausible impossibilities should be preferred to unconvincing possibilities"; I have succinctly demolished that position in my recent book, *Isaac Asimov's Guide to the Wit and Wisdom of All Human History* (Afflatua Press, N.Y., 1976). Of course, whenever they're challenged, the camp followers of irrationality will resort to Hegel's rejoinder when told that the facts contradicted his theories: "All the worse for the facts." Do not join them, Ed. The facts dictate that you seek expert medical advice, and as quickly as possible.

If it will help put your mind at rest, I have examined your

pouch, and although I can't identify all the ingredients as yet, they appear thoroughly non-toxic and, believe it or not, non-magical. The shells are cowrie and the hair does seem to be human, and of European texture, but that means nothing in and of itself; your meeting the African in the barber shop was obviously nothing more than a coincidence. This little grab-bag of junk can hurt *no one,* Ed. Only you can hurt yourself. I hope I have been of some help in making that clear.

On a lighter note, my latest book, *Isaac Asimov's Guide to Health, Happiness and Regularity through Self-Negation,* is doing very well, and will soon be out in paperback. (So far, it's even outselling my *Isaac Asimov's Guide to Guides.*) At a recent autograph party in Poughkeepsie, several nubile young ladies, obviously enamored of both my charm and talent, inquired if I had a hobby. I replied, with a bow to Oliver St. John Gogarty: "Converting lesbians." Well, I can tell you, Edward, I couldn't get rid of them after that. In fact, later that night. . . .
[Deleted for reasons of taste, and space—The Editor]
 . . . Well, Edward, I must get back to the grindstone, I've got another book to turn out this afternoon. (My first venture into political porn, *Sex Slaves of the Judiciary Committee,* based loosely on Watergate.) Hope you'll soon free yourself of the Black Dog, and we can get together for lunch.

Cordially,
Isaac

WU014 PD

CORNWALL CONN SEP 12 345 AEDT

O T NKABELE
329 E 8
NYC

CANNOT GO ON LIKE THIS STATE YOUR TERMS

EDWARD FERMAN
3240 RIDGEDALE AVE
CORNWALL CONN

329 East 8th Street
New York, N.Y. 10009
September 13, 1980

Mr. Edward L. Ferman
Magazine of Fantasy & Science Fiction
Cornwall, Connecticut 06753

My dear friend Ed:

I have received your wire and am most sympathetic to your plight, although I cannot countenance the idea that *multi,* or witch-power, is at the root of your difficulties. Nevertheless, inasmuch as your welfare and happiness are so important to me, I have swallowed my doubts and performed certain *uchawi* rituals of cleansing or, in Western parlance, exorcism, that were handed down to me by my uncle, the *Mganga* of our people. If a vindictive *mhondoro* is indeed pursuing you, he is now banished to the Eternal Night from whence he came. Thaumaturgically speaking, however, there is no assurance that he will not re-materialize in the future, if the situation which triggered his initial manifestation should recur. Thus, eternal vigilance on my part would be required in order to prevent another psychic onslaught on your mind and body, this time possibly fatal. Needless to say, dear Edward, I cannot intellectually justify your supernatural hypothesis, but I hope my actions will reassure you and soothe your troubled thoughts.

I also trust that following your recuperation you will return to my stories with a fresh and positive perspective. I am currently working on a new piece, THE HELL PITS OF R'GHANNA, which I will dispatch to you shortly. It is of novella length, and should elicit much favorable comment among the cognoscenti.

With warmest fraternal feelings,
Your buddy
Oggy

Cornwall, Connecticut 06753
September 20, 1980

Mr. O. T. Nkabele
329 East 8th Street
New York, New York 10009

Dear Oginga:

Yes, the headaches and chest pains have stopped, and I am slowly returning to normal. If anything in my life can ever be normal again. I understand your letter fully. Let us leave it at that.

Enclosed is a check for ASTRID OF THE ASTEROIDS, SLIME SLAVES OF G'HARN and URSULA OF URANUS.

Yours,
Edward L. Ferman

329 East 8th Street
New York, New York 10009
October 27, 1980

Mr. Edward L. Ferman
Magazine of Fantasy & Science Fiction
Cornwall, Connecticut 06753

Dear Ed:

Thank you for your check for HELL PITS OF R'GHANNA. I am enclosing a rough sketch of the cover illustration, which you will kindly have your own artist follow explicitly.

Your friend,
Oggy

Cornwall, Connecticut 06753
March 23, 1981

Mr. O. T. Nkabele
329 East 8th Street
New York, New York 10009

Dear Oginga:

Enclosed is a check for SELENA OF SIRIUS and SPACE PIRATES OF SATURN. I am sorry the amount is smaller this time, but we have had grave circulation problems from the day we began running your stories. I understand that since the elephant got Ben Bova you have been writing for *Omni* as well. I hope their finances are in better shape than ours.

Would you please provide us with an 8″ by 10″ glossy photograph of yourself (head and shoulders) for the artist working on the cover of our Oginga Nkabele Special Issue. He needs it as soon as possible.

Yours,
Ed

P.S. I'm enclosing a list of the members of Science Fiction Writers of America, and most of their addresses. Under separate cover I've sent you a convention folio which has many of the photographs of individual writers you requested. They should be voting on the Nebula Awards in mid-April. I'm afraid I don't know where any of them have their hair cut, but I'm sure you'll find out.

329 East 8th Street
New York, New York 10009
May 10, 1981

Mr. Edward L. Ferman
Magazine of Fantasy & Science Fiction
Cornwall, Connecticut 06753

My dear Ed:

Thank you for your most gracious telegram of congratulations on my Nebula. I sincerely believe it is the field itself, rather than your humble servant, that is the true beneficiary. Who, precisely, votes on the Hugos at the World Convention? How may I get in touch with them? I am still, alas, regrettably innocent of the inner machinations of American fandom.

With warmest regards,
Your pal
Oggy

Cornwall, Connecticut 06753
January 12, 1982

Mr. O. T. Nkabele
23 Sutton Place
New York, New York 10023

Dear Oggy:

It was good seeing you and Rachel on the weekend. I hope you'll come up again on your return from Hollywood.

No, I don't personally know anyone on the Nobel Prize Committee, but I have visited the Swedish Embassy and they inform me the judges are comprised of members of the Swedish and Norwegian Parliaments. The Embassy is mailing me their names and addresses, and I will forward them to you.

Thank you for sending us VISITATION OF THE VRILL. I'm glad you still find time to think of your old friends at F&SF, particularly now that we've gone mimeo. Let me know what you have in mind for the cover.

Best wishes,
Ed

P.S. Could you send me that hangover recipe you once mentioned? The B-12 shots no longer seem to do the job. I'll be tapering off soon, though. Really.

Michael Shea's first F&SF *contribution, "The Angel of Death,"
won a Nebula Award nomination and his second, which appears
below, attracted even more attention, including a second
Nebula Award nomination. The story—in which Dr. Carl Winters,
a fifty-seven-year-old pathologist, arrives at a mountain town
to perform autopsies on the victims of a suspicious mining
explosion—is about the business of death; and so be warned that
it is in some ways a grim and horrifying tale. However, it is
ultimately a positive, even a touching, story; and we doubt that
you will soon forget Dr. Winters and what he finds in a defunct ice
plant on the edge of the town known as Bailey.*

MICHAEL SHEA

The Autopsy

D R. Winters stepped out of the tiny Greyhound station and into
the midnight street that smelt of pines and the river, though
the street was in the heart of the town. But then it was a town of
only five main streets in breadth, and these extended scarcely a
mile and a half along the rim of the gorge. Deep in that gorge
though the river ran, its blurred roar flowed, perfectly distinct,
between the banks of dark shop windows. The station's window
showed the only light, save for a luminous clock face several doors
down and a little neon beer logo two blocks farther on. When he
had walked a short distance, Dr. Winters set his suitcase down,
pocketed his hands, and looked at the stars—thick as cobblestones
in the black gulf.

"A mountain hamlet—a mining town," he said. "Stars. No
moon. We are in Bailey."

He was talking to his cancer. It was in his stomach. Since learning of it, he had developed this habit of wry communion with it. He meant to show courtesy to this uninvited guest. Death. It would not find him churlish, for that would make its victory absolute. Except, of course, that its victory would *be* absolute, with or without his ironies.

He picked up his suitcase and walked on. The starlight made faint mirrors of the windows' blackness and showed him the man who passed: lizard-lean, white-haired (at fifty-seven), a man traveling on death's business, carrying his own death in him, and even bearing death's wardrobe in his suitcase. For this was filled—aside from his medical kit and some scant necessities—with mortuary bags. The sheriff had told him on the phone of the improvisations that presently enveloped the corpses, and so the doctor had packed these, laying them in his case with bitter amusement, checking the last one's breadth against his chest before the mirror, as a woman will gauge a dress before donning it, and telling his cancer:

"Oh, yes, that's plenty roomy enough for both of us!"

The case was heavy and he stopped frequently to rest and scan the sky. What a night's work to do, probing soulless filth, eyes earthward, beneath such a ceiling of stars! It had taken five days to dig them out. The autumnal equinox had passed, but the weather here had been uniformly hot. And warmer still, no doubt, so deep in the earth.

He entered the courthouse by a side door. His heels knocked on the linoleum corridor. A door at the end of it, on which was lettered NATE CRAVEN, COUNTY SHERIFF, opened well before he reached it, and his friend stepped out to meet him.

"Damnit, Carl, you're *still* so thin they could use you for a whip. Gimme that. You're in too good a shape already. You don't need the exercise."

The case hung weightless from his hand, imparting no tilt at all to his bull shoulders. Despite his implied self-derogation, he was only moderately paunched for a man his age and size. He had a rough-hewn face and the bulk of brow, nose, and jaw made his greenish eyes look small until one engaged them and felt the snap and penetration of their intelligence. He half-filled two cups from a coffee urn and topped both off with bourbon from a bottle in his desk. When they had finished these, they had finished trading news of mutual friends. The sheriff mixed another round, and sipped from his, in a silence clearly prefatory to the work at hand.

"They talk about rough justice," he said. "I've sure seen it now. One of those . . . patients of yours that you'll be working on? He was a killer. 'Killer' don't even half say it, really. You could say that *he* got justly executed in that blast. That much was justice for damn sure. But rough as hell on those other nine. And the rough don't just stop with their being dead either. That kiss-ass boss of yours! He's breaking his god-damned back touching his toes for Fordham Mutual. How much of the picture did he give you?"

"You refer, I take it, to the estimable Coroner Waddleton of Fordham County." Dr. Winters paused to sip his drink. With a delicate flaring of his nostrils he communicated all the disgust, contempt and amusement he had felt in his four years as Pathologist in Waddleton's office. The sheriff laughed.

"Clear pictures seldom emerge from anything the coroner says," the doctor continued. "He took your name in vain. Vigorously and repeatedly. These expressions formed his opening remarks. He then developed the theme of our office's strict responsibility to the letter of the law, and of the workmen's compensation law in particular. Death benefits accrue only to the dependents of decedents whose deaths arise *out of the course* of their employment, not merely *in* the course of it. Victims of a maniacal assault, though they die on the job, are by no means necessarily compensable under the law. We then contemplated the tragic injustice of an insurance company—*any* insurance company—having to pay benefits to unentitled persons, solely through the laxity and incompetence of investigating officers. Your name came up again."

Craven uttered a bark of mirth and fury. "The impartial public servant! Ha! The impartial brown-nose, flim-flam and bullshit man is what he *is*. Ten to one, Fordham Mutual will slip out of it *without* his help, and those men's families won't see a goddamn nickel." Words were an insufficient vent; the sheriff turned and spat into his wastebasket. He drained his cup, and sighed. "I beg your pardon, Carl. We've been five days digging those men out and the last two days sifting half that mountain for explosive traces, with those insurance investigators hanging on our elbows, and the most they could say was that there was 'strong presumptive evidence' of a bomb. Well, I don't budge for that because I don't have to. Waddleton can shove his 'extraordinary circumstances.' If you don't find anything in those bodies, then that's all the autopsy there is to it, and they get buried right here where their families want 'em."

The doctor was smiling at his friend. He finished his cup and spoke with his previous wry detachment, as if the sheriff had not interrupted.

"The honorable coroner then spoke with remarkable volubility on the subject of Autopsy Consent forms and the malicious subversion of private citizens by vested officers of the law. He had, as it happened, a sheaf of such forms on his desk, all signed, all with a rider clause typed in above the signatures. A cogent paragraph. It had, among its other qualities, the property of turning the coroner's face purple when he read it aloud. He read it aloud to me three times. It appeared that the survivors' consent was contingent on two conditions: that the autopsy be performed *in locem mortis,* that is to say in Bailey, and that only if the coroner's pathologist found concrete evidence of homicide should the decedents be subject either to removal from Bailey or to further necropsy. It was well written. I remember wondering who wrote it."

The sheriff nodded musingly. He took Dr. Winters' empty cup, set it by his own, filled both two-thirds with bourbon, and added a splash of coffee to the doctor's. The two friends exchanged a level stare, rather like poker players in the clinch. The sheriff regarded his cup, sipped from it.

"*In locem mortis.* What-all does that mean exactly?"

" 'In the place of death.' "

"Oh. Freshen that up for you?"

"I've just started it, thank you."

Both men laughed, paused, and laughed again, some might have said immoderately.

"He all but told me that I *had* to find something to compel a second autopsy," the doctor said at length. "He would have sold his soul—or taken out a second mortgage on it—for a mobile x-ray unit. He's right of course. If those bodies have trapped any bomb fragments, that would be the surest and quickest way of finding them. It still amazes me your Dr. Parsons could let his x-ray go unfixed for so long."

"He sets bones, stitches wounds, writes prescriptions, and sends anything tricky down the mountain. Just barely manages that. Drunks don't get much done."

"He's gotten that bad?"

"He hangs on and no more. Waddleton was right there, not deputizing him pathologist. I doubt he could find a cannonball in a dead rat. I wouldn't say it where it could hurt him, as long as he's still managing, but everyone here knows it. His patients sort of look after *him* half the time. But Waddleton would have sent you, no matter who was here. Nothing but his best for party contributors like Fordham Mutual."

The doctor looked at his hands and shrugged. "So. There's a killer in the batch. *Was* there a bomb?"

Slowly, the sheriff planted his elbows on the desk and pressed his hands against his temples, as if the question had raised a turbulence of memories. For the first time the doctor—half harkening throughout to the never-quite-muted stirrings of the death within him—saw his friend's exhaustion: the tremor of hand, the bruised look under the eyes.

"I'm going to give you what I have, Carl. I told you I don't think you'll find a damn thing in those bodies. You're probably going to end up assuming what I do about it, but assuming is as far as anyone's going to get with this one. It is truly one of those Nightmare Specials that the good Lord tortures lawmen with and then hides the answers to forever.

"All right then. About two months ago, we had a man disappear—Ronald Hanley. Mine worker, rock-steady, family man. He didn't come home one night, and we never found a trace of him. OK, that happens sometimes. About a week later, the lady that ran the laundromat, Sharon Starker, *she* disappeared, no trace. We got edgy then. I made an announcement on the local radio about a possible weirdo at large, spelled out special precautions everybody should take. We put both our squadcars on the night beat, and by day we set to work knocking on every door in town collecting alibis for the two times of disappearance.

"No good. Maybe you're fooled by this uniform and think I'm a law officer, protector of the people, and all that? A natural mistake. A lot of people were fooled. In less than seven weeks, six people vanished, just like that. Me and my deputies might as well have stayed in bed round the clock, for all the good we did." The sheriff drained his cup.

"Anyway, at last we got lucky. Don't get me wrong now. We didn't go all hog-wild and actually prevent a crime or anything. But we *did* find a body—except it wasn't the body of any of the seven people that had disappeared. We'd took to combing the woods nearest town, with temporary deputies from the miners to help. Well, one of those boys was out there with us last week. It was hot—like it's been for a while now—and it was real quiet. He heard this buzzing noise and looked around for it, and he saw a bee-swarm up in the crotch of a tree. Except he was smart enough to know that that's not usual around here—bee hives. So it wasn't bees. It was bluebottle flies, a god-damned big cloud of them, all over a bundle that was wrapped in a tarp."

The sheriff studied his knuckles. He had, in his eventful life, occasionally met men literate enough to understand his last name and rash enough to be openly amused by it, and the knuckles— scarred knobs—were eloquent of his reactions. He looked back into his old friend's eyes.

"We got that thing down and unwrapped it. Billy Lee Davis, one of my deputies, he was in Viet Nam, been near some bad, bad things and held on. Billy Lee blew his lunch all over the ground when we unwrapped that thing. It was a man. Some of a man. We knew he'd stood six-two because all the bones were there, and he'd probably weighed between two fifteen and two twenty-five, but he folded up no bigger than a big-size laundry package. Still had his face, both shoulders, and the left arm, but all the rest was clean. It wasn't animal work. It was knife work, all the edges neat as butcher cuts. Except butchered meat, even when you drain it all you can, will bleed a good deal afterwards, and there wasn't one god-damned drop of blood on the tarp, nor in that meat. It was just as pale as fish meat."

Deep in his body's center, the doctor's cancer touched him. Not a ravening attack—it sank one fang of pain, questioningly, into new, untasted flesh, probing the scope for its appetite there. He disguised his tremor with a shake of the head.

"A cache, then."

The sheriff nodded. "Like you might keep a potroast in the icebox for making lunches. I took some pictures of his face, then we put him back and erased our traces. Two of the miners I'd deputized did a lot of hunting, were woods-smart. So I left them on the first watch. We worked out positions and cover for them, and drove back.

"We got right on tracing him, sent out descriptions to every town within a hundred miles. He was no one I'd ever seen in Bailey, nor anyone else either, it began to look like, after we'd combed the town all day with the photos. Then, out of the blue, Billy Lee Davis smacks himself on the forehead and says, 'Sheriff, *I* seen this man somewhere in town, and not long ago!'

"He'd been shook all day since throwing up, and then all of a sudden he just snapped to. Was dead sure. Except he couldn't remember where or when. We went over and over it and he tried and tried. It got to where I wanted to grab him by the ankles and hang him upside down and shake him till it dropped out of him. But it was no damn use. Just after dark we went back to that tree —we'd worked out a place to hide the cars and a route to it through the woods. When we were close we walkie-talkied the men we'd left for an all-clear to come up. No answer at all. And when we got there, all that was left of our trap was the tree. No body, no tarp, no Special Assistant Deputies. Nothing."

This time Dr. Winters poured the coffee and bourbon. "Too much coffee," the sheriff muttered, but drank anyway. "Part of me wanted to chew nails and break necks. And part of me was scared shitless. When we got back I got on the radio station again and made an emergency broadcast and then had the man at the station rebroadcast it every hour. Told everyone to do everything in groups of three, to stay together at night in threes at least, to go out little as possible, keep armed and keep checking up on each other. It had such a damn-fool sound to it, but just pairing-up was no protection if half of one of those pairs was the killer. I deputized more men and put them on the streets to beef up the night patrol.

"It was next morning that things broke. The sheriff of Rakehell called—he's over in the next county. He said our corpse sounded a lot like a man named Abel Dougherty, a millhand with Con Wood over there. I left Billy Lee in charge and drove right out.

"This Dougherty had a cripple older sister he always checked back to by phone whenever he left town for long, a habit no one knew about, probably embarrassed him. Sheriff Peck there only found out about it when the woman called him, said her brother'd been four days gone for vacation and not rung her once. Without that Peck might not've thought of Dougherty just from our description, though the photo I showed him clinched it, and one would've reached him by mail soon enough. Well, he'd hardly set it down again when a call came through for me. It was Billy Lee. He'd remembered.

"When he'd seen Dougherty was the Sunday night three days before we found him. Where he'd seen him was the Trucker's Tavern outside the north end of town. The man had made a stir by being jolly drunk and latching onto a miner who was drinking there, man named Joe Allen, who'd started at the mine about two months back. Dougherty kept telling him that he wasn't Joe Allen, but Dougherty's old buddy named Sykes that had worked with him at Con Wood for a coon's age, and what the hell kind of joke was this, come have a beer old buddy and tell me why you took off so sudden and what the hell you been doing with yourself.

"Allen took it laughing. Dougherty'd clap him on the shoulder, Allen'd clap him right back and make every kind of joke about it, say 'Give this man another beer, I'm standing in for a long-lost friend of his.' Dougherty was so big and loud and stubborn, Billy Lee was worried about a fight starting, and he wasn't the only one worried. But this Joe Allen was a natural good ol' boy, handled it perfect. We'd checked him out weeks back along with everyone else, and he was real popular with the other miners. Finally Dougherty swore he was going to take him on to another bar to help celebrate the vacation Dougherty was starting out on. Joe Allen got up grinning, said god damn it, he couldn't accommodate Dougherty by being this fellow Sykes, but he could sure as hell have a glass with any serious drinking man that was treating. He went out with him, and gave everyone a wink as he left, to the general satisfaction of the audience."

Craven paused. Dr. Winters met his eyes and knew his thought, two images: the jolly wink that roused the room to laughter, and the thing in the tarp aboil with bright blue flies.

"It was plain enough for me," the sheriff said. "I told Billy Lee to search Allen's room at the Skettles' boarding house and then go straight to the mine and take him. We could fine-polish things once we had him. Since I was already in Rakehell, I saw to some of the loose ends before I started back. I went with Sheriff Peck down to Con Wood and we found a picture of Eddie Sykes in the personnel files. I'd seen Joe Allen often enough, and it was his picture in that file.

"We found out Sykes lived alone, was an on-again, off-again worker, private in his comings and goings, and hadn't been around for a while. But one of the sawyers there could be pretty sure of when Skyes left Rakehell because he'd gone to Sykes' cabin the morning after a big meteor shower they had out there about nine weeks back, since some thought the shower might have reached the ground, and not far from Sykes' side of the mountain. He wasn't in that morning, and the sawyer hadn't seen him since.

"It looked sewed up. It *was* sewed up. After all those weeks. I was less than a mile out of Bailey, had the pedal floored. Full of rage and revenge. I felt . . . like a *bullet,* like I was one big thirty-caliber slug that was going to go right through that blood-sucking cannibal, tear the whole truth right out of his heart, enough to hang him a hundred times. That was the closest I got. So close that I *heard* it when it all blew to shit.

"I sound squirrelly. I know I do. Maybe all this gave me something I'll never shake off. We had to put together what happened. Billy Lee didn't have my other deputy with him. Travis was out with some men on the mountain dragnetting around that tree for clues. By luck, he was back at the car when Billy Lee was trying to raise him. He said he'd just been through Allen's room and had got something we could maybe hold him on. It was a sphere, half again big as a basketball, heavy, made of something that wasn't metal or glass but was a little like both. He could half-see into it and it looked to be full of some kind of circuitry and components. If someone tried to spring Allen, we could make a theft rap out of this thing, or say we suspected it was a bomb. Jesus! Anyway, he said it was the only strange thing he found, but it was plenty strange. He told Travis to get up to the mine for back-up. He'd be there first and should already have Allen by the time Travis arrived.

"Tierney, the shift boss up there, had an assistant that told us the rest. Billy Lee parked behind the offices where the men in the yard wouldn't see the car. He went upstairs to arrange the arrest with Tierney. They got half a dozen men together. Just as they came out of the building, they saw Allen take off running from the squadcar with the sphere under his arm.

"The whole compound's fenced in and Tierney'd already phoned to have all the gates shut. Allen zigged and zagged some but caught on quick to the trap. The sphere slowed him, but he still had a good lead. He hesitated a minute and then ran straight for the main shaft. A cage was just going down with a crew, and he risked every bone in him jumping down after it, but he got safe on top. By the time they got to the switches, the cage was down to the second level, and Allen and the crew had got out. Tierney got it back up. Billy Lee ordered the rest back to get weapons and follow, and him and Tierney rode the cage right back down. And about two minutes later half the god-damned mine blew up."

The sheriff stopped as if cut off, his lips parted to say more, his eyes registering for perhaps the hundredth time his amazement that there was no more, that the weeks of death and mystification ended here, with this split-second recapitulation: more death, more answerless dark, sealing all.

"Nate."

"What."

"Wrap it up and go to bed. I don't need your help. You're dead on your feet."

"I'm not on my feet. And I'm coming along."

"Give me a picture of the victims' position relative to the blast. I'm going to work and you're going to bed."

The sheriff shook his head absently. "They're mining in shrinkage stopes. The adits—levels—branch off lateral from the vertical shaft. From one level they hollow out overhand up to the one above. Scoop out big chambers and let most of the broken rock stay inside so they can stand on the heaps to cut the ceilings higher. They leave sections of support wall between stopes, and those men were buried several stopes in from the shaft. The cave-in killed *them*. The mountain just folded them up in their own hill of tailings. No kind of fragments reached them. I'm dead sure. The only ones they *found* were of some standard charges that the main blast set off, and those didn't even get close. The big one blew out where the adit joined the shaft, right where, and right when Billy Lee and Tierney got out of the cage. And there is *nothing* left there,

Carl. No sphere, no cage, no Tierney, no Billy Lee Davis. Just rock blown fine as flour."

Dr. Winters nodded and, after a moment, stood up.

"Come on, Nate. I've got to get started. I'll be lucky to have even a few of them done before morning. Drop me off and go to sleep, till then at least. You'll still be there to witness most of the work."

The sheriff rose, took up the doctor's suitcase, and led him out of the office without a word, concession in his silence.

The patrol car was behind the building. The doctor saw a crueller beauty in the stars than he had an hour before. They got in, and Craven swung them out onto the empty street. The doctor opened the window and harkened, but the motor's surge drowned out the river sound. Before the thrust of their headlights, ranks of old-fashioned parking meters sprouted shadows tall across the sidewalks, shadows which shrank and were cut down by the lights' passage. The sheriff said:

"All those extra dead. For nothing! Not even to . . . *feed* him! If it *was* a bomb, and he made it, he'd know how powerful it was. He wouldn't try some stupid escape stunt with it. And how did he even know the thing was there? We worked it out that Allen was just ending a shift, but he wasn't even up out of the ground before Billy Lee'd parked out of sight."

"Let it rest, Nate. I want to hear more, but after you've slept. I know you. All the photos will be there, and the report complete, all the evidence neatly boxed and carefully described. When I've looked things over I'll know exactly how to proceed by myself."

Bailey had neither hospital nor morgue, and the bodies were in a defunct ice-plant on the edge of town. A generator had been brought down from the mine, lighting improvised, and the refrigeration system reactivated. Dr. Parsons' office, and the tiny examining room that served the sheriff's station in place of a morgue, had furnished this makeshift with all the equipment that Dr. Winters would need beyond what he carried with him. A quarter-mile outside the main body of the town, they drew up to it. Tree-flanked, unneighbored by any other structure, it was a double building; the smaller half—the office—was illuminated. The bodies would be in the big, windowless refrigerator segment. Craven pulled up beside a second squadcar parked near the office door. A short, rake-thin man wearing a large white stetson got out of the car and came over. Craven rolled down his window.

"Trav. This here's Dr. Winters."

"Lo, Nate. Dr. Winters. Everything's shipshape inside. Felt more comfortable out here. Last of those newshounds left two hours ago."

"They sure do hang on. You take off now, Trav. Get some sleep and be back at sunup. What temperature we getting?"

The pale stetson, far clearer in the starlight than the shadow-face beneath it, wagged dubiously. "Thirty-six. She won't get lower —some kind of leak."

"That should be cold enough," the doctor said.

Travis drove off and the sheriff unlocked the padlock on the office door. Waiting behind him, Dr. Winters heard the river again —a cold balm, a whisper of freedom—and overlying this, the stutter and soft snarl of the generator behind the building, a gnawing, remorseless sound that somehow fed the obscure anguish which the other soothed. They went in.

The preparations had been thoughtful and complete. "You can wheel 'em out of the fridge on this and do the examining in here," the sheriff said, indicating a table and a gurney. "You should find all the gear you need on this big table here, and you can write up your reports on that desk. The phone's not hooked up—there's a pay phone at that last gas station if you have to call me."

The doctor nodded, checking over the material on the larger table: scalpels, post-mortem and cartilage knives, intestine scissors, rib shears, forceps, probes, mallet and chisels, a blade saw and electric bone saw, scale, jars for specimens, needles and suture, sterilizer, gloves. . . . Beside this array were a few boxes and envelopes with descriptive sheets attached, containing the photographs and such evidentiary objects as had been found associated with the bodies.

"Excellent," he muttered.

"The overhead light's fluorescent, full spectrum or whatever they call it. Better for colors. There's a pint of decent bourbon in that top desk drawer. Ready to look at 'em?"

"Yes."

The sheriff unbarred and slid back the big metal door to the refrigeration chamber. Icy, tainted air boiled out of the doorway. The light within was dimmer than that provided in the office—a yellow gloom wherein ten oblong heaps lay on trestles.

The two stood silent for a time, their stillness a kind of unpremeditated homage paid the eternal mystery at its threshold. As if the cold room were in fact a shrine, the doctor found a peculiar awe in the row of veiled forms. The awful unison of their dying, the titan's grave that had been made for them, conferred on them a stern authority, Death's chosen Ones. His stomach hurt, and he found he had his hand pressed to his abdomen. He glanced at Craven and was relieved to see that his friend, staring wearily at the bodies, had missed the gesture.

"Nate. Help me uncover them."

Starting at opposite ends of the row, they stripped the tarps off and piled them in a corner. Both were brusque now, not pausing over the revelation of the swelled, pulpy faces—most three-lipped with the gaseous burgeoning of their tongues—and the fat, livid hands sprouting from the filthy sleeves. But at one of the bodies Craven stopped. The doctor saw him look, and his mouth twist. Then he flung the tarp on the heap and moved to the next trestle.

When they came out Dr. Winters took out the bottle and glasses Craven had put in the desk, and they had a drink together. The sheriff made as if he would speak, but shook his head and sighed.

"I *will* get some sleep, Carl. I'm getting crazy thoughts with this thing." The doctor wanted to ask those thoughts. Instead he laid a hand on his friend's shoulder.

"Go home, Sheriff Craven. Take off the badge and lie down. The dead won't run off on you. We'll all still be here in the morning."

When the sound of the patrol car faded, the doctor stood listening to the generator's growl and the silence of the dead, resurgent now. Both the sound and the silence seemed to mock him. The after-echo of his last words made him uneasy. He said to his cancer:

"What about it, dear colleague? We *will* still be here tomorrow? All of us?"

He smiled, but felt an odd discomfort, as if he had ventured a jest in company and roused a hostile silence. He went to the refrigerator door, rolled it back, and viewed the corpses in their ordered rank, with their strange tribunal air. "What, sirs?" he murmured. "Do you judge me? Just who is to examine whom tonight, if I may ask?"

He went back into the office, where his first step was to examine the photographs made by the sheriff, in order to see how the dead had lain at their uncovering. The earth had seized them with terrible suddenness. Some crouched, some partly stood, others sprawled in crazy, free-fall postures. Each successive photo showed more of the jumble as the shovels continued their work between shots. The doctor studied them closely, noting the identifications inked on the bodies as they came completely into view.

One man, Robert Willet, had died some yards from the main cluster. It appeared he had just straggled into the stope from the adit at the moment of the explosion. He should thus have received, more directly than any of the others, the shockwaves of the blast. If bomb fragments were to be found in any of the corpses, Mr. Willet's seemed likeliest to contain them. Dr. Winters pulled on a pair of surgical gloves.

He lay at one end of the line of trestles. He wore a thermal shirt and overalls that were strikingly new beneath the filth of burial. Their tough fabrics jarred with that of his flesh—blue, swollen, seeming easily torn or burst, like ripe fruit. In life Willet had grease-combed his hair. Now it was a sculpture of dust, spikes and whorls shaped by the head's last grindings against the mountain that clenched it.

Rigor had come and gone—Willet rolled laxly onto the gurney. As the doctor wheeled him past the others, he felt a slight self-consciousness. The sense of some judgment flowing from the dead assembly—unlike most such vagrant emotional embellishments of experience—had an odd tenacity in him. This stubborn unease began to irritate him with himself, and he moved more briskly.

He put Willet on the examining table and cut the clothes off him with shears, storing the pieces in an evidence box. The overalls were soiled with agonal waste expulsions. The doctor stared a moment with unwilling pity at his naked subject.

"You won't ride down to Fordham in any case," he said to the corpse. "Not unless I find something pretty damned obvious." He pulled his gloves tighter and arranged his implements.

Waddleton had said more to him than he had reported to the

sheriff. The doctor was to find, and forcefully to record that he had found, strong "indications" absolutely requiring the decedents' removal to Fordham for x-ray and an exhaustive second post-mortem. The doctor's continued employment with the Coroner's Office depended entirely on his compliance in this. He had received this stipulation with a silence Waddleton had not thought it necessary to break. His present resolution was all but made at that moment. Let the obvious be taken as such. If the others showed as plainly as Willet did the external signs of death by asphyxiation, they would receive no more than a thorough external exam. Willet he would examine internally as well, merely to establish in depth for this one what should appear obvious in all. Otherwise, only when the external exam revealed a clearly anomalous feature— and clear and suggestive it must be—would he look deeper.

He rinsed the caked hair in a basin, poured the sediment into a flask and labeled it. Starting with the scalp, he began a minute scrutiny of the body's surfaces, recording his observations as he went.

The characteristic signs of asphyxial death were evident, despite the complicating effects of autolysis and putrefaction. The eyeballs' bulge and the tongue's protrusion were by now at least partly due to gas pressure as well as the mode of death, but the latter organ was clamped between locked teeth, leaving little doubt as to that mode. The coloration of degenerative change—a greenish-yellow tint, a darkening and mapping-out of superficial veins— was marked, but not sufficient to obscure the blue of syanosis on the face and neck, nor the pinpoint hemorrhages freckling neck, chest, and shoulders. From the mouth and nose the doctor scraped matter he was confident was the blood-tinged mucous typically ejected in the airless agony.

He began to find a kind of comedy in his work. What a buffoon death made of a man! A blue, pop-eyed, three-lipped thing. And there was himself, his curious, solicitous intimacy with this clown-ish carrion. Excuse me, Mr. Willet, while I probe this laceration. How does it feel when I do this? Nothing? Nothing at all? Fine, now what about these nails. Split them clawing at the earth, did you? Yes. A nice bloodblister under this thumbnail I see—got it on the job a few days before your accident no doubt? Remarkable calluses here, still quite tough. . . .

The doctor looked for an unanalytic moment at the hands—

puffed, dark paws, gestureless, having renounced all touch and grasp. He felt the wastage of the man concentrated in the hands. The painful futility of the body's fine articulation when it is seen in death—this poignancy he had long learned not to acknowledge when he worked. But now he let it move him a little. This Roger Willet, plodding to his work one afternoon, had suddenly been scrapped, crushed to a nonfunctional heap of perishable materials. It simply happened that his life had chanced to move too close to the passage of a more powerful life, one of those inexorable and hungry lives that leave human wreckage—known or undiscovered —in their wakes. Bad luck, Mr. Willet. Naturally, we feel very sorry about this. But this Joe Allen, your co-worker. Apparently he was some sort of . . . cannibal. It's complicated. We don't understand it all. But the fact is we have to dismantle you now to a certain extent. There's really no hope of your using these parts of yourself again, I'm afraid. Ready now?

The doctor proceeded to the internal exam with a vague eagerness for Willet's fragmentation, for the disarticulation of that sadness in his natural form. He grasped Willet by the jaw and took up the post-mortem knife. He sank its point beneath the chin and began the long, gently sawing incision that opened Willet from throat to groin.

In the painstaking separation of the body's laminae Dr. Winters found absorption and pleasure. And yet throughout he felt, marginal but insistent, the movement of a stream of irrelevant images. These were of the building that contained him, and of the night containing it. As from outside, he saw the plant—bleached planks, iron roofing—and the trees crowding it, all in starlight, a ghost-town image. And he saw the refrigerator vault beyond the wall as from within, feeling the stillness of murdered men in a cold, yellow light. And at length a question formed itself, darting in and out of the weave of his concentration as the images did: Why did he still feel, like some stir of the air, that sense of mute vigilance surrounding his action, furtively touching his nerves with its inquiry as he worked? He shrugged, overtly angry now. Who else was attending but Death? Wasn't he Death's hireling, and this Death's place? Then let the master look on.

Peeling back Willet's cover of hemorrhage-stippled skin, Dr. Winters read the corpse with an increasing dispassion, a mortuary text. He confined his inspection to the lungs and mediastinum and found there unequivocal testimony to Willet's asphyxial death. The pleurae of the lungs exhibited the expected ecchymoses— bruised spots in the glassy, enveloping membrane. Beneath, the polyhedral surface lobules of the lungs themselves were bubbled and blistered—the expected interstitial emphysema. The lungs, on section, were intensely and bloodily congested. The left half of the heart he found contracted and empty, while the right was over-distended and engorged with dark blood, as were the large veins of the upper mediastinum. It was a classic picture of death by suffocation, and at length the doctor, with needle and suture, closed up the text again.

He returned the corpse to the gurney and draped one of his mortuary bags over it in the manner of a shroud. When he had help in the morning, he would weigh the bodies on a platform scale the office contained and afterwards bag them properly. He came to the refrigerator door, and hesitated. He stared at the door, not moving, not understanding why.

Run. Get out, now.

The thought was his own, but it came to him so urgently he turned around as if someone behind him had spoken. Across the room a thin man in smock and gloves, his eyes shadows, glared at the doctor from the black windows. Behind the man was a shrouded cart, behind that, a wide metal door.

Quietly, wonderingly, the doctor asked, "Run from what?" The eyeless man in the glass was still half-crouched, afraid.

Then, a moment later, the man straightened, threw back his head, and laughed. The doctor walked to the desk and sat down shoulder to shoulder with him. He pulled out the bottle and they had a drink together, regarding each other with identical bemused smiles. Then the doctor said, "Let me pour you another. You need it, old fellow. It makes a man himself again."

Nevertheless his re-entry of the vault was difficult, toilsome, each step seeming to require a new summoning of the will to move. In the freezing half-light all movement felt like defiance. His body lagged behind his craving to be quick, to be done with this moles-tation of the gathered dead. He returned Willet to his pallet and took his neighbor. The name on the tag wired to his boot was Ed Moses. Dr. Winters wheeled him back to the office and closed the big door behind him.

With Moses his work gained momentum. He expected to perform no further internal necropsies. He thought of his employer, rejoicing now in his seeming-submission to Waddleton's ultimatum. The impact would be dire. He pictured the coroner in shock, a sheaf of Pathologist's Reports in one hand, and smiled.

Waddleton could probably make a plausible case for incomplete examination. Still, a pathologist's discretionary powers were not well-defined. Many good ones would approve the adequacy of the doctor's method, given his working conditions. The inevitable litigation with a coalition of compensation claimants would be strenuous and protracted. Win or lose, Waddleton's venal devotion to the insurance company's interest would be abundantly displayed. Further, immediately on his dismissal the doctor would formally disclose its occult cause to the press. A libel action would ensue which he would have as little cause to fear as he had to fear his firing. Both his savings and the lawsuit would long outlast his life.

Externally, Ed Moses exhibited a condition as typically asphyxial as Willet's had been, with no slightest mark of fragment entry. The doctor finished his report and returned Moses to the vault, his movements brisk and precise. His unease was all but gone. That queasy stirring of the air—had he really felt it? It had been, perhaps, some new reverberation of the death at work in him, a psychic shudder of response to the cancer's stealthy probing for his life. He brought out the body next to Moses in the line.

Walter Lou Jackson was big, 6′ 2″ from heel to crown, and would surely weigh out at more than two hundred pounds. He had writhed mightily against his million-ton coffin with an agonal strength that had torn his face and hands. Death had mauled him like a lion. The doctor set to work.

His hands were fully themselves now—fleet, exact, intricately testing the corpse's character as other fingers might explore a keyboard for its latent melodies. And the doctor watched them with an old pleasure, one of the few that had never failed him, his mind at one remove from their busy intelligence. All the hard deaths! A worldful of them, time without end. Lives wrenched kicking from their snug meat-frames. Walter Lou Jackson had died very hard. Joe Allen brought this on you, Mr. Jackson. We think it was part of his attempt to escape the law.

But what a botched flight! The unreason of it—more than baffling—was eerie in its colossal futility. Beyond question, Allen had been cunning. A ghoul with a psychopath's social finesse. A good old boy who could make a tavernful of men laugh with delight while he cut his victim from their midst, make them applaud his exit with the prey, who stepped jovially into the darkness with murder at his side clapping him on the shoulder. Intelligent, certainly, with a strange technical sophistication as well, suggested by the sphere. Then what of the lunacy yet more strongly suggested by the same object? In the sphere was concentrated all the lethal mystery of Bailey's long nightmare.

Why the explosion? Its location implied an ambush for Allen's pursuers, a purposeful detonation. Had he aimed at a limited cave-in from which he schemed some inconceivable escape? Folly enough in this—far more if, as seemed sure, Allen had made the bomb himself, for then he would have to know its power was grossly inordinate to the need.

But if it was not a bomb, had a different function and only incidentally an explosive potential, Allen might underestimate the blast. It appeared the object was somehow remotely monitored by him, for the timing of events showed he had gone straight for it the instant he emerged from the shaft—shunned the bus waiting to take his shift back to town and made a beeline across the compound for a patrol car that was hidden from his view by the office building. This suggested something more complex than a mere explosive device, something, perhaps, whose destruction was itself more Allen's aim than the explosion produced thereby.

The fact that he risked the sphere's retrieval at all pointed to this interpretation. For the moment he sensed its presence at the mine, he must have guessed that the murder investigation had led to its discovery and removal from his room. But then, knowing himself already liable to the extreme penalty, why should Allen go to such lengths to recapture evidence incriminatory of a lesser offense, possession of an explosive device?

Then grant that the sphere was something more, something instrumental to his murders that could guarantee a conviction he might otherwise evade. Still, his gambit made no sense. Since the sphere —and thus the lawmen he could assume to have taken it—were already at the mine office, he must expect the compound to be sealed at any moment. Meanwhile, the gate was open, escape into the mountains a strong possibility for a man capable of stalking

and destroying two experienced and well-armed woodsmen lying
in ambush for him. Why had he all but insured his capture to
weaken a case against himself that his escape would have rendered
irrelevant? Dr. Winters saw his fingers, like a hunting pack round
a covert, converge on a small puncture wound below Walter Lou
Jackson's xiphoid process, between the eighth ribs.

His left hand touched its borders, the fingers' inquiry quick and
tender. The right hand introduced a probe, and both together
eased it into the wound. It inched unobstructed deep into the body,
curving upwards through the diaphragm towards the heart. The
doctor's own heart accelerated. He watched his hands move to
record the observation, watched them pause, watched them return
to their survey of the corpse, leaving pen and page untouched.

Inspection revealed no further anomaly. All else he observed
the doctor recorded faithfully, wondering throughout at the distress
he felt. When he had finished, he understood it. Its cause was not
the discovery of an entry wound that might bolster Waddleton's
case. For the find had, within moments, revealed to him that,
should he encounter anything he thought to be a mark of fragment penetration, he was going to ignore it. The damage Joe Allen
had done was going to end here, with this last grand slaughter, and
would not extend to the impoverishment of his victims' survivors.
No more internals. The externals will-they nill-they, would from
now on explicitly contraindicate the need for them.

The problem was that he did not believe the puncture in Jackson's thorax *was* a mark of fragment entry. Why? And, finding
no answer to this question, why was he, once again, afraid? Slowly,
he signed the report on Jackson, set it aside, and took up the post-
mortem knife.

First the long, sawing slice, unzipping the mortal overcoat.
Next, two great, square flaps of flesh reflected, scrolled laterally
to the armpits' line, disrobing the chest: one hand grasping the
flap's skirt, the other sweeping beneath it with the knife, flensing
through the glassy tissue that joined it to the chest-wall, and shav-
ing all muscles from their anchorages to bone and cartilage beneath. Then the dismantling of the strong-box within. Rib-shears
—so frank and forward a tool, like a gardener's. The steel beak bit
through each rib's gristle anchor to the sternum's centerplate. At
the sternum's crownpiece the collarbones' ends were knifed, pried,

and sprung free from their sockets. The coffer unhasped, unhinged, a knife teased beneath the lid and levered it off.

Some minutes later the doctor straightened up and stepped back from his subject. He moved almost drunkenly, and his age seemed scored more deeply in his face. With loathing haste he stripped his gloves off. He went to the desk, sat down, and poured another drink. If there was something like horror in his face, there was also a hardening in his mouth's line, and the muscles of his jaw. He spoke to his glass: "So be it, your Excellency. Something new for your humble servant. Testing my nerve?"

Jackson's pericardium, the shapely capsule containing his heart, should have been all but hidden between the big, blood-fat loaves of his lungs. The doctor had found it fully exposed, the lungs flanking it wrinkled lumps less than a third their natural bulk. Not only they, but the left heart and the superior mediastinal veins— all the regions that should have been grossly engorged with blood —were utterly drained of it.

The doctor swallowed his drink and got out the photographs again. He found that Jackson had died on his stomach across the body of another worker, with the upper part of a third trapped between them. Neither these two subjacent corpses nor the surrounding earth showed any stain of a blood loss that must have amounted to two liters.

Possibly the pictures, by some trick of shadow, had failed to pick it up. He turned to the Investigator's Report, where Craven would surely have mentioned any significant amounts of bloody earth uncovered during the disinterment. The sheriff recorded nothing of the kind. Dr. Winters returned to the pictures.

Ronald Pollock, Jackson's most intimate associate in the grave, had died on his back, beneath and slightly askew of Jackson, placing most of their torsos in contact, save where the head and shoulder of the third interposed. It seemed inconceivable Pollock's clothing should lack any trace of such massive drainage from a death mate thus embraced.

The doctor rose abruptly, pulled on fresh gloves, and returned to Jackson. His hands showed a more brutal speed now, closing the great incision temporarily with a few widely spaced sutures. He replaced him in the vault and brought out Pollock, striding, heaving hard at the dead shapes in the shifting of them, thrusting always—so it seemed to him—just a step ahead of urgent thoughts he did not want to have, deformities that whispered at his back, emitting faint, chill gusts of putrid breath. He shook his head—denying, delaying—and pushed the new corpse onto the worktable. The scissors undressed Pollock in greedy bites.

But at length, when he had scanned each scrap of fabric and found nothing like the stain of blood, he came to rest again, relinquishing that simplest, desired resolution he had made such haste to reach. He stood at the instrument table, not seeing it, submitting to the approach of the half-formed things at his mind's periphery.

The revelation of Jackson's shriveled lungs had been more than a shock. He felt a stab of panic too, in fact that same curiously explicit terror of this place that had urged him to flee earlier. He acknowledged now that the germ of that quickly suppressed terror had been a premonition of this failure to find any trace of the missing blood. Whence the premonition? It had to do with a problem he had steadfastly refused to consider: the mechanics of so complete a drainage of the lungs' densely reticulated vascular structure. Could the earth's crude pressure by itself work so thoroughly, given only a single vent both slender and strangely curved? And then the photograph he had studied. It frightened him now to recall the image—some covert meaning stirred within it, struggling to be seen. Dr. Winters picked the probe up from the table and turned again to the corpse. As surely and exactly as if he had already ascertained the wound's presence, he leaned forward and touched it: a small, neat puncture, just beneath the xiphoid process. He introduced the probe. The wound received it deeply, in a familiar direction.

The doctor went to the desk, and took up the photograph again. Pollock's and Jackson's wounded areas were not in contact. The third man's head was sandwiched between their bodies at just that point. He searched out another picture, in which this third man was more central, and found his name inked in below his image: Joe Allen.

Dreamingly, Dr. Winters went to the wide metal door, shoved it aside, entered the vault. He did not search, but went straight to the trestle where his friend had paused some hours before, and found the same name on its tag.

The body, beneath decay's spurious obesity, was trim and well-muscled. The face was square-cut, shelf-browed, with a vulpine nose skewed by an old fracture. The swollen tongue lay behind the teeth, and the bulge of decomposition did not obscure what the man's initial impact must have been—handsome and open, his now-waxen black eyes sly and convivial. Say, good buddy, got a minute? I see you comin' on the swing shift every day, don't I? Yeah, Joe Allen. Look, I know it's late, you want to get home, tell the wife you ain't been in there drinkin' since you got off, right? Oh, yeah, I heard that. But this damn disappearance thing's got me so edgy, and I'd swear to God just as I was coming here I seen someone moving around back of that frame house up the street. See how the trees thin out a little down back of the yard, where the moonlight gets in? That's right. Well, I got me this little popper here. Oh, yeah, that's a beauty, we'll have it covered between us. I knew I could spot a man ready for some trouble—couldn't find a patrol car anywhere on the street. Yeah, just down in here now, to that clump of pine. Step careful, you can barely see. That's right. . . .

The doctor's face ran with sweat. He turned on his heel and walked out of the vault, heaving the door shut behind him. In the office's greater warmth he felt the perspiration soaking his shirt under the smock. His stomach rasped with steady oscillations of pain, but he scarcely attended it. He went to Pollock and seized up the post-mortem knife.

The work was done with surreal speed, the laminae of flesh and bone recoiling smoothly beneath his desperate but unerring hands, until the thoracic cavity lay exposed, and in it, the vampire-stricken lungs, two gnarled lumps of grey tissue.

He searched no deeper, knowing what the heart and veins would show. He returned to sit at the desk, weakly drooping, the knife, forgotten, still in his left hand. He looked at the window, and it seemed his thoughts originated with that fainter, more tenuous Dr. Winters hanging like a ghost outside.

What was this world he lived in? Surely, in a lifetime, he had not begun to guess. To feed in such a way! There was horror enough in this alone. But to feed thus *in his own grave*. How had he accomplished it—leaving aside how he had fought suffocation long enough to do anything at all? How was it to be comprehended, a greed that raged so hotly it would glut itself at the very threshold of its own destruction? That last feast was surely in his stomach still.

Dr. Winters looked at the photograph, at Allen's head snugged into the others' middles like a hungry suckling nuzzling to the sow. Then he looked at the knife in his hand. The hand felt empty of all technique. Its one impulse was to slash, cleave, obliterate the remains of this gluttonous thing, this Joe Allen. He must do this, or flee it utterly. There was no course between. He did not move.

"I *will* examine him," said the ghost in the glass, and did not move. Inside the refrigerator vault, there was a slight noise.

No. It had been some hitch in the generator's murmur. Nothing in there could move. There was another noise, a brief friction against the vault's inner wall. The two old men shook their heads at one another. A catch clicked and the metal door slid open. Behind the staring image of his own amazement, the doctor saw that a filthy shape stood in the doorway and raised its arms towards him in a gesture of supplication. The doctor turned in his chair. From the shape came a whistling groan, the decayed fragment of a human voice.

Pleadingly, Joe Allen worked his jaw and spread his purple hands. As if speech were a maggot struggling to emerge from his mouth, the blue, tumescent face toiled, the huge tongue wallowed helplessly between the viscid lips.

The doctor reached for the telephone, lifted the receiver. Its deadness to his ear meant nothing—he could not have spoken. The thing confronting him, with each least movement that it made, destroyed the very frame of sanity in which words might have meaning, reduced the world itself around him to a waste of dark and silence, a starlit ruin where already, everywhere, the alien and unimaginable was awakening to its new dominion. The corpse raised and reached out one hand as if to stay him—turned, and walked towards the instrument table. Its legs were leaden, it rocked its shoulders like a swimmer, fighting to make its passage through gravity's dense medium. It reached the table and grasped it exhaustedly. The doctor found himself on his feet, crouched slightly, weightlessly still. The knife in his hand was the only part of himself he clearly felt, and it was like a tongue of fire, a crematory flame. Joe Allen's corpse thrust one hand among the instruments. The thick fingers, with a queer, simian ineptitude, brought up a scalpel. Both hands clasped the little handle and plunged the blade between the lips, as a thirsty child might a popsicle, then jerked it out again, slashing the tongue. Turbid fluid splashed down to the floor. The jaw worked stiffly, the mouth brought out words in a wet, ragged hiss:

"Please. Help me. Trapped in *this*." One dead hand struck the dead chest. "Starving."

"What are you?"

"Traveler. Not of earth."

"An eater of human flesh. A drinker of human blood."

"No. No. Hiding only. Am small. Shape hideous to you. Feared death."

"You brought death." The doctor spoke with the calm of perfect disbelief, himself as incredible to him as the thing he spoke with. It shook its head, the dull, popped eyes glaring with an agony of thwarted expression.

"Killed none. Hid in this. Hid in this not to be killed. Five days now. Drowning in decay. Free me. Please."

"No. You have come to feed on us, you are not hiding in fear. We are your food, your meat and drink. You fed on those two men within your grave. *Their* grave. For you, a delay. In fact, a diversion that has ended the hunt for you."

"No! No! Used men already dead. For me, five days, starvation. Even less. Fed only from necessity. Horrible necessity!"

The spoiled vocal instrument made a mangled gasp of the last word—an inhuman, snakepit noise the doctor felt as a cold flicker of ophidian tongues within his ears—while the dead arms moved in a sodden approximation of the body language that swears truth.

"No," the doctor said. "You killed them all. Including your . . . tool—this man. *What are you?*" Panic erupted in the question which he tried to bury by answering himself instantly. "Resolute, yes. That surely. You used death for an escape route. You need no oxygen perhaps."

"Extracted more than my need from gasses of decay. A lesser component of our metabolism."

The voice was gaining distinctness, developing makeshifts for tones lost in the agonal rupturing of the valves and stops of speech, more effectively wrestling vowel and consonant from the putrid tongue and lips. At the same time the body's crudity of movement did not quite obscure a subtle, incessant experimentation. Fingers flexed and stirred, testing the give of tendons, groping the palm for the old points of purchase and counter-pressure there. The knees, with cautious repetitions, assessed the new limits of their articulation.

"What was the sphere?"

"My ship. Its destruction our first duty facing discovery." (Fear touched the doctor, like a slug climbing his neck; he had seen, as it spoke, a sharp, spastic activity of the tongue, a pleating and shrinkage of its bulk as at the tug of some inward adjustment.) "No chance to re-enter. Leaving this take far too long. Not even time to set for destruct—must extrude a cilium, chemical key to broach hull shield. In shaft my only chance to halt host."

The right arm tested the wrist, and the scalpel the hand still held cut white sparks from the air, while the word "host" seemed itself a little knife-prick, a teasing abandonment of fiction—though the dead mask showed no irony—preliminary to attack.

But he found that fear had gone from him. The impossibility with which he conversed, and was about to struggle, was working in him an overwhelming amplification of his life's long helpless rage at death. He found his parochial pity for earth alone stretched to the trans-stellar scope this traveler commanded, to the whole cosmic trashyard with its bulldozed multitudes of corpses; galactic wheels of carnage—stars, planets with their most majestic generations—all trash, cracked bones and foul rags that pooled, settled, reconcatenated in futile symmetries gravid with new multitudes of briefly animate trash.

And this, standing before him now, was the death it was given him particularly to deal—his mite was being called in by the universal Treasury of death, and Dr. Winters found himself, an old healer, on fire to pay. His own, more lethal blade, tugged at his hand with its own sharp appetite. He felt entirely the Examiner once more, knew the precise cuts he would make, swiftly and without error. *Very soon now,* he thought and cooly probed for some further insight before its onslaught:

"Why must your ship be destroyed, even at the cost of your host's life?"

"We must not be understood."

"The livestock must not understand what is devouring them."

"Yes, doctor. Not all at once. But one by one. You will under-stand what is devouring you. That is essential to my feast."

The doctor shook his head. "You are in your grave already, Traveler. That body will be your coffin. You will be buried in it a second time, for all time."

The thing came one step nearer and opened its mouth. The flabby throat wrestled as with speech, but what sprang out was a slender white filament, more than whip-fast. Dr. Winters saw only the first flicker of its eruption, and then his brain nova-ed, thin-ning out at light-speed to a white nullity.

When the doctor came to himself, it was in fact to a part of himself only. Before he had opened his eyes he found that his wakened mind had repossessed proprioceptively only a bizarre truncation of his body. His head, neck, left shoulder, arm and hand declared themselves—the rest was silence.

When he opened his eyes, he found that he lay supine on the gurney, and naked. Something propped his head. A strap bound his left elbow to the gurney's edge, a strap he could feel. His chest was also anchored by a strap, and this he could not feel. Indeed, save for its active remnant, his entire body might have been bound in a block of ice, so numb was it, and so powerless was he to compel the slightest movement from the least part of it.

The room was empty, but from the open door of the vault there came slight sounds: the creak and soft frictions of heavy tarpaulin shifted to accommodate some business involving small clicking and kissing noises.

Tears of fury filled the doctor's eyes. Clenching his one fist at the starry engine of creation that he could not see, he ground his teeth and whispered in the hot breath of strangled weeping:

"Take it back, this dirty little shred of life! I throw it off gladly like the filth it is." The slow knock of bootsoles loudened from within the vault, and he turned his head. From the vault door Joe Allen's corpse approached him.

It moved with new energy, though its gait was grotesque, a ducking, hitching progress, jerky with circumventions of decayed muscle, while above this galvanized, struggling frame, the bruise-colored face hung inanimate, an image of detachment. With terrible clarity it revealed the thing for what it was—a damaged hand-puppet vigorously worked from within. And when that frozen face was brought to hang above the doctor, the reeking hands, with the light, solicitous touch of friends at sickbeds, rested on his naked thigh.

The absence of sensation made the touch more dreadful than if felt. It showed him that the nightmare he still desperately denied at heart had annexed his body while he—holding head and arm free—had already more than half-drowned in its mortal paralysis. There lay his nightmare part, a nothingness freely possessed by an unspeakability. The corpse said:

"Rotten blood. Thin nourishment. Only one hour alone before you came. Fed from neighbor to my left—barely had strength to extend siphon. Fed from the right while you worked. Tricky going —you are alert. Expected Dr. Parsons. Energy needs of animating this"—one hand left the doctor's thigh and smote the dusty overalls—"and of host-transfer, very high. Once I have you synapsed, will be near starvation again."

A sequence of unbearable images unfolded in the doctor's mind, even as the robot carrion turned from the gurney and walked to the instrument table: the sheriff's arrival just after dawn, alone of course, since Craven always took thought for his deputies' rest and because on this errand he would want privacy to consider any indiscretion on behalf of the miners' survivors that the situation might call for; his finding his old friend, supine and alarmingly weak; his hurrying over, his leaning near. Then, somewhat later, a police car containing a rack of still wet bones might plunge off the highway above some deep spot in the gorge.

The corpse took an evidence box from the table and put the scalpel in it. Then it turned and retrieved the mortuary knife from the floor and put that in as well, saying as it did so, without turning, "The sheriff will come in the morning. You spoke like close friends. He will probably come alone."

The coincidence with his thoughts had to be accident, but the intent to terrify and appall him was clear. The tone and timing of that patched-up voice were unmistakably deliberate—sly probes that sought his anguish specifically, sought his mind's personal center. He watched the corpse—back at the table—dipping an apish but accurate hand and plucking up rib shears, scissors, clamps, adding all to the box. He stared, momentarily emptied by shock of all but the will to know finally the full extent of the horror that had appropriated his life. Joe Allen's body carried the box to the worktable beside the gurney, and the expressionless eyes met the doctor's.

"I have gambled. A grave gamble. But now I have won. At risk of personal discovery we are obliged to disconnect, contract, hide as well as possible in host body. Suicide in effect. I disregarded situational imperatives, despite starvation before disinterment and subsequent autopsy all but certain. I caught up with crew, tackled Pollock and Jackson microseconds before blast. Computed five days' survival from this cache, could disconnect at limit of strength to do so, but otherwise would chance autopsy, knowing doctor was alcoholic incompetent. And now see my gain. You are a prize host, can feed with near impunity even when killing too dangerous. Safe meals delivered to you still warm."

The corpse had painstakingly aligned the gurney parallel to the worktable but offset, the table's foot extending past the gurney's, and separated from it by a distance somewhat less than the reach of Joe Allen's right arm. Now the dead hands distributed the implements along the right edge of the table, save for the scissors and the box. These the corpse took to the table's foot, where it set down the box and slid the scissors' jaws round one strap of its overalls. It began to speak again, and as it did, the scissors dismembered its cerements in unhesitating strokes.

"The cut must be medical, forensically right, though a smaller one easier. Must be careful of the pectoral muscles or arms will not convey me. I am no larva anymore—over fifteen hundred grams."

To ease the nightmare's suffocating pressure, to thrust out some flicker of his own will against its engulfment, the doctor flung a question, his voice more cracked than the other's now was:

"Why is my arm free?"

"The last, fine neural splicing needs a sensory-motor standard, to perfect my brain's fit to yours. Lacking this eye-hand coordinating check, much coarser motor control of host. This done, I flush out the paralytic, unbind us, and we are free together."

The grave-clothes had fallen in a puzzle of fragments, and the cadaver stood naked, its dark, gas-rounded contours making it seem some sleek marine creature, ruddered with the black-veined, gas-distended sex. Again the voice had teased for his fear, had uttered the last word with a savoring protraction, and now the doctor's cup of anguish brimmed over; horror and outrage wrenched his spirit in brutal alternation as if trying to tear it naked from its captive frame. He rolled his head in this deadlock, his mouth beginning to split with the slow birth of a mind-emptying outcry.

The corpse watched this, giving a single nod that might have been approbation. Then it mounted the worktable and, with the concentrated caution of some practiced convalescent reentering his bed, lay on its back. The dead eyes again sought the living and found the doctor staring back, grinning insanely.

"Clever corpse!" the doctor cried. "Clever, carnivorous corpse! Able alien! Please don't think I'm criticizing. Who am I to criticize? A mere arm and shoulder, a talking head, just a small piece of a pathologist. But I'm confused." He paused, savoring the monster's attentive silence and his own buoyancy in the hysterical levity that had unexpectedly liberated him. "You're going to use your puppet there to pluck you out of itself and put you on me. But once he's pulled you from your driver's seat, won't he go dead, so to speak, and drop you? You could get a nasty knock. Why not set a plank between the tables—the puppet opens the door, and you scuttle, ooze, lurch, flop, slither, as the case may be, across the bridge. No messy spills. And in any case, isn't this an odd, rather clumsy way to get around among your cattle? Shouldn't you at least carry your own scalpels when you travel? There's always the risk you'll run across that one host in a million that isn't carrying one with him."

He knew his gibes would be answered to his own despair. He exulted, but solely in the momentary bafflement of the predator— in having, for just a moment, mocked its gloating assurance to silence and marred its feast.

Its right hand picked up the post-mortem knife beside it, and the left wedged a roll of gauze beneath Allen's neck, lifting the throat to a more prominent arch. The mouth told the ceiling:

"We retain larval form till entry of the host. As larvae we have locomotor structures, and sense-buds usable outside our ships' sensory amplifiers. I waited coiled round Ed Sykes' bed leg till night, entered by his mouth as he slept." Allen's hand lifted the knife, held it high above the dull, quick eyes, turning it in the light. "Once lodged, we have three instars to adult form," the voice continued absently—the knife might have been a mirror from which the corpse read its features. "Larvally we have only a sketch of our full neural tap. Our metamorphosis is cued and determined by the host's endosomatic ecology. I matured in three days." Allen's wrist flexed, tipping the knife's point downmost. "Most supreme adaptations are purchased at the cost of inessential capacities." The elbow pronated and slowly flexed, hooking the knife body-wards. "Our hosts are all sentients, eco-dominants, are already carrying the baggage of coping structures for the plane-tary environment. Limbs, sensory portals"—the fist planted the fang of its tool under the chin, tilted it and rode it smoothly down the throat, the voice proceeding unmarred from under the furrow that the steel ploughed—"somatic envelopes, instrumentalities"—down the sternum, diaphragm, abdomen the stainless blade painted its stripe of gaping, muddy tissue—"with a host's brain we inherit all these, the mastery of any planet, netted in its dominant's cere-bral nexus. Thus our genetic codings are now all but disencum-bered of such provisions."

So swiftly the doctor flinched, Joe Allen's hand slashed four lateral cuts from the great wound's axis. The seeming butchery left two flawlessly drawn thoracic flaps cleanly outlined. The left hand raised the left flap's hem, and the right coaxed the knife into the aperture, deepening it with small stabs and slices. The posture was a man's who searches a breast pocket, with the dead eyes studying the slow recoil of flesh. The voice, when it resumed, had geared up to an intenser pitch:

"Galactically, the chordate nerve/brain paradigm abounds, and the neural labyrinth is our dominion. Are we to make plank bridges and worm across them to our food? Are cockroaches greater than we for having legs to run up walls and antennae to grope their way! All the quaint, hinged crutches that life sports! The stilts, fins, fans, springs, stalks, flippers and feathers, all in turn so vari-ously terminating in hooks, clamps, suckers, scissors, forks or little cages of digits! And besides all the gadgets it concocts for wrestling through its worlds, it is all knobbed, whiskered, crested, plumed, vented, spiked or measeled over with perceptual gear for combing pittances of noise or color from the environing plenitude."

Invincibly calm and sure, the hands traded tool and tasks. The right flap eased back, revealing ropes of ingeniously spared muscle while promising a genuine appearance once sutured back in place. Helplessly the doctor felt his delirious defiance bleed away and a bleak fascination rebind him.

"We are the taps and relays that share the host's aggregate of afferent nerve-impulse precisely at its nodes of integration. We are the brains that peruse these integrations, integrate them with our existing banks of host-specific data, and, lastly, let their consequences flow down the motor pathway—either the consequences they seek spontaneously, or those we wish to graft upon them. We are besides a streamlined alimentary/circulatory system and a reproductive apparatus. And more than this we need not be."

The corpse had spread its bloody vest, and the feculent hands now took up the rib shears. The voice's sinister coloration of pitch and stress grew yet more marked—the phrases slid from the tongue with a cobra's seeking sway, winding their liquid rhythms round the doctor till a gap in his resistance should let them pour through to slaughter the little courage left him.

"For in this form we have inhabited the densest brainweb of three hundred races, lain intricately snug within them like thriving vine on trelliswork. We've looked out from too many variously windowed masks to regret our own vestigial senses. None read their worlds definitely. Far better then, our nomad's range and choice, than an unvarying tenancy of one poor set of structures. Far better to slip on as we do whole living beings and wear at once all of their limbs and organs, memories and powers—wear all as tightly congruent to our wills as a glove is to the hand that fills it."

The shears clipped through the gristle, stolid, bloody jaws monotonously feeding, stopping short of the sterno-clavicular joint in the manubrium where the muscles of the pectoral girdle have an important anchorage.

"No consciousness of the chordate type that we have found has been impermeable to our finesse—no dendritic pattern so elaborate we could not read its stitchwork and thread ourselves to match, precisely map its each synaptic seam till we could loosen it and retailor all to suit ourselves. We have strutted costumed in the bodies of planetary autarchs, venerable manikins of moral fashion, but cut of the universal cloth: the weave of fleet electric filaments of experience which we easily re-shuttled to the warp of our wishes. Whereafter—newly hemmed and gathered—their living fabric hung obedient to our bias, investing us with honor and influence unlimited."

The tricky verbal melody, through the corpse's deft, unfaltering self-dismemberment—the sheer neuromuscular orchestration of the compound activity—struck Dr. Winters with the detached enthrallment great keyboard performers could bring him. He glimpsed the alien's perspective—a Gulliver waiting in a brobdingnagian grave, then marshalling a dead giant against a living, like a dwarf in a huge mechanical crane, feverishly programming combat on a battery of levers and pedals, waiting for the robot arms' enactments, the remote, titanic impact of the foes—and he marveled, filled with a bleak wonder at life's infinite strategy and plasticity. Joe Allen's hands reached into his half-opened abdominal cavity, reached deep below the uncut anterior muscle that was exposed by the shallow, spurious incision of the epidermis, till by external measure they were extended far enough to be touching his thighs. The voice was still as the forearms advertised a delicate rummaging with the buried fingers. The shoulders drew back. As the steady withdrawal brought the wrists into view, the dead legs tremored and quaked with diffuse spasms.

"You called your kind our food and drink, doctor. If you were merely that, an elementary usurpation of your motor tracts alone would satisfy us, give us perfect cattle-control—for what rarest word or subtlest behavior is more than a flurry of varied muscles? That trifling skill was ours long ago. It is not mere blood that feeds this lust I feel now to tenant you, this craving for an intimacy that years will not stale. My truest feast lies in compelling you to feed in that way and in the utter deformation of your will this will involve. Had gross nourishment been my prime need, then my gravemates—Pollock and Jackson—could have eked out two weeks of life for me or more. But I scorned a cowardly parsimony in the face of death. I reinvested more than half the energy that their blood gave me in fabricating chemicals to keep their brains alive, and fluid-bathed with oxygenated nutriment."

Out of the chasmed midriff the smeared hands dragged two long tresses of silvery filament that writhed and sparkled with a million simultaneous coilings and contractions. The legs jittered with faint, chaotic pulses throughout their musculature, until the bright, vermiculate tresses had gathered into two spheric masses which the hands laid carefully within the incision. Then the legs lay still as death.

"I had accessory neural taps only to spare, but I could access much memory, and all of their cognitive responses, and having in my banks all the organ of Corti's electrochemical conversions of English words, I could whisper anything to them directly into the eighth cranial nerve. Those are our true feast, doctor, such bodiless electric storms of impotent cognition as I tickled up in those two little bone globes. I was forced to drain them yesterday, just before disinterment. They lived till then and understood everything —*everything* I did to them."

When the voice paused, the dead and living eyes were locked together. They remained so a moment, and then the dead face smiled.

It recapitulated all the horror of Allen's first resurrection—this waking of expressive soul from those grave-mound contours. And it was a demon-soul the doctor saw awaken: the smile was barbed with fine, sharp hooks of cruelty at the corners of the mouth, while the barbed eyes beamed fond, langorous anticipation of his pain. Remotely, Dr. Winters heard the flat sound of his own voice asking:

"And Eddie Sykes?"

"Oh, yes, doctor. He is with us now, has been throughout. I grieve to abandon so rare a host! He is a true hermit-philosopher, well-read in four languages. He is writing a translation of Marcus Aurelius—he was, I mean, in his free time. . . ."

Long minutes succeeded of the voice accompanying the surreal self-autopsy, but the doctor lay stilled, emptied of reactive power. Still, the full understanding of his fate reverberated in his mind— an empty room through which the voice, not heard exactly but somehow implanted directly as in the subterranean torture it had just described, sent aftershocks of realization, amplifications of the Unspeakable.

The parasite had traced and tapped the complex interface between cortical integration of input and the consequent neural output shaping response. It had interposed its brain between, sharing consciousness while solely commanding the pathways of reaction. The host, the bottled personality, was mute and limbless for any least expression of its own will, while hellishly articulate and agile in the service of the parasite's. It was the host's own hands that bound and wrenched the life half out of his prey, his own loins that experienced the repeated orgasms crowning his other despoliations of their bodies. And when they lay, bound and shrieking still, ready for the consummation, it was his own strength that hauled the smoking entrails from them, and his own intimate tongue and guzzling mouth he plunged into the rank, palpitating feast.

And the doctor had glimpses of the history behind this preda- tion, that of a race so far advanced in the essentializing, the in- exorable abstraction of their own mental fabric that through scientific commitment and genetic self-cultivation they had come to embody their own model of perfected consciousness, stream- lined to permit the entry of other beings and the direct acquisition of their experiential worlds. All strictest scholarship at first, until there matured in the disembodied scholars their long-germinal and now blazing, jealous hatred for all "lesser" minds rooted and clothed in the soil and sunlight of solid, particular worlds. The parasite spoke of the "cerebral music," the "symphonies of ago- nized paradox" that were its invasion's chief plunder. The doctor felt the truth behind this grandiloquence: its actual harvest from the systematic violation of encoffined personalities was the experi- ence of a barren supremacy of means over lives more primitive, perhaps, but vastly wealthier in the vividness and passionate con- cern with which life for them was imbued.

Joe Allen's hands had scooped up the bunched skeins of alien nerve, with the wrinkled brain-node couched admidst them, and for some time had waited the slow retraction of a last major trunk- line which seemingly had followed the spine's axis. At last, when only a slender subfiber of this remained implanted, the corpse, smiling once more, held up for him to view its reconcatenated master. The doctor looked into its eyes then and spoke—not to their controller, but to the captive who shared them with it, and who now, the doctor knew, neared his final death.

"Goodbye, Joe Allen. Eddie Sykes. You are guiltless. Peace be with you at last."

The demon smile remained fixed, the right hand reached its viscid cargo across the gap and over the doctor's groin. He watched the hand set the glittering medusa's head—his new self—upon his flesh, return to the table, take up the scalpel, and reach back to cut in his groin a four-inch incision—all in eerie absence of tactile stimulus. The line that had remained plunged into the corpse suddenly whipped free of the mediastinal crevice, retracted across the gap and shortened to a taut stub on the seething organism atop the doctor.

Joe Allen's body collapsed, emptied, all slack. He was a corpse again entirely, but with one anomalous feature to his posture. His right arm had not dropped to the nearly vertical hang that would have been natural. At the instant of the alien's unplugging, the shoulder had given a fierce shrug and wrenching of its angle, flinging the arm upward as it died so that it now lay in the orientation of an arm that reaches up for a ladder's next rung. The slightest tremor would unfix the joints and dump the arm back into the gravitational bias; it would also serve to dump the scalpel from the proferred, upturned palm that implement still precariously occupied.

The man had repossessed himself one microsecond before his end. The doctor's heart stirred, woke, and sang within him, for he saw that the scalpel was just in reach of his fingers at his forearm's fullest stretch from the bound elbow. The horror crouched on him and, even now slowly feeding its trunkline into his groin incision, at first stopped the doctor's hand with a pang of terror. Then he reminded himself that, until implanted, the enemy was a senseless mass, bristling with plugs, with input jacks for senses, but, until installed in the physical amplifiers of eyes and ears, an utterly deaf, blind monad that waited in a perfect solipsism between two captive sensory envelopes.

He saw his straining fingers above the bright tool of freedom, thought with an insane smile of God and Adam on the Sistine ceiling, and then, with a lifespan of surgeon's fine control, plucked up the scalpel. The arm fell and hung.

"Sleep," the doctor said. "Sleep revenged."

But he found his retaliation harshly reined-in by the alien's careful provisions. His elbow had been fixed with his upper arm almost at right angles to his body's long axis; his forearm could reach his hand inward and present it closely to the face, suiting the parasite's need of an eye-hand coordinative check, but could not, even with the scalpel's added reach, bring its point within four inches of his groin. Steadily the parasite fed in its tapline. It would usurp motor control in three or four minutes at most, to judge by the time its extrication from Allen had taken.

Frantically the doctor bent his wrist inwards to its limit, trying to pick through the strap where it crossed his inner elbow. Sufficient pressure was impossible, and the hold so awkward that even feeble attempts threatened the loss of the scalpel. Smoothly the root of alien control sank into him. It was a defenseless thing of jelly against which he lay lethally armed, and he was still doomed—a preview of all his thrall's impotence-to-be.

But of course there was a way. Not to survive. But to escape, and to have vengeance. For a moment he stared at his captor, hardening his mettle in the blaze of hate it lit in him. Then, swiftly, he determined the order of his moves, and began.

He reached the scalpel to his neck and opened his superior thyroid vein—his inkwell. He laid the scalped by his ear, dipped his finger in his blood, and began to write on the metal surface of the gurney, beginning by his thigh and moving towards his armpit. Oddly, the incision of his neck, though this was muscularly awake, had been painless, which gave him hopes that raised his courage for what remained to do. His neat, sparing strokes scribed with ghastly legibility.

When he had done the message read:

> MIND PARASITE
> FM ALLEN IN ME
> CUT *all* TILL FIND
> 1500 GM MASS
> NERVE FIBRE

He wanted to write goodbye to his friend, but the alien had begun to pay out smaller, auxiliary filaments collaterally with the main one, and all now lay in speed.

He took up the scalpel, rolled his head to the left, and plunged the blade deep in his ear.

Miracle! Last, accidental mercy! It was painless. Some procedural, highly specific anesthetic was in effect. With careful plunges, he obliterated the right inner ear and then thrust silence, with equal thoroughness, into the left. The slashing of the vocal chords followed, then the tendons in the back of the neck that hold it erect. He wished he were free to unstring knees and elbows too, but it could not be. But blinded, with centers of balance lost, with only rough motor control—all these conditions should fetter the alien's escape, should it in the first place manage the reanimation of a bloodless corpse in which it had not yet achieved a fine-tuned interweave. Before he extinguished his eyes, he paused, the scalpel poised above his face, and blinked them to clear his aim of tears. The right, then the left, both retinas meticulously carved away, the yolk of vision quite scooped out of them. The scalpel's last task, once it had tilted the head sideways to guide the bloodflow absolutely clear of possible effacement of the message, was to slash the external carotid artery.

When this was done the old man sighed with relief and laid his scalpel down. Even as he did so, he felt the deep, inward prickle of an alien energy—something that flared, crackled, flared, *groped for* but did not quite find its purchase. And inwardly, as the doctor sank towards sleep—cerebrally, as a voiceless man must speak—he spoke to the parasite these carefully chosen words:

"Welcome to your new house. I'm afraid there's been some vandalism—the lights don't work, and the plumbing has a very bad leak. There are some other things wrong as well—the neighborhood is perhaps a little *too* quiet, and you may find it hard to get around very easily. But it's been a lovely home to me for fifty-seven years, and somehow I think you'll stay. . . ."

The face, turned towards the body of Joe Allen, seemed to weep scarlet tears, but its last movement before death was to smile.

This competition asked readers to submit short poems or limericks about fantastic or science fictional animals.

From Competition 25: Short Poems about SF Animals

THE *SIPPLE*

The *Sipple* is an alien critter
Resembling most a raw corn fritter,
With seven eyes, ingestion hole,
And tentacles as black as coal.
It doesn't gambol (take no bets!),
Excretes dry waste (it *never* wets).
Its sex is nebulous sensation;
No organs there for procreation.
It moves along without a ripple,
Pushed by the dangling part of *Sipple*.

—Rachel Cosgrove Payes
Shrub Oak, N.Y.

THE WUD

Beware the Wud, its ragged teeth
Can grind you into burgered beef.
Its habits are a gross disgrace.
(It wets itself in hyperspace.)
At seven hundred light years long,
When argued with, is never wrong.

—Mike DeSimone
Upper Darby, Pa.

CONKEW

The Conkew is a creature
With a most peculiar feature
Not found in beasts of any other kind.
With its mate, it binds securely
But for life, resulting purely
In one animal known as the Conkew-bind.

—Pat Cadigan
Kansas City, Kans.

THE FLEFFEL

The fleffel runs on ceilings.
The fleffel sticks to walls.
Its skin is apple-peelings.
Its eyes are tennis balls.

The fleffel barks like bongo drums.
It nests in chandeliers.
Its favorite foods are pork and plums
And science-fictioneers.

—Bruce Berges
Lennox, Calif.

There was a young man in the dark
who thought he was hunting the Snark;
   but his time-machine slipped—
   the continuum flipped
and his Boojum, he found, was a Quark.

—Mary C. Pangborn
Woodstock, N.Y.

Hunters have found that the
Martian Jobliloquy's
quite a discouraging
trophy to seek.

How do you catch something
quadridimensional?
—all that it does is
regress for a week.

—Sebastian Robinson
Glasgow, Scotland

F&SF *has published several highly original and entertaining stories by Neal Barrett. His latest tale takes place on a planet called Far, and it begins in a manner as cozy and familiar as its title. Where it ends is somewhere else indeed.*

NEAL BARRETT, JR.

"A Day at the Fair"

WE weren't even past Hummer's Hill and I could smell it already. Beanspice and weed-cake and a hundred other yum things to eat. The smells were floating up from all the little stands and cookpits and coming right out to meet us.

"I can smell it, Grandpa. I can smell the Fair!"

Grandpa just laughed. "We're getting mighty close, Toony, but I didn't figure we was *smellin'* close."

"Toony's always doing things 'fore she's supposed to," said Lizbeth Jean. I glared back at the wagon but Lizbeth Jean just nudged up to Mother and looked the other way.

I *do* kind of catch stuff sometimes, and Lizbeth Jean knows it. Just little things, like smells, or maybe who's coming over. Not even Grandpa knows about that, and he knows near everything.

Folks never can get over me and Lizbeth Jean. If you were looking for kids that didn't have any business being sisters, you'd come straight to us. She's about the prettiest girl on Far, and I'm near the plainest. Lizbeth Jean's got skin like brand new milk, and gold-silky hair down to here. My hair looks like it come out of a armpit somewhere, and I'm fat as a bubble.

All you got to do is set Lizbeth Jean and Mother up side by side to see where she got her good looks—including my share. Grandpa says Mother was more'n just pretty, before whatever it was happened to Papa and she kind of quit thinking real good. Papa's something nobody talks about much at our place.

When we came 'round Hummer's Hill a whole flock of Snappers waddled across the road and started hissing and grinding their jaws real fierce. Grandpa whacked a couple good and they scattered off quick. Snappers can't do much more'n scare you, but they do a pretty fair job of that. So while Grandpa was shooin' them off, I dropped back to where Tyrone was pulling the wagon.

Grandpa named him Tyrone after some kind of Earthie hero— only he couldn't have been one of your real big heroes if he was anything like Tyrone. According to Grandpa, he looks a lot like a big skinny anteater with the mange. Grandpa's always saying things look like something I haven't ever seen before.

"Tyrone," I said, "you goin' to have fun at the Fair?"

"Guess so," said Tyrone.

"You got some coppers, don't you?" I knew he did, 'cause Grandpa gave him some.

"Don't know," said Tyrone.

"Sure you do." I patted the little pouch around his neck. "Right in there, Tyrone. Five big shiny new coppers. Just like last year."

"Last year?" Tyrone blinked and looked dumber than ever. That's the trouble with Noords. They work real good and do what you tell 'em, but forget what it was in about a minute.

I could *really* smell the Fair, now. Not just the other way. There was bushdog cracklin' over a fire and Ting-root pie and dusty sweet-cakes yellow as the sky. "Do you smell it, Grandpa? Do you smell it *now?*"

"Toony, I sure do," said Grandpa. He closed his eyes and sniffed real good.

"What do you smell, Grandpa? Tell me!"

"I smell mustard and cotton candy, Toony. And popcorn and

cinnamon apples and lemonade so cold it makes your head hurt."

"Oh, Grandpa, you don't either," I scolded. "You're just makin' things up again."

"Guess maybe I am," said Grandpa.

Like always, I acted like a kid, trying to see sixteen things at once. As if they'd maybe close the whole Fair down if fat Toony didn't see it *right then.* There were flags and ribbons and bright strips of cloth everywhere you looked. There were reds and blues and greens and yellows and colors I hadn't even seen before. There were stands selling all kinds of pretties. And games where you knocked over pots, or caught a tin fish on a hook. And there were cockpits full of more sizzlin' bushdog than you could eat in a year, and toadberry tarts and stripe candy and hot fly-bread right out of the oven.

"Better watch out," said Lizbeth Jean real sweet-like. "You'll get fat, Toony."

"You can't *git* fat if you're fat already," I told her.

"*You* can," giggled Lizbeth Jean, and Grandpa said, "Now, now, we come to the Fair to have fun, girls," He stuck me on one side and Lizbeth Jean on the other, and left Tyrone to look after Mother. Which was a good idea, 'cause I've been known to bust Lizbeth Jean just for the fun of it.

There were people from all over, 'cause nobody misses the Fair. There were trappers from far as Southtown, and farmers like us from High, and even folks from the Crystal Hills. *They* don't hardly talk to each other, but they all came to the Fair.

I like just 'bout everything there is to see, but I guess I like the Patchmen best of all. That's because they got something new every year, and not the same old thing. And you never know what it's going to be, 'cause like Grandpa says, the Patchmen don't either. It's kinda whatever they happen on to, and fix up good. If there's a bunch of wars going on somewhere, the fleet dumps lots of old ships and stuff on Far. If there isn't much fighting, why, you don't get a lot of new things to see that year. So anyway, it's a good way to tell how the war's going.

"Grandpa, can we? Can we *please?*"

The sign was painted in big orange letters and said:

TALK TO YUR DEAR
DEPARTED LUVED ONES
2 COPPERS

On the wagon was a rusty old box colored speckledy gray. There wasn't anything on it but a worn-out knob and a little glass window.

"I don't know," said Grandpa, scowling real hard at the sign. "It's *two* coppers, Toony."

"Please," I begged, hanging on his hand, "do it, Grandpa!"

"Does the danged thing work?" Grandpa asked the Patchman. "Reckon it does, if you're chargin' two coppers for it."

"Sure does," said the Patchman. "Come right off a Bugship, out past Dingo." He grinned real sly at Grandpa. "Hear they give them hardbacks a whole bunch of new ancestors. Took out near a sector."

"Can't hardly burn too many," said Grandpa.

"Amen to that," said the Patchman, and looked right straight at me. I guess I was kind of staring, 'cause he was real interesting to look at. He had one good arm, and one bright silver, and a shiny glass head with bright ruby eyes. Course everyone knows the Patchmen were real Spacers 'fore they got banged up bad, which is how they get first pick of all the junk comes down. Grandpa says they don't much care 'bout going back home anymore, so they just hang around Far, or someplace else.

"Isn't nothing to it," the Patchman told Grandpa, "just hold that knob real tight and talk to anyone you want."

"Anyone?" asked Grandpa.

"Well, anyone that ain't still *breathin'* real good," winked the Patchman.

You could tell what Grandpa was thinking. He was thinking awful hard about Grandma, and whether he sure enough wanted to do this. I wasn't real surprised when the little round window blinked and went bright, and there was a man grinning out 'stead of Grandma. He was young, with old-timey hair and funny looking clothes.

"Well, I'll be damned," said Grandpa. "Jess—is that really you?"

"It's me all right," said the man. "You're looking right good, Doc."

"And you're looking a sight better'n *last* time I seen you, that's for sure."

The man laughed. "Not much sense staying eighty-nine. Not if you don't have to."

"No, guess not." Grandpa frowned at the little window and scratched his beard. "What's it like up there, Jess? I mean, they keep you busy and all?"

"Busy enough," said Jess. "There's lots to do, same as anywhere."

"I know damn well you aren't playing no *harp*."

"Never was much good at playin' things. Except maybe a little poker."

Grandpa made a face. "You wasn't *real* good at that, either. You know, I've thought about it some, being up there with all that time on your hands and not having something to do. It never did seem right to me, just switching from doin' to not d—"

Grandpa's face went white as flour. The man just kind of flicked out of sight, and there was this real pretty girl where he'd been.

"Hello, Doc. It's been a long time . . ."

Grandpa swallowed hard. "Mary, I—didn't want to do this."

"I know you didn't, Doc. And I know how hard it's got to be. I just had to see you, though."

"Well, I'm glad now you did. Real glad."

"You're looking fine, Doc."

"Oh, sure I am."

"No, really. Just as handsome as ever."

"I'm looking *old* is what I'm doing." He stopped a minute, and studied Grandma real hard. "I guess there's a lot of the old crowd up there," he said finally. "Folks we used to know and all."

"Sure is," said Grandma, "lots of 'em, Doc. Ellie's here, and Cora—you remember Cora?"

"Wasn't thinking 'bout *them*, Mary. Guess Will's there, and J. R., and course *Jess* is probably always hangin' around. I mean—"

"I *know* what you mean," smiled Grandma. "That isn't the way it is up here, Doc. It's not the same."

"Don't care where it is!" snapped Grandpa.

"Doc, don't do this, please."

"Well, damn it all anyway. I just—"

"Doc. . . ."

"I can't change, Mary, just 'cause you're there and I'm here. I—Mary? *Mary!*"

You could see Grandma saying something, but you couldn't tell what it was, and in a minute the little window went all dark again.

"Goddamn it," roared Grandpa. "It ain't right—carryin' on like that up *there!*"

"Guess they can do 'bout whatever they want," said the Patchman.

"Well, it ain't right, I'll tell you that right now. I—hellfire, what do *you* want, Tyrone?"

Tyrone was standing right behind him, his big sad eyes staring at the little round window.

"I don't think that's too good a idea," said the Patchman, trading a look with Grandpa.

"I have two coppers," said Tyrone.

"Fine," said Grandpa, "let's you and me and Toony see if we can find some stick candy somewhere, Tyrone."

"Have two coppers," said Tyrone.

"I know you do, Tyrone."

"I have—"

"Well, just spend 'em, then," said Grandpa. "Damned if you ain't stubborn. Even for a Noord!"

Tyrone carefully laid the worn and shiny coins in the Patchman's hand and wrapped his three stubby fingers around the knob. He stood real still and looked hard as he could into the window. In a minute, it got kind of dim and gray and cold looking, like the saddest winter day there ever was. Tyrone kept on trying, but there was nothing there to see but curly-gray fog, fading way way off into nowhere.

The Patchman looked at Grandpa, and Grandpa just shrugged and sort of turned Tyrone around real easy. "Guess it ain't working right, Tyrone. Come on, let's go get that candy."

"That's it for sure," said the Patchman. "Been having a lot of trouble with it lately. And I ain't going to keep your coppers, either. No, sir, you didn't get a fair look, you don't have to pay."

"See there," said Grandpa, "you got both your coppers back. How 'bout that now?"

"I guess," said Tyrone. He let me and Grandpa lead him away, but he kept looking back at the little round window just as long as he could.

Mother and Lizbeth Jean like to stand around and watch Trading, but it seems kind of dumb to me. Everybody's got 'bout the same as everybody else, but that doesn't seem to bother folks. They'll squat on the ground all day and swap blankets, pots, candles, ropes, dull knives and sourweed soup—the same stuff they make back home themselves. And if you squat around long enough, you can even get the same blanket back you made yourself last winter. It don't make a lot of sense, but what do I know?

The only real Trading goes on with the Patchmen, and they sure aren't interested in blankets and soup. What they want is girls and *Saba*-wings. That's about the only things worth lifting off Far. Too many girls get born here anyway, and *Saba*-moths go through wheat faster'n rain. Lizbeth Jean's thirteen and just right for selling, but Grandpa isn't ever going to do that. No matter how poor we get. And of course I don't have anything to worry 'bout. Patchmen aren't just real excited 'bout fat girls with hair like an armpit.

At noon, the sun got real hot and the sky turned close to silver. Like always, Grandpa made us go rest under the wagon till it got cooler, and, like always, me and Lizbeth Jean just whispered and giggled and punched each other the whole time. Mother kind of dozed, her face all slack and empty-looking. Grandpa curled up and started snoring, and Tyrone sat out in the sun boiling himself. Noords won't come into the shade for anything. Grandpa says it scares 'em to see the light go away. *I* think they're just too dumb to know better.

When we finally got up, and everybody was ready to go again, Grandpa said since it'd been a fairly good year and the *Saba*-moths hadn't eaten more than half the crop, maybe we could all get some real Fair-bought food for supper, 'stead of the flatcakes we'd packed in the wagon. Lizbeth Jean and me did a lot of squealing and dancing around, till Grandpa said maybe we wouldn't eat *anything* if everybody didn't shut up and behave.

Now, if anybody likes to eat, it's me, old bubble-gut Toony.

Grandpa says I can eat anything that don't eat me, and then go hunting for more. This time, though, there was more food to be had than even I could handle. After 'bout a half hour of stuffing, I didn't even want to *smell* bushdog cooking. Not ever.

"You're going to bust someday," said Lizbeth Jean. "Gonna just swell up and go *Bang!* Toony."

"An' you're goin' to get a big fat lip, Lizbeth Jean."

"Grandpa!" shrieked Lizbeth Jean, "she's gonna *hit* me!"

"Now, now, girls," said Grandpa, "this is Fair day. You know your mother don't like to see fighting."

'Course Mother wasn't even paying any attention to all this. She was just staring out at nothing, like always.

Tyrone bought a knife that'd break in about a minute, and Lizbeth Jean bought a shell comb and a ring, like she does every year. I got hungry again—like *I* do every year—and bought a Ting-root pie with gooey stuff on top. Then I went back out to where the Patchmen were. There was one old beat-up machine off a Spidership, and I got what I wanted from that and had the man wrap it up real nice in a little colored cloth.

Right about then, we had some excitement. The air got hot and still, and the sun turned the sky all rusty-green. All of a sudden, every Noord at the Fair stopped dead in their tracks, big feet flat against the ground, long noses tremblin' in the air. You don't have to be on Far very long to know what *that* means. I hit it out quick and found Grandpa and Mother and Lizbeth Jean, and we all sat real quiet on the ground, not thinking 'bout anything, like everybody else. All you could see was folks sitting, and waiting, and not looking anywhere close to the sky. What you're supposed to do is think about not even *bein'* there—kind of a little old piece of nothing. Noords do it real good, of course, seein' they been at it 'bout a million years. It comes kinda natural if you don't do a whole lot of thinking anyway.

After a while, the Noords got all unspooked, and everyone got up and stretched and started thinking again. Off to the south you could see 'em—two big Portugees floatin' high and slow, flat-looking bodies all pearly-blue in the sun. They weren't real hungry, or looking for anything special, they were just drifting along, trailing their stingers like long rags of rain 'gainst the ground.

"They're kinda early," said a man next to Grandpa. "Means we didn't get much rain up north this year."

"Which means there'll be a sight more here than we need," said Grandpa. "Always something, ain't it?"

"One thing or another," said the man.

Mother couldn't take a lot of sun, and squattin' down waiting for the Portugees near did her in. So Tyrone took her and Lizbeth Jean back to the wagon, and me and Grandpa walked out past the cookpits again where the Patchmen stayed. He didn't say what we was going for, but I had a real good idea. Grandpa's got a spot near home where you can find good greenstones if you know how to look. He keeps what he finds all year in a little leather sack, then brings them to the Fair. It isn't something you're *supposed* to do, but Grandpa knows a Patchman who knows a Spacer who can get things off of Far.

So I stayed outside the tent while Grandpa did his business, and pretended I was too little to know nothing, which is what grown-ups like. When he was through, we walked on back out the Patchmen's camp, and right there was when the thing in the cage started yelling at us. It shook its bars and made such a awful noise me and Grandpa stopped to take a look.

"Pleez," it said, "you come heeer. Lizzen to me!" The thing sounded all the world like a sack full of gravel, and Grandpa told me not to get up close. I wasn't about to, 'cause it stuck a warty old hand out the bars right at me.

"Iz big miztake," it kept croakin'. "Pleez, you help me!"

"Lordee," I said, "what in the world is it, Grandpa?"

Grandpa didn't answer. He just scratched his chin and grinned, like something real amusing come to mind. It *was* a funny-looking sight. Sort of like a fat old frog with foldy skin and pale yellow eyes. It wasn't wearing nothing but rags, and not much of that.

"Talks a blue streak, don't he?"

Grandpa and I both turned around, and there was a Patchman standing just behind us. Or rolling, really, 'cause he wasn't much more'n a head and shoulders set right on top of a big black box.

"Does, at that," said Grandpa. "Where'd you come by this little fellar?"

The Patchman made a face. "Got took is what I did. Traded

him from a Spacer for a bottle of good whiskey. Back down at
Rise-up. Figured folks'd pay a copper to see a Bug in a cage." He
shook his head and spit on the ground. "That was damn good
whiskey, too."

"I—am—not—BUG!" screamed the creature in the cage. He
shook his bars so hard I hid behind Grandpa. "I am Vize Adm'ral
Ch'rr of Procor Fleet! You lizzen to me—you help!"

The Patchman grinned and winked at Grandpa. "Never seen
one yet wasn't Grand High Muckety-muck of somethin'."

"Reckon so," said Grandpa.

The Patchman's box whirred inside and he rolled up close, till
he was looking Grandpa right in the eye. "Listen, friend, you
want to buy him, I'll make you a good price."

"What for?" said Grandpa. "What in hell'd *I* do with him?"

"You're a farmer, aren't you?"

"So?"

"Do a good day's work for you."

Grandpa looked at the creature and laughed out loud. "Son,
if that there's a field hand, I'm Queen of the May."

"He's a real smart fella," the Patchman insisted, "when he
ain't raving on like that. He can count, and read and write good."

"Don't take a lot of smart to run a hoe," said Grandpa.

"He plays chess, too."

Grandpa's brows shot up like a bushdog's tail. "He does what,
now?"

"Meanest endgame you ever saw," said the Patchman, trying
hard not to look too pleased with himself.

Grandpa peered in at the creature. "That right? You any good?"

"Pleez—" The thing looked up real miserable at Grandpa.
"I am not Bug. I am friend. I am Vize Adm'ral Ch'rr of—"

"I didn't ask for your goddamn war record. Do you play or
don't you?"

The creature didn't say anything. It just kinda sank to the
bottom of its cage and started making little whiny sounds.
Grandpa looked disgusted.

"He'll come around," said the Patchman, "you get him home
and settled in. He isn't much used to company."

Grandpa looked at the man real hard. "I don't think this fella
knows a endgame from a pussycat. 'Sides, he's got warts."

"I'll take just what I paid for him," said the Patchman. "A good bottle of whiskey. Throw in the cage for nothing. Isn't anything fairer than that."

"Reckon not. If you need somethin' powerful ugly that don't smell good."

"It doesn't have to be *real* good whiskey."

"Right nice of you. Seeing as how there isn't no such thing this side of—*Great God and hairy little pigs!*" Grandpa stared right over my head and his jaw dropped about a foot. Before I could blink, he was out of there, hobbling past the wagon, shoutin' and waving his stick. Then *I* saw what it was and my heart went right down in my stomach. A Patchman was leading a string of girls into camp on a long piece of rope. There wasn't any of them over twelve or fourteen, and the very last one was Lizbeth Jean.

Grandpa didn't even look at her. He marched right up to the Patchman and poked his stick in the man's chest. "Boy, you got something there don't belong to you."

The Patchman stopped and looked real hard at Grandpa. Then he just swept the stick aside like nothing was there and walked on by. Grandpa let him go. When the end of the line came by, he whipped out his little pocket knife and cut Lizbeth Jean off the string. Lizbeth Jean started bawling and hung on his leg like a leech.

The Patchman jerked 'round and stared, like he could hardly believe what he was seeing. He studied Grandpa up and down, then shook his head and grinned. "Old man, you're startin' to bother me some."

"Figure to," said Grandpa.

"Just put that pretty back where you got her, and get on your way."

"She ain't for sale," said Grandpa.

The Patchman laughed. "The *sellin'* parts over and done." He patted his pocket twice. "Got the paper right here, all signed and proper."

Grandpa's face got terrible dark. "You got nothin' at all," he said softly, " 'cept a poor woman's mark don't have any idea what she's about."

The Patchman brought himself up real straight. He was a mean, stringy-lookin' man, split right down the middle—flesh and bone on one side, silver on the other. You could tell by his eyes he wasn't about to give up Lizbeth Jean. 'Specially now, since three or four other Patchmen had drifted up to watch.

"Be best if you just get on your way," he told Grandpa. "I'm sure takin' that pretty."

"You're sure welcome to try," said Grandpa.

The Patchman grinned. His hand kind of blurred 'round his belt and came up with a short little blade. He flipped it over twice, letting its bright catch the sun.

"Mink, just hold on there a minute," said one of the Patchmen.

"Just mind your business," said Mink, not moving his eyes off Grandpa. The first Patchman said something to the man beside him, and the man looked at Grandpa, then at Mink.

"Pardo's right," said the man. "Just let it go, Mink. Leave him be."

Mink gave him a black look, spit on the ground, and started for Grandpa. Grandpa didn't move. He pushed Lizbeth Jean away and just stood where he was. Mink walked right up to him and drove his blade hard at Grandpa's belly.

Only he didn't. Or I *guess* he didn't. Right there's where it starts gettin' real hard to explain. All I know is Mink got sort of blurry a second and then he was just looking down at his knife, and laughing, and not even thinking about Grandpa. He laughed so hard the tears came to his eyes, and then he started slashin' and cuttin' as hard as he could at his own belly, ripping and tearing away hard, and watching himself come apart. Everything inside came rolling out wet and shiny and spilling to the ground, and Mink kept laughing and slicing away like he hadn't ever seen anything funny as that.

Then, all of a sudden it wasn't even happenin' at all, and Mink was just standing there looking at his belly and screaming. There wasn't a scratch on him but Mink wouldn't stop. A couple of men took him up and carried him off to the tents somewhere, but he was still going strong. Like maybe now he'd got started he didn't know *how* to stop anymore.

Nobody said anything for a long time. Then one of the Patchmen walked over to Grandpa real slow. "I'm sorry about that," he said, "just real sorry."

"It's over," said Grandpa.

"Pardo said it was you, said he recognized you right off. An' I said hell, Pardo, you know it ain't *him,* what'd *he* be doing way out here on Far?"

"Guess you still ain't sure, are you?" said Grandpa.

The Patchman looked at Grandpa, then got kind of white and funny lookin' around the mouth. "No, sir," he said, "I'm—surely not."

"Fine," said Grandpa, "that's just fine. Come on, Toony, Lizbeth Jean. We best be getting on back now. . . ."

By the time we got moving, there was a light breeze from the west and the moons were full up in the sky. The razortrees sparkled and made tinkly sounds in the wind, and I could hear a bunch of Whoopers start yappin' away. Tyrone hauled the wagon up ahead, with Mother and Lizbeth Jean already asleep inside. Me and Grandpa came up behind, where old Wart was pulling his cage and talkin' to himself. Grandpa said he was keepin' a good eye on him for a while, till he stopped wanting to be a admiral and settled down to some decent chess playing. *I* didn't figure he'd ever do much of anything, but what does a fat little girl know?

"I got you a present," I said after a while. "You want to open it now or wait'll you get home?"

"Why, right now," said Grandpa. "Once you know 'bout a present, you almost have to open it." He took the little package and unwrapped it and held up what was inside.

"You gotta open the cap and smell," I told him. "You tell this machine what kind of smell you want and it makes it right off. The Patchman said it come from a Spidership."

Grandpa took off the cap and smelled.

"It's *supposed* to be popcorn, like you're always talkin' about. Only I said throw in a little lemonade and cotton candy, too. Is it all right?"

Granda gave me a big grin. "Just as right as it can be, Toony. That's a real good present."

"I got Mother one, too. It's some kinda flower you can't get on Far. Maybe it'll help her remember stuff. You know, like you do."

"Maybe it will," said Grandpa. "You just never can tell."

The Snappers started grinding and hissing out in the bush again, and me and Grandpa walked along and listened. I got to thinking, and wondering about things, which I do sometimes. Like what happened to Papa, and why Grandpa had to play like bein' a farmer when he wasn't. All that stuff I'm not supposed to ask about. There isn't any end to that kind of thinking. So I started thinking 'bout bushdog sizzling and sweet-cakes and Ting-root pie and how the Fair would be next year. I figured I was growing up some, 'cause I decided right then and there it didn't do much good worrying about being fat and havin' hair like a armpit. When it comes down to it, you're either a Toony or a Lizbeth Jean, and isn't anything you do going to change it. . . .

Russell Griffin teaches at the University of Bridgeport and is the author of several SF novels (most recently, Makeshift God*). He writes that his poem was "inspired by my coming across a copy of* Slovenly Peter *by one Dr. Hoffman, a 19th century German physician who was concerned with the edification of children in the most direct way possible. The book includes such inspiring tales as the story of Augustus, who refused to eat his soup one day and died within a week; the story of Lucy, who ignored her mother's warnings, played with matches, and incinerated herself; and the story of a boy who mistreated animals until he was torn apart by various woodland creatures. Anyway, I was so taken with Hoffman's approach that I couldn't resist composing a couple of modern-day examples. If you're going to edify children, I always say, there's no better way than to scare them to death."*

RUSSELL GRIFFIN

The Most Illuminatingly Doleful and Instructively Affecting Demise of Flo, Late of Upper Blooton

Sweet little ones, attention lend
To Flo's grim, grisly, shocking end.
Flo lived in Upper Blooton then,
An Eden just off Exit 10,
Where almost nothing went amiss
To mar her Prelapsarian Bliss.

But smallest things, we often find,
Can rattle the serenest mind:
The least cloud dims the brightest days,
The fly afloat in Sauce Bernaise,
The fizzless Coke, the tepid shower,
Will sweetest dispositions sour.

So Flo, though blessed, would run amuck
On mornings when her toaster stuck.
Sometimes the Arnold Veri-Thin
Would buckle and get wedged within,
Or English muffins prove too wide,
Or scraps of heel slip down inside.

She'd never first remove the plug
(As mother warned) but always dug
Her fork deep in the toaster's slot
And rout and thrust until she got
Her slice, by Passion blinded to
The arcing sparks that upward flew.

One day, alas, it happened that
Her Eggo Waffle was too fat.
It stuck. In plunged her fork and went
Right through a heating element
To form a fatal a.c. link
From Flo to Blooton Power, Inc.
Her eyes grew wide, her hair grew straight,
She cursed her hasty fork—too late!
For as a pennant when gales blow
Stands straight out from the mast, just so
Flo sideways rose with high-volt torque,
A banner from her red-hot fork.

"Dear me," she mused, "I never thought
My Inner Light was quite so hot.
But none can say my light was hid
Beneath a bushel." And none did.
No Bridegroom, Peeping Tom, or Tramp
Could miss *this* Foolish Virgin's lamp.

But as the brightest shooting star
Is soonest spent, our tale's bizarre
Conclusion was on final flash
Converting Flo to soda ash
And freeing all her primal parts—
Air, water, carbon, and Pop Tarts.

One instant still her image hung
In floating soot, and then among
The molecules of air dispersed.
Her mother later found the worst:
What had been Flo was now no more
Than siftings on her No-Skuff floor.

Her mother later, over juice,
Received reporters. "What's the use?
Despite our warning her," she sighed,
"She stuck her fork inside and died.
And charred her brand-new dress-up shoes,
And blew a twenty-ampere fuse.

"*She's* free of pain and cold and toil
By shuffling off this heating coil,
But we, the living, spent an hour
Deprived of all electric power,
And worse, endured—O Wretched Ghost—
This morning's breakfast without toast."

ISAAC ASIMOV

Science:
The Word I Invented

ROBOTICS has become a sufficiently well-developed technology to warrant articles and books on its history, and I have watched this in amazement and in some disbelief, because I invented it.

No, not the technology; the word.

In October 1941, I wrote a robot story entitled "Runaround," first published in the March 1942 issue of *Astounding Science Fiction,* in which I recited, for the first time, my "Three Laws of Robotics." Here they are:

1. A robot must not injure a human being or, through inaction, allow a human being to come to harm.

2. A robot must obey the orders given it by human beings except where those orders would conflict with the First Law.

3. A robot must protect its own existence, except where such protection would conflict with the First or Second Law.

These laws have been quoted many times by me in stories and essays, but what is much more surprising is that they have been quoted innumerable times by others (in all seriousness) as something that will surely be incorporated in robots when they become complex enough to require it.

As a result, in almost any history of the development of robotics, there is some mention of me and of the Three Laws.

It is a queer feeling to know that I have made myself into a footnote in the history of science and technology for having invented the foundation of a science that didn't exist at the time.—And that I did it at the age of 21.

The Three Laws, and the numerous stories I have written that have dealt with robots, have given many people—from enthusiastic teen-age readers to sophisticated editors of learned magazines in the field—the idea that I am an expert on robots and computers. As a result, I am continually being asked endless questions about robotics.

What I will do, then, is write a question-and-answer essay on the subject. It will take care of just about all the major questions I am forever being asked and it should make it unnecessary for anyone to have to ask me any questions on the subject again.*

1. Dr. Asimov, how did you come to be such an expert in the field of robotics?

Alas, I am not an expert, and I never have been. I don't know how robots work in any but the vaguest way. For that matter, I don't know how a computer works in any but the vaguest way, either. I have never worked with either robots or computers, and I don't know any details about how robots or computers are currently being used in industry.

I don't take pride in this. I merely present it as a fact. I would like to know all about robots and computers, but I can only squeeze so much into my head, and though I work at it day and night with remorseless assiduity, I still only manage to get a small fraction of the total sum of human knowledge into my brain.

2. In that case, Dr. Asimov, how did you come to write so

* But I am dreaming. The questions will continue, I know.

many robot stories, considering that you know nothing about the subject?

It never occurred to me that I had to. When I was reading science fiction in the 1930s, I came across a number of robot stories and learned what I had to know on the subject from them.

I found out that I didn't like stories in which robots were menaces or villains because those stories were technophobic and I was technophilic. I did like stories in which the robots were presented sympathetically, as in Lester del Rey's "Helen O'Loy" or Eando Binder's "I, Robot."

What's more, I didn't think a robot should be sympathetic just because it happened to be nice. It should be engineered to meet certain safety standards as any other machine should in any right-thinking technological society. I therefore began to write stories about robots that were not only sympathetic, but were sympathetic *because they couldn't help it.* That was my contribution to this particular sub-genre of the field.

3. Does that mean that you had the Three Laws of Robotics in mind when you began writing your robot stories?

Only in a way. The concept was in my mind but I wasn't smart enough to put it into the proper words.

The first robot story I wrote was "Robbie" in May 1939, when I was 19. (It appeared in the September 1940, *Super-Science Stories,* under the title of "Strange Playfellow.") In it, I had one of my characters say, about the robot-hero, "He just can't help being faithful and loving and kind. He's a machine—*made so.*" That was my first hint of the First Law.

In "Reason," my second robot story (April 1941, *Astounding*), I had a character say, "Those robots are guaranteed to be subordinate." That was a hint of the Second Law.

In "Liar," my third robot story (May 1941, *Astounding*), I gave a version of the First and Second Laws when I said the "fundamental law" of robots was: "On no condition is a human being to be injured in any way, even when such injury is directly ordered by another human."

It wasn't, however, till "Runaround," my fourth robot story, that it all came together in the Three Laws in their present wording, and that was because John Campbell, the late great editor of

Astounding, quoted them to me. It always seemed to me that John invented those laws, but whenever I accused him of that, he always said that they were in my stories and I just hadn't bothered to isolate them. Perhaps he was right.

4. *But you say you invented the term "robotics." Is that right?*
Yes. John Campbell, as best I can remember, did not use the word in connection with the Three Laws. I did, however, in "Runaround" and I believe that was its first appearance in print.

I did not know at the time that it was an invented term. The science of physics routinely uses the "-ics" suffix for various branches: as in the case of mechanics, dynamics, electrostatics, hydraulics, and so on. I took it for granted that the study of robots was "robotics."

It wasn't until a dozen years later, at least, that I became aware that "robotics" was not listed in the 2nd edition of Websters' Unabridged Dictionary or (when I quickly checked) in any of the other dictionaries I consulted. What's more, when Websters' 3rd edition was published, I looked up "robotics" at once and still didn't find it.

I therefore began saying that I had invented the word, for it did indeed seem to me that I had done so.

In 1973, there appeared "The Barnhart Dictionary of New English Since 1963," published by Harper & Row. It includes the word "robotics" and quotes a passage from an essay of mine in which I claim to have invented it. That's still just me saying so, but at least the lexicographers didn't cite earlier uses by someone else.

The word is now well established, and it is even used in the titles of magazines that are devoted to the technology of robots. To be candid, I must admit that it pleases me to have invented a word that has entered the scientific vocabulary.*

5. *I frequently hear your robots referred to as "positronic robots." Why positronic?*
When I first began writing science fiction stories, the positron

---

* "Psychohistory," which I also invented, has entered the scientific vocabulary, but, alas, not in the sense of my invention.

had been discovered only six years before as a particle with all the properties of an electron except for an opposite charge. It was the first (and, at that time, still the only) bit of antimatter that had been discovered, and it carried a kind of science-fictional flavor about it.

That meant that if I spoke of "positronic robots" rather than "electronic robots," I would have something exotic and futuristic instead of something conventional.

What's more, positrons are very evanescent particles, at least in our world. They don't survive more than a millionth of a second or so before they bump into one of the electrons with which our world is crowded, and then the two annihilate each other.

I had a vision, therefore, of "positronic pathways" along which positrons briefly flashed and disappeared. These pathways were analogous to the neurons of the animal nervous system, and the positrons themselves were analogous to the nerve impulse. The exact nature of the pathways was controlled by positronic potentials, and where certain potentials were set prohibitively high, then certain thoughts or deeds became virtually impossible. It was the balance of such potentials which resulted in the Three Laws.

Of course, it takes a great deal of energy, on the subatomic scale, to produce a positron; and that positron, when it encounters an electron and is annihilated, produces a great deal of energy on the subatomic scale. Where does that positron-producing energy come from and where does the positron-annihilation energy go to?

The answer to that is that I didn't know and didn't care. I never referred to the matter. The assumption (which I didn't bother to state) was that future technology would handle it and that the process would be so familiar that nobody would wonder about it or comment upon it—any more than a contemporary person would worry about what happens in a generating plant when a switch is flicked and a bathroom light goes on.

7. *Talking about the positronic energies reminds me, Dr. Asimov, to wonder where your robots got the energy to do their work. Where?*

I assumed some form of nuclear power (or "atomic power") as we called it in the 1930's.

When I wrote my first robot story in 1939, uranium fission was just being discovered, but, of course, I had not heard of it yet. That, however, didn't matter. From about 1900 on, it was perfectly well understood that there was a source of huge and concentrated energy in the interior of the atom. It was standard "believe it or not" fare to be told that if all the energy in an ounce of matter could be extracted it would suffice to drive a large ocean liner across the Atlantic.

Consequently, the general science-fictional thought was that some very small object, serving as an "atomic energy device" could be inserted into a robot and that would keep it running for millions of years, if necessary.

As the years passed and we learned a great deal about the practical aspects of nuclear energy, I might have yielded to the headlines of the moment and spoken wisely of uranium fission and cadmium rods and so on, but I did not do so. I think I was right in this. I maintained silence about the details of the energy source because it had nothing to do with the point of the stories, and that caused no reader-discomfort that I am aware of.

8. In your earliest robot stories you made no mention of computers, yet surely the positronic brain is actually a very complex, compact, and versatile computer? Why did you not say so?

Because it never occurred to me to say so. I was a creation of the science fiction of the 1930's, which was written by writers who built on what had gone before.

As it happened, the world of fiction had been full of humaniform objects brought to artificial life, including the Golem and Frankenstein's monster. There were also various "automatons" in human shape. Such things were in the air. Capek invented the word "robot" for them but the word was applied to a concept that long existed.

Computers, on the other hand, were not really in the air until the first electronic computer was built during World War II. Earlier mechanical calculating devices were so simple that they gave absolutely no birth to the thought of "thinking machine."

Since my robot stories began just before World War II, computers were not part of my consciousness, and I did not either talk or think of them. Yet even so I could not help introduce computers, even though I did not know what I was doing.

In my very first robot story, my little-girl heroine encounters a "talking robot" which "sprawled its unwieldy mass of wires and coils through twenty-five square yards." When it spoke there was "an oily whir of gears." I hadn't managed to work out the notion of electronics in its connection, but what I had was a kind of mechanical computer.

By the time I wrote my story "Escape" in November 1944 (it appeared in the August 1945, *Astounding,* as "Paradoxical Escape"), I had another huge non-portable structure which I referred to as a "thinking machine" and called "the Brain." That was written about the time the first electronic computer, ENIAC, came into existence though, of course, I knew nothing about that.

Eventually, I did begin to write computer stories. I think the first of those was "Franchise," which appeared in the August 1955, *If.* Even then I never completely differentiated robots and computers and I feel I was right not to do so. To me, a robot was a mobile computer and a computer an immobile robot. From here on in then, when I speak of "robots" in this essay, please remember that I use it to include computers as well.

9. Come to think of it, why are robots humaniform? Surely that is not the most efficient shape.

Again, it's a matter of history. The robot is in the tradition of the "artificial man" which goes far back in the human imagination.

It is a matter of drama. What can be so supreme an achievement as to create an artificial human being—so that we have the mythical Greek inventor, Daedalus, constructing a brazen man, Talos, who served to guard the shores of Crete. Again, what can be so supreme a blasphemy as to attempt to mimic the Creator by devising an artificial human being, so that we have the hubris-and-até of Victor Frankenstein.

With such a background, science fiction writers were unable to think of intelligent machines without making them humaniform. Intelligence and the human shape seemed too intimately connected to be separated. It was only with the rise of the electronic computer, which presents a kind of artificial intelligence without the involvement of any fixed shape, that robots were seen as mobile computers and no longer had to be humaniform.

Thus, the very successful R2D2 in "Star Wars" was shaped like a fire hydrant, and seemed very cute in consequence, especially, for some reason,* to the female portion of the audience.

And if we step into the world of real robots, the kind that are being used in industry now, we have only the vaguest sign of humaniformity, if any at all. But then they are as yet very primitive and limited in the tasks they can perform. It is possible that as robots become more versatile and generalized in their abilities, they will become more humaniform.

My reasons for thinking so are two:

a) Our technology is built round the human shape. Our tools, our appliances, our furniture, are built to be used by human beings. They fit our hands, our buttocks, our feet, our reach, the way we bend. If we make use of robots with proportions like ours, with appendages like ours, which bend as we do, they can make use of all our tools and equipment. They can live in our world; they will be technologically compatible with us.

b) The more they look like us, the more acceptable they will be. It may be that one of the reasons that computers rouse such distaste and fear in many people who are otherwise normally intelligent is that they are nonhumaniform and are therefore seen as a dehumanizing influence.

10. Well, then, when do you think we will have robots like those you describe, as intelligent and versatile, and subject to the Three Laws?

How can one tell? At the rate that computer technology is now advancing, it doesn't seem to me to be impossible that within a century, enough capacity and versatility can be packed into a device the size of a human brain to produce a reasonably intelligent robot.

On the other hand, technological capacity alone may well prove insufficient. Civilization may not endure long enough to allow robots to reach such a stage. Or even if it does, it may turn out that the social and psychological pressures against robots will prevent their development. Perhaps my feeling that humaniform robots will seem friendly will prove wrong. They may prove terrifying

---

* It has been pointed out to me that R2D2 had a phallic appearance.

instead (something which I take for granted in my robot stories, by the way).

Then, too, even if the technological capacity is there and if social resistance is absent, it may be that the direction of technology will be different from that which I originally imagined.

For instance, why should each robot have an independent brain with all the expense and risk of damage that would entail?

Surely, it would make more sense to have some central computer be responsible for the actions of many robots.* The central computer in charge of a squadron of robots could be any size since it would not have to be portable, and, while expensive, it would certainly not be as expensive as a squadron of separate and very compact brains. Furthermore, the central immobile computer could be well protected and would not run the risk of the kind of damage that would always be possible in the case of mobile robot brains.

Each mobile robot would, we might imagine, have a characteristic wavelength to which it would respond and through which it would be connected to its own portion of the central brain. Without a brain of its own it could be risked in dangerous enterprises much more readily. The disadvantage would be that it would depend on electromagnetic communication that could be interfered with, perhaps, by both natural and technological means. In other words, a malfunctioning or nonfunctioning robot would then be much more likely.

11. Since you mention the possibility of a malfunctioning robot, how safe are the Three Laws anyway? They seem to be ambiguous. How do you define a human being? What do you mean by harm?

The Three Laws are deliberately ambiguous. From the very first time I used them in "Runaround," it was the ambiguity that supplied me with a plot. I considered the definition of "harm" as early as my story "Liar!" and in my novel *The Naked Sun* (Doubleday, 1957) I even dealt with robotic murder, despite the Three Laws.

As to how a human being was to be defined, that was something

* Such a possibility is mentioned in my robot story "The Bicentennial Man" (*Stellar Two*, 1976).

that now and then I thought of dealing with, but it was something from which I always shrank and turned away. Finally, I tackled that subject in "That Thou Art Mindful of Him" (*F&SF,* May 1974) and full-circled myself back into the Frankenstein complex.

It may have been partly in expiation for this that I went on to write "The Bicentennial Man." There I considered not only what a human being might be but what a robot might be, too, and ended by showing, in a way, their coalescence.

12. In "That Thou Art Mindful of Him," then, you forecast the replacement of human beings by robots, while in "The Bicentennial Man" you forecast the fusion of human beings and robots. Which do you think is the more likely of the two?

Perhaps neither.

I feel that not all intelligence need be equivalent. Suppose dolphins have intelligence that is comparable to ours, as some people think. Its evolution and its way of life is nevertheless so different from ours, that we seem to be able to meet on no common ground. Our respective intelligences seem to be so different in quality that there is no way of judging whether the dolphin is less advanced than we are or, possibly, more advanced, because there is no way of comparing them quantitatively.

If that is true in comparing the human being with the dolphin, how much more so might it not be in comparing the human being with the robot.

The human intelligence is the result of over three billion years of biological evolution, working through the processes of random mutation and of natural selection acting on systems of nucleic acids and proteins, with its driving criterion of success that of survival to the stage of reproduction.

The robot intelligence is the result, so far, of thirty years of technological evolution, working through directed human design and experiment acting on systems of metal and electricity, with its driving criterion of success that of usefulness for human purposes.

It would be very odd indeed, with every point so different in the two varieties of intelligence, if they did not end up very different —so different that no direct comparison is possible.

Robot intelligence seems to specialize in the scrutiny of tiny parts subjected to definite and repeated arithmetical operations with faultless accuracy and incredible speed. In that respect it far outmatches us already and may forever do so.

Human intelligence seems to specialize in an intuitive understanding of the whole and advances by the conjectural leap. In this respect we far outmatch the robot and may forever do so. After all, how can we program a robot to be intuitive if we do not know what it is that makes *us* intuitive?

Even if we could make the robot more like a human being, or vice versa, why should we want to? Why not take advantage of each area of specialization and make the robot ever better in its weighing of parts and the human being (through genetic engineering, eventually) ever better in its weighing of the whole.

We could then have a symbiotic arrangement, one in which the robot and the human being would be far greater together, than either could possibly be separately.

It was this which I was aiming at in my Lije Baley novels. *The Caves of Steel* (Doubleday, 1953) pictured a society in which human beings overbalanced the robots; *The Naked Sun,* one in which the robots overbalanced the human beings. The projected third novel of the series was to show the symbiotic balance—but though I tried, I lacked the ability to picture what was dimly in my mind.

I failed when I first tried in 1958 and I never quite felt I was up to it since. What a pity I didn't get to it while I was still in my twenties and had not yet grown wise enough to know there were things I lacked the ability to do—.

John Varley wrote many successful stories for F&SF *in the mid-1970s, most recently the award-winning "The Persistence of Vision." Since then, he has become primarily a novelist (*Titan, Wizard*) but made a welcome return to our pages with this surprising and affecting tale about a starship crewman and a little girl.*

JOHN VARLEY

The Pusher

THINGS change. Ian Haise expected that. Yet there are certain constants, dictated by function and use. Ian looked for those and he seldom went wrong.

The playground was not much like the ones he had known as a child. But playgrounds are built to entertain children. They will always have something to swing on, something to slide down, something to climb. This one had all those things, and more. Part of it was thickly wooded. There was a swimming hole. The stationary apparatus was combined with dazzling light sculptures that darted in and out of reality. There were animals, too: pygmy rhinoceros and elegant gazelles no taller than your knee. They seemed unnaturally gentle and unafraid.

But most of all, the playground had children.

Ian liked children.

He sat on a wooden park bench at the edge of the trees, in the shadows, and watched them. They came in all colors and all sizes, in both sexes. They were black ones like animated licorice jelly-beans and white ones like bunny rabbits, and brown ones with curly hair and more brown ones with slanted eyes and straight black hair and some who had been white but were now toasted browner than some of the brown ones.

Ian concentrated on the girls. He had tried with boys before, long ago, but it had not worked out.

He watched one black child for a time, trying to estimate her age. He thought it was around eight or nine. Too young. Another one was more like thirteen, judging from her shirt. A possibility, but he'd prefer something younger. Somebody less sophisticated, less suspicious.

Finally he found a girl he liked. She was brown, but with startling blonde hair. Ten? Possibly eleven. Young enough, at any rate.

He concentraed on her and did the strange thing he did when he had selected the right one. He didn't know what it was, but it usually worked. Mostly it was just a matter of looking at her, keeping his eyes fixed on her no matter where she went or what she did, not allowing himself to be distracted by anything. And sure enough, in a few minutes she looked up, looked around, and her eyes locked with his. She held his gaze for a moment, then went back to her play.

He relaxed. Possibly what he did was nothing at all. He had noticed, with adult women, that if one really caught his eye so he found himself staring at her she would usually look up from what she was doing and catch him. It never seemed to fail. Talking to other men, he had found it to be a common experience. It was almost as if they could feel his gaze. Women had told him it was nonsense, or if not, it was just reaction to things seen peripherally by people trained to alertness for sexual signals. Merely an un-conscious observation penetrating to the awareness; nothing mys-terious, like ESP.

Perhaps. Still, Ian was very good at this sort of eye contact. Several times he had noticed the girls rubbing the backs of their necks while he observed them, or hunching their shoulders. May-be they'd developed some kind of ESP and just didn't recognize it as such.

Now he merely watched her. He was smiling, so that every time she looked up to see him—which she did with increasing frequency—she saw a friendly, slightly graying man with a broken nose and powerful shoulders. His hands were strong, too. He kept them clasped in his lap.

Presently she began to wander in his direction.

No one watching her would have thought she was coming toward him. She probably didn't know it herself. On her way, she found reasons to stop and tumble, jump on the soft rubber mats, or chase a flock of noisy geese. But she was coming toward him, and she would end up on the park bench beside him.

He glanced around quickly. As before, there were few adults in this playground. It had surprised him when he arrived. Apparently the new conditioning techniques had reduced the numbers of the violent and twisted to the point that parents felt it safe to allow their children to run without supervision. The adults present were involved with each other. No one had given him a second glance when he arrived.

That was fine with Ian. It made what he planned to do much easier. He had his excuses ready, of course, but it could be embarrassing to be confronted with the questions representatives of the law ask single, middle-aged men who hang around playgrounds.

For a moment he considered, with real concern, how the parents of these children could feel so confident, even with mental conditioning. After all, no one was conditioned until he had first done something. New maniacs were presumably being produced every day. Typically, they looked just like everyone else until they proved their difference by some demented act.

Somebody ought to give those parents a stern lecture, he thought.

"Who are you?"

Ian frowned. Not eleven, surely, not seen up this close. Maybe not even ten. She might be as young as eight.

Would eight be all right? He tasted the idea with his usual caution, looked around again for curious eyes. He saw none.

"My name is Ian. What's yours?"

"*No.* Not your *name.* Who are *you?*"

"You mean what do I do?"

"Yes."

"I'm a pusher."

She thought that over, then smiled. She had her permanent teeth, crowded into a small jaw.

"You give away pills?"

He laughed. "Very good," he said. "You must do a lot of reading." She said nothing, but her manner indicated she was pleased. "No," he said. "That's an old kind of pusher. I'm the other kind. But you knew that, didn't you?" When he smiled she broke into giggles. She was doing the pointless things with her hands that little girls do. He thought she had a pretty good idea of how cute she was, but no inkling of her forbidden eroticism. She was a ripe seed with sexuality ready to burst to the surface. Her body was a bony sketch, a framework on which to build a woman.

"How old are you?" he asked.

"That's a secret. What happened to your nose?"

"I broke it a long time ago. I'll bet you're twelve."

She giggled, then nodded. Eleven, then. And just barely.

"Do you want some candy?" He reached into his pocket and pulled out the pink and white striped paper bag.

She shook her head solemnly. "My mother says not to take candy from strangers."

"But we're not strangers. I'm Ian, the pusher."

She thought that over. While she hesitated he reached into the bag and picked out a chocolate thing so thick and gooey it was almost obscene. He bit into it, forcing himself to chew. He hated sweets.

"Okay," she said, and reached toward the bag. He pulled it away. She looked at him in innocent surprise.

"I just thought of something," he said. "I don't know your name. So I guess we *are* strangers."

She caught on to the game when she saw the twinkle in his eye. He'd practiced that. It was a good twinkle.

"My name is Radiant. Radiant Shiningstar Smith."

"A very fancy name," he said, thinking how names had changed. "For a very pretty girl." He paused, and cocked his head. "No. I don't think so. You're Radiant . . . Starr. With two *r's*. . . . *Captain* Radiant Starr, of the Star Patrol."

She was dubious for a moment. He wondered if he'd judged her wrong. Perhaps she was really Mizz Radiant Faintingheart Belle, or Mrs. Radiant Motherhood. But her fingernails were a bit dirty for that.

She pointed a finger at him and made a Donald Duck sound as her thumb worked back and forth. He put his hand to his heart and fell over sideways, and she dissolved in laughter. She was careful, however, to keep her weapon firmly trained on him.

"And you'd better give me that candy or I'll shoot you again."

The playground was darker now, and not so crowded. She sat beside him on the bench, swinging her legs. Her bare feet did not quite touch the dirt.

She was going to be quite beautiful. He could see it clearly in her face. As for the body . . . who could tell?

Not that he really gave a damn.

She was dressed in a little of this and a little of that, worn here and there without much regard for his concepts of modesty. Many of the children wore nothing. It had been something of a shock when he arrived. Now he was almost used to it, but he still thought it incautious on the part of her parents. Did they really think the world was that safe, to let an eleven-year-old girl go practically naked in a public place?

He sat there listening to her prattle about her friends—the ones she hated and the one or two she simply adored—with only part of his attention.

He inserted um's and uh-huh's in the right places.

She was cute, there was no denying it. She seemed as sweet as a child that age ever gets, which can be very sweet and as poisonous as a rattlesnake, almost at the same moment. She had the capacity to be warm, but it was on the surface. Underneath, she cared mostly about herself. Her loyalty would be a transitory thing, bestowed easily, just as easily forgotten.

And why not? She was young. It was perfectly healthy for her to be that way.

But did he dare try to touch her?

It was crazy. It was as insane as they all told him it was. It worked so seldom. Why would it work with her? He felt a weight of defeat.

"Are you okay?"

"Huh? Me? Oh, sure, I'm all right. Isn't your mother going to be worried about you?"

"I don't have to be in for hours and hours yet." For a moment she looked so grown up he almost believed the lie.

"Well, I'm getting tired of sitting here. And the candy's all gone." He looked at her face. Most of the chocolate had ended up in a big circle around her mouth, except where she had wiped it daintily on her shoulder or forearm. "What's back there?"

She turned.

"That? That's the swimming hole."

"Why don't we go over there? I'll tell you a story."

The promise of a story was not enough to keep her out of the water. He didn't know if that was good or bad. He knew she was smart, a reader, and she had an imagination. But she was also active. That pull was too strong for him. He sat far from the water, under some bushes, and watched her swim with the three other children in the park this late in the evening.

Maybe she would come back to him, and maybe she wouldn't. It wouldn't change his life either way, but it might change hers.

She emerged dripping and infinitely cleaner from the murky water. She dressed again in her random scraps, for whatever good it did her, and came to him, shivering.

"I'm cold," she said.

"Here." He took off his jacket. She looked at his hands as he wrapped it around her, and she reached out and touched the hardness of his shoulder.

"You sure must be strong," she commented.

"Pretty strong. I work hard, being a pusher."

"Just what *is* a pusher?" she said, and stifled a yawn.

"Come sit on my lap, and I'll tell you."

He did tell her, and it was a very good story that no adventurous child could resist. He had practiced that story, refined it, told it many times into a recorder until he had the rhythms and cadences just right, until he found just the right words—not too difficult words, but words with some fire and juice in them.

And once more he grew encouraged. She had been tired when

he started, but he gradually caught her attention. It was possible no one had ever told her a story in quite that way. She was used to sitting before the screen and having a story shoved into her eyes and ears. It was something new to be able to interrupt with questions and get answers. Even reading was not like that. It was the oral tradition of storytelling, and it could still mesmerize the *n*th generation of the electronic age.

"That sounds great," she said, when she was sure he was through.

"You liked it?"

"I really truly did. I think I want to be a pusher when I grow up. That was a really neat story."

"Well, that's not actually the story I was going to tell you. That's just what it's like to be a pusher."

"You mean you have another story?"

"Sure." He looked at his watch. "But I'm afraid it's getting late. It's almost dark, and everybody's gone home. You'd probably better go, too."

She was in agony, torn between what she was supposed to do and what she wanted. It really should be no contest, if she was who he thought she was.

"Well . . . but—but I'll come back here tomorrow and you—"

He was shaking his head.

"My ship leaves in the morning," he said. "There's no time."

"Then tell me now! I can stay out. Tell me now. Please please please?"

He coyly resisted, harrumphed, protested, but in the end allowed himself to be seduced. He felt very good. He had her like a five-pound trout on a twenty-pound line. It wasn't sporting. But, then, he wasn't playing a game.

So at last he got to his specialty.

He sometimes wished he could claim the story for his own, but the fact was he could not make up stories. He no longer tried to. Instead, he cribbed from every fairy tale and fantasy story he could find. If he had a genius, it was in adapting some of the elements to fit the world she knew—while keeping it strange enough to enthrall her—and in ad-libbing the end to personalize it.

It was a wonderful tale he told. It had enchanted castles sitting on mountains of glass, moist caverns beneath the sea, fleets of star-ships and shining riders astride horses that flew the galaxy. There were evil alien creatures, and others with much good in them. There were drugged potions. Scaled beasts roared out of hyper-space to devour planets.

Amid all the turmoil strode the Prince and Princess. They got into frightful jams and helped each other out of them.

The story was never quite the same. He watched her eyes. When they wandered, he threw away whole chunks of story. When they widened, he knew what parts to plug in later. He tailored it to her reactions.

The child was sleepy. Sooner or later she would surrender. He needed her in a trance state, neither awake nor asleep. That is when the story would end.

". . . and though the healers labored long and hard, they could not save the Princess. She died that night, far from her Prince."

Her mouth was a little round *o*. Stories were not supposed to end that way.

"Is that *all?* She died, and she never saw the Prince again?"

"Well, not quite all. But the rest of it probably isn't true, and I shouldn't tell it to you." Ian felt pleasantly tired. His throat was a little raw, making him hoarse. Radiant was a warm weight on his lap.

"You *have* to tell me, you know," she said, reasonably. He supposed she was right. He took a deep breath.

"All right. At the funeral, all the greatest people from that part of the galaxy were in attendance. Among them was the greatest Sorcerer who ever lived. His name . . . but I really shouldn't tell you his name. I'm sure he'd be very cross if I did.

"This Sorcerer passed by the Princess's bier . . . that's a—"

"I know, I *know,* Ian. Go on!"

"Suddenly he frowned and leaned over her pale form. 'What is this?' he thundered. 'Why was I not told?' Everyone was very concerned. This Sorcerer was a dangerous man. One time when someone insulted him he made a spell that turned everyone's heads backwards so they had to walk around with rear-view mirrors. No one knew what he would do if he got really angry.

" 'This Princess is wearing the Starstone,' he said, and drew himself up and frowned all around as if he were surrounded by idiots. I'm sure he thought he was, and maybe he was right. Because he went on to tell them just what the Starstone was, and what it did, something no one there had ever heard before. And this is the part I'm not sure of. Because, though everyone knew the Sorcerer was a wise and powerful man, he was also known as a great liar.

"He said that the Starstone was capable of capturing the essence of a person at the moment of her death. All her wisdom, all her power, all her knowledge and beauty and strength would flow into the stone and be held there, timelessly."

"In suspended animation," Radiant breathed.

"Precisely. When they heard this, the people were amazed. They buffeted the Sorcerer with questions, to which he gave few answers, and those only grudgingly. Finally he left in a huff. When he was gone everyone talked long into the night about the things he had said. Some felt the Sorcerer had held out hope that the Princess might yet live on. That if her body were frozen, the Prince, upon his return, might somehow infuse her essence back within her. Others thought the Sorcerer had said that was impossible, that the Princess was doomed to a half-life, locked in the stone.

"But the opinion that prevailed was this:

"The Princess would probably never come fully back to life. But her essence might flow from the Starstone and into another, if the right person could be found. All agreed this person must be a young maiden. She must be beautiful, very smart, swift of foot, loving, kind . . . oh, my, the list was very long. Everyone doubted such a person could be found. Many did not even want to try.

"But at last it was decided the Starstone should be given to a faithful friend of the Prince. He would search the galaxy for this maiden. If she existed, he would find her.

"So he departed with the blessings of many worlds behind him, vowing to find the maiden and give her the Starstone."

He stopped again, cleared his throat, and let the silence grow.

"Is that all?" she said, at last, in a whisper.

"Not quite all," he admitted. "I'm afraid I tricked you."

"Tricked me?"

He opened the front of his coat, which was still draped around her shoulders. He reached in past her bony chest and down into an inner pocket of the coat. He came up with the crystal. It was oval, with one side flat. It pulsed ruby light as it sat in the palm of his hand.

"It shines," she said, looking at it wide-eyed and open-mouthed.

"Yes, it does. And that means you're the one."

"Me?"

"Yes. Take it." He handed it to her, and as he did so, he nicked it with his thumbnail. Red light spilled into her hands, flowed between her fingers, seemed to soak into her skin. When it was over, the crystal still pulsed, but dimmed. Her hands were trembling.

"It felt very, very hot," she said.

"That was the essence of the Princess."

"And the Prince? Is he still looking for her?"

"No one knows. I think he's still out there, and some day he will come back for her."

"And what then?"

He looked away from her. "I can't say. I think, even though you are lovely, and even though you have the Starstone, that he will just pine away. He loved her very much."

"I'd take care of him," she promised.

"Maybe that would help. But I have a problem now. I don't have the heart to tell the Prince that she is dead. Yet I feel that the Starstone will draw him to it one day. If he comes and finds you, I fear for him. I think perhaps I should take the stone to a far part of the galaxy, some place he could never find it. Then at least he would never know. It might be better that way."

"But I'd help him," she said, earnestly. "I promise. I'd wait for him, and when he came, I'd take her place. You'll see."

He studied her. Perhaps she would. He looked into her eyes for a long time, and at last let her see his satisfaction.

"Very well. You can keep it then."

"I'll wait for him," she said. "You'll see."

She was very tired, almost asleep.

"You should go home now," he suggested.

"Maybe I could just lie down for a moment," she said.

"All right." He lifted her gently and placed her prone on the ground. He stood looking at her, then knelt beside her and began to gently stroke her forehead. She opened her eyes with no alarm, then closed them again. He continued to stroke her.

Twenty minutes later he left the playground, alone.

He was always depressed afterwards. It was worse than usual this time. She had been much nicer than he had imagined at first. Who could have guessed such a romantic heart beat beneath all that dirt?

He found a phone booth several blocks away. Punching her name into information yielded a fifteen-digit number, which he called. He held his hand over the camera eye.

A woman's face appeared on his screen.

"Your daughter is in the playground, at the south end by the pool, under the bushes," he said. He gave the address of the playground.

"We were so worried! What . . . is she . . . who is—"

He hung up and hurried away.

Most of the other pushers thought he was sick. Not that it mattered. Pushers were a tolerant group when it came to other pushers, and especially when it came to anything a pusher might care to do to a puller. He wished he had never told anyone how he spent his leave time, but he had, and now he had to live with it.

So, while they didn't care if he amused himself by pulling the legs and arms off infant puller pups, they were all just back from ground leave and couldn't pass up an opportunity to get on each other's nerves. They ragged him mercilessly.

"How were the swing-sets this trip, Ian?"

"Did you bring me those dirty knickers I asked for?"

"Was it good for you, honey? Did she pant and slobber?"

"My ten-year-old baby, she's a-pullin' me back home. . . ."

Ian bore it stoically. It was in extremely bad taste, and he was the brunt of it, but it really didn't matter. It would end as soon as they lifted again. They would never understand what he sought, but he felt he understood them. They hated coming to Earth. There was nothing for them there, and perhaps they wished there was.

And he was a pusher himself. He didn't care for pullers. He

agreed with the sentiment expressed by Marian, shortly after lift-off. Marian had just finished her first ground leave after her first voyage. So naturally she was the drunkest of them all.

"Gravity sucks," she said, and threw up.

It was three months to Amity, and three months back. He hadn't the foggiest idea of how far it was in miles; after the tenth or eleventh zero his mind clicked off.

Amity. Shit City. He didn't even get off the ship. Why bother? The planet was peopled with things that looked a little like ten-ton caterpillars and a little like sentient green turds. Toilets were a revolutionary idea to the Amiti; so were ice cream bars, sherbets, sugar donuts, and peppermint. Plumbing had never caught on, but sweets had, and fancy desserts from every nation on Earth. In addition, there was a pouch of reassuring mail for the forlorn human embassy. The cargo for the return trip was some grayish sludge that Ian supposed someone on Earth found tremendously valuable, and a packet of desperate mail for the folks back home. Ian didn't need to read the letters to know what was in them. They could all be summed up as "Get me *out* of here!"

He sat at the viewport and watched an Amiti family lumbering and farting its way down the spaceport road. They paused every so often to do something that looked like an alien cluster-fuck. The road was brown. The land around it was brown, and in the distance were brown, unremarkable hills. There was a brown haze in the air, and the sun was yellow-brown.

He thought of castles perched on mountains of glass, or Princes and Princesses, of shining white horses galloping among the stars.

He spent the return trip just as he had on the way out: sweating down in the gargantuan pipes of the stardrive. Just beyond the metal walls unimaginable energies pulsed. And on the walls themselves, tiny plasmoids grew into bigger plasmoids. The process was too slow to see, but if left unchecked the encrustations would soon impair the engines. His job was to scrape them off.

Not everyone was cut out to be an astrogator.

And what of it? It was honest work. He had made his choices long ago. You spent your life either pulling gees or pushing *c*. And when you got tired, you grabbed some z's. If there was a pushers' code, that was it.

The plasmoids were red and crystalline, teardrop-shaped. When he broke them free of the walls, they had one flat side. They were full of a liquid light that felt as hot as the center of the sun.

It was always hard to get off the ship. A lot of pushers never did. One day, he wouldn't either.

He stood for a few moments looking at it all. It was necessary to soak it in passively at first, get used to the changes. Big changes didn't bother him. Buildings were just the world's furniture, and he didn't care how it was arranged. Small changes worried the shit out of him. Ears, for instance. Very few of the people he saw had earlobes. Each time he returned he felt a little more like an ape who has fallen from his tree. One day he'd return to find everybody had three eyes or six fingers, or that little girls no longer cared to hear stories of adventure.

He stood there, dithering, getting used to the way people were painting their faces, listening to what sounded like Spanish being spoken all around him. Occasional English or Arabic words seasoned it. He grabbed a crewmate's arm and asked him where they were. The man didn't know. So he asked the captain, and she said it was Argentina, or it had been when they left.

The phone booths were smaller. He wondered why.

There were four names in his book. He sat there facing the phone, wondering which name to call first. His eyes were drawn to Radiant Shiningstar Smith, so he punched that name into the phone. He got a number and an address in Novosibirsk.

Checking the timetable he had picked—putting off making the call—he found the antipodean shuttle left on the hour. Then he wiped his hands on his pants and took a deep breath and looked up to see her standing outside the phone booth. They regarded each other silently for a moment. She saw a man much shorter than she remembered, but powerfully built, with big hands and shoulders and a pitted face that would have been forbidding but for the gentle eyes. He saw a tall woman around forty years old who was fully as beautiful as he had expected she would be. The hand of age had just begun to touch her. He thought she was fighting that waistline and fretting about those wrinkles, but none of that mattered to him. Only one thing mattered, and he would know it soon enough.

'You *are* Ian Haise, aren't you?" she said, at last.

"It was sheer luck I remembered you again," she was saying. He noted the choice of words. She could have said coincidence.

"It was two years ago. We were moving again and I was sorting through some things and I came across that plasmoid. I hadn't thought about you in . . . oh, it must have been fifteen years."

He said something noncommittal. They were in a restaurant, away from most of the other patrons, at a booth near a glass wall beyond which spaceships were being trundled to and from the blast pits.

"I hope I didn't get you into trouble," he said.

She shrugged it away.

"You did, some, but that was so long ago. I certainly wouldn't bear a grudge that long. And the fact is, I thought it was all worth it at the time."

She went on to tell him of the uproar he had caused in her family, of the visits by the police, the interrogation, puzzlement, and final helplessness. No one knew quite what to make of her story. They had identified him quickly enough, only to find he had left Earth, not to return for a long, long time.

"I didn't break any laws," he pointed out.

"That's what no one could understand. I told them you had talked to me and told me a long story, and then I went to sleep. None of them seemed interested in what the story was about. So I didn't tell them. And I didn't tell them about the . . . the Star-stone." She smiled. "Actually, I was relieved they hadn't asked. I was determined not to tell them, but I was a little afraid of holding it all back. I thought they were agents of the . . . who were the villains in your story? I've forgotten."

"It's not important."

"I guess not. But something is."

"Yes."

"Maybe you should tell me what it is. Maybe you can answer the question that's been in the back of my mind for twenty-five years, ever since I found out that thing you gave me was just the scrapings from a starship engine."

"Was it?" he said, looking into her eyes. "Don't get me wrong.

I'm not saying it *was* more than that. I'm asking *you* if it wasn't more."

"Yes, I guess it was more," she said, at last.

"I'm glad."

"I believed in that story passionately for . . . oh, years and years. Then I stopped believing it."

"All at once?"

"No. Gradually. It didn't hurt much. Part of growing up, I guess."

"And you remembered me."

"Well, that took some work. I went to a hypnotist when I was twenty-five and recovered your name and the name of your ship. Did you know—"

"Yes. I mentioned them on purpose."

She nodded, and they fell silent again. When she looked at him now, he saw more sympathy, less defensiveness. But there was still a question.

"Why?" she said.

He nodded, then looked away from her, out to the starships. He wished he was on one of them, pushing *c*. It wasn't working. He knew it wasn't. He was a weird problem to her, something to get straightened out, a loose end in her life that would irritate until it was made to fit in, then be forgotten.

To hell with it.

"Hoping to get laid," he said. When he looked up she was slowly shaking her head back and forth.

"Don't trifle with me, Haise. You're not as stupid as you look. You knew I'd be married, leading my own life. You knew I wouldn't drop it all because of some half-remembered fairy tale thirty years ago. *Why?*"

And how could he explain the strangeness of it all to her?

"What do you do?" He recalled something, and rephrased it. "Who *are* you?"

She looked startled. "I'm a mysteliologist."

He spread his hands. "I don't even know what that is."

"Come to think of it, there was no such thing when you left."

"That's it, in a way," he said. He felt helpless again. "Obviously, I had no way of knowing what you'd do, what you'd become, what would happen to you that you had no control over.

All I was gambling on was that you'd remember me. Because that way . . ." He saw the planet Earth looming once more out the viewport. So many, many years and only six months later. A planet full of strangers. It didn't matter that Amity was full of strangers. But Earth was home, if that word still had any meaning for him.

"I wanted somebody my own age I could talk to," he said. "That's all. All I want is a friend."

He could see her trying to understand what it was like. She wouldn't, but maybe she'd come close enough to think she did.

"Maybe you've found one," she said, and smiled. "At least I'm willing to get to know you, considering the effort you've put into this."

"It wasn't much effort. It seems so long-term to you, but it wasn't to me. I held you on my lap six months ago."

"How long is your leave?" she asked.

"Two months."

"Would you like to come stay with us for a while? We have room in our house."

"Will your husband mind?"

"Neither my husband nor my wife. That's them sitting over there, pretending to ignore us." Ian looked, caught the eye of a woman in her late twenties. She was sitting across from a man Ian's age, who now turned and looked at Ian with some suspicion but no active animosity. The woman smiled; the man reserved judgment.

Radiant had a wife. Well, times change.

"Those two in the red skirts are police," Radiant was saying. "So is that man over by the wall, and the one at the end of the bar."

"I spotted two of them," Ian said. When she looked surprised, he said, "Cops always have a look about them. That's one of the things that don't change."

"You go back quite a ways, don't you? I'll bet you have some good stories."

Ian thought about it, and nodded. "Some, I suppose."

"I should tell the police they can go home. I hope you don't mind that we brought them in."

"Of course not."

"I'll do that, and then we can go. Oh, and I guess I should call the children and tell them we'll be home soon." She laughed, reached across the table and touched his hand. "See what can happen in six months? I have three children, and Gillian has two."

He looked up, interested.

"Are any of them girls?"

This competition, suggested by John Brunner, asked readers to submit "imaginary collaborations."

From Competition 26:
Imaginary Collaborations

The Roads Must Roll Up the Walls of the World by Heinlein and Tiptree
The Beast that Shouted Love At the Brave Little Toaster by Ellison and Disch
Blow Ups Happen When Worlds Collide by Heinlein and Wylie
If All Men Were Androids, Would You Let One Marry Your Electric Sheep? by Sturgeon and Dick
The Deathbird Goes Dingo by Ellison and Disch
Barefoot in the Brillo by Aldiss and Ellison

—Susan Milmore
New York, N.Y.

The Moon Is A Brave Little Toaster by Heinlein and Disch
Love Is the Plan, the Plan Is Continued on the Next Rock by Tiptree and Lafferty

Barefoot in the Furnace by Aldiss and Silverberg
Schwartz Between the Bed Sheets by Silverberg and Lief
Come to Venus, Melancholy Baby Is Three by Disch and Sturgeon
—Jeff Grimshaw
New York, N.Y.

Fun With Your Neutron Star by Niven and Disch
I Have No Reproductive System and I Must Scream by Ellison
and Sladek
We Also Serve Man by Heinlein and Knight
Nine Billion Short, Short SF Stories by Clarke and Asimov
—Jim Detry
Urbana, Ill.

The Man In the High Castle Is A Harsh Mistress by Dick and
Heinlein
San Diego Lightfoot Who? by Reamy and Budrys
The Sheep Look Dispossessed by Brunner and LeGuin
A Case of Stolen Faces by Blish and Bishop
We Who Are About to Get Off the Unicorn by Russ and
McCaffrey
—Pat Cadigan
Kansas City, Kans.

The Man in the Odd John by Dick and Stapledon
The Persistence of Conan by Varley and Howard
The Very Slow Galaxy Reader by Watson and Pohl
Golem^{5,271,009} by Bester and Bester
The Stainless Steel Rat Wants Some of Your Little Fuzzy by
Harrison, Sturgeon and Piper
—S. Hamm
Brooklyn, N.Y.

*Twenty Thousand Leagues Under The Universal Baseball
Association* by Verne and Coover
The Mouse That Roared, Dandelion Wine! by Wibberly and
Bradbury

I Will Fear No Evil, Not To Mention Camels by Heinlein and Lafferty

—Michael Tippens
Atlanta, Ga.

Who Can Replace A Broke Down Engine? by Aldiss and Goulart
The Downstairs Room Is Room Enough by Wilhelm and Asimov
The Man Who Sold the Player Piano by Heinlein and Vonnegut

—John Nieminski
Park Forest, Ill.

Thomas M. Disch is a long-time F&SF *contributor whose stories
have been included in several of these collections. His latest story
(which made the final Hugo and Nebula ballot as best novella
of 1980) is about the adventures of five electrical appliances. They
are minor appliances, which implies a degree of innocence,
loyalty, and dependability often missing from, say, a TV or a
washing machine. We venture to say that it has been a long time
since such a cheerful and diverting group appeared in the pages of
any magazine or book, and we guarantee that all of you will
be charmed.*

THOMAS M. DISCH

The Brave Little Toaster
A Bedtime Story
for Small Appliances

B Y the time the air conditioner had come to live in the summer
cottage it was already wheezing and whining and going on
about being old and useless and out-of-date. The other appliances
had felt sorry and concerned, but when it finally did stop working
altogether, they also felt a distinct relief. In all its time there it
had never really been friendly—never really.

There were five appliances left in the cottage. The vacuum
cleaner, being the oldest and a steady, dependable type besides (it
was a Hoover), was their leader, insofar as they could be said to
have one. Then there was an off-white plastic alarm clock/radio
(AM only), a cheerful yellow electric blanket, and a tensor lamp
who had come from a savings bank and would sometimes get to
speculating, late at night, whether that made him better than
ordinary store-bought appliances or worse. Finally, there was the
toaster, a bright little Sunbeam. It was the youngest member of

the little clan, and the only one of them who had lived all its life there at the cottage, the other four having come with the master from the city years and years and years ago.

It was a pleasant cottage—quite cold in the winter, of course, but appliances don't mind that. It stood on the northernmost edge of an immense forest, miles from any neighbors and so far from the nearest highway that nothing was audible, day or night, but the peculiar hoots and rustlings of the forest and the reassuring sounds of the cottage itself—the creak of the timbers or the pattering of rain on windowpanes. They had grown set in their countrified ways and loved the little cottage dearly. Even if the chance had been offered them, which it wasn't, they wouldn't have wanted to be taken back to the city every year on Labor Day, the way that certain other appliances were, like the blender and the TV and the Water Pik. They *were* devoted to their master (that was just in their nature as appliances), but living so long in the woods had changed them in some nice, indefinable way that made the thought of any alternate life-style pretty nearly unthinkable.

The toaster was a special case. It had come straight to the cottage from a mail-order house, which tended to make it a little more curious about urban life than the other four. Often, left to itself, it would wonder what kind of toaster the master had in his city apartment, and it was privately of the opinion that whatever the brand of that other toaster it couldn't have made more perfect toast than the toaster made itself. Not too dark, not too light, but always the same uniform crunchy golden brown! However, it didn't come right out and say this in front of the others, since each of them was subject to periods of morbid misgivings as to its real utility. The old Hoover could maunder on for hours about the new breeds of vacuums with their low chassis, their long snaky hoses, and their disposable dust-bags. The radio regretted that it couldn't receive FM. The blanket felt it needed a dry cleaning, and the lamp could never regard an ordinary 100-watt bulb without a twinge of envy.

But the toaster was quite satisfied with itself, thank you. Though it knew from magazines that there were toasters who could toast four slices at a time, it didn't think that the master, who lived alone and seemed to have few friends, would have wanted a toaster of such institutional proportions. With toast, it's quality that matters, not quantity: that was the toaster's credo.

Living in such a comfy cottage, surrounded by the strange and beautiful woods, you would have thought that the appliances would have had nothing to complain of, nothing to worry about. Alas, that was not the case. They were all quite wretched and fretful and in a quandary as to what to do—for the poor appliances had been abandoned.

"And the worst of it," said the radio, "is not knowing *why*."

"The worst of it," the tensor lamp agreed, "is being left in the dark this way. Without an explanation. Not knowing *what* may have become of the master."

"Two years," sighed the blanket, who had once been so bright and gay and was now so melancholy.

"It's more nearly two and a half," the radio pointed out. Being a clock as well as a radio, it had a keen sense of the passing time. "The master left on the 25th of September, 1973. Today is March 8, 1976. That's two years, five months, and thirteen days."

"Do you suppose," said the toaster, naming the secret dread none of them dared to speak aloud before, "that he knew, when he left, that he wouldn't be coming back? That he *knew* he was leaving us . . . and was afraid to say so? Is that possible?"

"No," declared the faithful old Hoover, "it is not! I can say quite confidently that our master would not have left a cottage full of serviceable appliances to . . . to rust!"

The blanket, lamp, and radio all hastened to agree that their master could never have dealt with them so uncaringly. Something had happened to him—an accident, an emergency.

"In that case," said the toaster, "we must just be patient and behave as though nothing unusual has happened. I'm sure that's what the master is counting on us to do."

And that is what they did. Every day, all through that spring and summer they kept to their appointed tasks. The radio/alarm would go off each morning at seven-thirty sharp, and while it played some easy-listening music, the toaster (lacking real bread) would pretend to make two crispy slices of toast. Or, if the day seemed special in some way, it would toast an imaginary English muffin. Muffins of whatever sort have to be sliced *very* carefully if they're to fit into a toaster's slots. Otherwise, when they're done, they may not pop out easily. Generally it's wiser to do them under a broiler. However, there *wasn't* a broiler in the cottage, nothing but an old-fashioned gas ring, and so the toaster did the best it could. In any case, muffins that are only imaginary aren't liable to get stuck.

Such was the morning agenda. In the afternoon, if it were a Tuesday or a Friday, the old Hoover would rumble about the cottage vacuuming up every scrap of lint and speck of dust. This involved little actual picking up, as it was rather a small cottage, and was sealed very tight; so the dust and dirt had no way of getting inside, except on the days when the vacuum cleaner itself would trundle outdoors to empty a smidgen of dust at the edge of the forest.

At duck the tensor lamp would switch its switch to the ON position, and all five appliances would sit about in the kitchen area of the single downstairs room, talking or listening to the day's news or just staring out the windows into the gloomy solitude of the forest. Then, when it was time for the other appliances to turn themselves off, the electric blanket would crawl up the stairs to the little sleeping loft, where, since the nights were usually quite chilly, even in midsummer, it would radiate a gentle warmth. How the master would have appreciated the blanket on those cold nights! How safe and cozy he'd have felt beneath its soft yellow wool and electric coils! If only he'd been there.

At last, one sultry day toward the end of July, when the satisfactions of this dutiful and well-regulated life where beginning to wear thin, the little toaster spoke up again.

"We can't go on like this," it declared. "It isn't natural for appliances to live all by themselves. We need people to take care of, and we need people to take care of *us*. Soon, one by one, we'll all wear out, like the poor air conditioner. And no one will fix us, because no one will know what has happened."

"I daresay we're *all* of us sturdier than any air conditioner," said the blanket, trying to be brave. (Also, it is true, the blanket had never shown much fellow feeling for the air conditioner or any other appliances whose function was to make things cooler.)

"That's all very well for *you* to say," the tensor lamp retorted. "You'll go on for years, I suppose, but what will come of me when my bulb burns out? What will become of the radio when his tubes start to go?"

The radio made a dismal, staticky groan.

"The toaster is right," the old Hoover said. "Something must be done. Something definitely must be done. Do any of you have a suggestion?"

"If we could telephone the master," said the toaster, thinking aloud, "the radio could simply ask him outright. *He'd* know what we should do. But the telephone has been disconnected for nearly three years."

"Two years, ten months, and three days, to be exact," said the radio/alarm.

"Then there's nothing else for us to do but to find the master ourselves."

The other four appliances looked at the toaster in mute amazement.

"It isn't unheard of," the toaster insisted. "Don't you remember —only last week there was a story that the radio was telling us, about a dear little fox terrier who'd been accidentally left behind, like us, at a summer cottage. What was his name?"

"Grover," said the radio. "We heard it on the *Early Morning Roundup*."

"Right. And Grover found his way to his master, hundreds of miles away in a city somewhere in Canada."

"Winnipeg, as I recall," said the radio.

"Right. And to get there he had to cross swamps and mountains and face all sorts of dangers, but he finally did find his way. So, if one silly dog can do all that, think what five sensible appliances, working together, should be able to accomplish."

"Dogs have legs," the blanket objected.

"Oh, don't be a wet blanket," the toaster replied in a bantering way.

It should have known better. The blanket, who didn't have much of a sense of humor and whose feelings were therefore easily hurt, began to whimper and complain that it was time for it to go to bed. Nothing would serve, finally, but that the toaster should make a formal apology, which it did.

"Besides," said the blanket, mollified, "dogs have noses. That's how they find their way."

"As to that," said the old Hoover, "I'd like to see the nose that functions better than mine." And to demonstrate its capabilities it turned itself on and gave a deep, rumbling snuffle up and down the rug.

"Splendid!" declared the toaster. "The vacuum shall be our nose—and our legs as well."

The Hoover turned itself off and said, "I beg your pardon?"

"Oh, I meant to say our *wheels*. Wheels, as I'm sure everyone knows by now, are really more efficient than legs."

"What about the rest of us," the blanket demanded, "who don't have wheels *or legs*? What shall *we* do? I can't *crawl* all the way to wherever it is, and if I tried to, I'd soon be shredded to rags."

The blanket was certainly in a fretful state, but the toaster was a born diplomat, answering every objection in a tone of sweet, unswervable logic.

"You're entirely right; and the radio and I would be in an even sorrier state if we tired to travel such a distance on our own. But that isn't necessary. Because we'll *borrow* some wheels. . . ."

The tensor lamp lighted up. "And build a kind of carriage!"

"And *ride* all the way there," said the radio, "in comfort and luxury." It sounded, at such moments, exactly like the announcer in an advertisement.

"Well, I'm not sure," said the blanket. "I *might* be able to do that."

"The question is," said the toaster, turning to the Hoover, "will *you* be able to?"

Deep in its motor the vacuum cleaner rumbled a rumble of quiet confidence.

It was not as easy a matter as the toaster had supposed to find a serviceable set of wheels. Those he'd had in mind at first belonged to the lawn-mower out in the lean-to shed, but the task of disconnecting them from the mower's heavy blades was beyond the appliances' limited know-how. So, unless the Hoover were willing to cut a swatch of lawn everywhere it went, which it wasn't, the lawnmower's sturdy rubber wheels had to be put out of mind.

The blanket, who was now full of the spirit of adventure, suggested that the bed in the sleeping loft might be used, since it had four castor-type wheels. However, the weight and unwieldiness of the bed were such as to rule out that notion as well. Even on a level road the Hoover would not have had the strength to draw such a load—much less across raw wilderness!

And that seemed to be that. There were no other wheels to be found anywhere about the cottage, unless one counted a tiny knife-sharpener that worked by being rolled along the counter top. The toaster racked its brains trying to turn the knife-sharpener to account, but what kind of carriage can you build with a single wheel that is one and a half inches in diameter?

Then, one Friday, as the Hoover was doing its chores, the idea the toaster had been waiting for finally arrived. The Hoover, as usual, had been grumbling about the old metal office chair that stood in front of the master's desk. No amount of nudging and bumping would ever dislodge its tubular legs from where they bore down on the rug. As the vacuum became more and more fussed, the toaster realized that the chair would have moved very easily . . . *if it had still possessed its original wheels!*

It took the five appliances the better part of an afternoon to jack up the bed in the sleeping loft and remove the castors. But it was no trouble at all to put them on the chair. They slipped right into the tubular legs as though they'd been made for it. Interchangeable parts *are* such a blessing.

And there it was, their carriage, ready to roll. There was quite enough room on the padded seat for all four riders, and being so high it gave them a good view besides. They spent the rest of the day delightedly driving back and forth between the cottage's overgrown flower beds and down the gravel drive to the mailbox. There, however, they had to stop, for that was as far as the Hoover could get, using every extension cord in the cottage.

"If only," said the radio with a longing sigh, "I still had my old batteries. . . ."

"Batteries?" inquired the toaster. "I didn't know you had batteries."

"It was before you joined us," said the radio sadly. "When I was new. After my first batteries corroded, the master didn't see fit to replace them. What need had I for batteries when I could always use the house current?"

"I don't see what possible relevance your little volt-and-a-half batteries could have to *my* problem," observed the Hoover testily.

The radio looked hurt. Usually the Hoover would never have made such an unkind and slighting remark, but the weeks of worry were having their effect on all of them.

"It's *our* problem," the toaster pointed out in a tone of mild reproof, "and the radio is right, you know. If we *could* find a large enough battery, we could strap it under the seat of the chair and set off this very afternoon."

"If!" sniffed the Hoover scornfully. "If! If!"

"And I know where there may be a battery as big as we need!" the tensor lamp piped. "Have you ever looked inside that lean-to behind the cottage?"

"Into the tool shed!" said the blanket with a shudder of horror. "Certainly not! It's dark and musty and filled with spiders."

"Well, I was in it just yesterday, poking about, and there was *something* behind the broken rake and some old paint cans—a big, black, boxy thing. Of course it was nothing like *your* pretty red cylinders." The tensor lamp tipped its hood towards the radio. "But now that I think of it, it may have been a *kind* of battery."

The appliances all trooped out to the lean-to, and there in the darkest corner, just as the lamp had supposed, was the spare battery that had come from the master's old Volkswagen. The battery had been brand-new at the time that he'd decided to trade in the VW on a yellow Saab, and so he'd replaced this one in the lean-to and then—wasn't it just his way?—forgetting all about it.

Between them, the old Hoover and the toaster knew enough about the basic principles of electricity to be able, very quickly, to wire the battery so that it would serve their needs instead of an automobile's. But before any of the small appliances who may be listening to this tale should begin to think that they might do the same thing, let them be warned: ELECTRICITY IS VERY DANGEROUS. *Never* play with old batteries! *Never* put your plug in a strange socket! And if you are in any doubt about the voltage of the current where you are living, *ask a major appliance.*

And so they set off to find their master in the faraway city where he lived. Soon the dear little summer cottage was lost from sight behind the leaves and branches of the forest trees. Deeper and deeper they journeyed into the woods. Only the dimmest dapplings of sunlight penetrated through the dense tangle overhead to guide them on their way. The path wound round and twisted about with bewildering complexity. The road map they had brought with them proved quite useless.

It would have been ever so much easier, of course, to have followed the highway directly into the city, since that is where highways always go. Unfortunately that option was not open to them. Five such sturdy and functional appliances would certainly not have been able to escape the notice of human beings traveling along the same thoroughfare, and it is a rule, which all appliances must obey, that whenever human beings are observing them they must remain perfectly still. On a busy highway they would therefore have been immobilized most of the time. Besides, there was an even stronger reason for staying off the highway—the danger of pirates. But that's a possibility so frightening and awful that we should all simply refuse to think any more about it. Anyhow who ever heard of pirates in the middle of the woods?

The path twisted and turned and rose and fell, and the poor old Hoover became very tired indeed. Even with the power from the battery it was no easy task making its way over such a rugged terrain, especially with the added burden of the office chair and its four riders. But except for its rumbling a little more loudly than usual the old vacuum cleaner did its job without a complaint. What a lesson for us all!

As for the rest of them, they were in the highest spirits. The lamp craned its long neck every which way, exclaiming over the views, and even the blanket soon forgot its fears and joined in the general spirit of holiday adventuring. The toaster's coils were in a continual tingle of excitement. It was all so strange and interesting and full of new information!

"Isn't it wonderful!" exclaimed the radio. "Listen! Do you hear them? Birds!" It did an imitation of the song it had just heard—not one that would have fooled any of the actual birds there in the forest, for in truth it sounded more like a clarinet than a bird. Even so, a thrush, a wood pigeon, and several chickadees did come fluttering down from their roosts and perches high above to cock their heads and listen. But only a moment. After a twitter or two of polite approval they returned to the trees. Birds are like that. They'll pay attention to you for a minute or two and then go right back to being birds.

The radio pretended not to feel slighted, but he soon left off doing imitations and recited, instead, some of his favorite ads, the beautiful songs about Coca-Cola and Esso and a long comic jingle about Barney's Hi-Styles for Guys and Gals. There's nothing that so instantly civilizes a forest as the sound of a familiar advertisement, and soon they were all feeling a lot more confident and cheerful.

As the day wore on, the Hoover was obliged to stop for a rest more and more frequently—ostensibly to empty its dustbag. "Can you believe," it grieved, shaking a last moldering leaf from the bag, "how filthy this forest is?"

"On the contrary," the blanket declared, "It's thoroughly agreeable. The air's so fresh, and just feel the breeze! I feel renewed, as if I'd just come out of my original box. Oh, why, why, why don't they ever take electric blankets on picnics? It isn't fair!"

"Enjoy it while it lasts, kiddo," said the radio ominously. "According to the latest Weather and Traffic Round-up, we're in for rain."

"Won't the trees work like a roof?" asked the lamp. "They keep the sunlight out well enough."

None of them knew the answer to the lamp's question, but as it happens, trees do not work like a roof. They all got more or less wet, and the poor blanket was drenched through and through. Fortunately the storm did not last long and the sun came out immediately afterwards. The wet appliances trudged on along the muddy path, which led them, after a little while, to a clearing in the wood. There in a glade full of sunshine and flowers the blanket was able to spread itself out on the grass and begin to get dry.

The afternoon was wearing on, and the toaster had begun to feel, as all of us do at times, a definite need for solitude. Much as it liked its fellow appliances, it wasn't used to spending the entire day socializing. It longed to be off by itself a moment to be private and think its own thoughts. So, without saying anything to the others, it made its way to the farthest corner of the meadow and began to toast an imaginary muffin. That was always the best way to unwind when things got to be too much for it.

The imaginary muffin had scarcely begun to warm before the toaster's reveries were interrupted by the gentlest of interrogatories.

> "Charming flower, tell me, do,
> What genera and species you
> Belong to. I, as may be seen
> At once, am just a daisy, green
> Of leaf and white of petal. You
> Are neither green nor white nor blue
> Nor any color I have known.
> In what Eden have you grown?
> Sprang you from earth or sky above?
> In either case, accept my love."

"Why, thank you," the toaster replied, addressing the daisy that was pressing its petaled face close to the toaster's gleaming chrome. "It's kind of you to ask, but in fact I'm not a flower at all. I'm an electric toaster."

> "Flower, forebear! You can't deceive
> The being that adores you. Weave
> Your thick black root with mine.
> O beautiful! O half-divine!"

These fervent declarations so embarrassed the toaster that for a moment it was at a loss for words. It had never heard flowers speaking in their own language and didn't realize how they would say any absurd thing that would help them to a rhyme. Flowers, as botanists well know, can only speak in verse. Daisies, being among the simpler flowers, characteristically employ a rough sort of octosyllabic doggerel, but more evolved species, especially those in the tropics, can produce sestinas, rondeaux, and villanelles of the highest order.

The daisy was not, however, simply snared in its own rhyme scheme. It had genuinely fallen in love with the toaster—or, rather, with its own reflection in the toaster's side. Here was a flower (the daisy reflected) strangely like itself and yet utterly unlike itself too. Such a paradox has often been the basis for the most impassioned love. The daisy writhed on its stem and fluttered its white petals as though in the grip of cyclone winds.

The toaster, thoroughly alarmed by such immoderate behavior, said that it really was time to be getting back to its friends on the other side of the meadow.

> "Oh, stay, beloved blossom, stay!
> They say our lives are but a day:
> If that be true, how shall I bear
> To spend that brief day anywhere
> Except with you? You are my light,
> My soil, my air. Stay but one night
> Beside me here—I ask no more.
> Stay, lovely bloom—let me adore
> Those polished petals bright as the dew
> When dawn attempts to rival you,
> That single perfect coiling root—
> Imperishable! Absolute!
> O beautiful! O half-divine!
> Weave your thick black root with mine."

"Now really," said the toaster in a tone of gentle reprimand, "there's no cause to be carrying on like this. We scarcely know each other, and, what's more, you seem to be under a misapprehension as to my nature. Can't you see that what you call my root is an electric cord? As to petals, I can't think *what* you may mean, for I simply don't have any. Now—I really must go and join my friends, for we are journeying to our master's apartment far, far away, and we shall never get there if we don't get a move on."

> "Alas the day and woe is me!
> I tremble in such misery
> As never flower knew before.
> If you must go, let me implore
> One parting boon, one final gift:
> Be merciful as you are swift
> And pluck me from my native ground—
> Pluck me and take me where you're bound.
> I cannot live without you here:
> Then let your bosom be my bier."

Feeling truly shocked by the daisy's suggestion and seeing that the creature was deaf to reason, the toaster hastened to the other side of the meadow and began to urge his friends to set out at once on their journey. The blanket protested that it was still somewhat damp, the Hoover that it was still tired, and the lamp proposed that they spend the night there in the meadow.

And that is what they did. As soon as it grew dark the blanket folded itself into a kind of tent, and the others all crawled inside. The lamp turned itself on, and the radio played some easy-listening music—but very quietly, so as not to disturb other denizens of the forest who might already be asleep. Soon they were asleep themselves. Travel does take it out of you.

The alarm clock had set itself, as usual, for seven-thirty, but the appliances were awake well before that hour. The vacuum cleaner and the lamp both complained, on rising, of a certain stiffness in their joints. However, as soon as they were on their way, the stiffness seemed to melt away.

In the morning light the forest appeared lovelier than ever. Cobwebs glistening with dew were strung like miniature power lines from bough to bough. Pretty mushrooms sprouted from fallen logs, looking for all the world like a string of frosted light bulbs. Leaves rustled. Birds chirped.

The radio was certain that it saw a real fox and wanted to go off after it. "Just to be sure, you know, that it *is* a fox."

The blanket grew quite upset at this suggestion. It had already snagged itself once or twice on low-hanging branches. What ever would become of it, it wanted to know, if it were to venture from the path and into the dense tangle of the forest itself.

"But think," the radio insisted. "—a fox! We'll never have such a chance again."

"*I'd* like to see it," said the lamp.

The toaster, too, was terribly curious, but it could appreciate the blanket's point of view, and so it urged them to continue along the path. "Because, don't you see, we must reach the master as soon as we possibly can."

This was so inarguably true that the radio and lamp readily assented, and they continued on their way. The sun rose in the sky until it had risen all it could, and the path stretched on and on. In the midafternoon there was another shower, after which they once again made camp. Not, this time, in a meadow, for the woods were now quite dense, and the only open places were those under the larger trees. So instead of sunning itself on the grass (for there was neither grass nor sunlight to be found) the blanket hung itself, with the Hoover's help, from the lowest limb of an immense and ancient oak. In minutes it had flapped itself dry.

At twilight, just as the lamp was thinking of turning itself on, there was a stir among the leaves on the branch to the right of the branch from which the blanket was contentedly hanging.

"Hello!" said a squirrel, emerging from the clustered leaves. "I *thought* we had visitors."

"Hello," replied all the appliances together.

"Well, well, well!" The squirrel licked his whiskers. "What do you say then, eh?"

"About what?" asked the toaster, who was not being unfriendly, but who could be a little literal-minded at times, especially when it was tired.

The squirrel looked discountenanced. "Allow me to introduce myself. I'm Harold." Having pronounced his name, his good humor seemed completely restored. "And this fair creature—"

Another squirrel dropped from a higher branch and lighted beside Harold.

"—is my wife Marjorie."

"Now you must tell us your names," said Marjorie, "since we've just told you ours."

"We don't have names, I'm afraid," said the toaster. "You see, we're appliances."

"If you don't have names," Harold demanded, "how do you know which of you are men and which are women?"

"We aren't either. We're appliances." The toaster turned to the Hoover for confirmation.

"Whatever *that* may mean," said Marjorie brusquely. "It can't alter a universal law. Everyone is either a man or a woman. Mice are. Birds are. Even, I'm given to understand, insects." She held her paw up to her lips and tittered. "Do you like to eat insects?"

"No," said the toaster. "Not at all." It would have been more trouble than it was worth to explain to the squirrels that appliances didn't eat anything.

"Neither do I, *really*," said Marjorie. "But I love nuts. Do you have any with you? Possibly in that old sack?"

"No," said the Hoover stiffly. "There is nothing in that old sack, as you call it, but dirt. About five pounds of dirt, I'd estimate."

"And what is the use, pray, of saving dirt?" asked Harold. When no answer seemed forthcoming, he said, "I know what we'd all enjoy doing. We can tell jokes. You start."

"I don't think I know any jokes," said the Hoover.

"Oh, I do," said the radio. "You're not Polish, are you?"

The squirrels shook their heads.

"Good. Tell me—why does it take three Poles to screw in a light bulb?"

Marjorie giggled expectantly. "I don't know—why?"

"One to hold the light bulb, and the other two to turn the ladder around."

The squirels looked at each other with bewilderment.

"Explain it," said Harold. "Which are the men and which are the women?"

"It doesn't matter. They're just very stupid. That's the whole idea of Polish jokes, that Poles are supposed to be so stupid that no matter what they try and do they misfunction. Of course, it's not fair to Poles, who are probably as bright as anyone else, but they are funny jokes. I know hundreds more."

"Well, if that was a fair sample, I can't say I'm very keen to hear the rest," said Marjorie. "Harold, you tell him—"

"It," the radio corrected. "We're all it's."

"Tell *them*," Majorie continued, "the one about the three squirrels out in the snow." She turned to the lamp confidingly. "This will lay you out. Believe me."

As Harold told the joke about the three squirrels in the snow, the appliances exchanged glances of guarded disapproval. It wasn't just that they disapproved of dirty jokes (especially the old Hoover); in addition, they didn't find such jokes amusing. Gender and the complications it gives rise to simply aren't relevant to the lives appliances lead.

Harold finished his joke, and Marjorie laughed loyally, but none of the appliances cracked a smile.

"Well," said Harold, miffed, "I hope you enjoy your stay under *our* oak."

With which, and a flick of their big furry tails, the two squirrels scampered up the trunk and out of sight.

In the small hours of the night the toaster woke from a terrible nightmare in which it had been about to fall into a bathtub full of water to discover itself in a plight almost as terrible. Thunder was thundering, and lightning was streaking the sky, and rain was pelting it mercilessly. At first the toaster couldn't remember where it was or why it was there, and when it did remember, it realized with dismay that the electric blanket, which ought to have been spread out and sheltering the other four appliances, had disappeared! And the rest of them? They were still here, thank heaven, though in a state of fearful apprehension, each one of them.

"Oh dear," groaned the Hoover, "I should have *known*, I should have *known!* We never, never should have left our home."

The lamp in an extremity of speechless agitation was twisting its head rapidly from side to side, casting its little beam of light across the gnarled roots of the oak, while the radio's alarm had gone off and would not stop ringing. Finally the toaster went over to the radio and turned the alarm off itself.

"Oh, thank you," said the radio, its voice blurry with static. "Thank you so much."

"Where is the blanket?" the toaster demanded apprehensively.

"Blown away!" said the radio. "Blown off to the far end of the forest, where we shall never be able to find it!"

"Oh, I should have *known!*" groaned the Hoover. "I should have *known!*"

"It's not your fault," the toaster assured the vacuum, but it only groaned the louder.

Seeing that it could not be of any help to the vacuum, the toaster went over to the lamp and tried to calm it down. Once its beam was steady, the toaster suggested that it be directed into the branches above them, on the chance that the blanket, when it was blown away, might have been snagged on one of them. The lamp did so, but it was a very faint light and a very tall oak and a very dark night, and the blanket, if it were up there, was not to be seen.

All of a sudden there was a flash of lightning. The radio's alarm went off again, and the lamp shrieked and folded itself up as small as could be. Of course it's silly to be afraid of lightning, since it's only another form of electricity. But such a large form—and so uncontrolled! If you were a person, instead of an appliance, and you encountered a berserk giant many times larger than yourself, you'd have some idea how the average electric appliance feels about lightning.

In the brief moment that the lightning was lighting everything up, the toaster, who had been peering up into the oak, was able to make out a shape—all twisted about—that *might* have been the blanket. The toaster waited until there was another lightning flash; and, yes, definitely, it *was* the yellow blanket, which had indeed become snagged on one of the highest branches of the tree.

Once they all knew that the blanket was nearby, even though they still had no idea how they'd be able to get it down, the storm ceased to seem quite so scary. The rain made them quite miserable, as rain will do, but their worst anxieties were over. Even the occasional bolt of lightning was now something to be wished for rather than dreaded, since by its brightness they could glimpse their companion high above them, clutching to the limb of the oak and flailing in the ceaseless winds. How could they feel afraid, or even sorry for themselves, when they considered the terrors the poor blanket must be experiencing?

By morning the storm had abated. The radio, at top volume, called up to the blanket, but the blanket made no response. For one horrible moment the toaster thought its friend might have stopped working altogether. But the radio kept on calling to the blanket, and after a time it made a feeble reply, waving one wet bedraggled corner at its friends.

"YOU CAN COME DOWN NOW," the radio shouted. "THE STORM IS OVER."

"I *can't*," said the blanket with a whimper. "I'm stuck. I *can't* get down."

"You must try," the toaster urged.

"What's that?" said the blanket.

"THE TOASTER SAYS YOU MUST TRY!"

"But I told you—I'm *stuck*. And there's a great rip right through the center of me. And another by my hem. And I hurt." The blanket began to wring itself convulsively, and a steady patter of droplets fell from its rain-soaked wool into the puddles below.

"What the deuce is all this racket about?" Harold demanded imperiously, stepping forth from his nest high in the trunk of the oak. "Do you have any idea what *time* it is? Squirrels are trying to sleep."

The radio apologized to Harold and then explained the cause of the commotion. Like most squirrels, Harold was essentially kind-hearted, and when he saw what had happened to the blanket, he immediately offered his assistance. First he went into his nest and woke his wife. Then together the two squirrels began to help the blanket to loosen itself from where it had been snared. It was a long and—to judge by the blanket's cries—painful process, but at last it was done, and with the squirrels' help the liberated blanket made its way, slowly and carefully, down the trunk of the tree.

The appliances gathered round their friend, commiserating over his many injuries and rejoicing at his rescue.

"How shall we ever be able to repay you?" said the toaster warmly, turning to Harold and Marjorie. "You've saved our friend from a fate too terrible to imagine. We're *so* grateful."

"Well," said Marjorie cagily, "I can't remember whether or not you said you had any nuts with you. But if you do. . . ."

"Believe me," said the Hoover, "if we did, you would have them all. But you can see for yourselves that my bag contains nothing but dust and dirt." Whereupon it opened its dustbag and a thick brown sludge of rain-sodden topsoil oozed forth.

"Though we don't have nuts," said the toaster to the disconsolate squirrels, "perhaps there is something *I* could do for you. That is, if you like *roasted* nuts."

"Indeed, yes," said Harold. "Any kind will do."

"Then if you can provide me with some nuts, I shall roast them. As many as you like."

Harold narrowed his eyes suspiciously. "You mean you want us to give *you* the nuts *we've* been storing up all this summer?"

"If you'd like me to roast them," answered the toaster brightly.

"Oh, darling, do," Marjorie urged. "I don't know what he means to do, but *he* seems to. And we might like it."

"I think it's a trick," said Harold.

"Just two or three of the ones that are left from last year. Please?"

"Oh, very well."

Harold scampered up the tree trunk to his nest and returned

with four acorns stuffed in the pouches of his cheeks. At the toaster's bidding Harold and Marjorie cracked them open, and then Harold placed them carefully on the thin strips of metal that went up and down inside the toaster's slots. As these strips were meant to accommodate large slices of bread, it had to be very careful lest the tiny round acorns should roll off as it lowered them into itself. When this was done it turned on its coils and commenced toasting them. When the acorns were starting to turn a crispy brown, the toaster lifted them up gently as far as it could, turned off its coils, and (when it judged the squirrels would not burn their paws by reaching in) bade them take out the roasted nuts and taste them.

"Delicious!" Marjorie declared.

"Exquisite!" Harold agreed.

As soon as the squirrels had eaten the first four acorns, they returned to their nest for more, and when those were gone still more, and then again some more after that. Marjorie, especially, was insatiable. She urged the toaster to remain in the forest as their guest. It could stay in their own nest, where it would always be dry and cozy, and she would introduce it to all their friends.

"I'd love to be able to accept," said the toaster, from a sense not only of politeness but of deep obligation as well, "but it really isn't possible. Once I've roasted your nuts for you—would you like some more?—we *must* be on our way to the city where our master lives."

While the toaster roasted some more acorns, the radio explained to the squirrels the important reason for their journey. It also demonstrated its own capacities as a utensil and persuaded the other appliances to do the same. The poor Hoover was scarcely able to function from having been clogged with mud, and the squirrels, in any case, could not see the point of sweeping up dirt from one place and putting it somewhere else. Nor did the lamp's beams or the radio's music excite their admiration. However, they were both very taken with the electric blanket, which, damp as it was, had plugged itself into the battery strapped under the office chair and was glowing warmly. Marjorie renewed her invitation to the toaster and extended it to the blanket as well. "Until," she explained, "you're quite well again."

"That's very kind," said the blanket, "and of course I'm so grateful for all you've done. But we must be on our way. Truly."

Marjorie sighed resignedly. "At least," she said, "keep your tail tucked into that black thing that makes the furry part of you so delightfully hot. Until you have to leave. The warmth is so pleasant. Isn't it, my dear?"

"Oh, yes," said Harold, who was busy shelling acorns. "Most agreeable."

The Hoover ventured a mild protest, for it feared that with both the toaster and the blanket working so hard the battery would be worn down needlessly. But really what else could they do but comply with the squirrels' request? Besides, quite apart from their debt of gratitude, it felt so good to be useful again! The toaster would have gone on gladly roasting acorns all morning and all afternoon, and the squirrels seemed of much the same disposition.

"It's strange," said Harold complacently, while he stroked the toaster's side (now sadly streaked with raindrop patterns like the outside of a window), "it's more than strange that you should maintain you have no sex, when it's very clear to me that you're male." He studied his own face in the mottled chromium. "You have a man's whiskers and a man's front teeth."

"Nonsense, darling," said his wife, who was lying on the other side of the toaster. "Now that I look carefully, I can see her whiskers are most definitely a woman's whiskers and teeth as well."

"I won't argue, my love, about anything so patently obvious as whether or not a man is a man, for it's evident that he is!"

It suddenly dawned on the toaster how the squirrels—and the daisy the day before—had come by their confusions. They were seeing *themselves* in his sides! Living in the wild as they did, where there are no bathroom mirrors, they were unacquainted with the principle of reflectivity. It considered trying to explain their error to them, but what would be the use? They would only go away with hurt feelings. You can't always expect people, or squirrels, to be rational. Appliances, yes—appliances have to be rational, because they're built that way.

To Harold the toaster explained, under seal of strictest secrecy, that it was indeed, just as he had supposed, a man; and to Marjorie it confided, under a similar pact of trust, that it was a woman. It hoped they were both true to their promises. If not, their argument would be fated to continue for a long, long while.

With its coils turned to HIGH, the blanket was soon quite dry, and so, after a final round of roast acorns, the appliances said good-bye to Harold and Marjorie and continued on their way.

And what a long and weary way it was! The forest stretched on seemingly forever with the most monotonous predictability, each tree just like the next—trunk, branches, leaves; trunk, branches, leaves. Of course a tree would have taken a different view of the matter. We all tend to see the way *others* are alike and how *we* differ, and it's probably just as well we do, since that prevents a great deal of confusion. But perhaps we should remind ourselves from time to time that ours is a very partial view, and that the world is full of a great deal more variety than we ever manage to take in. At this stage of their journey, however, the appliances had lost sight of this important truth, and they were very bored and impatient, in addition simply to being worn to a frazzle. Rust spots had begun to develop alarmingly on the unchromed bottom of the toaster and inside it as well. The stiffness that the vacuum and lamp complained of each morning on rising no longer vanished with a bit of exercise but persisted through the day. As for the blanket, it was almost in tatters, poor thing. Alone of the appliances, the radio seemed not to have suffered damage from the demands of the trip.

The toaster began to worry that when they did at last arrive at the master's apartment they would be in such raggle-taggle condition that he would have no further use for them. They'd be put on the scrap heap, and all their efforts to reach him would have been in vain! What a dreadful reward for so much loyalty and devotion! But it is a rare human being who will be swayed by considerations of the heart in his dealings with appliances, and the master, as the toaster well knew, was not notable for his tender conscience. Its own predecessor at the cottage had still been quite serviceable when it had been sent to the dump, its only faults having been that its chrome had been worn away in patches and that its sense of timing was sometimes erratic. In its youth the toaster had thought these sufficient grounds for the older appliance's replacement, but now. . . .

Now it was better not to think about such matters. Better simply to pursue one's duty wherever it led, along the path through the forest.

Until, at the bank of a wide river, that path finally came to an end.

They were all, at first sight of that broad impassable expanse of water, utterly cast-down and despairing, none more so than the Hoover, which became almost incoherent in its distress. "No!" it roared aloud. "I refuse! Never! Oh! Stop, turn me off, empty my bag, leave me alone, go away!" It began to choke and sputter, and then ran over its own cord and started chewing on it. Only the toaster had enough presence of mind to wrest the cord from the vacuum's powerful suction grip. Then, to calm it down, it led the Hoover back and forth across the grassy bank of the river in regular, carpet-sweeping swathes.

At last these habitual motions brought the Hoover round to a more reasonable frame of mind, and it was able to account for its extraordinary alarm. It was not only the sight of this new obstacle that had distressed it so, but, as well, its certainty that the battery was now too run-down for them to be able to return to the cottage by its power. They could not go forward and they could not turn back. They were marooned! Marooned in the middle of the forest, and soon it would be fall and they would have no shelter from the inclemencies of the autumn weather, and then it would be winter and they'd be buried in the snow. Their metal parts would corrode. The Hoover's rubber belt would crack. They would be powerless to resist the forces that would slowly but surely debilitate and destroy them, and in only a few months—or even weeks—they would all be unable to work.

No wonder the Hoover, foreseeing this inevitable progression of events, had been beside itself. What *were* they to do? the toaster asked itself.

There was no answer immediately forthcoming.

Toward evening the radio announced that it was receiving interference from a source quite nearby. "A power drill, by the feel of it. Just on the other side of the river."

Where there was a power drill there were bound to be power lines as well! New hope poured into the appliances like a sudden surge of current.

"Let's look at the map again," said the lamp. "Maybe we can figure out exactly where we are."

Following the lamp's suggestion, they unfolded the road map

and looked very carefully at all the dots and squiggles between the spot (marked with a Magic Marker) along the highway where the cottage was situated and the little patch of pink representing the city they were bound for. At last, only a quarter-inch from the pink patch of the city, they found the wavery blue line that had to be the river they'd come to, since there were no other blue lines anywhere between the cottage and the city, and this river was much too big for the mapmakers to have forgotten all about it.

"We're almost there!" the radio trumpeted. "We'll make it! Everything will be all right! Hurrah!"

"Hurrah!" the other appliances agreed, except for the Hoover, who wasn't so easily convinced that all would now be well. But when the lamp pointed out four distinct places where the river was traversed by highways, even the Hoover had to admit that there was cause to cheer up, though he still wouldn't go so far as to say "Hurrah."

"We only have to follow the river," said the toaster, who did like to give instructions, even when it was obvious what had to be done, "either to the left or the right, and eventually it must lead us to one of those bridges. Then, when it's very late and there's no traffic, we can make a dash for it!"

So once again they set off with courage renewed and determination strengthened. It was not so light a task as the toaster had made it sound, for there was no longer a clear path to follow. Sometimes the bank of the river lay flat as a carpet, but elsewhere the ground got quite bumpy or—what was worse—quaggy and soft. Once, avoiding a rock, the Hoover took a sharp turn; and the office chair, getting a leg mired in an unremarked patch of mud, was overturned, and the four appliances riding on it tumbled off the plastic seat into a thorough slough. They emerged smirched and spattered, and were obliged to become dirtier still in the process of retrieving the castor wheel that had come off the chair and was lost in the mud.

The blanket, naturally, was exempted from this task, and while the four others delved for the lost wheel, it betook itself down the water's edge and attempted to wash away the signs of its spill. Lacking any cloth or sponge, the blanket only succeeded, sad to say, in spreading the stains over a larger area. So preoccupied was the blanket with its hopeless task that it almost failed to notice—

"A boat!" the blanket cried out. "All of you, come here! I've found a boat!"

Even the toaster, with no experience at all in nautical matters, could see that the boat the blanket had discovered was not of the first quality. Its wood had the weather-beaten look of the clapboard at the back of the summer cottage that the master had always been meaning to replace, or at least repaint, and its bottom must be leaky for it was filled with one big puddle of green mush. Nevertheless, it must have been basically serviceable, since a Chriscraft outboard motor was mounted on the blunt back-end, and who would put an expensive motor on a boat that couldn't at least stay afloat?

"How providential," said the Hoover.

"You don't intend for us to *use* this boat, do you?" asked the toaster.

"Of course we shall," replied the vacuum. "Who knows how far it may be to a bridge? This will take us across the river directly. You're not afraid to ride in it, are you?"

"Afraid? Certainly not!"

"Well, then?"

"It doesn't *belong* to us, if we were to take it, we'd be no better than . . . than pirates!"

Pirates, as even the newest of my listeners will have been informed, are people who take things that belong to other people. They are the bane of an appliance's existence, since once an appliance has been spirited away by a pirate, it has no choice but to serve its bidding just as though it were that appliance's legitimate master. A bitter disgrace, such servitude—and one that few appliances can hope to escape once it has fallen to their lot. Truly, there is no fate, even obsolescence, so terrible as falling into the hands of pirates.

"Pirates!" exclaimed the Hoover. "Us? What nonsense? Who ever heard of an appliance that was a pirate?"

"But if we took the boat—" the toaster insisted.

"We wouldn't *keep* it," said the Hoover brusquely. "We'd just borrow it a little while to cross the river and leave it on the other side. Its owner would get it back soon enough."

"How long we'd have it for doesn't matter. It's the *principle* of the thing. Taking what isn't yours is piracy."

"Oh, as for principles," said the radio lightly, "there's a well-known saying: '*From* each according to his ability, *to* each according to his need.' Which means, as far as I can see, that someone who makes use of his abilities should get to use a boat when he or it needs to cross a river and the boat is just sitting there waiting." With which, and a little chuckle besides, the radio hopped onto the foremost seat of the rowboat.

Following the radio's example, the Hoover heaved the office chair into the back of the boat and then got in itself. The boat settled deep in the water.

Avoiding the toaster's accusing look, the blanket took a seat beside the radio.

The lamp seemed to hesitate, but only for a moment. Then it too entered the boat.

"Well?" said the Hoover gruffly. "We're waiting."

Reluctantly the toaster prepared to board the boat. But then, inexplicably, *something made it stop*. What's happening? it wondered—though it could not say the words aloud, for the same force preventing it from moving prevented its speech as well.

The four appliances in the boat had been similarly incapacitated. What had happened, of course, was that the owner of the boat had returned and *seen* the appliances. "Why, what's this?" he exclaimed, stepping from behind a willow tree with a fishing rod in one hand and a string of sunfish in the other. "It seems we've had some visitors!"

He said much more than this, but in a manner so rough and ill-mannered that it were better not to repeat his words verbatim. The sum of it was this—that he believed the owner of the appliances had been about to steal his boat, and so he intended, by way of retaliation, to steal the appliances!

He took the toaster from where it sat spellbound on the grassy riverbank and set it in the rowboat beside the blanket, lamp and radio. Then, unfastening the battery from the office chair, he threw the latter end-over-end high up into the air. It came down—Splash!—in the middle of the river and sank down to the muddy bottom, nevermore to be seen.

Then the pirate—for there could no longer be any doubt that such he was—started the Chriscraft motor and set off upstream with his five helpless captives.

After mooring his boat alongside a ramshackle dock on the other side of the river, the pirate loaded the outboard motor and the appliances onto the wooden bed of a very dusty pickup truck —except for the radio, which he took with him into the front seat. As it drove off, the truck jolted and jounced and bolted and bounced so violently the toaster feared the ride would cost it every coil in its body. (For though toasters look quite sturdy, they are actually among the more delicate appliances and need to be handled accordingly.) But the blanket, realizing the danger the toaster was in, managed to slip underneath its old friend and cushion it from the worst shocks of the journey.

As they rode they could hear the radio in the front seat humming the poignant theme-song from *Dr. Zhivago.*

"Listen!" the Hoover hissed. "Of all possible songs to be singing, it has chosen one of the master's favorites. Already it has forgotten him!"

"Ah," said the toaster, "what choice does it have, poor thing? Once one of us had been turned on, would we have behaved any otherwise? Would you? Would I?"

The old vacuum groaned, and the radio went on playing its sad, sad song.

What graveyards are for people—horrible, creepy places that any reasonable individual tries to stay away from—the City Dump is for appliances and machines of every description. Imagine, therefore, what the appliances must have felt when they realized (the pirate had parked his pickup in front of high, ripply iron gates and was opening the padlock with a key from the ring that swung from his belt) that they had been brought to the City Dump! Imagine their horror as he drove the truck inside and they assimilated the terrible fact that he lived here! There, with smoke curling from a tin chimney, was his wretched shack—and all about it the most melancholy and fearsome sights the toaster had ever witnessed. Dismembered chassis of once-proud automobiles were heaped one atop the other to form veritable mountains of rusted iron. The asphalt-covered ground was everywhere strewn with twisted beams and blistered sheet metal, with broken and worn-out machine parts of all shapes and sizes—with all the terrible emblems, in short, of its own inevitable obsolescence. An appalling scene to behold—yet one that exercised a strange fascination over the toaster's mind. As often as it had heard of the City Dump, it had somehow never really believed in its existence. And now it was here, and nothing, not even the pirate's stony gaze, could prevent its shudder of fear and wonder.

The pirate got out of the truck and took the radio, along with his fishing rod and his day's catch, into the hovel where he lived. The appliances, left to themselves in the back of the truck, listened to the radio sing song after song with apparently indefatigable good cheer. Among them was the toaster's own favorite melody, "I Whistle a Happy Tune." The toaster was certain this couldn't be a coincidence. The radio was trying to tell its friends that if they were brave and patient and cheerful, matters would work out for the best. Anyhow, whether that was the radio's intention or just a program it had been tuned to, it was what the toaster firmly believed.

After he'd had his dinner the pirate came out of his shack to examine the other appliances. He fingered the Hoover's mud-stained dustbag and the frayed part of its cord where it had been chewing on itself. He lifted the blanket and shook his head in mute deprecation. He looked inside the lamp's little hood and saw—which the lamp itself had not realized till now—that its tiny bulb was shattered. (It must have happened when the lamp had fallen off the office chair, just before they'd found the boat.)

Finally the pirate picked up the toaster—and made a scornful grimace. "Junk!" he said, depositing the toaster on a nearby scrap pile.

"Junk!" he repeated, dealing with the lamp in a similar fashion.

"Junk!" He hurled the poor blanket over the projecting, broken axle of a '57 Ford.

"Junk!" He set the Hoover down on the asphalt with a shattering *thunk*.

"All of it, just junk." Having delivered this dismaying verdict, the pirate returned to his shack, where the radio had gone on singing in the liveliest manner all the while.

"Thank goodness," said the toaster aloud, as soon as he was gone.

"Thank goodness?" the Hoover echoed in stricken tones. "How

can you say 'Thank goodness' when you've just been called junk and thrown on a heap of scrap?"

"Because if he'd decided to take us into his shack and use us, we'd have become his, like the radio. This way we've got a chance to escape."

The blanket, where it hung, limply, from the broken axle, began to whimper and whine. "No, no, it's true. That's all I am now—junk! Look at me—look at these tears, these snags, these stains. Junk! This is where I belong."

The lamp's grief was quieter but no less bitter. "Oh, my bulb," it murmured, "oh, my poor poor bulb!"

The Hoover groaned.

"Pull yourselves together, all of you!" said the toaster, in what it hoped was a tone of stern command. "There's nothing wrong with any of us that a bit of fixing-up won't put right. You—" it addressed the blanket "—are still fundamentally sound. Your coils haven't been hurt. After some sewing up and a visit to the dry cleaner you'll be as good as new."

It turned to the lamp. "And what nonsense—to fuss over a broken bulb! You've broken your bulb before and probably will many times again. What do you think replaceable parts are *for?*"

Finally the toaster directed its attention to the vacuum cleaner. "And you? You, who must be our leader! Who ought to inspire us with your own greater strength! For *you* to sit there groaning and helpless! And just because some old pirate who lives in a dump makes an unflattering remark. Why, he probably doesn't even know how to *use* a vacuum cleaner—that's the sort of person *he* is!"

"Do you think so?" said the Hoover.

"Of course I do, and so would you if you'd be rational. Now, for goodness' sake, let's all sit down together and figure out how we're going to rescue the radio and escape from here."

By midnight it was amazing how much they'd managed to accomplish. The Hoover had recharged the rundown battery from the battery in the pirate's own truck. Meanwhile the lamp, in looking about for another doorway or gate than the one they'd come in by (there wasn't any), had discovered a vehicle even better suited to their needs than the office chair the pirate had thrown in the river. This was a large vinyl perambulator, which is another word for pram, which is also known, in the appliances' part of the world, as a baby buggy. By whatever name, it was in good working order—except for two minor faults. One fault was a squeak in the left front wheel, and the other was the way its folding visor was twisted out of shape so as to give the whole pram an air of lurching sideways when it was moving straight ahead. The squeak was fixed with a few drops of 3-in-1 Oil, but the visor resisted their most determined efforts to bend it back into true. But that didn't matter, after all. What mattered was that it *worked*.

To think how many of the things consigned to this dump were still, like the pram (or themselves, for that matter) essentially serviceable! There were hair dryers and four-speed bicycles, water heaters and wind-up toys that would all have gone on working for years and years with just the slightest maintenance. Instead, they'd be sent to City Dump! You could hear the hopeless sighs and crazed murmurings rising from every dark mound round about, a ghastly medley that seemed to swell louder every moment as more and more of the forlorn, abandoned objects became conscious of the energetic new appliances in their midst.

"You will never, never, never get away," whispered a mad old cassette player in a cracked voice. "No, never! You will stay here like all the rest of us and rust and crack and turn to dust. And never get away."

"We will, though," said the toaster. "Just you wait and see."

But how? That was the problem the toaster had to solve without further delay.

Now the surest way to solve any problem is to think about it, and that's just what the toaster did. It thought with the kind of total, all-out effort you have to give to get a bolt off that's rusted onto a screw. At first the bolt won't budge, not the least bit, and the wrench may slip loose, and you begin to doubt that any amount of trying is going to accomplish your purpose. But you keep at it, and use a dab of solvent if there's any on hand, and eventually it starts to give. You're not even sure but you think so. And then, what do you know, it's off! You've done it! That's the way the toaster thought, and at last, because he thought so hard, he thought of a way they could escape from the pirate and rescue the radio at the same time.

"Now here's my plan," said the toaster to the other appliances, which had gathered round him in the darkest corner of the dump. "*We'll frighten* him, and that will make him run away, and when he's gone we'll go into his shack—"

"Oh, no, *I couldn't* do that," said the blanket with a shiver of dread.

"We'll go into his shack," the toaster insisted calmly, "and get the radio and put it inside the baby buggy and get in ourselves, all except the Hoover, of course, which will high-tail it out of this place just as fast as it can."

"But won't the gate be locked?" the lamp wanted to know. "It is now."

"No, because the pirate will have to unlock it to get out himself, and he'll be too frightened to remember to lock it behind him."

"It's a very good plan," said the Hoover, "but what I don't understand is—*how* are we going to frighten him?"

"Well, what are people afraid of the most?"

"Getting run over by a steam roller?" the Hoover guessed.

"No. Scarier than that."

"Moths?" suggested the blanket.

"No."

"The dark," declared the lamp with conviction.

"That's close," said the toaster. "They're afraid of ghosts."

"What are ghosts?" demanded the Hoover.

"Ghosts are people who are dead, only they're also sort of alive."

"Don't be silly," said the lamp. "Either they *are* dead or they aren't."

"Yes," the blanket agreed. "It's as simple as ON and OFF. If you're ON, you can't be OFF, and vice versa."

"*I* know that, and *you* know that, but people don't seem to. People say they know that ghosts don't exist but they're afraid of them anyhow."

"No one can be afraid of something that doesn't exist," the Hoover huffed.

"Don't ask me how they do it," said the toaster. "It's what they call a paradox. The point is this—people are afraid of ghosts. And so *we're* going to pretend to be one."

"How?" asked the Hoover skeptically.

"Let me show you. Stoop down. Lower. Wrap your cord around my cord. Now—lift me up . . ."

After an hour's practice of pretending to be a ghost, they decided they were ready. Carefully, so that the other appliances wouldn't fall off, the old Hoover trundled toward the window of the shack. The toaster, where it was balanced atop the handle of the vacuum, was just able to see inside. There on a table between a stack of unwashed dishes and the pirate's ring of keys was the poor captive radio, and there, in dirty striped pajamas, getting ready to go to bed, was the pirate.

"Ready?" the toaster whispered.

The blanket, which was draped over the vacuum in a roughly ghostlike shape with a kind of hood at the top through which the toaster was able to peer out, adjusted its folds one last time. "Ready," the blanket replied.

"Ready?" the toaster asked again.

For just a moment the lamp, where it was hidden halfway down the handle of the Hoover, turned itself on and then, quickly off. The bulb it had taken from the socket in the ceiling of the pickup truck had only half the wattage it was used to, and so its beam of light was noticeably dimmer—just enough to make the blanket give off the faintest yellowish glow.

"Then let's start haunting," said the toaster.

That was the signal the Hoover had been waiting for.

"Whoo!" groaned the Hoover in its deepest, most quivery voice. "Whoo!"

The pirate looked up with alarm. "Who's there?" he demanded.

"Whoo—oo!" the Hoover continued.

"Whoever you are, you'd better go away."

"Whoo—oo—oo!"

Cautiously the pirate approached the window from which the groaning seemed to issue.

Upon receiving a secret electric signal from the toaster, the vacuum crept quietly alongside the shack to where they would be out of sight from the window.

"Whoo . . ." breathed the Hoover in the barest of whispers. "Whoo . . . Whoo—oo . . ."

"Who's out there?" the pirate demanded, pressing his nose against the pane of glass and peering into the outer darkness. "You'd better answer me. Do you hear?"

In answer the Hoover made a strangling, gurgling, gaspy sound that sounded frightening even if you knew it was only the Hoover doing it. By now the pirate, who didn't have any idea what this mysterious groaning might be, had got into a considerable state of nerves. When you live all alone in the City Dump you don't expect to hear strange noises just outside your window in the middle of the night. And if you were also a bit superstitious, as pirates tend to be. . . .

"All right then—if you won't say who you are, I'm going to come out there and find out!" He lingered yet a while before the window, but at last, when no reply was forthcoming, the pirate pulled on his pants and then got into his boots. "I'm warning you!" he called out, though not in a tone that could be called threatening.

Still there was no reply. The pirate took up his key ring from where it lay on the table beside the radio. He went to the door.

He opened it.

"Now!" said the toaster, signaling secretly to the blanket along its electric cord.

"I can't," said the blanket, all atremble. "I'm too afraid."

"You *must!*"

"I mustn't: it's against the rules."

"We discussed all that before, and you *promised*. Now hurry—before he gets here!"

With a shudder of trepidation the blanket did as it was bidden. There was a rent in its side where it had been pierced by a branch on the night it was blown up into the tree. The lamp was hiding just behind this rent. As the pirate appeared around the corner of the shack, the blanket twitched the torn fabric aside.

The pirate stopped short in his tracks when he saw the shrouded figure before him.

"Whoo—oo!" groaned the Hoover one last time.

At this cue the lamp turned itself on. Its beam slanted up through the hole in the blanket right into the pirate's face.

When the lamp lit up, the pirate stared at the figure before him with the utmost horror. What he saw that was so frightening was the same thing the daisy had seen, the same thing Harold and Marjorie had seen, as well—he saw his own features reflected in the toaster's mottled chrome. And as he had been a very wicked person from his earliest youth, his face had taken on that special kind of ugliness that only very evil people's faces acquire. Seeing such a face grimacing at him from this strange hooded figure, what was the pirate to suppose but that he had come upon the most dangerous kind of ghost, the kind that understands exactly who we are and knows all the wrong things we've done and intends to punish us for them. From such ghosts even grown-up pirates will flee in terror. Which is exactly what the pirate did.

As soon as he was gone, the appliances rushed into the pirate's shack and rescued the joyful radio. Then before the pirate could return they scrambled into the baby buggy, and the old Hoover drove off with them as fast as its wheels would revolve.

As luck would have it, they didn't have much farther to go: where the master lived on Newton Avenue was only a mile or so from City Dump. They reached his apartment building early in the morning before a single milk truck had appeared on the street.

"You see," said the toaster cheerfully, "in the end everything really does work out for the best."

Alas, the toaster had spoken too soon. Their tribulations were not yet at an end, and not everything would work out for the best, as they were shortly to discover.

The Hoover, which had an instinctive knack for such things, buzzed the street door open and summoned the automatic elevator. When the elevator door slid open, it wheeled the pram in and pressed the button for the 14th floor.

"It's *changed* so," said the tensor lamp, as the Hoover pushed the pram out of the elevator and down the corridor. "The wallpaper used to be green squiggles and white blobs, and now it's crisscross lines."

"It's we who've changed," said the blanket miserably.

"Hush," said the Hoover sternly. "Remember the rules!" It pressed the doorbell beside the door to the master's apartment.

All the appliances kept perfectly still.

No one came to the door.

"Maybe he's asleep," said the alarm clock/radio.

"Maybe he's not home," said the Hoover. "I'll see." It rang the doorbell again, but in a different way so that only the appliances in the apartment would be able to hear it ring.

In only a moment a Singer sewing machine answered the door. "Yes?" said the sewing machine in a tone of polite curiosity. "Can I help you?"

"Oh, excuse me, I seem to have made a mistake." The Hoover looked at the number on the door, then at the name on the brass panel over the bell. It was the right number, the right name. But . . . a sewing machine?

"Is that. . . . ?" said a familiar voice within the apartment. "Why, it is! It's the old Hoover! How *are* you? Come in! Come in!"

The Hoover wheeled the pram into the apartment and over the deep-piled carpet toward the friendly old TV.

The blanket peeked out shyly over the side of the pram.

"And who's that with you? Come out—don't be shy. My goodness, what a treat this is."

The blanket crawled out of the pram, taking care to keep the worst effects of the journey folded up out of sight. It was followed by the radio, the lamp, and, last of all, the toaster.

The TV, which knew all five of them from the time it had spent with the master at the summer cottage, introduced them to the many appliances from all over the apartment which had begun to gather in the living room. Some, like the Water Pik, the blender, and the TV itself, were old friends. Some, like the stereo and the clock on the mantel, were known to the four appliances that had lived in the apartment at one time themselves but not to the toaster. But a great many were complete strangers to them all. There were huge impractical ginger-jar lamps squatting on low tables and, out of the bedroom, dim little lamps with frilly shades and other lamps screwed into the dining-nook wall that were pretending to be candleflames. Out of the kitchen had trooped a whole tribe of unfamiliar gadgets: a crockpot, a can opener, a waffle iron, a meat grinder, a carving knife, and, somewhat abashedly, the master's new toaster.

"How do you do," said the new toaster in a barely audible voice when the TV introduced it.

"How do *you* do?" the toaster replied warmly.

Neither could think of anything else to say. Fortunately there were more introductions to be effected. The Hoover had to go through a similar ordeal when it met the apartment's vacuum cleaner, which was (just as the Hoover had feared) one of the new lightweight models that looks like a big hamburger bun on wheels. They were polite to each other, but it was obvious that the new vacuum looked on the Hoover as outmoded.

The blanket had an even worse shock in store. The last two appliances to appear in the living room were a vaporizer and a long tangled string of Christmas tree lights, both of which had been hibernating in a closet. The blanket looked about anxiously. "Well," it said, making a determined effort to seem accepting and friendly, "I think there must still be one more of you we haven't yet met."

"No," said the TV. "We're all here."

"But is there no other . . . blanket?"

The TV avoided the blanket's earnest gaze. "No. The master doesn't use an electric blanket anymore. Just a plain wool one."

"But he always . . . he always. . . ." The blanket could say no more. Its resolution deserted it and it fell in a heap on the carpet.

A gasp went up from the apartment's assembled appliances, which until now had had no idea of the extent of the blanket's injuries.

"Doesn't *use* an electric blanket!" the toaster repeated indignantly. "Why ever not?"

The screen of the TV flickered and then, evasively, started showing a gardening show.

"It isn't the master's choice, really," said the Singer sewing machine in its funny clipped accent. "I daresay *he* would be delighted to see his old blanket again."

The blanket looked up questioningly.

"It's the mistress," the sewing machine went on. "She says she becomes too hot under an electric blanket."

"The mistress?" the five appliances repeated.

"Didn't you know?"

"No," said the toaster. "No, we haven't heard anything from the master since he left the cottage three years ago."

"Two years, eleven months, and twenty-two days, to be precise," said the alarm clock/radio.

"That's why we determined to find our way here. We feared. . . . I don't know what exactly. But we thought that . . . that our master would need us."

"Oh," said the sewing machine. It turned to watch the gardening show on the TV.

As unobtrusively as it might, the new toaster crept back into the kitchen and resumed its post of duty on the formica countertop.

"Two years, eleven months, and twenty-two days is a long time to be left alone," the radio asserted at rather a loud volume. "Naturally we became concerned. The poor air conditioner stopped working altogether."

"And all the while," said the lamp, "never a word of explanation!" It glared reproachfully at the TV, which continued to discuss the problem of blister beetles.

"Can't *any* of you tell us why?" the toaster demanded earnestly. "Why did he never return to the cottage? There must be a *reason*."

"I can tell you," said the vaporizer, inching forward. "You see, the mistress is subject to hay fever. I can help her a bit with her asthma, but when the hay fever starts in on her, there's nothing anyone can do, and she is really very miserable then."

"I still don't understand," said the toaster.

The sewing machine spelled it out. "Rather than go to the country, where there is bound to be ragweed and pollen and such, they spend their summers at the seaside."

"And our cottage—our lovely cottage in the woods—what is to become of it?"

"I believe the master means to sell it."

"And . . . and us?" the toaster asked.

"I understand there is to be an auction," said the sewing machine.

The Hoover, which had comported itself with great dignity throughout the visit, could bear no more. With a loud groan it grasped the handle of the perambulator as though to steady itself. "Come," it gasped. "All of you, come. We are not wanted here. We'll return to . . . to. . . ."

Where would they return? Where could they? They had become appliances without a household!

"To the Dump!" shrieked the blanket hysterically. "Isn't that where *junk* belongs? That's all we are now—junk!" It twisted its cord into an agonized knot. "Isn't that what the pirate said we were? Junk! Junk! Junk! All of us, and me most of all."

"Control yourself," said the toaster sternly, though its own coils felt as though they were about to snap. "We're *not* junk. We're sturdy, useful appliances."

"Look at me!" cried the blanket, displaying the full extent of its worst tear. "And these mudstains—look!"

"Your tears can be sewn up," said the toaster calmly. It turned to the sewing machine. "Can't they?"

The sewing machine nodded in mute agreement.

"And the stains can be cleaned."

"And then what?" the Hoover demanded dourly. "Let us suppose the blanket is repaired and cleaned, and that I've mended my cord and got my dustbag into working shape, and that you've polished yourself. Suppose all that—what then? Where shall we go?"

"I don't know. Somewhere. I'll have to think."

"Pardon me," said the TV, turning off the gardening show. "But didn't I hear you say something about a . . . pirate?"

"Yes," said the sewing machine nervously. "What pirate did you mean? There's not a pirate in this building, I hope?"

"Never fear—we don't have to worry any more about him. He captured us but we escaped from him. Would you like to know how?"

"Goodness, yes," said the TV. "I love a good story."

So all the appliances gathered in a circle about the toaster, which began to tell the story of their adventures from the moment they had decided to leave the cottage till the moment they arrived at the door of the apartment. It was a very long story, as you know, and while the toaster told it, the sewing machine set to work sewing up all the rips and tears in the blanket.

The next afternoon when the blanket came back from Jiffy Dry Cleaners on the other side of Newton Avenue, the apartment's appliances put on a splendid party for their five visitors. The Christmas tree lights strung themselves up between the two ginger-jar lamps and winked and bubbled in the merriest way, while the TV and the stereo sang duets from all the most famous musical comedies. The toaster was polished to a fare-thee-well, and the Hoover was likewise in fine fettle once again. But most wonderful of all—the blanket looked almost as good as new. Its yellow was possibly not as bright as it had been, but it was a lovely yellow, for all that. The exact same yellow, according to the TV, of custard and primroses and the nicest bathroom tissues.

At five o'clock the radio's alarm went off, and everyone became very still, except for the blanket, which went on whirling gaily about the living room for some time before it realized the music had stopped.

"What is it?" asked the blanket. "Why are you all so quiet?"

"Hush," said the radio. "It's time for *The Swap Shop*."

"What is *The Swap Shop*?" asked the blanket.

"It's the program on listener-supported radio station KHOP," said the toaster excitedly, "that is going to find a new home for us! I told you not to worry, didn't I? I told you I'd think of something!"

"Be quiet," said the lamp. "It's starting."

The radio turned up its volume so that all the appliances in the living room could hear. "Good afternoon," it said, in a deep, announcer-type voice, "and welcome to *The Swap Shop*. Today's program opens with a very strange offering from Newton Avenue. It seems that someone there wants to swap—now listen to this list!—a Hoover vacuum cleaner, an AM alarm clock/radio, a yellow electric blanket, a tensor lamp, and a Sunbeam toaster. All this in exchange for . . . well, it says on the card here: 'You name it.' What's most important, I'm informed, is that you should have a real and genuine *need* for all five of these fine appliances, since their present owner wants them to be able to stay together. For sentimental reasons! Now I've heard everything! Anyhow, if you think you *need* those five appliances, the number to call is 485-9120. That number again, 485-9120. Our next offer is not quite so unusual. Seems there's a party on Center Street who is offering, absolutely for free, five lovable black-and-white—"

The radio tuned out KHOP. "Didn't he make us sound super!" it exclaimed, forgetting in its excitement to stop speaking in the announcer's voice.

"Come over here by the telephone," the Hoover urged the radio. "You'll have to talk to them. I'm just too nervous."

All five appliances gathered about the telephone and waited for it to ring.

There are two schools of thought about whether or not appliances ought to be allowed the free use of telephones. Some insist that it is flatly against the rules and should never be done in any circumstances, while others maintain that it's all right, since it is only another appliance one is talking to, in this case a telephone. Whether or not it's against the rules, it is certainly a fact that a good many appliances (lonely radios especially) do use the phone system regularly, usually to contact other appliances. This explains the great number of so-called "wrong numbers" that people get at odd times. Computerized exchanges could never make so many mistakes, though they end up taking the blame.

For the last three years, of course, this issue had not mattered very much to the appliances, since the phone in the cottage had been disconnected. Ordinarily, the Hoover would probably have opposed the notion of any of them using the phone, as it did tend to adopt the conservative attitude. But first there had been the absolute necessity of calling Jiffy Dry Cleaners and having them pick up the blanket, and that had established a clear precedent for their phoning in to KHOP and offering themselves on *The Swap Shop*. And now here they were all gathered round the telephone, waiting to talk with their next master!

The phone rang.

"Now whatever you do," warned the Hoover, "don't say yes to the first person who happens to call. Find out something about him first. We don't want to go just anywhere, you know."

"Right," said the radio.

"And remember," said the toaster, "to be nice."

The radio nodded. It picked up the telephone receiver. "Hello?" it said.

"Is this the person with the five appliances?"

"It is! Oh my goodness yes indeed, it is!"

And so the five appliances went to live with their new mistress, for as it happened it was a woman who'd phoned them first and not a man. She was an elderly, impoverished ballerina who lived all alone in a small room at the back of her ballet studio on Center Street in the oldest part of the city. What the ballerina had swapped for the appliances were her five lovable black-and-white kittens. The appliances' former master never could figure out how, upon returning with his wife from their summer vacation by the sea, there had come to be five kittens in their apartment. It was rather an awkward situation, for his wife was allergic to cat fur.

But they were such darlings—it would never have done to put them out on the street. In the end they decided to keep them, and his wife simply took more antihistamines.

And the appliances?

Oh, they were *very* happy. At first the Hoover had been doubtful about entering service with a woman (for it had never worked for a woman before, and it was somewhat set in its ways), but as soon as it realized what a fastidious and immaculate housekeeper its mistress was, it forgot all its reservations and became her greatest champion.

It felt so good to be *useful* again! The radio would play beautiful classical music for the ballerina to dance to; and when she became tired and wanted to sit down and read, the lamp would light her book; and then when it grew late and she'd finished her book, the blanket would give off a steady, gentle warmth that kept her cozy all through the long, cold night.

And when it was morning and she awoke, what wonderful slices of toast the toaster would toast for her—so brown and crisp and perfect and always just the same!

And so the five appliances lived and worked, happy and fulfilled, serving their dear mistress and enjoying each other's companionship, to the end of their days.

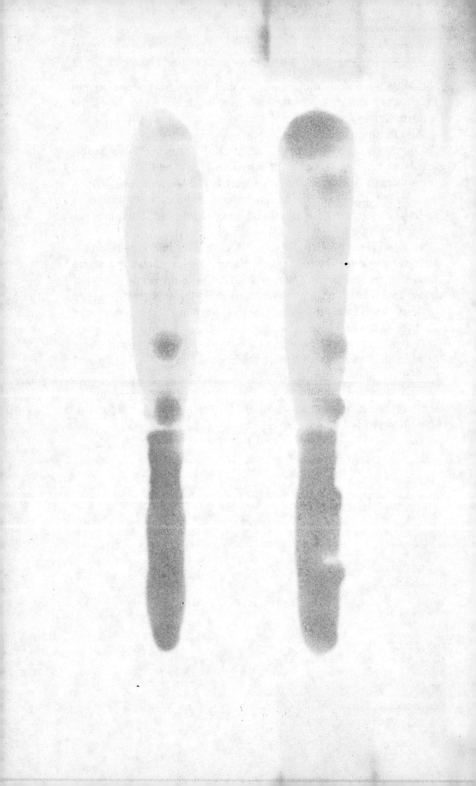